At first the only thing happening was Hiblit Rahms standing there in the midst of everyone, screaming. Head thrown back, eyes closed tight, fists held up and clenched, Hiblit looked like a tortured soul in the Caverns of the Damned.

And then others began to scream as small gouts of flame erupted to life in more than half a dozen places. Some of the places were the clothing of those people still closest to Hiblit, and the rest described a circle of sorts around the screaming man. Almost a protective circle, Delin thought, one meant to keep people from reaching Hiblit. Guardsmen had come rushing in from the hall when the screams first began, and now they stood with members of the Five's personal guard, clearly at a loss about what to do.

"Look at that," Bron said, pointing to a woman whose costume skirt had begun to blaze. "The flames just went out, and the skirt isn't even singed. It looks like all the clothing fires have been put out, and now the ring around Hiblit is being extinguished. Damned strong talent, whoever he is."

CHALLENGES

Book Three of THE BLENDING

SHARON GREEN

AVON · EOS

AVON BOOKS
A division of
The Hearst Corporation
1350 Avenue of the Americas
New York, New York 10019

Copyright © 1998 by Sharon Green
Published by arrangement with the author
Visit our website at **http://www.AvonBooks.com/Eos**
Library of Congress Catalog Card Number: 97-94882
ISBN: 0-380-78809-8

First Avon Eos Printing: May 1998

AVON EOS TRADEMARK REG. U.S. PAT. OFF. AND IN OTHER COUNTRIES, MARCA REGISTRADA, HECHO EN U.S.A.

Printed in the U.S.A.

WCD   10 9 8 7 6 5 4 3 2

*For the two greatest partners in the world,
in alphabetical order: Zane Melder and
Debbora Wiles*

*And to the memory of
Ariane Randie W.;
Child of my heart, dream sweetly forever.*

Yes, I know, this time I dropped the story right in the middle of that costumed ball they made us attend. By now you've probably forgotten what was happening then, so I'll remind you: the testing authority was scheming, our opponents were scheming, and we were scheming. See, that wasn't so difficult.

And it wasn't much harder to live through, at least, not the beginning of it. The palace of the Seated Five was big and beautiful, the music was nice, the snacks delicious. The other people there, however. . . . They were all members of the nobility, and were staring at us as though they considered us trained but still dangerous animals. What we assumed were our first-scheduled opponents—they came over and insulted us, then ambled away. A member from another noble Blending-to-be had tried to get information from Rion by lying to him, but Rion had caught him at it. Vallant Ro managed to get in touch with Pagin Holter, who had previously been in our residence, and found out the location of his new residence.

All of which was only the beginning of the evening, and doesn't even say anything about personal feelings. The only one really trying to keep our group moving forward was Jovvi, ignoring the emotional storms of the rest of us in an effort to put us in the best possible position for the competitions. That meant gathering as much information as we could, every item available from the store of data the testing authority had been

*keeping secret. We hadn't made much progress with that,
but Jovvi's determination refused to let us stop trying.*

*And so we continued with the evening, having very
little idea of what still lay ahead of us. . . .*

ONE

Jovvi brushed at the skirt of her costume, a blue that was
nicely set off by the silver sequins of the gown's top, her
thoughts filled with faint satisfaction. Rion had resisted that
noble's tempting offer all by himself, showing the strength
of personality they'd all begun to expect from him. The
changes in him had been nothing short of incredible, and
even the noble who had tried to get information out of him
had been surprised. The man was a member of one of the
noble challenging Blendings, and hadn't been quite as
strong as Jovvi had thought he would be.

She paused to smile encouragingly at a still-nervous
Tamrissa, then went back to her musing. Possibly the noble
hadn't been using his full strength in Spirit magic on Rion,
and that's why she'd been able to block his attempts so
easily. It would be dangerous to start believing that the
nobles weren't any good, even though it would be nice to
think so. That would give her and the others an even better
chance to win the Fivefold Throne. . . .

Sight of Vallant closed that line of thought rather
abruptly. Vallant had actually managed to get in touch with
Pagin Holter, and the small ex-groom who had originally
been in their residence had given Vallant more than the
address of his new residence. He'd also found out that the
betting on the upcoming competitions was completely one-
sided, all the gold having been placed on one or another of

the noble groups. That no one was betting on one of the common groups meant those with the gold knew something everyone else didn't: that the common groups had no chance at all, no matter how strong they were.

"Is something wrong?" a voice asked, and Jovvi looked up to see Lorand staring down at her. His worry was clear despite the mask hiding most of his features, so she smiled at him.

"Nothing more than the usual," she replied, working to sound more lighthearted than she felt. "Vallant managed to speak to Pagin Holter, and learned from Holter that no one is betting on any of the common challenging Blendings to win. That doesn't count the ordinary man or woman who bets a few coppers or even a piece of silver. Those with gold to bet are placing it only on the noble groups."

"That doesn't sound very good," Lorand said with a frown, his dark eyes filled with disturbance. "It means that they intend to do something to make us lose, and the . . . 'smart money' knows it. Do you think we'll be able to find a way around whatever it is?"

"First we'll have to find out what it is," Jovvi replied, sharing his disturbance. "I don't expect it to be something simple, like the drugged tea they tried to give us before the qualifying tests, but we'll still have to keep that in mind. If we eat or drink anything before the competitions, we'll deserve to lose."

"Is that why they tried so hard to get me to drink that tea?" Lorand asked, now looking surprised. "I hadn't realized it was drugged . . . so now I have something else to thank Eskin Drowd for. If I hadn't seen him there, smirking and expecting me to fail, I probably *would* have taken the tea."

"Holter also said that Drowd was added to his residence to replace the man who went insane during that supposed competition," Jovvi told him, her thoughts now busy with this new point. "From what you said about his very late appearance at the testing and qualifying area, it's possible they added him to that group without first making him qualify. If so, that suggests something else I don't like very much."

"That they don't care how good or bad one of us is, as long as they have the required number of warm bodies,"

Lorand agreed, putting her thoughts into words. "That seems to confirm the theory that we'll just be there to make the event look good, and the idea is beginning to get me angry. I don't like having people use me for their own purposes without caring what *I* want."

"But that's all we can expect from the testing authority," Jovvi pointed out. "They're there to make sure their fellow nobles look good when they win, so anything we accomplish will have to be done on our own. That's one of the reasons I want us to try our best: to get even with the testing authority for treating us so badly. If we actually manage to win, we can tell those cheats to go home and not come back."

"Right now that's a better incentive than winning the Throne," Lorand said with a grin. "Kicking them out after telling them what incompetents they are should also get even for all the people they ganged up on. And the others should enjoy it as much as we will."

The laughter they shared had felt wonderful to Jovvi, but after no more than a moment Lorand's grin faltered and died.

"I . . . think I've bothered you enough," he said, his gaze no longer meeting hers. "I know you want me to stay away from you, and except for matters involving the group, I mean to do exactly that. I care for you too much to want to see you upset. . . ."

He began to turn away then, his thoughts and emotions a roiling mess, and Jovvi found it impossible to let that go on.

"Lorand, don't," she said, stopping him with a hand to his arm. "You've been incredibly wonderful about understanding how I feel, something most men wouldn't have found possible. It isn't *you* I'm trying to avoid, it's the uncertainty brought about by your fear of burnout. Uncertainty is something *I* can't handle, so you could say we both have problems that need to be worked on. And since we're both still here, maybe we can work on them together. . . ."

Jovvi hadn't known she was going to say that, but the hunger she felt for Lorand had been growing stronger rather than fading. He'd come to mean more to her than any other man she'd ever known, and a stab of pain flared in her chest when he slowly shook his head.

"I don't deserve to be made an offer like that," he said in a choked voice, very deliberately not looking at her. "I thought I'd gotten past the fear of burnout and I felt twelve feet tall—until I discovered that the fear was still right where it had always been. I'm a helpless fool, Jovvi, and I love you too much to saddle you with someone like me. You deserve better, and as long as I stay out of the way I'm sure you'll get it."

This time he did move away, and Jovvi's frantic thoughts could find nothing to say that would stop him. She'd been the one who had told him how much she needed security in her life, something his fear kept him from giving her. Neither one of them had changed, so there *were* no words to keep him beside her. Jovvi could look at his tall, broad-shouldered, blond-haired form and ache to have his arms around her again, but finding a way to bring them together again seemed impossible.

Rather than staring at him where he stood only a few steps away, Jovvi turned to look elsewhere as she fought not to cry.

Two

Rion didn't deliberately listen to the conversation between Jovvi and Lorand Coll, but he wasn't so far away that not hearing it would have been possible. It could have become a matter of embarrassment if either of them had noticed, but both seemed too wrapped in pain to see the trivial. Which Rion could understand, once he thought about it for a moment. Jovvi and Coll had been attracted to one another almost from the first moment they'd all entered the residence. They were the last two people Rion would have expected to have trouble between them, but it had happened anyway. Tamrissa and Vallant Ro had spent more time disagreeing than getting along, so the coolness between those two was perfectly understandable, but—

Rion's thoughts on personal interaction came to a sudden halt, shoved aside by an abrupt and unpleasant idea. He considered it alone for a moment, then moved over to where Vallant Ro stood. Ro glanced at him, then shook his head with a small grimace.

"That wasn't any fun to overhear," Ro said softly, clearly knowing Rion would understand his meaning. "Someone might think I'm glad not to be the only one with woman trouble, but that isn't so. Those two are too decent for anyone to be enjoyin' their pain."

"I agree," Rion answered just as softly with a nod. "They shouldn't be having that problem, but speaking of problems, I think we all have one. Do you remember when Holter said he'd never be chosen over you to round out our group because he didn't belong? We were in the coach coming back from practice at the time."

"Of course I remember," Ro agreed, his brows raised behind the mask. "What about it?"

"It just occurred to me that he *was* beginning to belong, and that could be why he was transferred to another residence," Rion replied slowly, searching for the proper words of explanation. "A short while ago, a former acquaintance of mine came over to . . . chat. He's a member of one of the noble challenging Blendings, and what he most wanted to chat about was Tamrissa's weak points. He said something about Fire being the most important aspect in a Blending."

"I think I see what you're gettin' at," Ro said after a moment, his brow furrowed in thought. "Holter was gettin' along with Tamrissa and I'm not, and that's why I was the one who stayed. I told her once that she and I *had* to be close or the Blendin' wouldn't work, and at the time I thought it was somethin' I made up. Looks like I might have been tellin' the truth after all."

"I'm afraid so," Rion agreed, still disturbed by the idea.

"We knew that the testing authority was doing its best to sabotage us, and now we seem to have discovered one of its methods. I wonder just how important this will turn out to be."

"If that noble was questionin' you about it, the answer's probably very important," Ro replied, his frown beginning to look permanent. "The next answer we need is what to do about it, but that one's not as easy to find."

Rion felt the urge to say that it wasn't as difficult as Ro seemed to think, but he held the words back as a struggling understanding of Ro's position forced its way to his notice. Rion liked Tamrissa and had no trouble getting along with her, but Ro couldn't say the same—at least not about the getting along part. The matter might turn out to be even more of a problem than Rion had first imagined.

The conversation with Ro might have gone on a bit longer, but a definite stir in the crowd took their attention. Rion joined everyone else in looking toward the entrance doors, and saw that someone of apparently great importance had just arrived. It was also possible to see that another common challenging Blending had arrived earlier, the members of which, in silver and orange, now stood closer to the entrance than their own group did.

People swirled around the new arrivals, but when they approached the group in silver and orange it was possible to see the ones who had been surrounded. There were five of them, all dressed in white, which told Rion that the Seated Blending had arrived. The Blending always wore white for formal public appearances, and Eltrina Razas, their residence's testing authority representative, wasn't far from the Five. She seemed to be introducing the participants in silver and orange, most of whom looked nervous and awed despite their masks.

"It looks like we'll be next," Ro commented from Rion's right. "I know this is supposed to be a great privilege, but if they passed us by I would not sit down and start cryin'."

"Nor I," Rion agreed, oddly pleased to find that his groupmate seemed less impressionable than the fools in the orange group. He'd never been as close to the Five as Mother was and therefore hadn't had much to do with them, but he'd seen them from a distance on more than one occasion. They'd seemed as petty and vicious as any other noble, and he'd never really wanted a closer acquaintance-ship.

But that didn't stop the entire entourage from heading for them. Tamrissa moved to Jovvi's side as the crowd approached, Coll came to stand on Rion's left, and then all three men drifted a bit closer to the ladies. Personal difficulties or not, they were a group who had begun to support each other automatically. Eltrina Razas hurried ahead of the very important newcomers, and when she reached the group she wore a frown.

"Will you people stop looking as though you're about to be attacked?" she hissed, annoyance and a touch of being harried clear in her manner. "You're going to be *introduced* to the Five, not set in opposition against them. Smile!"

Obeying her own order about smiling, Eltrina turned just in time to greet the arrival of the entourage. Most of the Five looked bored and sullen, leaving all of the interacting to Damilla Sytoss, their Water magic member.

"And this, Excellencies, is the second group," Eltrina purred in a sleekly burbling way that Rion had seen others use many times before. "In order, they are Tamrissa Domon, Fire magic, Jovvi Hafford, Spirit magic, Lorand Coll, Earth magic, Clarion Mardimil, Air magic, and Vallant Ro, Water magic. They're—"

"That's Rion Mardimil, not Clarion," Rion interrupted to correct, ignoring Eltrina's immediate outrage and the expressions of startlement on most of the Five. "If you insist on doing this, you can at least make an effort to get it right."

"How dare you speak to us like that?" Eltrina gasped, now reddening with embarrassment. "Haven't you learned *yet* that you're of no consequence whatsoever? You—"

"Nonsense," Jovvi took her turn at interrupting, adding to Eltrina's fury. "If he—and the rest of us—are of no consequence at all, why are we here and going through this farce? You really can't have it both ways, you know."

"The girl is quite right, Eltrina," Damilla Sytoss said with a grin, also interrupting the testing authority representative. "These people aren't of no consequence, not when they'll be formed into a challenging Blending at the start of the new week. I was supposed to have the pleasure of telling you that, my dears, but obviously you already knew. That leaves me nothing to do but congratulate you and wish you luck, and yet that's actually quite enough. Perhaps we'll meet again when the last of the competitions is over."

Her smile showed too much amusement for that final word of encouragement to have much meaning, and then they were all drifting on toward the next group in silver and yellow. All but Eltrina, that is, who gestured to a young man to hurry ahead and be ready to make the introductions, while she lingered for a moment with another purpose in mind.

"I meant to pass on this news earlier, but with the group in orange arriving late I simply couldn't manage it." The one Eltrina addressed was Jovvi, and the older woman's expression had turned to one of sly satisfaction. "That person from your hometown and her two cohorts—they were arrested today, and a special session of court will be held tomorrow at which they will be tried and sentenced. Attempting to kidnap a participant in these competitions will bring fearful penalties if they're convicted, which I have no doubt they will be. We won't need your testimony, but you may attend if you like. The particulars are here."

She thrust a folded sheet of paper at Jovvi, then hurried off after the entourage with an almost gleeful step. Rion didn't understand why that was until he saw Jovvi's pallor and the way she held the paper crumpled in her fist. Clearly she was disturbed by what she'd been told, and Tamrissa put an arm about her shoulders.

"That was a disgusting thing for her to do," Tamrissa commiserated while patting Jovvi's hands. "She wanted to get you upset, and used the one way she could be sure of. I wonder how they found out about the kidnapping attempt."

When Jovvi simply shook her head, Ro stirred where he stood to Rion's right.

"There were servants bringin' you food and drink when you told me about it in the dinin' room," Ro said in a musing way. "If that was the only time you mentioned it in the house, that must be when it was overheard. And I'll bet the bitch expected you to blame one of *us* for informin'. Anythin' to drive us as far apart as possible.''

"Yes, you're probably right," Jovvi agreed after taking a deep breath, obviously working to pull herself together. "I hate the idea of getting anyone involved with the authorities and the courts, and my feelings must have been perfectly clear.''

"For all we know, the servant listening could have had Spirit magic," Tamrissa pointed out, her exasperated annoyance clear. "Talk about taking unfair advantage! We'll have to be a bit more careful from now on, but in the meantime, what are you going to do? You don't *have* to attend the trial, you know. . . .''

"Actually, I do," Jovvi said, her sigh filled with resignation. "I know I'm not responsible for Allestine's stupidities, but I still need to be there to find out what happens to her. I just wonder why they don't need me to testify. How else can they get the details of what happened?''

"Personally, *I'd* like some details about what happened," Coll put in, his brow creased with disturbance. "And am I the only one who didn't know about this?''

"I hadn't heard about it either," Rion said, which calmed Coll's intense stare to a small degree. "Would someone like to inform us now?''

"That woman Allestine, who ran the residence where Jovvi was a courtesan, tried to kidnap her after one of the practice sessions," Tamrissa said when Jovvi herself hesitated. "She and those two bullies forced Jovvi into a coach, and were going to drag her back to the town she came from. Jovvi used her talent to stop them, and that's why she was so exhausted the night you and I helped Rion, Lorand. That's probably also why you didn't know. There were too many other things going on to remember about an attempt that didn't work.''

"Yes, you're right about us being involved in other things," Coll agreed, most of the intensity now gone from him. "And if Jovvi didn't want the authorities to find out about it, I can understand why no one discussed it. But I'd also like to know why they don't need her to testify.''

"Probably because it's a criminal trial," Ro put in when

everyone else either shrugged or shook their head. "I saw part of one once, when a member of my crew was involved, and they don't have anyone testifyin' but the people who are accused. They get the truth out of them somehow, because my crewman was cleared."

"I expect I'll find out all about it tomorrow," Jovvi said, her smile still on the weak side. "Right now I'd like to tell you all how wonderful you are, working so hard to make me feel better. And we still haven't even discussed that official announcement. It's now no longer a secret that we'll be a challenging Blending."

"No, and I wonder how many of the groups had the nerve to tell *them*, rather than wait to *be* told," Rion said, glad to help change the subject. "Damilla considered the matter amusing, but her sense of humor has become notorious over the years. Her Blendingmates seemed more annoyed."

"They're annoyed about this entire affair," Jovvi supplied, her smile slightly better now. "They hate being put on parade like a team of dressed-up horses, but they had no more choice about coming tonight than we did. And I couldn't help noticing that their Spirit magic user hadn't even the most tenuous hold on the power. What about the others?"

Rion had to think only for a moment before he realized that the same was true of the Air magic user. Keeping a touch on the power had become automatic with *him*, but apparently the Air magic member of the Seated Five didn't do the same.

"The woman doin' all the talkin' for them flexed her talent for a moment," Ro offered with a shrug. "It was when Mardimil said his piece, and she seemed to be reactin' to that. But it wasn't a very strong response, and then it died away again completely."

"And she was the only one?" Jovvi asked, looking around to get everyone's nod of agreement. "Now isn't that strange. I'd have to really work at it to sever myself completely from the power, and I'm certain the rest of you are in the same position. So why does the reigning Five do it differently? Because there's a danger in maintaining contact that we don't know about, or. . . ."

Or because the members of the Five are so ordinary, they never should have been seated. Rion finished Jovvi's uncompleted sentence silently, and judging by their expressions the others were doing the same. Both parts of that speculation gave them something to think about . . . as though they needed any more. . . .

THREE

Delin Moord stood watching the Five making the round of introductions to the commoners, his expression carefully free of what his mind felt. Those five people represented the most power it was possible to have, the highest social and political positions, the ultimate in safety and independence. He needed all that to be his, his and his group's, and there was nothing he would refuse to do in order to satisfy that need. Nothing whatsoever. . . .

"Now isn't that interesting," Kambil Arstin murmured from Delin's left, also watching the Five. The Blending had paused in front of the peasants in silver and blue, the group meant to be first to face—and lose to—the Advisors' chosen noble Blending.

"What is there to find interesting?" Delin asked languidly, automatically covering his annoyance with Kambil. The man was the only other member of the group Delin could depend on to be really effective where subtlety was concerned, but that didn't mean he liked him. Anyone who made cryptic comments without immediately explaining them *had* to consider himself superior on one level or another.

"What was interesting was the combined reaction of the entire Blending," Kambil answered without looking away from the Five, who were now moving on toward the third peasant group. "Something that was said surprised them, and it wasn't a pleasant surprise. Damilla is the one doing all the talking, and she shifted rather quickly to being amused. I think we both know what *that* means."

"It means she was picturing someone being hurt, most probably badly hurt," Delin replied at once. "I wonder if she intends to continue indulging her private pleasures once her Blending has been retired. If so, we may be asked to take action against her."

"With her strong habit of being discreet, I doubt we'll have the problem," Kambil returned with amusement. "Everyone knows what she's like, but I've never heard anyone claim to have seen her doing it. Now that we're discussing it, I wonder if it's true after all."

"You think she encouraged the rumors for her own reasons?" Delin asked in startlement, suddenly realizing that what Kambil had said was true. "That could very well be the truth. If you want to keep people from trying to take advantage of you, the first step is to make them afraid of you. I wouldn't have expected such clear and intelligent thinking from a woman."

"You'd be wise not to judge all women by Selendi and—the other women you know," Kambil advised, his words and tone gentle. "Underestimating people can and does lead to disaster, and with our current undertaking we'll do well to avoid as much obvious disaster as possible."

Delin murmured neutral agreement, but on the inside his mind seethed. Was Kambil really lecturing *him*, the true leader of their group? The fool had some nerve trying to tell *him* how to behave, not to mention diplomatically holding back on what he'd originally meant to say. Kambil had clearly intended to mention Selendi and Delin's mother as examples, and at the last instant had changed his mind. Delin had caught the hesitation, and fiercely resented having the point brought up even obliquely.

Because Delin's mother was even worse than Selendi. Lady Talvine Moord had never had an original thought in her life, and paid attention only to what her husband told her. She doted on the man as the force which powered her own life, and put him and his wishes above everything else in the world—including her children. Delin could still remember that first time with his father, a small boy terrified of what would be done to him. He'd run to his mother, expecting to be protected, but his mother had smiled vaguely and turned her back, pretending she saw nothing when her husband dragged her sobbing son back with him. . . .

Delin shuddered as he always did at that memory, the one that returned to him time and again in dreams. It had been his first experience with his father's ways but not his last, and to this day Delin couldn't imagine himself standing up to the man. Even though they stood eye to eye physically and Delin's talent was worlds stronger, the least thought of disobeying the man sent Delin into a trembling funk. Challenging the man simply wasn't possible, not on any level whatsoever. Being out of his house and in a position where he couldn't simply be ordered back was an incredible relief, but Delin still *needed* more. . . .

"Delin," Kambil hissed, and Delin looked up to find that he'd fallen into the blackout time of his memories again. More time had passed than he'd expected, and the Five's entourage was leaving the vicinity of Adriari Fant's group and heading toward his own. He'd thought they would only have the peasants introduced to them, but apparently everyone was to be given the "honor."

"And here is the next to last group," Hiblit Rahms said as the entourage approached, his speech and mannerisms distinct despite the costume and mask he wore. Hiblit had replaced Rigos as the one in charge of the noble challenging Blendings when Rigos had been arrested for the murder of Elfini Weil, and at first Delin had been delighted to have someone other than Rigos assigned to watch them. Delin's group wasn't meant to win the Fivefold Throne, Adriari's group had been chosen for that, but Delin and his groupmates meant to forceably change that decision. Rigos would have seen what they were up to and would have reported them immediately, but Rigos's replacement wasn't likely to be as observant or vindictive.

And Hiblit *was* completely different, only not in a way that would prove beneficial to Delin and the others. There was something seriously wrong with the man in that he moved as though his clothes were filled with pins that constantly stuck into him, and he never made eye contact with those he spoke to. He merely recited what he'd obviously been told to say, and had even refused a simple cup of tea because he "wasn't allowed" to eat or drink anywhere but at home. That statement had been made without any visible emotions, but Kambil, who was their Spirit talent, said the man was twisted impossibly tight on the inside. Not only would Hiblit never take a bribe to ignore what Delin's group would be doing, but he'd certainly report the bribe attempt itself.

"The people in this group are as follows," Hiblit said as the Five's entourage stopped in front of them, his tone distant and his gaze fixed on some invisible object in the distance. "Lord Bron Kallan, Fire magic, Lord Kambil Arstin, Spirit magic, Lord Delin Moord, Earth magic, Lady Selendi Vas, Air magic, and Lord Homin Weil, Water magic. The empire greatly appreciates their cooperation in this matter."

"Of course it does," Damilla Sytoss said with one of her enigmatic smiles, clearly ignoring the emotionlessness of the recital Hiblit had made. "We all appreciate their cooperation. And how is your father, Lord Homin? Recovering from his ordeal, I trust?"

"He—he's gone to our country house to recuperate, Excellency," Homin stuttered in answer, obviously startled to be addressed personally. Then the fat little man startled Delin by pulling himself together and rising to the occasion. "When I see him again, I'll be sure to mention that you asked after him."

"Yes, please do," Damilla told him with a wider smile, and then they were all moving on toward the last of the noble groups. Hiblit led the way, but Delin had the feeling that the man walked alone through a completely private world.

"Wasn't that impressive?" Selendi cooed, and Delin turned to see that she'd taken Homin's arm. "The only one of us spoken to directly was Homin, and I was the one standing right next to him."

"What do you think that makes *you*?" Bron commented with a snort of ridicule while Homin's flabby chest swelled with Selendi's praise. "Most of us were standing next to him, and I certainly didn't even see *him* turned magically into someone important. He's the same short, fat—"

"Bron, I need your help," Delin interrupted immediately, before the fool could finish insulting Homin and starting a fight. "You know we still have to talk to the group we'll be facing in the first competition, and since you're our leader I have to ask your advice. Will you step over to one side with me for a moment?"

"Oh, all right," Bron grudged, obviously unhappy about being torn away from the sport of picking on the helpless, but still willing to go. So far he'd always responded to the nonsense about his being the group's leader, although from the sneers of derision on the faces of Selendi and Homin, Bron was the only one who still believed the lie. And would probably continue to believe it no matter what anyone said, as long as the ploy wasn't used to extremes. Bron was truly stupid, but even the terminally stupid eventually saw the light if it was shined in their eyes often enough.

Delin led the way to a spot a short distance away from the others, then he began to fabricate the problem he wanted Bron's "help" with. He was in the midst of mentioning the obvious, that the first group they would face was composed of three men and two women, when an interruption came. But not an ordinary interruption, and Delin turned with Bron and everyone else to watch what was happening in the middle of the dance floor.

At first the only thing happening was Hiblit Rahms standing there in the midst of everyone and screaming. Head thrown back, eyes closed tight, fists held up and clenched, Hiblit looked like a tortured soul in the Caverns of the Damned. His screams sent a chill through Delin, and he could see he wasn't alone in feeling that way. All the people who had been dancing were backing away from the man, most of them with shudders of fear. The scream was like that, something to bring unknown and unexplained fear to all those who heard it.

"What's wrong with him?" Bron demanded unsteadily in a low voice. "Why is he doing that, and why doesn't someone stop him?"

Bron's bewilderment was clear, but this time Delin felt

that it wasn't stupidity making the man say what he had. He, too, wished someone would stop Hiblit, most especially as he himself seemed helpless to accomplish the task. To stop the man, one would have to go close to him, and somehow Delin was certain that even his talent would be fouled if he sent it to touch the screaming man. Obviously, Kambil had been right about how tightly strung Hiblit was on the inside.

And then others began to scream as small gouts of flame erupted to life in more than half a dozen places. Some of the places were the clothing of those people still closest to Hiblit, and the rest described a circle of sorts around the screaming man. Almost a protective circle, Delin thought, one meant to keep people from reaching Hiblit. Guardsmen had come rushing in from the hall when the screams first began, and now they stood with members of the Five's personal guard, clearly at a loss about what to do.

"Look at that," Bron said, pointing to a woman whose costume skirt had begun to blaze. "The flames just went out, and the skirt isn't even singed. It looks like *all* the clothing fires have been put out, and now the ring around Hiblit is being extinguished. Damned strong talent, whoever he is. I can feel the vibrations in the power without needing to reach out."

"Reaching out might be a good idea," Delin said, trying not to snarl through his teeth. "It would help to know *who* has a talent that strong, especially if the person turns out to be a member of one of the peasant groups. Give it a try, Bron, and tell me what you learn."

"Oh, all right," the mindless fool grumbled, as though the point were completely unimportant. Everyone in the room had probably reached for the power automatically, even those with minimal talent. It was a reflex of self protection in which Delin had fully participated, but awareness of the power used by someone of a different aspect wasn't possible. Only same aspect awareness worked, and anyone but an imbecile like Bron would already know the source of the great strength he'd mentioned.

"It's gone now," the imbecile announced after a moment with a dismissive shrug. "He put out all the fires then released the power, so I can't tell who it was. But it was probably Edril Lanton, the Five's Fire magic user. It's certainly something he should have done."

Delin limited himself to a noncommittal grunt as he felt the Earth magic members of the guard begin to exert magical force on Hiblit, but on the inside he was furious. Edril Lanton was as lazy and unimaginative as Bron, so he was probably the last—after Bron—to have wielded his talent. It might even have been Adriari showing off for her group, the group that the Advisors meant to have Seated this time, but now Delin would never know. And all because Bron was such an incredible ignoramus . . . !

"They've put him to sleep, for all the good it's done," Kambil's voice came as the man stopped beside Delin. "Those little noises he's making mean he's still screaming even though he's unconscious. I have a feeling we'll be getting another new agent . . . and I'm curious about who put those fires out. Would you like to ask Bron, or shall I?"

"I already have, and he doesn't know," Delin growled, finding controlling his anger almost beyond him. "He said a large amount of strength was being used, but didn't bother to find out who was using it. By the time he tried, the user stopped. I'm now wondering if it was Adriari, showing off to everyone without putting the arrogance into words."

"If it was, we may have a problem," Kambil murmured as Delin watched the guard members carefully carrying Hiblit out. "I couldn't sense the amount of power being used myself, of course, but I also couldn't miss the fact that no one and nothing were actually burned. Both clothing and flesh should have been charred, and that it wasn't can only be attributed to the user's quick response and greater than ordinary ability."

"Faster and better than Bron, you mean," Delin murmured back, the very important point pushing his anger aside. "It won't be possible to get the results from the testing of Adriari's group no matter how much gold we try to offer, so we might be wisest assuming the worst. If Adriari *is* stronger than Bron, we certainly do have a problem."

"One which would be less troublesome if we didn't have to face her group," Kambil agreed with a sigh. "But it's foolish to think about that, as there's only one way we can avoid facing them. That way isn't at all practical, so we'll have to think of a way that is."

Delin was about to ask what the impractical way was when the answer suddenly became clear. If Adriari's group lost in the first set of competitions, Delin's group would be able to forget about them. But that would mean having the peasants defeat them, which wasn't about to happen. The Advisors had made certain that the peasants *couldn't* defeat them. . . .

Various ideas flitted through Delin's mind, their appearance and disappearance like the flickering flame of a candle. There *was* a way to let the peasants win after all, and the thought of having to face them later with his own group caused not the slightest bit of worry. He and his people were good enough to defeat *any* peasants, especially if they happened to have personal problems. Delin decided to look into the matter, and then he'd make his final decision. . . .

FOUR

I didn't quite feel shaky as they carried the unconscious man out, but that was only because I still held onto the power. Once I released it and my usual reactions took over again, I'd probably tremble like a hut in an earthquake. That screaming had been so horrible, so utterly lost and abandoned. . . .

"That was a marvelous exhibition you put on, Tamma," Jovvi said very softly from beside me. "When those flames appeared, all I could picture was fire spreading and burning everything in reach, including us."

"That's what I pictured, so I had to stop it," I whispered

back. "The man isn't even a Middle talent so it wasn't hard, but I can't believe that no one else tried to do the same. There are supposed to be *how* many High practitioners in this room?"

"I think you've just discovered that there's a big difference between 'supposed to be' and 'are,' " she murmured, letting her gaze move around the room. "Almost everyone in here was terrified, and their reaching for the power forced me to use my ability to protect myself rather than help even a little. But before I blocked everything out, I got a small look into that man's mind. It was horribly painful but it was also strange, only I don't know in what way. If I'd had even a minute or two longer. . . ."

"Everything in this place seems to be strange," I said, joining Jovvi in gazing around. "The Five are leaving through a door other than the one the guardsmen carried that man through, and now everyone else looks to be getting ready to leave. What really bothers me, though, is that most of those people seemed to know the man who had the fit, but not one of them is following along to find out how he'll be when he wakes up. Maybe they know where he'll be taken and mean to follow after he's taken there, but somehow I doubt it."

"You're unusually perceptive," Jovvi said with a nod of agreement, still studying people. "They're all working very hard to forget what happened, and most of them even seem to have managed it. They're treating it like a bad dream you're best off not even discussing, but they can't stay here and do it. That's why they're getting ready to leave, so they can put the incident out of their minds."

"Which means they'll make no effort to find out why it happened," I said, hearing the disgust in my voice. "They stroll around pretending to be so very superior to commoners, but they're no better than my parents and their cronies. Why are decent human beings so rare in this empire?"

"They're rare because you usually have to be raised by decent human beings in order to become one yourself," Jovvi answered, finally turning back to look at me. "Most of us in the group seem to be exceptions to that rule, but largely it came about after we all met. And now I think it's just about time for us to leave, since Lady Eltrina is hurrying in this direction. Apparently there's a benefit in having been one of the last groups to arrive."

"Please stay together, people," Lady Eltrina said as she came up to us, again looking harried. "Your coaches will have to be moved in order to let the other guests' carriages out, so you might as well be taken back to your residence. I'll call you in just a few minutes, and when I do I'll expect you all to come as quickly as possible."

With that she was off again, probably to keep one of us from saying something that would upset her even more. I thought about the fairly large amount of power I still held to, wondering if I should release it to be sure *I* wasn't the one who said something I'd certainly be sorry about later—but decided not to. I'd really been looking forward to seeing the palace, but now I felt that I'd be much happier if I held to the power until I was out of there.

"Excuse me, Dama Domon, but I need to speak to you privately for a moment."

The male voice was so serious that I had to turn and look before I was completely certain it was Vallant Ro who had spoken. There was the oddest air about him, which was why I didn't flatly refuse the way he'd refused me just a short while ago. The urge was definitely there, but curiosity won out.

"All right, Dom Ro," I said just as formally once I'd followed him a few steps away from the others. "What is it you wanted to talk about?"

"Not many minutes ago, it was pointed out to me that I was the one left in the residence rather than Holter because you and I aren't gettin' along," he said, not quite meeting my gaze. "The doin' is part of the testin' authority's plan to ruin us as a Blendin', so continuin' with our . . . disagreement would just be playin' into their hands. For the good of the group, I want to propose a truce."

"A truce," I echoed, staring straight up at him. "And for the good of the group. You chase after me until I can't think straight and then suddenly won't even speak to me, and that's what you call a disagreement? Anyone else would have come to me with *some* kind of explanation, but you—you just want to foil the plans of the testing authority. All right, Dom Ro, if that's the most pressing thing on your mind, let's by all means foil the testing authority. Consider me one hundred percent willing."

By then his direct stare had a frown to keep it company, and he parted his lips to say something else. But I no longer had any interest in anything he might say, so I turned and stalked back to the others before he produced the first syllable. Distantly I knew that if I hadn't still been in touch with the power I'd probably be in tears, but that realization didn't do much to calm my anger. I'd barely been able to keep him out of every thought I had, and all *he'd* apparently thought about was getting even with the testing authority.

Jovvi glanced at me with her own frown, but she seemed to know better than to ask me any questions—which was very wise of her, since I was more than ready to make a scene even worse than that unknown Fire talent. I suddenly understood that when frustration reaches a certain level, the only possible reaction becomes the screaming out of it for all the world to hear. But I wasn't quite at that level yet, since I would have much preferred making someone else do the screaming. . . .

Dom Ro actually tried to speak to me again, but Jovvi quickly drew him aside and saved his breeches as well as any sense of modesty he might have had. The desire to burn the pants off him was an almost living thing inside me, and if you don't believe I could have done it without harming him in the least, you haven't been following our adventures very closely. He would have been bare before he could even think about protecting himself with Water magic, and the picture that evoked drove me even crazier. I had to push it away with another thought, and my mind came up with just the thing.

Rion had gone to join Jovvi and Dom Ro, so Lorand now stood all alone. He gazed toward the place where the group in orange and silver had stood, possibly watching the way every noble in sight moved with the sort of short, jerky motions that proclaimed them to be horribly annoyed. Their annoyance probably stemmed from the fact that they couldn't simply leave when they wanted to, but had to wait around like commoners until it became their turn. My parents would have fit in perfectly, but I didn't care to waste time realizing that you don't need a title to be self-centered and heartless.

Instead I walked over to Lorand, trying to forget what I'd heard pass between him and Jovvi. They really cared for each other, and there shouldn't be so much pain between people who cared so deeply. Maybe I could help to make *him* forget for a while, too. . . .

"You don't look like yourself," Lorand observed suddenly, proving he wasn't as distracted as he'd seemed. "Is something wrong?"

"I'm about as angry as it's possible to get without exploding," I told him, "but I'm really trying to calm down. This is no place to lose control, especially not when you're still touching the power."

"That must be it," he said with sudden understanding in his voice. "You're still touching the power. I seem to be a different person too when I'm still in touch with it, one who's a good deal more confident. Does this mean you were the one who stopped those fires earlier?"

"Somebody had to do it," I answered with a shrug. "Our very noble hosts and fellow guests seemed to find it beyond them, so I made the effort. Wouldn't you have helped to put that poor man to sleep if the guard hadn't been able to do it?"

"It so happens I did," he admitted, looking rueful. "I doubt if anyone noticed, though, because I discovered that I could . . . disguise my efforts by hiding them behind the efforts of others. I have no idea how I was able to do that, and standing here thinking about it hasn't given me any answers."

"I've noticed an odd ability growing up every now and then too," I said, feeling the frown I'd developed. "I think this is something we ought to discuss with the entire group, but not in *this* place. Besides, I actually came over to ask you a favor. There's a very good chance you won't want to, and if so that's perfectly all right, but I still thought I would ask. Do you mind?"

"If you ask?" he said with brows raised. "Of course not. We do happen to be friends, so if I can I'll do it. What's the favor?"

"I need to be distracted from something," I admitted,

distantly wondering how I could say all that so calmly and coherently. "If you feel the same, you might not mind lying with me even though we don't mean something special to one another. If you really don't think you should, I'll understand completely."

His mouth opened and closed a few times, as though he couldn't decide what to say first, and then he shook his head.

"Someday I'll have to tell you how hearing that made me feel," he said, his smile odd. "Right now I don't think I can find the proper words to describe it, so let me say instead that most girls don't make that offer quite so . . . flatly and openly. If they do it at all they just sort of hint around, so if I looked surprised, that's the reason."

"I suppose most girls have more experience with this sort of thing," I said with a nod for the information he'd given me. "I'm only first starting to get that experience, so I'm bound to do *something* wrong. Does your response mean you aren't interested?"

"No, it so happens it doesn't," he answered with a grin. "I'm really not used to talking to you with you showing such an . . . overt personality, and the experience is fascinating. What I was going to say is that you're right about my need to be distracted, but wrong to think you don't mean something special to me. I may not be the sort of man a woman can count on every minute of her lifetime, but that doesn't mean I can't do an occasional favor for a very good friend. Were you thinking about tonight?"

"Tonight or tomorrow," I agreed, now studying him with my head to one side. "But you don't really believe that nonsense, do you? About you not being a man a woman can count on? Jovvi may have said that at some time, but that hasn't stopped her from constantly worrying about you. Or thinking about you. You're as important to her as she seems to be to you, so why can't you take it a bit easier on yourself?"

"Mainly because I'm a disappointment to myself," he said, the grin long gone. "When we spoke that night we had dinner together, I actually believed I was over my problem of fearing burnout. It didn't take long to find I was mistaken, though, so I'm completely disgusted with myself. Wouldn't you be?"

"I usually am when it comes to standing up for myself without leaning on the power," I told him. "I can't seem to act or speak or feel the way I want to when it's just me, and that's very frustrating. But then I remind myself that no serious problem disappears overnight, and that I've actually made a lot of progress when you consider how I used to be. I'm not a fully independent person *yet*, but someday I will be."

"You know, that's something I'll have to consider," he said, his expression less intense and more pensive. "If you stop to think about it, I've made *some* progress, but I just don't know if it's enough. Well, that's for later, so let's change the subject. What is it that you need distracting from?"

"Vallant Ro," I pronounced, struggling to keep that giant rush of anger from returning. "The man's impossible, even more now than he used to be. Do you know what he had the nerve to say?"

"I'm almost afraid to ask," Lorand ventured, his brows high again. "And I thought he'd decided to avoid you."

"So did I," I agreed with a short nod. "After trapping me into agreeing to lie with him and then making me wait most of the night before it became clear that he wasn't coming after all—now he wants us to put aside our *'disagreement'* for the good of the *group*. When he said that, I almost set his breeches on fire."

"I'm glad you didn't," Lorand said after choking just a little, an odd glint dancing in his eyes. "And not just because our Blending will need him. But what was that about waiting for him most of the night? Am I wrong in thinking you sounded . . . disappointed when you said that?"

"Well, maybe I *was* looking forward to the time just a little," I grudged, discovering that the subject was hard to discuss even in the presence of the power. "He drove me so crazy that he was almost the only thing I could think about, and then he—"

"Didn't show up," Lorand finished when I couldn't. A tiny amount of tears had begun to moisten my eyes, mostly from the unavoidable realization that the man I found so attractive had lost all interest in me. And the memory of how alone and abandoned I'd felt that night, almost as much as I'd felt since the day my parents married me to a monster. . . .

"But I can't really blame him for stepping clear of the difficulty I represent," I said, blinking away those foolish tears. "I seem to attract powerful men who like to own things, and my father's plans are far from secret. No sensible man would want to get in the way of all that, so— Oh, look. There's Lady Eltrina, waving at us. Our coaches must be here . . . Lorand, would you mind if we waited until tomorrow to lie together? I—don't think I'm quite up to it tonight."

"No, I don't mind," he replied gently as he took my hand and put it on his arm. "But right now I insist on escorting you to the coach, and I don't care *who* doesn't like it."

I gave him as strong a smile as I could just now, then joined him in heading out of the ballroom. The music had started up again a few minutes earlier, but I hadn't noticed. Not that it mattered. All I wanted to do right now was get back to my apartment and release my hold on the power. After that . . . well, I thought I knew what would happen. Tears and Water magic do go rather well together, don't you think?

FIVE

Vallant watched Tamrissa Domon march away from him, giving him no chance to say the ten things he wanted to— all at the same time. She'd agreed with his suggestion just the way he'd hoped she would, but not quite in the *expected*

way. There was something odd about her, something different, and what had she said during her controlled tirade about how she felt? That was something else he felt a strong need to question her on, but when he followed her back to the immediate vicinity of the rest of the group, Jovvi stepped out to block his way to her.

"No, Vallant, you don't want to speak to her again right now, take my word for it," Jovvi admonished, urging him back a few steps. "She was the one who stopped the fires a few minutes ago, and she's still touching the power. I promise you that if you try to speak to her now, her anger will make you truly regret it. What in the world did you say to *get* her that angry?"

"All I did was propose a truce between us for the sake of the group," Vallant replied, finding it difficult to keep his voice down—and his eyes away from Tamrissa. "Are you tryin' to tell me she's actin' so strange because she's still touchin' the power? Why should that make any difference at all? *I* don't get strange when I'm touchin' the power."

"You mean being fully open doesn't change you at all?" Jovvi asked, the question gentle but sounding as if she already knew the answer to it. "Personally, I always feel different with the power coursing through me. I'm more alive and alert, more ready to cope with anything that might happen. But you're not affected in any way?"

"I didn't say I wasn't affected," Vallant pointed out, still oddly disturbed. "I get the same feelin's you do, and a sense of . . . freedom, I suppose it is, as well. But I don't get all strange and different, which Tamrissa has. Are you absolutely certain there's nothin' wrong with her?"

"What's wrong is what her natural personality has been made into," Rion interjected, drawing Vallant's attention. "She's a sweet, warm, and lovely person who hasn't been allowed to exhibit any of those traits. Being in touch with the power makes her more whole and assured, the same way it does with me. Perhaps I should have mentioned that since coming to Gan Garee, I've been more or less in touch with the power all the time. Living with Mother has given me the strong habit of circumspection at all times, and that's probably why you weren't aware of the situation."

"That, Rion, could be why you've changed so much so quickly," Jovvi said, just about taking the words out of Vallant's mouth. "You were able to see what more normal behavior consisted of, and the power helped you to adapt to it. I wonder why no one ever mentioned the power can do things like that."

"There's a lot about the power that no one ever mentioned," Vallant said, and this time Rion looked as though the words had been taken from between *his* teeth. "We need to do some discussin' on the point, but first things need to come first. Rion told me that that noble who came to talk to him wanted most to know about Tamrissa. He said somethin' about the Fire talent bein' the most important one in a Blendin'."

"Oh, dear," Jovvi said with raised brows, and Vallant had the impression she would have preferred to have used a stronger phrase, but had limited herself to the understated. "Do you think he was telling the truth, Rion? Misleading us would be easy since we don't know any better, and it could only be a benefit to our opponents."

"The way he approached the subject leads me to believe that misdirection wasn't his goal," Rion answered with a small headshake. "The very first thing he asked was about Tamrissa's flaws and problems, and that was when he fully expected me to answer. When I simply said she was a lovely lady, he tried to press the point. Finally he urged me to speak about everyone else first if I found it easier, but he still wanted me to come back to Tamrissa."

"You're right, Rion, there's too much there for it to be subtle misdirection," Jovvi said with a distant look. "Comparing your emotions with his at the time, he knew you were about to say something and he felt elation and victory. The satisfaction wouldn't have been so strong if his goal had simply been to pass on false information."

"You remember emotions the way other people remember words?" Vallant asked, curiosity suddenly piqued. "That's somethin' else I didn't know. It looks like we'll have a lot to talk about, but we still haven't settled the other matter. And a strange thought just came to me: Coll and I discovered that the testin' authority knows all about our respective problems. If everythin's set up for the nobles to win, wouldn't they be told all about us? The answer ought to be yes, so why would that group need to hear it from one of *us*?''

Jovvi frowned over the point, obviously agreeing, and so did Mardimil. They all considered the question in silence for a moment, and then Mardimil made a sound of understanding.

"Of course, I should have thought of this immediately," he said then. "I simply keep forgetting what my former peers are like. It's common knowledge that the Advisors never leave anything to chance if the matter is important, so it's hardly likely that they've left the matter of who the next Blending will be to that same chance. They'll already have chosen one of the groups, and that group alone will have all its support.''

"So the others have to find out for themselves, or do without the information," Vallant summed up with a nod. "Now it makes sense, along with why that friend of yours came over. He and his group don't want to end up lookin' like fools by bein' unprepared and maybe losin' to us.''

"But according to the colors of our costumes, we won't be facing them first," Jovvi pointed out, again looking thoughtful. "Why would they bother to question *us* . . . unless . . . Rion, is it possible that your friend and his group have decided to go against the wishes of the Advisors and intend to try to win the Throne themselves?''

"Certainly," Rion agreed with a shrug. "Backstabbing and intrigue are the favorite pastimes of the noble class. If they're successful they won't have anything to worry about, but a question still remains: why us? I saw nothing to show that they approached the other groups as well, so singling us out makes no sense.''

"It does if they've had access to our test results," Jovvi countered, which statement immediately shifted Vallant away from supporting Mardimil's. "We don't really know how we did, remember, but we weren't able to hold back *too* far. We could well have ended up close to the top of the list. . . .''

"Which would make us a force they decided they'd have to reckon with," Vallant finished when Jovvi let her words trail off. "That should also mean we're expected to win in the first competition—shouldn't it?"

"I'd rather not count on that, and I'm glad to see that you're as doubtful as I am," Jovvi replied. "The noble groups know a good deal more than we do, but Rion has pointed out that they don't know it all. We'll have to think long and hard about this. . . ."

"And finish discussing it at another time," Mardimil added, looking past them. "Eltrina is over there and gesturing at us, which ought to mean our coaches are here. What a disappointment that we have to leave so early."

Vallant made a sound of amused support for that sarcasm, and Jovvi chuckled her own agreement. For a group of "peasants who were being honored," they weren't being very appreciative. Instead they lost no time following Coll and Tamrissa, who once again seemed to be extremely friendly. Vallant had once discussed the matter with Coll, and had been very relieved to learn that it was Jovvi in whom Coll was most interested. But considering the discussion Vallant had overheard earlier between Coll and Jovvi, it might be time to raise the matter again—

Vallant forced himself away from that line of thought with disgust, wondering if he would ever learn and remember. How many times did Tamrissa have to show her extreme disinterest in him before he got the message? And how many times would he have to decide to stay away from *all* women before he could make his inner mind remember it? If Tamrissa and Coll became more than friends, it was none of his business. Even if it did hurt like blazes. . . .

What seemed like hundreds of nobles stood around in dozens of groups, and all of them glared at the commoners who were getting to leave before them. Vallant could see the rest of his group ignoring the glares so he did the same, but the urge to teach the useless fools some manners was really strong. If they hadn't been so aware of his presence, he might have indulged in some of those childhood tricks everyone played once their talent grew strong enough.

Like lining someone's shoes with a very thin layer of frozen water. Vallant grinned to himself as he remembered the ploy, which was designed not to be noticed immediately. The ice simply sucked the heat out of the victim's body through the soles of his feet, and before he knew it, the poor victim was shivering with cold. The moisture involved wasn't enough to let you *know* what was happening, at least not until you began to squish a bit when you walked. That usually let the cat out of the bag—or the ice out of the shoe.

"Since there's no longer a need for me to accompany the ladies, I've decided to return to my usual place," Mardimil said when they stopped at their coach. "Not to mention the fact that Coll needs to be filled in about our discussion."

"Before we get back to the residence and all those ears," Vallant agreed, lowering his voice just the way Mardimil had. Coll had looked at them with quickly suppressed startlement, and Vallant had had to keep his own feelings out of his expression. His problem with Tamrissa was *not* Coll's fault, a fact he kept reminding himself about as he climbed into the coach after his two groupmates. It isn't Coll's fault, so *don't* start a fight with the man. . . .

Settling back in the seat next to Mardimil, Vallant worked to keep to his decision. He listened to Mardimil's recital of what they and Jovvi had talked about, and even added a comment or two of his own. Coll was just as surprised to learn of Tamrissa's importance as they'd been, and finally he shook his head.

"I don't know how she's going to take finding that out," he said, sounding worried. "She seems to be really strong when she's touching the power, but I have a feeling it's more . . . cover than reality. She lacks the confidence of a truly strong personality, which means all her doubts and uncertainties are still there under the surface. What are we going to do if she can't handle it?"

"She *can* handle it, and she will," Vallant found himself stating very flatly. "She may have her doubts, but *I* know she's strong enough to handle anythin' *they* throw at her. As long as the rest of us are there to support her, she'll do just fine."

"That's a fairly strange sentiment coming from a man who's treated her the way you have," Coll said, and it seemed to Vallant that the man's tone had grown considerably colder. "If your idea of supporting her is to make

her cry, we'll probably all be better off if you support our
opponents instead.''

"Make her *cry*?" Vallant echoed with a snort, beginning
to lose control of his temper. "You seem to have missed
the fact that she tore me to shreds before stalking off in a
fury. If that's the sort of thing makin' her cry, I won't mind
seein' the practice stopped here and now.''

"Are you trying to claim that your attitude had nothing
to do with it?" Coll demanded, the ice in his words beginning to heat up. " 'He drove me so crazy he was almost
all I could think about,' she said. 'He trapped me into
agreeing to lie with him and I waited most of the night, but
he never showed up,' she said. If that's what you consider
you being torn to shreds, you'd better get some help with
your definitions. You—''

"Wait just a minute," Vallant interrupted, stunned and
disbelieving. "She was never thinkin' about *me*, not with
the way she spoke to me. And she hated the idea of lyin'
with me, so why would she stay up waitin' most of the
night? You've got to be mistakin' what she said.''

"Ro, I'm not mistaken," Coll said slowly and clearly,
his anger having backed off quite a bit. "She had trouble
admitting that she actually looked forward to being with
you, but when she had to say you never showed up, she
couldn't even get the words out. She almost cried instead,
but being in close touch with the power let her refuse to
allow it to happen. But that doesn't mean it didn't *start* to
happen.''

"But . . . I still don't understand," Vallant groped, not
caring how bewildered and lost he sounded. "If she really
was interested, why did she keep pushin' me away?''

"I believe it's because she fears beginning a relationship," Mardimil put in, speaking as gently as Coll had.
"Her first experience with one was so far from pleasant
that the idea of starting a second must be nothing short of
terrifying.''

"She also said she didn't blame you for stepping out of
the way of the plans of very powerful men," Coll added.
"She took that as the reason for your sudden avoidance of
her, which seemed a fairly safe guess. Nothing else had

happened which would have explained your abrupt lack of interest.''

''I . . . thought I was doin' what *she* wanted,'' Vallant muttered, his head spinning. ''She kept snappin' at me and tellin' me to leave her alone . . . I decided I was bein' pathetic, chasin' after a woman who didn't want me around. I knew she wasn't sure about associatin' with a man after what her husband put her through but I thought she didn't want to know me.''

Vallant knew his speech was just short of plaintive, but he was still too stunned to care about that, either. Tamrissa *didn't* hate him? She'd almost cried at the thought of his not coming to her? Well, he'd just have to change *that* oversight. . . .

''You seem to have changed your mind again,'' Mardimil remarked, apparently staring at him through the darkness of the coach. ''If so, perhaps I ought to remind you about the beliefs of the testing authority. If you and Tamrissa suddenly stop feuding, it's possible the testing authority will decide to replace you in the group.''

''Or her,'' Coll added in startled agreement. ''They could suddenly decide that she gets along too well with the rest of us, and replace her with someone none of us could stomach. We were blind for not considering this sooner, but I think there's a way we can fix it. Tomorrow we'll have to have a group discussion that ends in a five-way fight.''

''Now, that sounds like an excellent idea,'' Mardimil said with a grin clear in his voice. ''Not only will Ro still be feuding with Tamrissa, but the rest of us will have started to bicker as well. If the testing authority has any thoughts involving shifting us around, that should end them. They'll decide that any changes can only make the situation better rather than worse, and better won't be what they want.''

''That's fine for the rest of you, but what about Tamrissa and me?'' Vallant demanded, only just suppressing the urge to curse. ''She's miserable thinkin' I don't care any longer, and I've *got* to tell her the truth. There's a lot I want to tell her, and it's waited too long already.''

''Ro, it's just going to have to wait a bit longer,'' Coll said, sounding as though he were forcing patience. ''If it doesn't, you and she could find yourselves in separate residences. What good will it do you to make up with her if the two of you are immediately separated?''

"And it shouldn't be for long," Mardimil added, as though he could sense the wall of stubbornness which had risen high in Vallant. "Once they actually form us into a Blending, there shouldn't be any more danger of relocation. In the meanwhile, you can ask Jovvi to tell Tamrissa the truth. That will stop Tamrissa's being miserable without putting your places in the group in jeopardy."

That suggestion made Vallant pause, even though he still hated the idea of waiting. As long as he knew Tamrissa wasn't suffering it would be easier for *him* to wait, but he still didn't like the restriction. He wanted to go straight up to Tamrissa, take her in his arms, tell her how wonderful it felt not to be hated by the woman he loved, and then kiss her. He also burned to give her his physical love, but that didn't have to happen right away. A delay of an hour or two would be perfectly acceptable. . . .

"All right, you've both made your point," Vallant conceded after a moment, knowing they were waiting to hear his decision. "I'll tell Jovvi to pass on the word to Tamrissa and then I'll join all the rest of you in pretendin' to fight, but only until we're formed into a Blendin'. After that. . . .''

Adding details was unnecessary, especially since the details were no one's business but his and Tamrissa's. He'd need to find a time to speak privately to Jovvi, though. Possibly tomorrow, if no one else decided to go with her to that trial. But she'd need someone with her anyway, so he'd definitely plan on going. . . . After she got through the unpleasantness, there would be time enough to talk. . . .

And tonight he could dream about Tamrissa without calling himself names. Vallant grinned despite the impatience choking him, feeling as though a great burden had been lifted from his shoulders. Hopefully he'd be there to see Tamrissa's expression when she found out the truth. It would be wonderful, absolutely wonderful. . . .

SIX

Jovvi came down early to breakfast, expecting to find that everyone else had slept late. She and Tamrissa had gone directly to their respective beds last night when they got home, and the men had done the same. But Jovvi hadn't been able to sleep, and the fact that the others seemed to have the same trouble had added to her wakefulness. She'd finally had to be firm with herself and use an exercise that forced sleep, partly by cutting her off from an awareness of the people around her.

So when she walked into the dining room to find Vallant and Rion already there, her brows rose in surprise. They both looked up and nodded to her, but then Vallant gestured to his eyes and produced a broad wink. Even more surprisingly Rion did the same, and then Rion held up a finger.

"Ro here is being rather foolish," he said, sounding petulantly annoyed but not looking or feeling the same. "He's decided to accompany you to court this morning, and that despite my disapproval. His being there will make it seem as though you're unable to act for yourself and by yourself."

"Mardimil still doesn't understand what it means to be a gentleman," Vallant put in, the annoyance in his voice also unmatched by his emotions. "My goin' with you will be seen as nothin' more than common courtesy, somethin' his sort has given up on. But then it *is* called common, so what else can you expect?"

"From you?" Rion countered stiffly, greatly amused on the inside. "No more than what I usually get. What a pity

35

that your jealousy over my already knowing the palace and some of its people has gotten completely out of hand.''

Vallant made a loud sound of ridicule, but went back to his food rather than adding to the argument. But it wasn't a real argument, Jovvi realized as she continued on to the buffet. They'd warned her with gestures that they were about to do something and then they'd started their unreal argument. Obviously they were doing it for the benefit of the servants who were surely listening, but the reason behind it would have to be found out only after she and Vallant were out of the house.

Jovvi filled a plate and took it to the table, discovering that she was hungrier than she'd expected to be. There was no question that she would go to court to see what happened to Allestine, but the prospect of going alone had tied her stomach in knots. She never minded doing things by herself, but this time. . . . Thank the Highest Aspect that Vallant had decided to go with her.

The rest of the meal was coldly silent, with Vallant and Rion deliberately ignoring each other. Right at the beginning Jovvi wondered if they were unobserved and actually wasting their time, but spreading her senses just a bit showed immediately that they weren't. One of the male servants stood just out of sight near the kitchen, probably pretending to be on hand just in case one of them wanted something not on the buffet. But the eagerness with which he listened said he was there for another reason entirely, certainly so that he'd have what to report later. Luckily, though, there was no trace of his using Spirit magic.

Rion was the first to leave, which he did with a courtly bow to Jovvi while ignoring Vallant as though the second man were a piece of furniture. Vallant snorted again to show his opinion of that, but Rion ignored the reaction as well. As soon as he was gone, Vallant looked at Jovvi.

''We both know Mardimil was just bein' foolish,'' he said, actually sounding somewhat stuffy. ''Women *need* a man to lean on, so I'll be right there to supply the shoulder. When are we leavin'?''

''Right after breakfast,'' Jovvi told him, doing her part by adding stiffness to her voice. If Vallant hadn't winked again to show he wasn't serious, she *would* have been good and insulted. As it was. . . . "You really don't need to bother going, you know. I can—"

"Now, now, not another word," he interrupted, definitely sounding stuffy. "A true gentleman never finds somethin' like this a bother, so we'll say no more about it."

Jovvi nearly giggled at the way Vallant rolled his eyes after saying that, knowing exactly how narrowminded he sounded. Instead of laughing she simply sighed in exasperation, thereby making sure his playacting wasn't wasted. She could always giggle later—*before* they got to court.

Vallant waited until she was finished eating, and then he escorted her out of the house. The coach she'd arranged for last night was just pulling up, so they waited for it to stop and then climbed in. Once they were settled and the coach was moving again, Jovvi eyed Vallant.

"I think you can tell me now what you and Rion were doing," she said. "And in case you're interested, there was a servant standing just out of sight, taking it all in."

"Actually, I already knew that," he replied with a grin. "It came to me that I can judge if any people are nearby by the amount of body water humans have. And Mardimil and I were doin' what he and I and Coll agreed to do last night: make sure the testin' authority has no reason to break us up. If they think we're gettin' too friendly, they just might do that."

"You're absolutely right!" Jovvi exclaimed. "I missed that, but happily you three didn't. You and Rion will be arguing with Lorand next, I suppose?"

"Mardimil first and then me," Vallant agreed with a nod. "At first we were goin' to do it after the next group meetin', but then we decided we might not have the time to wait. It's gettin' too close to the time they'll be formin' us into a Blendin', and we're hopin' they won't do any separatin' afterward. If they think we can't stand each other, they ought to leave us alone."

"I certainly hope so," Jovvi agreed fervently. "I'll have to speak to Tamma as soon as we get back, to let her know what's going on. After that I can blame her for the fact that Allestine was arrested, and she'll know I'm not serious."

"Coll and Mardimil are supposed to tell her while we're

gone," Vallant said. "They'll both try to get her alone, and
at least one of them ought to succeed."

His words stopped there, but Jovvi could see that there
was something he ached to add. His emotions had rippled
wildly when he'd mentioned Tamma, and Jovvi couldn't
stand it.

"You might as well tell me whatever you're holding
back on," she said, smiling faintly at his startlement. "If
you don't, we'll probably both explode."

"But imposin' now would be wrong," he protested, actually meaning it. "This court business has got to be botherin' you, and I meant to say right away that I don't have
to go in with you if you really don't want company. I can
walk around outside the buildin' until the whole thing is
over—"

"Vallant, please," she interrupted, leaning forward to
touch his hand where it rested on his knee. "I'm very glad
to have you going with me, and talking about what's bothering you won't be imposing. I'm badly in need of something to distract me, so you'd actually be doing me a
favor."

"To tell the truth, I feel like a damned fool just thinkin'
about it," he admitted heavily, his very handsome face
strained. "Talkin' about it is worse, but neither is as bad
as not doin' somethin' to change it. Last night Tamrissa
said some things to Coll, and he got mad and repeated them
to *me*. It seems I was wrong to believe she has no feelin's
for me."

"I think I tried to tell you that at one point, but you were
in too much pain to hear me," Jovvi commented with a
smile and a nod. "I expect Lorand put it a bit less delicately
than I did . . . And now you've decided to do—what?
Change your mind again?"

"The only reason I changed it the first time was to keep
from botherin' a woman who wanted nothin' to do with
me." Now his expression was just serious, and it was clear
that he was telling the truth. "I also felt pretty worthless,
to have a woman like Tamrissa hate me so much."

"It wasn't hate, it was fear," Jovvi felt compelled to tell
him. "She's very much afraid of getting involved again,
and the fact that she only treated *you* that way said clearly

how attracted she was to you. It was rather easy for me to see that, but discussing it without her permission was another matter entirely.''

"And now we have an even bigger problem," he said, leaning forward to rest his arms on his knees and clasp his hands. "I was all for talkin' to her right away and gettin' the misunderstandin' straightened out, but Coll and Mardimil talked me out of it. They pointed out that I was probably kept in the residence while Holter was moved elsewhere because he was startin' to fit in too well. And he also got along with Tamrissa, which seems to be the major point. If *I* start gettin' along with her, I could end up bein' transferred elsewhere.''

"Yes, you certainly could." Jovvi was forced to agree even while she hated the idea. "So that means you can't change the way you've been acting with Tamma, but she has to be told *something*. The way things are now, she's completely miserable."

"And I refuse to let her go on feelin' like that," Vallant said flatly. "This happened because I acted like a fool, and I won't have her sufferin' over my mistake. I'd like you to tell her the truth—and that I'll be lookin' for a chance to get her alone. What the testin' authority doesn't know can't hurt us."

"Well, I'll tell her, of course, but I'm not sure how she'll take it," Jovvi said, needing to tell the man the truth. "She took a very big step forward when she decided to try a relationship with you, but that was just before *you* apparently changed your mind. Now that you've changed it back, there's no guarantee she'll do the same."

"I feel like I'm ridin' a runaway horse," Vallant said after letting out a long, deep breath. "And not only runaway, we're both blindfolded. But you can tell Tamrissa that I offer my apologies in advance, because this time I won't be changin' my mind back again. She'd better do the same, or she'll end up very unhappy with me."

"Vallant, you have to promise me that you won't push her *too* much," Jovvi asked, suddenly nervous. "She's gotten into the habit of reaching to the power in order to protect herself, and she could accidentally cause you a great deal of harm. You have to remember what she's been through—''

"I do remember, but it's time *she* forgot," Vallant said as he sat back, his mind solidly made up. "I won't ever do anythin' to harm her, but it may be time to stop thinkin' of her as breakable. Real women aren't that fragile, and she's as real as they come."

His thoughts slipped into a private area then, and Jovvi didn't have to work very hard to guess which one. She felt the definite urge to press her warning, but usually tried to avoid wasting her time and breath. Vallant's earlier determination about Tamma was like a single flame to the current conflagration raging inside him, and Jovvi could only hope that the comparison would not turn out to be literal.

Having no more conversation to distract her, Jovvi looked out the coach window to see that they were entering an area of the city that seemed to have a large number of official-looking buildings. The sight caused her to shiver just a little, so similar was it to that time she'd had her own brush with the law. The official-looking buildings appeared just the same, only slightly less imposing than they'd been to a very frightened young girl.

The time had been just after she'd met the family which had offered to take her in, but before she'd decided to accept the offer. The people had seemed unbelievably decent, but young Jovvi had seen too much of the other sort to give her trust that easily—even if her gift tried to tell her they were sincere. She'd eaten the food they'd given her and then had returned to the streets, going back to the house twice in five days when finding food elsewhere proved impossible. Each time they'd told her she could stay and live with them, but they hadn't tried to keep her from leaving again.

And then the day came when the guardsmen suddenly appeared everywhere, their aim being to arrest every street child they could catch. There had finally been too many complaints about burglary and trespassing in locked warehouses for the officials to ignore, so they sent out a large number of guardsmen to sweep up the dregs who were causing so much trouble. Very few of the children and older street people avoided the net, and Jovvi wasn't one of them.

She'd been caught easily and thrown into one of the cages-on-wheels the guardsmen had brought along to hold their prizes, and had been too frightened to use her ability in an effort to escape.

There had been so many others in the cage that Jovvi had found it difficult to breathe despite all the open spaces between the cage's bars. It had also been almost impossible to stand, especially when the wagon the cage was sitting in began to move. Everyone had reeked of fear even before that; once they were definitely on the way out of the neighborhood some of them never left, the fear turned to choking terror.

They'd passed the official-looking buildings before the wagon was driven into the back of one, and then they'd been pulled out of the cage and dragged to a series of large cells. The cells afforded more room, but the stink of urine and vomit added to terror and hopelessness had made Jovvi throw up. The filthy straw underfoot hadn't really absorbed what she'd produced, even though it wasn't much. She hadn't had a decent meal in a few days, so there'd been little more than liquid to give up.

They'd been kept in that cell for three days, and once each day they'd been given a bowl of thick gruel and a cup of water. Jovvi had had to force herself to eat the terrible stuff, which had tasted worse than day-old garbage, but she hadn't been able to force herself to sleep. At most she'd catnapped, and then only for a few minutes at a time. Constant fear is exhausting, but it also refuses to let its victim rest. When Jovvi was finally taken out of the cell with five of the other children she knew, she was close to complete collapse.

Before that day Jovvi had never been in a courtroom, but she had no difficulty recognizing it when she and the others were dragged inside. They were made to sit down on a bench at the front of the wood-paneled room, and a man seated at a nearby table had risen to address the panel of judges. He recited the list of crimes they were accused of, and the first of Jovvi's group, a boy she knew and disliked, was pulled off the bench to stand in front of the judges' dais. One of the judges asked if there was anyone in the courtroom who was willing to be responsible for the boy, and when no one spoke up to volunteer, the boy was told he'd been found guilty and was then sent away to work off his sentence.

The fact that they weren't told what the sentence was only made things worse for Jovvi and the others. She sat there in pure terror as one by one the other children were done the same as the first, and finally it was her turn. She waited numbly for her fate to be sealed—but suddenly a voice spoke out, saying *it* would be responsible for her. The voice belonged to the father of the family which had invited her to live with them, and Jovvi never understood why she hadn't fainted with relief.

The man had been required to pay three silver dins in reparation for her crimes, just about every penny the family had. After feeling dizzying relief Jovvi had felt guilty, but Nolin, the man, had just told her she could pay him back when she grew up. He'd taken her home, his wife Minara had helped her to bathe before giving her an old but clean dress to wear, and then they'd fed her. By then it had been impossible for Jovvi to keep her eyes open, and she'd ended up sleeping for a full day. And she'd never gone back to the streets again. . . .

But now she was going back to a courtroom, and the thought of it threatened to make her throw up all over again.

SEVEN

It took some doing, but by the time the coach stopped in front of the large stone building, Jovvi was projecting outward calm. Inward was another matter entirely, but she refused to let herself think about that.

"This whole neighborhood looks like a ghost town," Vallant commented as he helped her out of the coach. "I haven't even seen anybody walking in the street for two or three blocks."

"This is supposed to be the second rest day," Jovvi reminded him with a brief smile of thanks for his help. "It's odd that they didn't wait until tomorrow to hold this trial, and I'm tempted to think there's an ulterior motive involved. But the whole thing might just be standard practice, and I'm simply being overly suspicious."

"In our position, overly suspicious is the safest thing to be," Vallant murmured as they started up the wide stone steps. "Don't forget that I'll be actin' superior and insufferable, and maybe you ought to be actin' more than a little upset. If they're doin' this just to ruin your balance, it would be a shame to make them think they wasted the effort."

Jovvi considered that an excellent idea, especially since it would be easy to arrange. Showing her true feelings rather than hiding them would do it, and that way even another Spirit magic practitioner would be convinced. Yes, that was definitely the way to play it, and the realization made her even more glad that Vallant was there. Normally she would probably have come up with the idea herself, but where courtrooms were concerned there was nothing normal about her reactions.

The heavy wooden front doors of the building were unlocked, and just inside was a guardsman standing a post. He directed them to the room where the trial was being held, on the second floor and in the daylight court, whatever that was. She and Vallant produced rather loud footsteps as they crossed the wide, empty floor to the proper stairway, and Jovvi was relieved to see that her companion was only faintly disturbed about being indoors. With all that emptiness around them, there wasn't much feeling of confinement.

The second-floor corridor had windows at either end, but there were still lamps lit around the first set of double doors on the right. Opening one of the doors showed them where everyone had gathered, more than a dozen people in addition to the defendants. But the three high chairs up on the dais were empty, which meant that court wasn't yet in session. An older man dressed like a bailiff stood near the doors they entered by, and when he saw them he came over.

"Good mornin'," he greeted them pleasantly, his accent sounding just like Vallant's. "Can I help you folks with somethin'?"

"This lady is here to observe the trial," Vallant answered with a smile. "She's the one they tried kidnappin', but the officials said they wouldn't need her testimony. Is it all right if she and I just sit down back here somewhere?"

"You're welcome to sit anyplace you like," the bailiff replied with a smile of his own, one that seemed a bit warmer than the first one he'd produced. "If anyone has a right to observe the trial, I'd say this lady is it. And if one of you has any questions about what you see, don't hesitate to ask."

"That's really lovely of you," Jovvi told him with one of her own best smiles. "I just might have some questions, so we'll sit down right here."

The bailiff nodded to show that it was fine with him, so Jovvi urged Vallant to move to the bench first and let her sit on the end. Vallant hesitated very briefly, but the room was rather large and he wasn't far from the door. It was possible to feel his clench-jawed efforts at self-control, but they were successful enough to let him do as she wanted.

Once they were seated, Jovvi made herself look around a bit more deliberately. Ark and Bar were seated not far from Allestine at the front of the room, but her two bullies were wearing chains while she was not. Jovvi had expected to find Allestine frantic and terrified, but in point of fact the woman was calm and a bit impatient. It was as though she considered the proceeding a formality, and was just waiting to have it over and done with.

For a moment Jovvi wondered whether someone had lied to Allestine about what would happen, and then she realized that it didn't matter. Someone could have lied, but it was just like the spoiled brat Allestine to expect to get away with whatever she did. She'd gotten her own way for so many years that it was probably beyond her to picture any other outcome. Jovvi sighed and braced herself, anticipating

what would happen if things went against the woman.
Which they probably would. . . .

Everyone sat or stood around for a number of minutes,
some of those at the front of the courtroom speaking together in soft, secretive voices. They were the prosecuting
officials, Jovvi suddenly understood, and their thought patterns suggested that they didn't know why they were there
on a rest day. So much for the practice being an ordinary
one.

And there was someone probing gently at Jovvi with
Spirit magic. She'd noticed as soon as the attempt began,
but had made no effort to keep the practitioner away from
her surface thoughts and emotions. As Vallant had said, if
they were trying so hard to upset her, it would be foolish
to make them think their efforts were wasted. Not to mention the fact that she *was* upset.

At the end of the double handful of minutes, a door
opened on the left side of the room and three men appeared.
They all wore the heavy purple robes of judges, and filed
up onto the dais and took their places. Once they were
seated, everyone in the courtroom stood up and bowed their
respect. The judge in the center, the presiding judge, nodded acknowledgment to let everyone sit again. The judge
on the right, who oversaw the procedures used by the pros-
ecution, and the judge on the left, charged with looking out
for the accused, made no effort to add their own nods.

"Now," the presiding judge said, once everyone was
settled. "Will someone please tell me why we're all here
this morning?"

"The circumstances are rather special, Your Honor," the
chief prosecutor said after getting to his feet. The man had
Spirit magic, and although he was no more than a Low-to-
Middle talent, he must certainly be able to feel the judge's
vast annoyance.

"As I'm sure the Court knows," he continued, "we're
in the midst of preparing for the competitions which will
choose our next Seated Blending. The matter before you
this morning concerns the attempted kidnapping of one of
the participants who qualified for the competitions. The
special section of Advisory law therefore comes into play,
which mandates the speediest trial possible."

"I can't see that waiting one more day would have caused the entire system to break down," the judge grumbled, dissatisfaction clear on his broad, middle-aged face. "But since we're already here, we might as well get on with it. Go ahead and start giving us the facts."

"Really, Judge, this is all such foolishness," Allestine interrupted as she rose gracefully to her feet. "The charges are absolutely untrue, and—"

"Dama, this isn't the time," the judge on the left interrupted in turn, his face expressionless. "You'll be allowed your say, but not until the prosecutor has his. Sit down now, and wait until you're asked to speak."

Allestine was extremely annoyed, but she still nodded and smiled at the judge and resumed her seat. She seemed to think that she'd done something to help her cause, but Jovvi knew better. All three of the judges were Low talent Spirit magic users, and not one of them had missed Allestine's very transparent emotions.

The prosecutor went on to describe the attempted kidnapping in surprising detail, ending with the fact that the victim hadn't tried to press charges. That was why the empire, much less softhearted and forgiving than a young, inexperienced woman, was bringing the matter before the bar.

"Very simply put, Your Honor, this isn't an attempt that can or should be overlooked," the prosecutor wound up. "Qualified participants for the competitions are rare enough that they must be thoroughly protected, so that no one tries the same again. We respectfully ask the court to make an example of this woman and her cohorts."

"Why are the two men in chains?" the judge on the right asked after the prosecutor bowed. "Since there's a squad of guardsmen around them, chains seem rather unnecessary."

"A squad of guardsmen was also sent to arrest the three, Your Honor," the prosecutor explained, faint embarrassment over the omission clear in the man's thoughts. "The two men still tried to resist, apparently at the orders of the defendant. They're in chains now to avoid a repetition of the incident."

"Very commendable," the judge on the right commented dryly, his tone telling the prosecutor that the point was an important one and shouldn't have been overlooked. His thoughts seemed to indicate that the man was new, and therefore wasn't yet used to all parts of the proper procedures.

"All right, Dama, now it's your turn," the judge on the left said to Allestine. "Were you telling us earlier that the charges are a bit harsh?"

"Not harsh, Judge, completely untrue," Allestine said as she rose again, completely ignoring the hint given her by the judge. "That silly bit of fluff was lying when she told everyone what happened. The truth is that I'd come to say goodbye to her, and she begged me to take her back to Rincammon with me. She said she hated everything about this city and wanted to go home, back to my residence in our city. I tried to be as gentle as possible when I refused her, but she still flew into a rage. She made me stop the coach then and there to let her out, but not before she said I'd be sorry for refusing her. I had no idea what she meant until the guardsmen came to arrest us. Her story is a lie, Your Honor, from beginning to end."

She used her smile on all three of the judges then, moving her body very slowly and gracefully. Jovvi recognized the subtle movement as one all courtesan are taught, to show prospective patrons that the courtesan is completely available. Allestine considered her speech—and offer—a full success, but that was because she had Low level Fire magic. Spirit magic showed Jovvi how unhappy the three judges were with Allestine's story, the judge on the left disgusted with the way she'd ignored his suggested defense.

"Dama, are you saying you weren't overcome by emotional loss and therefore found yourself doing something foolish?" he tried again, this time spelling it out for her. "The young lady had lived in your residence long enough for you to become sisterly—or motherly—fond of her, so perhaps you weren't able to face the idea of leaving her behind all alone. That would explain—"

"Nonsense, Your Honor," Allestine interrupted with a small laugh, actually trying to make the words sound coy. "The girl was a terrible troublemaker in the residence, and she wasn't even particularly popular with my patrons. With that in mind, you can see that the idea of my trying to kidnap her is pure nonsense. The truth is that I was very relieved to be rid of her.''

"So that's the truth, is it?" the judge on the right said while the one on the left sighed with exasperated resignation. "Then why don't you tell us, Dama, why you came all this way just to visit a girl you don't like? You've conducted no business of any sort in this city, nor have you visited anyone else. Court investigators checked the point thoroughly, so there's no mistake.''

"I'm afraid they weren't quite as thorough as all that,'' Allestine disagreed, apparently prepared for the question. "I came to Gan Garee to see if it was practical to open a residence here. I've been thinking about expanding for quite some time, and finally decided to look into the matter. Courtesy forced me into visiting that stupid girl while I was here, which I certainly now wish I hadn't.''

"Looking into expanding your business would mean seeing what properties are available and assessing the competition you would face,'' the judge on the right pursued, his expression hard and unyielding. "You may now tell this court how you found out what was available, and the method you used to gauge your future competition.''

"Why, Your Honor, the answer to those questions is very simple,'' Allestine purred, privately feeling a ridiculing delight. "I *meant* to do those things, but I'm afraid I disliked this city the moment I laid eyes on it. As soon as I got here I decided against opening a residence after all, and so had no need to do any investigating.''

"I see,'' the judge on the right responded stiffly, vastly annoyed with Allestine's inner amusement. "You came all the way from Rincammon just to change your mind once you got here. Would you now like to explain how a woman with High ability in Spirit magic can possibly make an unpopular courtesan? Or how such a woman could possibly prefer the life of an unpopular courtesan to the chance of becoming one of the new Seated Blending? Those points are still rather unclear.''

"Not to me they aren't,'' Allestine all but snapped, resenting the fact that the prosecuting judge had brought up the very same argument Jovvi had. "The girl just isn't very bright, and she never seemed to realize that my patrons didn't like her. She would boast about having first standing in the residence, and never noticed that the other girls were laughing at her. That, Your Honor, was the way it was."

"That, Dama, is a crock," the prosecuting judge countered, completely out of patience. "A High practitioner in Spirit magic would have to be dead not to notice unpopularity and laughter at her expense. You leave me no choice but to ask for an unbiased accounting."

He looked at the other two judges then, and the defense judge simply shrugged and nodded. It seemed to Jovvi that he couldn't think of a reason to counter the request and therefore was forced to agree to it. The presiding judge nodded when he saw that, and then raised his arm.

"It's the unanimous decision of this court that the defendant be required to give an unbiased accounting," he announced to everyone in general. "The chief court clerk is authorized to make the necessary preparations."

People got up and began to move around and talk to each other then, leaving Allestine feeling confused and vaguely worried. Jovvi was also confused, so she took the opportunity to turn to the friendly bailiff.

"Can you tell me what that's all about?" she asked in a soft voice, looking up at him. "I've never heard that phrase before."

"It's used only when the defendant denies all the charges lodged," the bailiff replied just as softly after bending to her. "The court wants to know the truth, and the only one here who can give it to them without question is the defendant herself. She'll be given the drink, and once it starts workin' on her she'll tell the court everythin' it wants to know."

"What drink is that?" Jovvi asked with a frown. "Is it a truth drug of some kind?"

"Better than those phony truth drugs," the man replied with a smile. "It's called Puredan, and when it's inside somebody they have to do as they're told. They keep a careful eye on the stuff, because once somebody under its influence is told somethin', they'll still obey the command once the Puredan wears off. And since it's supposed to taste like funny water, people could have it fed to them without knowin' about it. That's why they're so careful about who can use it.''

Jovvi nodded her thanks and turned back to what was going on in the courtroom again. Allestine was in the process of drinking a glass of clear liquid which one of the men in the room had brought to her, and the judges were watching carefully as she drank. Her mind said she didn't know what it was that she drank, but had accepted it despite her annoyance over the delay in her release.

And then Jovvi started as an unexpectedly swift reaction began in Allestine. The woman hadn't even finished the entire glass of liquid when her thought processes came to a sudden halt. All voluntary cogitation seemed to be gone, and she stopped drinking until the court clerk quietly urged her to finish the liquid. She did so immediately, then stood in docile thoughtlessness, waiting patiently for the next thing she would be told.

There was something of a stir over near where Ark and Bar sat, and Jovvi suddenly noticed how agitated their minds were. It had taken them a moment to realize what Allestine was being given, and by the time they tried to interfere it was too late to stop her from drinking. The guardsmen got the two bullies quieted down again, and by then Jovvi had noticed the two men seated a few rows behind the squad of guardsmen. They weren't at all happy about what was going on, but the frustration level inside them said there was nothing they could do to stop it.

"Why don't we start with a simple but obvious point," the prosecuting judge said suddenly, quieting all other conversation in the room. "In your initial statement, Dama, you said that your two male companions didn't realize at first that they were resisting arrest. You claimed that they thought they were protecting you from some sort of attack, and now I ask if that statement was true."

"Of course not," Allestine responded at once, her voice soft and entirely free of reluctance. "They knew the guardsmen were there to arrest us, so they tried to prevent that from happening. It was what they were supposed to do."

A not-quite ripple went through the people in the room, a voiceless reaction to the easy and damning admission. Jovvi could tell she wasn't the only one who had never seen the results of Puredan use, and the others seemed as shaken as Jovvi felt.

"That sounds more like it," the prosecuting judge said with satisfaction. "And now you may tell us about the reason for your presence in Gan Garee. Did you really come here to see about expanding your business?"

"It would be rather impractical for me to expand all the way here," Allestine replied calmly. "The residence at home requires my close personal supervision, and so would any other residence I opened. I might be able to divide my time if the two were in the same city, but not with them being so far apart. No, the only reason I came here was to see what Jovvi was doing."

"Didn't you know what she was doing?" the judge asked next. "She came here to test for High practitioner, didn't she?"

"Certainly, and that's why I had to follow," Allestine agreed. "She's always been so quick to do just the right thing for herself that I knew she would choose to stay here if she passed those tests. And maybe even if she didn't, since any residence in the city would have accepted her gladly. But she brings in more gold than all the rest of my ladies combined, so I simply couldn't afford to let her go. I made up my mind to come after her and bring her back, knowing no one would notice the absence of one single girl."

"Didn't you realize that she's more than just another girl?" the judge pursued. "How could you think no one would notice the disappearance of a competitions entrant?"

"Everyone knows that competition business is nonsense," Allestine said, almost adding a small laugh. "Real people never bother about it, so why should I? Besides, I *wanted* her back in my residence, and I usually get what I want. Ark and Bar make sure of that, so why shouldn't I have tried to kidnap her? It didn't even matter that she said she would report me to the authorities. I *wanted* her back."

"Is that why you didn't leave the city when your attempt failed?" the judge asked next. "You had all your possessions with you and you'd paid your inn charges in full, our investigators told us, but then you went back to the inn. Were you going to try again?"

"Of course, but that isn't why I didn't leave," Allestine answered, her hands folded comfortably in front of her. "It wasn't possible to leave, it just wasn't, and that's why I decided to try again. We would have made sure she was unconscious that second time, but I'm not certain about what I would have done with her. It wasn't possible to leave. . . ."

Allestine's voice trailed off as though she were confused about something, but she really had nothing in her mind that could *be* confusing. Jovvi, however, wasn't in the same position, and she was both confused and disturbed. Something wasn't right here, she knew, but before she was able to figure out what, the defense judge spoke.

"Did you regret your actions at all?" he asked, his mind weary with the necessity. "Weren't you the least bit sorry that you tried what you did? Wasn't there the smallest chance that you would have changed your mind about trying again?"

"No, I wasn't sorry," Allestine admitted quickly and easily. "Why would I be sorry about taking back what's mine? She belongs to me, you know, and always will. Just like the other girls in the residence, only she's much more valuable than them. When I get her back, she'll make my fortune even larger than it already is."

"I think that's clear enough," the presiding judge said while Jovvi's insides twisted and knotted. Allestine really did consider her a slave, and would not have hesitated to keep her a prisoner if she'd gotten her back to the residence. "I now direct the senior court clerk to bring the defendant out of it, so that she'll be fully aware when sentence is pronounced."

As the clerk approached Allestine again, the three judges began to speak softly among themselves. The prosecuting and defending judges seemed to be making suggestions, and the presiding judge listened and asked an occasional question. Jovvi could feel his effort to keep an open mind, but it wasn't possible to deny completely that he'd already made a decision. In the interim the clerk had been speaking to Allestine, and now her thoughts had returned as quickly as they'd previously disappeared. When the clerk walked away from her, she looked up at the three judges with faint puzzlement.

"Does the defendant have anything she'd like to add?" the presiding judge asked, sounding downright solemn. "This, Dama, will be your last opportunity to do so."

"How many times can I repeat that the silly little chit is lying?" Allestine asked sleekly, as though she had no idea about what she'd said only a few moments ago. "I'm completely innocent, and I think I've shown that no one can prove differently."

Once again she didn't quite smirk, but that was only on the outside. The presiding judge saw the same thing Jovvi did, but wasn't nearly as upset by it.

"But the opposite of your claims *has* been proven, and in a way no one can doubt or discredit," the presiding judge said in a ponderous voice. "Allestine Tromin, stand forward and hear the penalty for your crimes."

"What are you talking about?" Allestine tried to shrill, suddenly frightened by what she'd heard. "Who could have—"

"Allestine Tromin, you have been found guilty of a terrible crime through the testimony of your own words," the judge plowed on, overriding Allestine's protests. "Kidnapping with the intent to enslave is vile enough, but to take as your victim a rare resource of the empire is unforgivable."

Allestine now stood with her mouth opening and closing, but no sound emerged. Her face had gone completely pale and her mind clanged with shock. No one had ever challenged her word before, and now it was not only challenged but declared a lie. Jovvi could see that she began to believe the scene unreal, as though it were nothing but a nightmare.

"For these reasons I shall pronounce an equally monstrous sentence," the presiding judge continued, his talent closed down to separate him from the woman he spoke to. "You are hereby remanded to the department of justice, which will transport you to one of the empire's deep mines. There you will remain, performing hard labor, for five full years. And those two men, who accompanied you in perfidy, will also accompany you in your sentence. They will suffer the same fate, but at two other mines, to exclude the possibility of continuing your mutual support. Take them all away.''

The final ritual words seemed to release everyone, meaning Ark and Bar began to fight being taken out. A guardsman went and wrapped a big hand around Allestine's arm, but she refused his urging to go with him. She simply stood there and shook her head, denying everything she couldn't accept, and the guardsman had to call someone to help him with her. When the two men began to drag her out she started to scream and struggle, and the screaming didn't stop until a door closed to cut off the sound.

"Jovvi, are you all right?" Vallant asked, somehow from a long distance off. "Just hold on, it's all over with now. Would you mind fetchin' her some water?"

The last was to the bailiff, Jovvi knew in a dreamy, distant way, and then she became aware of how Vallant had begun to rub her hand and wrist. The brisk action brought her back a short way, and that was when deep shock moved aside for extreme pain.

"No, it's all right," Vallant said quickly and softly when she started to sob. "That sentence was terrible, but no one can say she didn't earn it. She was the one who came after *you*, and no one was makin' her do it. She went ahead and acted as she pleased because she refused to believe she'd ever be caught and punished. This is all *her* fault, not yours.''

"I . . . should have . . . looked harder for . . . a way to . . . stop her," Jovvi sobbed, dizzy with guilt and horror. "It's all . . . my fault, and . . . now she'll die just . . . like my father did.''

That part was the hardest for Jovvi to bear, the knowledge that Allestine had been sent to the deep mines. They were a hundred times worse than the mine her father had died in, and all the workers were prisoners. Allestine was a hundred times more likely to die, and Jovvi knew it was all *her* fault.

"That witch won't die," Vallant said as Jovvi cried against him, holding her tight in his arms. "Once she comes out of the shock, she'll start hatin'. She'll hate the man who made her pay for what she did, she'll hate the law that let him do it, and she'll hate you for bein' the cause of it all. It won't be her own greed and stupidity that caused her downfall, it'll be all *your* fault. So you see you don't have to blame yourself, because she'll be doin' it for you.''

That line of reasoning was so absurd that it got Jovvi's attention, and after a moment she was forced to admit that Vallant was probably right. It took away only a very small amount of the pain, but enough of it that she was able to sit straight and accept the water the bailiff brought. After sipping at it she noticed that they were the last ones left in the room, everyone else having gone without her seeing it.

"As soon as you feel a bit stronger, we'll start to take you home," Vallant said, and oddly enough his tone had shifted to pomposity again. "I knew a weak little thing like you couldn't handle somethin' like this alone, and I mean to tell Mardimil I was right as soon as we get back to the residence."

Vallant had reverted to the game he and Rion had been playing earlier that morning, and Jovvi didn't understand why—until she suddenly realized that there was someone lurking behind one of the partially closed doors at the front of the room. The someone was a Spirit magic user, and he was delighted with what he heard and felt.

"I'm not weak," Jovvi protested stiffly as soon as she understood what was going on, putting the proper sense of insult on the surface of her mind. "This was all a terrible shock, and anyone in my position would have reacted the same."

"Of course any woman would have acted the same," Vallant returned with grating indulgence. "But that just proves I know women a lot better than Mardimil does. Are you ready to get goin' yet? I promised myself a good long soak in the bath house, and I'm lookin' forward to it."

"Yes, certainly I'm ready," Jovvi muttered as she handed the water glass back to the bailiff, who was fighting not to show his extreme disapproval. Then she rose stiffly to her feet, her inner self rigid because of the contact with Vallant's supporting arm, and let herself be urged out of the room. She felt as though she'd been put through that very first test again, and was incredibly grateful that Vallant had noticed that eavesdropper. Now they were leaving the properly false impression behind them, and they could go home feeling they'd accomplished something.

But it would be quite some time before Jovvi got over what she'd been forced to witness.

EIGHT

Delin Moord glanced into the dining room as he passed it, but only Selendi and Homin were in there, giggling as they fed each other. It came as no surprise that it was breakfast which they fed each other, even though normal people were almost ready to have lunch. Despite their early return to the house last night, Selendi, Homin, and Bron had still slept late. Kambil was awake, however, and when Delin joined him in the sitting room Kambil looked up.

"I heard you leaving this morning, and wondered whether it was a woman or business which got you out of bed so early," Kambil said with a smile. "Then I realized that you were more determined than anticipating, and immediately ruled out the ladies. I can see you were successful in whatever the business was, so I'll ask only if it concerns our joint project."

"It certainly does, and you're very much a spoilsport," Delin answered, finding it impossible to hold back a pleased grin. "I wanted to make an announcement, but now you've ruined it. I have just what we need to know, and all it cost me was five gold dins."

"Now, that's a reasonable price," Kambil said with raised brows. "How could someone with all the knowledge we needed ask so little?"

"It was because the man didn't have it, he only guarded it," Delin said with a laugh. "I paid a visit to the main offices of the testing authority—wearing plain clothes and a gentleman's privacy mask—and discovered that there was only one guard on duty on the premises. The man had been drinking and was dead asleep and snoring, and he never even stirred when I walked past him. On the way out I left five gold dins in his uniform pocket, where he's certain to find them. If our luck continues to hold, he'll drink himself to death before anyone realizes someone might have gotten past him to the complete records."

"Just how complete are we talking about?" Kambil asked, leaning forward in his chair to stare at Delin. "Just the commoners—or the noble groups as well?"

"The answer is both, but don't get your hopes *too* high," Delin replied, a shadow passing over his pleasure. "The records concerning Adriari's group weren't with the others, leading me to guess that the Advisors consider them no one else's business. That means we can't confirm or disprove the surmise that it was Adriari who put out those fires last night."

"And so, in the absence of proof either way, we have to assume the worst," Kambil said, leaning back again. "Believing anything else would be kidding ourselves, and we can't afford to do that. But you did find out about the commoners in orange? When we missed our chance to question them last night, I thought Hiblit might have taken us down to oblivion with him."

"No, all the information we'll need was right there," Delin said, turning to the tea service and beginning to pour himself a cup. "They really are the strongest of all the peasant groups, but a memorandum at the beginning of the file recommends that some of them be shifted around before a Blending is formed. Apparently they get along a bit too well."

"And they'll probably be told that the change is for the good of the group," Kambil said with amusement. "I'll admit I'm surprised, but I suppose I shouldn't be. If we were defeated easily by commoners, our loss would reflect on the entire nobility."

"But two of our groups *will* be defeated," Delin reminded him, turning with his cup of tea to find a chair. "Now that I've seen exactly who's involved, I can appre-

ciate the point. The two groups are composed of the lowest
segment of nobility, and the offspring of those who are out
of favor with—or have annoyed—the Advisors.''

"Neither of whom will know they're *meant* to lose,''
Kambil said, nodding. "And the strongest commoner group
will be broken up. I now suspect we may have judged Rigos a bit too harshly. And what of the group Mardimil is
in, the second strongest? Will they also be broken up?''

"The memorandum mentioned proposed attempts to disrupt their friendliness with one another,'' Delin supplied
after sipping at his tea. "If the disruptions work, they'll be
left alone to form a Blending that will never operate properly. If the disruptions are a failure, various members will
be replaced despite the duplication of the plan used with
the first group. Everything in the memorandum, however,
leads me to realize that *we* are badly in need of adjusting
of our own.''

"What sort of adjusting?'' Kambil asked, his brows
high. "I thought our progress with our abilities was perfectly acceptable.''

"It is, but we need to do better there as well,'' Delin
said, feeling the frown that creased his brow. "Our test
results show us to be no more than the equals of the second
strongest peasant group, and that will never do. We have
to be the absolute best, but that isn't our greatest problem.
There were only hints in what I read, but everything suggests that Bron will keep us from Blending properly.''

"Because of his jealousy over Selendi and Homin?''
Kambil asked, still obviously surprised but clearly understanding what Delin had meant. "That won't be difficult to
fix, not when Selendi has that driving need to be with every
man she meets. We'll just tell Bron that it's now all right
for him to lie with her, and—''

"Yes, I think you see the rest of the problem now,''
Delin said when Kambil's words broke off abruptly. "At
the moment Bron is jealous of Homin, but once he lies with
Selendi his jealousy will become contempt again. Homin's
new self-confidence will never let him accept that contempt, and I noticed that he's become aware of how I've
been controlling Bron. Homin will counter Bron's contempt
with a taunt about how Bron is a fool to believe he's our

leader, and that will cause an explosion to tear the entire group apart.''

"So something has to be done about one or the other of them,'' Kambil concluded, nodding again. "Weakening Homin's self-confidence would be easiest, but that would leave Bron as a continuing problem for the rest of us. I think it's him we have to do something about.''

"Such as what?'' Delin challenged sourly. "How do we turn a loudmouthed, obnoxious fool into someone we can Blend with? I racked my brain all the way back here, but not a single idea tumbled forth. If you've had better luck, I'll be delighted to hear it.''

"I do have something of an idea, it's just not fully formed yet,'' Kambil said with a wave of his hand. "Give me a little while, and then we should be able to do something. Did you find out anything else in those reports?''

"One other thing,'' Delin agreed, forcing himself to push aside the problem Bron represented. "That memorandum was highly confidential, so it included the triggering phrase used on the peasants which will control them during the competitions. They'll be forced to obey whomever uses the phrase, and if they're told to lose, they will.''

"If the commoners are controlled *that* tightly, why are they going through all this rigamarole about separating groups and breaking up friendships?'' Kambil demanded. "All they would have to do is tell them to compete for a while before losing realistically, and the rest of the nonsense could be forgotten.''

"That's what I thought, but apparently the Advisors prefer to be a bit more subtle,'' Delin replied with a shrug. "They'll use the phrase on the group facing Adriari's people first, but not on the others. The two peasant groups able to win will be allowed to do so, and only if they prove stronger than the two noble groups meant to face them in the second competition will the phrase be used again. If not, the noble groups will simply be allowed to win on their own. The observers' group *will* be watching closely, so that's probably the best way to handle it.''

"The observers' group composed of commoner leaders,'' Kambil remembered aloud. "Yes, I'd almost forgotten about them. Have they ever lodged a really serious

protest over the outcome of one of the competitions? You'd
think it would be easier to buy them off rather than try to
fool them.''

"They're a bunch of malcontents and discontents who
would rather make trouble than have gold," Delin informed
him. "I'm quoting my father there, but there's no reason
to think his assessment is wrong. They're all proven rab-
blerousers who have a common hatred for their betters, and
they've made trouble more than once. The Advisors clearly
have no desire to cause a riot, so they use subtlety rather
than gold.''

"Which doing, if I'm not mistaken, you intend to put to
your own use," Kambil said, studying him narrowly.
"Would you like to share whatever it is you have in
mind?''

"Well, you were the one who brought the point up in
the first place," Delin responded with a smile, enjoying
himself again. "You said, in effect, that we would be best
off if we never had to face Adriari's group. But there was
only one way to accomplish that, and the single way was
impossible. Do you still consider it so impossible?''

"You intend to help the commoners win against them?"
Kambil demanded, satisfyingly quick to understand. "From
what you've said I assume you mean to tell them about the
keying phrase, and trust them to find a way around the need
to respond to it. But even assuming their Blending works
and they're able to win, what about when *we* have to face
them? You said our two groups are equally strong.''

"What would you propose as an alternative plan?" Delin
countered, privately contemptuous of the man's cowardice.
"Figure out which group will face Adriari's second? That
group will be *us* if our plans go right, and for all we know
they'll be stronger rather than just our equals. No, we have
to take a chance here, but it's one that offers us an edge
beyond the fact that the peasants are actually our inferiors
rather than our equals. It seems that the members of that
group have their little . . . quirks.''

"What do you mean by quirks?" Kambil asked, still
clearly concerned but now a bit calmer. "Will they all faint
if we yell 'Boo!' together?''

"Your sarcasm isn't far off the mark," Delin allowed

with a grin. "It seems that their lady of Fire is easily frightened and cowed, the sort of lady who trembles and weeps. She spent two years married to a sadistic merchant and never once even singed his toes."

"Really?" Kambil said, his brows high again. "No wonder Mardimil refused to discuss her. She's probably the only woman he's ever known who hasn't told him what to do."

"And our acquaintance Mardimil has his dear mother still riding on his back," Delin continued. "He's changed his given name in an effort to free himself from her, but the one time she barged into the residence she nearly succeeded in dragging him out with her. If we arrange for her to visit him again at just the wrong time. . . ."

"He'll be so disconcerted he probably won't be able to function at all," Kambil finished for him, nodding approvingly. "And if we have trouble arranging a visit, we can always send a note supposedly from her that will rattle his teeth. What about the others?"

"The Earth magic member has a morbid fear of burnout, and the Water magic user is a claustrophobe," Delin supplied. "They'll be childishly simple to manipulate, assuming they manage an actual Blending to begin with. And on top of that, the Water magic user has managed to start a feud with the lady of Fire, which has to indicate some sort of higher talent on his part. Earth magic and Spirit magic were more than close to begin with, but now the two work to avoid each other. Again, they all may find it impossible to Blend, but if they manage it we can safely set them against Adriari's group."

"That's a rather large if," Kambil observed, crossing his legs as he finally reached for his teacup. "But you haven't said anything about that Spirit magic user. What's his or her quirk?"

"Her, and she doesn't seem to have one," Delin replied, looking down into the depths of his tea. "That disturbed me at first, but in the absence of a quirk she has a weakness. She strongly dislikes the idea of becoming involved with the legal system, so they've arranged for someone close to her to be tried and sentenced today. I don't know all the details, but she was involved in some way and they expect her to blame herself for whatever happens."

"Which will ruin her balance, at least for a time," Kambil said, once again nodding with approval. "And if we should need it, reminding her of the incident at the proper time will affect her balance again. Yes, I can see now why you want to help them against Adriari's group. If they make it through far enough to face us, we won't have any trouble handling them. So now what?"

"Now all that's left is to find out who will be taking Hiblit's place," Delin said with a sigh. "I'd suggest that the next one can't possibly be as bad as the first two, but something tells me we haven't yet seen the worst. Our luck has been too good everywhere else for it to continue to hold here."

"Well, it won't be long before we find out," Kambil said, something about him suggesting that he found Delin's pessimism amusing. "A messenger came by earlier with word that our most recent Advisory agent would call on us later today. We were therefore asked to remain in the residence, but you'd already gone. I didn't mention that, of course, and planned to point out that you couldn't have known you were supposed to have stayed in if the agent got here before you returned."

"Well, that's one piece of luck in our favor," Delin allowed, feeling fractionally better. "I'm here and he's not, so we have no excuses or explanations to make. I wonder—"

Delin's comment was interrupted by a knock at the door, which was immediately followed by the entrance of one of the servants. There was a figure behind the servant, which probably meant the new agent had arrived. Delin began to put his teacup on the table next to him but froze in midmotion when the figure behind the servant came forward to where he could be easily seen.

"The Advisory agent," the servant announced unnecessarily. "Lord Rigos Baril."

NINE

Eltrina Razas entered the meeting oozing friendliness and calm, but on the inside she was filled with annoyance. Once again she was being forced to do something Ollon Capmar should have been doing, with her there only to convince everyone that she was the one who'd actually done the work. She'd had to *do* the work instead of simply pretending, and now she was missing the dinner engagement she'd made with a very interesting man. When she finally managed to cause Ollon's death, her satisfaction would be double what she originally had expected it to be.

"Good evening, Lady Eltrina," High Lord Embisson Ruhl said in greeting, his smile as cold and unreal as usual. "We were expecting Ollon to be back in his usual place. Hasn't he returned yet?"

"He's done no more than send word, Lord Embisson," Eltrina answered carefully, having no wish to insult the man even accidentally. He was so powerful, he took meals with the Advisors on a regular basis. . . . "He's still terribly broken up over the tragic death of his sister, and apparently can't bring himself to return to work. He asked me to sit in for him again and give your committee the final report on the commoners—final, that is, until they're formed into Blendings."

"Yes, we're aware of which 'final' this is, dear," Lord Embisson told her with cold condescension that cut like ice shards. The man was so ancient his hair was completely white, but his bulky body was still straight and apparently strong. It was said that this was his *third* twenty-fifth year, and that was just possible. Eltrina firmly kept herself from blushing over the faux pas she'd made and took her seat at the large table as gracefully as possible.

"You don't seem to have brought many files with you," Lord Embisson observed once she was settled. "One thin folder . . . Ollon usually brings everything."

"I'm afraid I lack Lord Ollon's physical strength," Eltrina replied with a smile when she would have preferred to tell the stupid old man just how much of a fool he really was. And he was the only member of his committee who ever spoke. . . . "In view of that lack I use my memory instead, so I'm just as prepared to render a full report. Shall I begin?"

Lord Embisson waited for the two youngest members of his committee—men who must have been at least forty—to pick up their pens and poise them over blank paper, and then he nodded his permission to proceed.

"As you know," Eltrina began, "this year we have six viable groups rather than five. I've kept the sixth group unofficial, of course, as I planned to use them when and if necessary to fill in any gaps. I've also discovered that some people simply aren't able to Blend, and if that happens with one of the five original groups, we'll have the unofficial sixth to put in their place."

A very soft murmur went around the table, and there was even a faint flicker in Lord Embisson's eyes. Eltrina had had to find something to justify the existence of a group that should never have been formed, and a search of the archives had given her the answer. During the last twenty-fifth year, one of the five chosen peasant groups hadn't been able to Blend. It had taken a lot of scrambling around to find substitutes for one member after another, and they'd achieved a Blending only at the very last minute. There was no danger of the same happening this time, but even better, there was no way for Lord Embisson to give the credit to Ollon.

"In the interim," Eltrina continued, "the five primary groups have been finalized according to their test ratings. The three weakest groups are of no concern, but they've still been given members who can't possibly get along well enough to Blend fully. The strongest group has had two of its members replaced, which should also keep *them* from

Blending properly. The last group, the second strongest, has been kept intact.''

"Is that wise?" Lord Embisson asked with a frown. "They're the ones who traditionally face the chosen Noble Blending, and it would be foolish to court disaster by overlooking them."

"I agree completely, my lord, and that's why they haven't been overlooked," Eltrina replied with the same smile. "I had a report from the observer in their residence only two hours ago, and it was that report which convinced me to leave them just as they are. It will also help if the competition observers try to complain about substitutions in the other groups."

"You still haven't told us what was in that report," Lord Embisson pointed out testily. Eltrina could see that he wanted to find something to prove that she wasn't doing the job properly, but he'd have to do better than question what she'd learned.

"The report covered all five members of the group," Eltrina purred, dragging out disclosure of the details as long as possible. "The Spirit magic member was given some difficulty by a former associate, and when the observer reported the incident I had the former associate arrested. The trial was held this morning, and the Spirit magic member couldn't stay away. The accused was found guilty and sentenced to a severe punishment, and the Spirit magic member was devastated. Despite not having reported the incident herself, she nevertheless felt that the associate's plight was her fault. Her feelings were confirmed by a Spirit magic user I sent there to check on the matter."

"After undoubtedly informing the young lady of the trial yourself," Lord Embisson commented dryly. "So the unifying member of the potential Blending doesn't even have control of herself, not to mention everyone else. And you're certain of that?"

"The observer at the trial said she nearly fainted when she heard the sentence pronounced," Eltrina agreed with a nod. "Later, when she and her escort, the Water magic user, returned to the residence, she nearly snapped his head off for the condescending way he'd been treating her. She also accused the Fire magic user of breaking her word to keep silent about the incident which had culminated in the trial, and the Fire magic user ran to her apartment in tears.

"The Water magic user, insulted over the way the Spirit magic user had denigrated his efforts to assist her, then turned on the Air magic user and started an argument. The Air magic user, having already had words with the Earth magic user, found no reason not to join the argument with enthusiasm. The observer felt that if the Spirit magic user hadn't finally screamed at the both of them to be quiet, they might well have turned a verbal argument physical.

"As it was they both stalked out of the room, leaving behind the definite impression that the matter wasn't yet settled. The observer feels that they've all been harboring resentments toward one another, but the Spirit magic user has been smoothing things over. Now that she's out of control, actual emotions are pouring out of the others. Even if she manages to regain control, things have been said that can't possibly be forgotten—or forgiven."

"So any change in the membership of the group can only strengthen it," Lord Embisson mused, obviously having no trouble seeing the point. "Soon they may even be taking sides against one another, but that brings forward a different problem. If they despise each other so thoroughly, they'll probably find it impossible to Blend."

"If that happens we'll replace them with the spare group, but I don't expect it to happen," Eltrina said, showing the last of her cards. "They knew about being formed into a Blending before they were told, you see, and made the expected decision to win the Throne. That decision should hold them together long enough to Blend, but afterward they'll certainly get in each other's way."

"Yes, they certainly will," Lord Embisson chuckled, which let the others show amusement as well. "And even if they don't, it won't really matter. They'll be given very explicit instructions before they face Lady Adriari's group, instructions they won't be able to refuse. Let them try their best *then* and see where it gets them."

The amusement really spread and grew with that, and Eltrina joined in with a smile as she sat back. She had her own reasons for not wanting to break up that group, and they all came down to revenge. She would make those peasants sorry for the way they'd embarrassed her in front of the Five, and they had immunity only until the moment they lost. After that they were hers, and she knew exactly what she would do with them. She would enjoy it immensely, but the same could not be said for them. . . .

Sweet daydreams kept the smile on Eltrina's face until the committee finished laughing, and then she calmly went on with the rest of her report.

TEN

Dinner was an artistically silent affair, with everyone pretending to be angry or insulted or both. I made sure to force myself into the emotion of feeling unjustly accused so that any eavesdropping servant with Spirit magic would believe I actually felt the way I pretended to. The others must have been doing the same, as Warla became very upset when she came into the dining room to speak to me about some household matter. No one was any more pleasant or polite to her than they were to anyone else, and after spending a number of useless minutes trying to cheer everyone up, she left just short of tears.

I felt tempted to go after the girl who'd been my companion for two years and tell her the truth, but common sense forced me to drop the idea. Warla was terrible at hiding her feelings, and if she suddenly became unconcerned, the spy in the household would certainly notice. So I continued to sit silently among the others, at a table which had been too big for five people but which was now obviously too small. Lorand sat fairly close to me for a reason, but even he and I didn't talk.

I'd originally meant to go to the library after dinner, but

at the last moment decided to go to my apartment instead. I could read for a while in the sitting room just as easily, and that way would avoid the possibility of needing to talk to anyone. Pretending to be angry and hurt is easier when you're not associating with people you actually like quite a lot.

I'd had a small tea service brought and had settled into a chair with a book when I heard something out in the hall. I looked up at a low knock at the door, and then Jovvi was entering fast and closing the door quickly behind her.

"None of the servants is upstairs right now, so I thought I'd take advantage of the privacy to come visiting," she said softly, her smile strained and the words a lot lighter than the disturbance in her eyes. "I wanted to be certain you knew I wasn't serious about blaming you for what happened to Allestine."

"Of course I know, and I'm so sorry," I said at once, putting aside my book and getting up to go to her. "What that woman did was terrible, but the sentence was even more horrible. Are you sure you're all right?"

By then I'd hugged her and had a supporting arm around her shoulders. Her smile grew even worse and she shook her head.

"Actually, I'm not all right at all," she admitted, the strain having intensified. "I feel as though I'm personally responsible for what Allestine did and the sentence she got, even though I know I'm not. It will take awhile before my balance is restored, but it helps to know that I have the strong support of good friends to lean on."

"You certainly do, so lean all you like," I told her firmly, leading her toward one of the couches. "And you can also sit down, because there's something you need to be told: Lorand and I will be out of the house for a while tomorrow morning."

The look she gave me was somewhat peculiar, but she simply sat at the same time I did and waited for me to explain.

"A man came to the house late this afternoon, while you were up here in your bedchamber," I continued. "He's someone who's come to see Lorand before over a matter I won't go into now, but this time he came to say he had news. He's finally located Lorand's friend Hat, and he told Lorand where Hat will be tomorrow morning. The idiot was going to go alone, but I insisted on going with him.''

"I'm glad you did,'' she said with a better smile as she patted my hand. "Even the strong need support in times of difficulty, and if I can't be with him, I'm glad it's you in my place. Now there's something *you* need to know about. Vallant asked me to speak to you, and—''

By then I had stood up and turned away from her, but that probably wasn't what had caused her words to end so abruptly. The chaos in my mind surely had more to do with it, whirling madly in all directions like a fireworks display out of control.

"I'm glad you're taking this so well,'' she continued, the words extremely dry. "The lack of true surprise in that . . . great blend of emotions tells me Lorand must have mentioned the same subject. I gathered from Vallant that he'd spoken to the other men before mentioning the matter to me.''

"Yes, Lorand told me,'' I admitted without turning. "The only reason Vallant began to ignore me was because he thought that that was what I wanted, but now he's learned differently, so he's right back to where he was. Except that he can't say anything to me directly, or he'll probably be transferred out of the residence.''

"Yes, that almost sums it up,'' she admitted, now sounding cautious. "And the last I heard, you were prepared to tell him about your interest and risk starting a relationship. That's why I don't understand all this sudden . . . distress.''

"It's there because I'd finally managed to make myself understand he was right not to get involved with me,'' I explained slowly, trying to get it clear for my own benefit as well. "Even forgetting about the virtual certainty that the testing authority will send him away if they find out about us, there's still my father and that beast he wants me to marry, and that noble who all but promised to claim me. Putting someone you care about into the middle of all that makes no sense, so I can't picture myself doing it. We'll all be much better off if things go back to the way they were.''

"In other words, you're chickening out.'' Her tone was

flat, with a lot of exasperation behind the comment. "The idea of a relationship has frightened you again, so you're trying to back away from it a second time. The only trouble with making that decision is someone named Vallant. If you thought you had his interest before, you'd better think again. This time there won't be any stopping him."

"But that's absolutely mindless!" I protested, finally turning to face her again. "He has to have *some* idea of what he's putting himself in the middle of, and not caring just says he's a fool. Am I supposed to get involved with a fool simply because he refuses to face reality?"

"I'd say *you* were the one refusing to face reality," she stated bluntly, her hands calmly folded in her lap. "You're attracted to Vallant and he's attracted to you, and he's determined to see if something can come of that. The only thing that stopped him earlier was the belief that you wanted something else. Now that he knows better, he's properly ignoring the testing authority's wants, your father and his friend's wants, and that noble's wants. The only wants which are relevant here are yours and Vallant's, a reality *you* refuse to face. All the rest of it is a pile of excuses you're trying to hide behind, but if you can't see that yourself, there's nothing I can say to make you believe it."

It was rather a long speech that she'd made, and at the end of it she just sat there and glared at me. At first I didn't know what to say in answer, then I finally decided on the truth.

"But he could be hurt," I whispered, putting my greatest fear into words. "He'll be in the middle of the entire mess, and if he's hurt it will be all *my* fault. I'd die if that happened, Jovvi, I'd curl up and die."

"No, you'd just want to," she corrected gently as she stood and came over to put a comforting arm around my shoulders. "But I do understand what's bothering you, and I really sympathize. What you have to make yourself understand is that the choice is Vallant's, and there's really nothing you can do to stop him. That leaves you only the option of going along with it, which could turn out to be extremely pleasant. Vallant said to tell you that he'll be looking for opportunities to get you alone."

She chuckled at the immediate blush coloring my cheeks, gave me a hug while telling me it was time she left, and then she stepped out of the room again. I stood staring at the closed door for a number of minutes, my mind and body busy with reacting to the idea of Vallant's getting me alone, and then another thought pushed its way through.

Jovvi had said that I had no choice but to accept Vallant's decision, and that had triggered a relatively new process inside me. The process involved finding options whenever someone said I had no choice about something, and it had developed to counter what my parents told me. Now it had countered Jovvi's pronouncement, and in a way I hadn't expected.

"If I can't protect him by refusing to associate with him, what if I *do* associate with him?" I murmured aloud, a wicked smile beginning to curve my lips. "Dom Ro may be the only one able to change his own mind, but what's there to say I can't give him a bit of unmentioned help? Then he'll be safe again, and I'll have some marvelous memories. . . ."

And his being safe would make it all worthwhile. I'd be able to stand the loneliness if I knew he was safe and happy, so I couldn't wait to start my brand new plan. . . .

ELEVEN

Jovvi made it back to her bedchamber without being seen and took a moment to breathe deeply while hating the need for all that sneaking around. But at least the requirements of secrecy were taking her mind off the devastating experience she'd had that morning. Not to mention the attention she'd had to give Tamma and her problem. It would be interesting to see how that worked out, especially since it had been fairly clear that Tamma wasn't about to give up her worries.

And thinking about worries brought Jovvi back to her own. She'd spent a good part of the day trying to regain her balance, as there were things she'd seen at the trial that she knew she needed to think about. What had kept her from doing it was the fact that she had to replay the trial in her mind in order to consider what needed examining, and she wasn't yet able to do that. The anguish and guilt were still too fresh and painful. . . .

For the hundredth time Jovvi was forced to shy away from the too-vivid memories, and getting frustrated was simply making things worse. What she needed was another distraction, and the perfect one would also help her sleep. To her mind that meant a relaxing soak in the bath house, something she'd meant to do earlier but had forgotten. Well, better late than never, everyone said. . . .

It didn't take long for Jovvi to change into a wrap, and it took the same amount of time for her to decide that she wanted none of the house's multitude of spies to follow along and ruin her relaxation. So once she was ready to go, she sent her ability out ahead of her to make sure no one discovered her presence or destination. A maid in the midst of a late-evening chore was out in the hall, but the task was quickly seen to so that the maid could go to her own room.

When the hall was empty again, Jovvi slipped out. No one hovered in corners or shadows or behind doors as she quietly descended the stairs, but a surprising number of servants were still up and about in the kitchen. Or perhaps the number wasn't quite that surprising. People who needed information to sell to their secret patrons had to be available to gather that information when there was a chance it would occur, and most of the members of the soon-to-be Blending were awake. Spies get to go to bed only when the objects of their spying do, which more than served them right.

One of the male servants lurked in a deep shadow not far from the back door, but he might as well have been holding a stable lantern for all the good the shadow did in hiding him from Jovvi. She paused far enough away so that he had no idea she was there, and then took a moment to consider the situation. The man had apparently been at his post for quite some time, and seemed to have no intention of leaving it yet despite the discomfort which had not yet reached his conscious mind—

Jovvi smiled, realizing that that was her answer. Rather than standing there for hours waiting for the man to leave or finding a window to climb out of, she just had to encourage the growing discomfort of his body. He'd apparently brought a supply of tea along to keep him company during his vigil, and when tea wants to leave you it becomes rather insistent. Jovvi just had to focus his awareness on that insistence, and then let nature take its course.

As soon as the man had hurried off to relieve himself, Jovvi slipped outside and did her own hurrying toward the bath house. An intensive scan in all directions showed no one aware of her at all, which was exactly the way she wanted it. The door to the bath house opened easily in the dim colored light of the paper lanterns, and Jovvi stepped inside—only to discover that the place was already occupied. For a heart-stopping moment she thought it was Lorand, but he and Rion only looked alike physically. In their minds the two men were completely different individuals.

"Oh, I'm sorry, Rion, I should have realized I'd be intruding on someone's peace and quiet," she said at once when he sat up abruptly from one of the bath's headrests. "That servant waiting in the shadows near the back door . . . He must have been waiting to see if anyone came out secretly to join you."

"And now *you* have," he pointed out calmly, beginning to get to his feet. "Obviously the only thing I can do is leave at once, which ought to make him think we aren't hatching any secret plots."

"Even though we are," Jovvi agreed with a smile as she gestured to him. "But don't leave unless you really want to. The servant was forced to abandon his post for a moment or two, so he missed seeing me come out here. As far as he knows, you're still alone."

"You won't mind if I stay?" Rion asked as he settled back to watch Jovvi walk over to the soap cabinet. "My presence won't keep you from enjoying the water as well?"

"No, I'm used to bathing in mixed company," Jovvi

said, then turned back to him as she realized something. "Rion, you're making progress again. You've noticed that men and women don't usually bathe together, and I think you're trying to understand why."

"Yes, I am," he acknowledged with a smile, one hand pushing back wetness from his dripping hair. "When I first got here, all I knew was that I was supposed to bathe alone. Being in a group changed *that* pretty quickly, and of course I noticed that you and Tamrissa didn't bathe with the rest of us. I suppose I thought that was because you didn't want to be crowded, but when I accidentally walked in on Warla a short while ago, I learned differently. She'd put up the occupied sign, and I simply hadn't seen it."

"Oh, dear," Jovvi said as she slipped out of her wrap, leaving it on the bench near her slippers. "It's terrible to laugh at something like that, especially with someone like Warla involved. But the girl could use some shaking up, which just might put some starch into her backbone."

"There seemed to be plenty of starch all through her when she began to scream," Rion told her ruefully. "At first I thought I'd gotten here just in time to save her from some horrible but invisible fate, and it took me a moment to realize that *I* was the horror. She made me turn my back before she would leave the water, and while she dressed she kept apologizing for having to blame me for intruding. That was one point I didn't even try to understand."

"I don't blame you a bit," Jovvi said with a laugh, aware of the way he looked straight at her as she entered the water. "I'd rather avoid it myself, although I'm usually not this much of a coward. It's supposed to be my place to help people with emotional problems if I can, but right now I have too many of my own."

"Which our . . . friends at the testing authority want you to have, according to Ro," Rion said, leaning forward again. "Coll and Ro and I found a few moments of privacy during the afternoon, and he told us about the trial—as well as about that secret observer with Spirit magic. The man seemed completely taken in?"

"As far as I could tell, he was only able to see surface emotions," Jovvi said, feeling the warm water begin to take the knots out of her muscles. "I had plenty of those at the time, and all of them were the sort those people were apparently trying to produce. I still have them, of course, but don't intend to let them be as crippling as those people wanted them to be. When you know what people are about, you find it easier to meet their ploys."

"Not always," Rion said, a dark shadow passing over his mind as his gaze began to see something inward. "There are times you can actually watch what people are about, but it becomes impossible to figure out why—and what you can do about it. That's something else I've recently learned, and I wish I hadn't."

"I'd say you need to talk about the situation," Jovvi observed, heading for the side of the bath where she'd left her soap. "If you'll hold on until I've washed, I'll be more than happy to listen."

"But you said yourself just now that you have enough of your own problems," he protested in confusion. "How can I add to that without feeling that I'm taking advantage of a friend?"

"Actually, I'm in the process of learning something new myself," Jovvi replied, turning to look at him. "I'm beginning to realize that if it weren't for my friends' willingness to share their feelings with me, I'd never be able to share mine with them. And then I'd be locked up all alone in my head with the horror I now feel, and nothing would be able to relieve it. It isn't necessary for someone to be able to do something about your problem; very often it's just their willingness to listen which helps."

"You're only just now learning that?" Rion asked with amusement obviously offered up for sharing. "I learned that myself days ago, only hadn't realized I had. Go ahead and do your washing, and then we'll exchange problems."

Jovvi matched his smile before turning to her bath, which didn't take very long. Once she'd pushed back her freshly clean hair with both hands to rid herself of dripping water, she moved to the rest area near Rion's and slid down into it.

"Okay, I'm all ready to listen now," she said, feeling the calm patience he'd been showing all along. "What is it that's bothering you?"

"It . . . seems I've lost my lady, but not in the usual

way,'' he began, his former calm definitely rippling. ''Tamrissa and Coll helped me to avoid Mother's watchdogs so that I might go to see Naran in her new place of residence, and we had a marvelous time together. Afterward I left to come back here, but it occurred to me that I didn't have to be here until morning. So I went back to the house where she'd been, only to find her—and all trace of her—gone. It was almost as though I'd imagined her, but I happen to know I didn't. She should have been living in that house, but instead she'd disappeared.''

''Is it possible that your mother's people found her?'' Jovvi asked, hating to bring up the point but knowing it was necessary. ''You might have been followed without your knowing it, and those people might have spirited her away.''

''I discovered I *was* followed, but not closely enough for them to know which house I went to,'' Rion answered with a dismissive headshake. ''The next day I was told they meant to find out, but Naran was gone by then. And not only were there no signs of a struggle in the empty house, the rooms we used had been tidied.''

''That's very strange,'' Jovvi said with a frown. ''Are you sure the house was where she was supposed to live? Is it possible she really lives elsewhere and only used the house as a place to meet you?''

''I was about to say it *isn't* possible, but that's not true,'' Rion replied, his brows high with surprise. ''Naran's note gave me the address, where she said she would be *that night*. If I recall correctly, it never actually said she would be living there. I wonder why she would bring me to a place other than where she's living?''

''Possibly because there's a danger you might be followed,'' Jovvi suggested, swallowing down the other possibility: that Rion's Naran was married. The idea might have to be suggested to him, but not right now. Some other time, when his spirits hadn't suddenly soared out of their previous pit.

''And I never thought of that!'' he exclaimed, his handsome face alight with relief and gladness. ''The most obvious answer of all, and I needed to have it pointed out. I feel like a fool, but at least a thoroughly delighted one.''

"That's the best kind of fool to be," Jovvi said, smiling at his grin. "When you see Naran next you can speak to her about it, but at least for now your worry is put to rest."

"So it is," he agreed, his expression softening as he turned a bit more toward her. "And now it's your turn. Share the horror you went through with me, so that you won't be trapped alone in your head with it."

Jovvi hadn't really intended to talk about her own thoughts, but realizing that Rion waited to listen rather than to judge made her start to tell the story of her own experience with the law. As her mind went back to it again, it almost felt as though she were reliving the time. The helplessness, the uncertainty, the terror of being completely alone . . . by the time she reached the part about her rescue, she came back to the present to find that she huddled against Rion, held tightly in his arms. She was also trembling, and he made small sounds of comfort and soothing.

"There, now, you see?" he murmured, gently rocking her a bit. "You weren't all alone after all, and you certainly aren't alone now. We're all here for you, sweet lady, anytime you might need us. Please believe that, as it happens to be true."

"Yes, you're absolutely right," Jovvi said, raising her face to his without trying to leave his arms. "If anyone should know that we're all prepared to be there for each other, I'm certainly the one. But until now I knew it only with my mind, not with my heart and inner being. Thank you, Rion, for helping me to see it in the proper way."

"The pleasure was mine," he responded, his beautiful smile warming again. "Another thing I've been learning is that it isn't an imposition to help real friends, it's a delight. I considered mentioning the point to my mother and telling her she was wrong, but then I realized that she wasn't wrong. Since none of the people she knows really is her friend, she'll never find it possible to experience what we do. Eventually I may come to pity her."

"If someone else in your place said that, I would doubt their ever actually reaching that point." Jovvi looked at him with both her eyes and her talent, her hands to his arms, and there was no doubt at all. "You, however, are almost there already, and somehow I'm not surprised. But I think you'd better let me go now, unless you plan to stay here a good deal longer. Every time we speak I find you more and more attractive, and I'm not in the habit of ignoring attractive men who happen to be both naked and holding me.''

"I was about to ask if you found my holding you upsetting," he replied slowly, studying her as carefully as she had done with him. "I may be mistaken, but the question seems unnecessary. Am I correct in thinking that you aren't upset in the least?"

"Yes, it so happens you are," Jovvi told him with a bit more of a smile. "What I am is becoming aroused, a perfectly natural reaction when you're with someone you consider attractive. But in this case the someone I'm with has a lady he's very much involved with, and it would be inconsiderate to offer him a joining that he might well want to refuse."

"But—why would I want to refuse?" Rion asked, and Jovvi could see that he was honestly puzzled. "If Naran were here my complete attention would be hers, as I love her with every fiber of my being. But she doesn't happen to be here now, so I would scarcely be turning my back on her. To—join, as you called it, with another woman won't lessen my love for Naran in the least, and especially not if you're the other woman. What I feel for you and Tamrissa is a good deal more than fondness."

"Yes, it is, isn't it," Jovvi murmured distractedly as she examined the emotion he'd mentioned. It wasn't romantic love, which Rion felt for Naran and she herself felt for Lorand, but it was definitely a kind of love. There had been a hint of the same thing when Tamma had spoken about Rion, and surprisingly enough Jovvi could just detect the same thing growing in her own thoughts about Rion. Another oddness to be thought about after she got around to the prior ones, but definitely not at this moment.

Rather than saying anything else, Jovvi leaned a bit closer and touched her lips to Rion's. She wondered if he would understand, and his chuckle and response answered her question immediately. Until now he'd been holding her supportively rather than intimately, which is always a matter of attitude rather than the presence or absence of clothing. After the kiss, however. . . .

After the kiss, Rion needed no further encouragement. His big hands began to stroke her body slowly as he started a much longer kiss, his own body made available for any caresses *she* might wish to give. With the help of her talent, Jovvi was able to touch him just where and how he most wanted the touches, and his flaring passion drew her irresistibly in his wake. His moans of pleasure and complete abandon were like nothing she had ever experienced before, an assessment which would have shocked her during a more levelheaded time.

But Jovvi had already been pulled so deeply into his passion that she no longer had the capacity for rational, critical thought. Her own moans joined his all by themselves, and it actually took a long moment to understand what they were suddenly lying on. They hadn't left the bath, so Rion must have supplied a bed of thickened air to keep them—and especially her—from drowning. By the time she reached that conclusion Rion was entering her, sharing rather than taking without having to be told.

And then their thoughts merged even more closely than their bodies, which couldn't possibly get any closer. Jovvi closed her eyes and simply moved with Rion, losing herself to pure sensation. It was the most marvelous experience she'd ever had . . . except for one . . . which she couldn't let herself think about now. But she *would* have that other again some day, she *would* . . . !

Even though she was the one who had chased him away. Her eyes closed tight, Jovvi shared pleasure with Rion . . . and even in mindlessness thought only of Lorand. . . .

TWELVE

Delin heard the servant say, "Lord Rigos Baril," and his shock was so deep that he simply couldn't move. In his mind, Delin had already filed Rigos away as a previously solved problem. Not solved in the best way, of course, which would have put Rigos in Delin's power rather than simply being under arrest for murder, but still acceptably solved. The man Delin hated would never again be in a position of power . . . so how could he possibly be here in the same position he'd previously had?

"Rigos?" Kambil said in startlement, taking a step toward the small, dark man who now strolled into the room. "I'd say that this was a surprise, but the understatement would be ludicrous. How did you manage to be reinstated?"

"When they cleared me, they had no choice but to re-instate me," Rigos answered, sounding to Delin just as arrogant and superior as he'd always sounded. "And they did clear me, twice, using two different methods."

"And what methods were those?" Delin heard himself asking, just as though nothing at all were wrong. "People said there was real evidence against you, and that's why you were arrested."

"The evidence, such as it was, had to be discarded," Rigos drawled, stopping to adjust one of his shirt cuffs as he looked lazily back and forth between the two larger men. "The first thing they did was arrange an interview for me with the Earth magic Adept the Advisors themselves consult. The man apparently listened to my protestations of innocence with every bit of his ability, and then told the Advisors that I spoke the truth. You should know something about that, Delin, isn't that so?''

Delin gave the man what he hoped was an enigmatic smile, a reaction he worked rather hard to force. He had no idea how someone with Earth magic could tell truth from lie, but he would die sooner than admit it to Rigos. He'd never even *heard* of people using the ability in that way. . . .

''And what was the second method used?'' Kambil asked smoothly while gesturing Rigos to a chair. ''I hope it's something I've heard about, unlike that first method.''

''Oh, I'm sure you're familiar with the second method,'' Rigos said, inspecting the chair briefly before sitting in it. ''It's the same method they use in a court of law, where the accused speaks nothing but the truth. Puredan isn't supposed to be used by anyone but a panel of judges, but the Advisors do insist on exercising their privileges whenever the mood strikes. Happily the mood struck in my case, and they tell me I cleared myself completely.''

''You're right, I do know about Puredan,'' Kambil said, exchanging a brief glance with Delin. ''There's never any doubt when that drug is used, so allow me to offer my congratulations. And I must say your timing is excellent. It seems you were cleared just as Hiblit vacated the position. How is he, by the way?''

''Hiblit is a raving lunatic, and will probably remain one for the rest of his life,'' Rigos answered, a shadow passing quickly across his expression. ''They have to keep him full of attar of goldflower, I hear, or he starts to scream and doesn't stop. His physician said something about it being a response to unbearable pressure of more than one sort, but Hiblit's father is too powerful for *any* physician to go into details. Did either of you know Hiblit before he was given the post?''

''We didn't, but Homin did,'' Kambil replied, his gaze troubled. ''Homin told us what the poor soul was like as a boy, but there was nothing left of the original in the grown man. Very frankly, he disturbed every one of us.''

''You weren't the only ones,'' Rigos muttered, for once looking almost human. ''I've known him since our teenage years, when he wasn't quite as bad. His father always wanted him to get anything I happened to earn . . . but Hiblit is all through with his father, isn't he?''

Rigos's sudden smile was much too bright, but it still brought back the man's original attitudes. He'd dropped his guard for one brief moment, but his expression said that was all over and done with.

"I can't tell you how much at home I feel," Rigos continued in the drawl he'd been using only a minute earlier. "You and Delin, Kambil, and not a sign of the rest of your group. Are they in the house somewhere, or did their drivers get them lost forever on their way here?"

"Homin and Selendi are in the dining room, and Bron is still asleep," Kambil answered with a chuckle that looked and sounded perfectly real. "There was nothing scheduled for us to do, so there's really no reason for all of us to be together."

"There *was* nothing scheduled, but now there is," Rigos responded with spiteful amusement. "Send for them, please, while I pour myself a cup of tea."

Delin saw Kambil's very brief hesitation as Rigos got up and headed for the tea service, and was forced to admit that Kambil had a bit more self-control than he did himself. If Rigos had just given *him* orders as if he were a servant, Delin knew he would probably have exploded. All Kambil did, however, was hesitate briefly, and then he walked toward a bell pull. Delin stood where he was for a moment, then chose his own chair to sit in. He would listen to what Rigos had to say, and later he would find a better and more permanent way to get rid of him.

Homin and Selendi reached the room rather quickly, and then they all waited for Bron to arrive. Rigos actually went through the explanation a second time when Selendi and Homin began to pelt him with questions, and he didn't even seem overly annoyed. He did, however, speak mostly to Homin, as though it were important that the fat little man really believe in Rigos's innocence. And Homin, the fool, calmly told Rigos that he was glad the agent was free again, all but absolving Rigos of anything and everything he might have done.

Delin spent the waiting time for Bron listing all the things Homin *should* have said to Rigos, things that would have haunted Rigos and maddened him. It was highly unlikely that Rigos would go the same way Hiblit had, but if he ever did, Delin would be the last to cry. . . .

"What kind of sick joke is this?" Bron suddenly demanded from the doorway, drawing everyone's attention. He wore a wrap casually belted at his middle and obviously nothing else—except for an expression that showed him to be completely outraged.

"Bron, this isn't any sort of joke," Kambil told the fool soothingly, obviously trying to quiet him. "Lord Rigos has been cleared of all charges and released, so it's only natural that he's back to work with us. He—"

"Natural?" Bron interrupted, his voice harsh and accusing. "You think it's natural for us to work with a murderer? I don't care *what* kind of story he's telling, I don't intend to swallow it. If he's been cleared it's because his father *bought* him clear, so let his father work with him. If they try to force *me* to do it, I'll quit the group."

And with that Bron turned and stalked out of the room. There was no doubt whatsoever that the man had meant every word he'd said, and Rigos had gone as pale as Delin had ever seen him. At first Delin thought the pallor came from anger, but a second glance showed something else entirely. Rigos was actually in pain over the lack of belief, and Delin suddenly realized that Bron wasn't the only one who would be likely to believe that Rigos's father had bought him free. Most people would believe it, which meant that *Bron* had found the perfect way to be rid of Rigos!

"Try to ignore that outburst," Kambil was in the process of saying to Rigos, acting like the fool that he was. "I'm sure you can tell that not all of us feel the same way, so—"

"No," Delin interrupted, this time letting his voice quiver the least little bit. "Don't lie to the man, Kambil, not when you have to know that I feel just the way Bron does. If admitting that I'm uneasy being in the same room with Rigos makes me less of a man, then so be it. I may not have had the nerve to say the words first, but now that they've been said I'll certainly stand with Bron behind them."

Rigos's color still hadn't come back, especially since

Homin and Selendi were studiously avoiding his gaze. It probably hadn't occurred to the pair at first that Rigos's father might have used his gold and influence, but once suggested, the idea was more than possible. Everyone who heard that particular accusation would believe it, and the truth would be entirely beside the point. Delin watched Rigos being forced to accept that, and a small thrill of pleasure ran down his back.

"I—won't lower myself to argue the prejudices of fools," Rigos said at last, his voice unsteady and his gaze on his hands. "I came here for a purpose, so let's get on with it."

Delin caught Kambil's minute headshake, which hopefully meant that Rigos was lying about deciding to be unaffected. There was very little else he *could* have said, which made Delin love the entire idea.

"I'm here to inform your group that tomorrow you'll be formed into a Blending," Rigos continued, still looking nowhere but at his hands. "You'll pay very close attention to what you're told, and you'll follow directions exactly. If one or more of you decide to do things your own way, you probably won't Blend. You'll—be given more information when your mentor arrives, so make sure you're here and ready to work with him."

Delin had the impression that there was more Rigos had meant to say, but instead of saying it he simply got up and headed out of the room. Kambil waited a moment before following, and when he returned after another moment he was in the process of shaking his head.

"Well, he certainly didn't stroll out *this* time," Kambil announced. "He was barely in the carriage when he ordered his driver to go, and the man obeyed immediately. I think if he'd stayed here even five minutes longer, he'd have broken down and cried. I got the impression he was afraid this would happen, and now that it has he's devastated."

"Devastated enough to resign his position?" Delin asked, trying not to hope too hard. "Bron can't be the only one who will feel that way, and if we're lucky he won't be the only one who says it. And I thought the loathsome little deficient hadn't been affected at all by what happened to him."

"He almost had me fooled as well, but I could tell that something wasn't quite right," Kambil said as he stopped in the middle of the room. "There was an . . . expectation inside him that was composed mainly of fear. If this happens to him even one more time, he might very well resign."

"He should never have come back in the first place," Selendi pronounced as she got to her feet. "It isn't as if he murdered someone unimportant, after all. Come on, Homin, let's go talk about something more interesting."

"Of course, Selendi," Homin said with a smile as he got hurriedly to his feet. "Anything your lovely little heart desires. All I want to say is . . . I'm still grateful."

Homin's final words were addressed to Delin, who knew that the fat little man meant he was grateful to Rigos for having killed Elfini, the woman Homin's father had married. Delin could understand that, but his estimate of Homin went up a grudging notch. He obviously wouldn't have minded working with Rigos, but had kept silent for the sake of the group.

"What now?" Kambil asked softly after Homin and Selendi were gone. "Trying to soothe the man was a mistake on my part even if the attempt was automatic, and I'm grateful that you were able to correct it. Now I'd like to know what our next step is."

"The first has to be finding out how the members of the other groups feel," Delin said, smiling easily at the wonderful luck they were having. "If necessary we'll stir things up against Rigos, but hopefully it won't be necessary. One way or another we should be rid of him soon, and—"

Delin paused to take a deep, excited breath, feeling very much like a child with a gift. "And tomorrow," he finished, "tomorrow we become a Blending!"

THIRTEEN

Lorand returned to his bedchamber briefly after breakfast, and when he came downstairs again he found Tamrissa waiting for him in the hall, just as she was supposed to. She examined him as he descended the stairs, and smiled as he approached her.

"See?" she said, still looking him over. "That shirt and coat look perfect on you, worlds better than they ever did on my husband. Don't you feel silly now for being reluctant about taking them?"

"Yes, of course," he muttered, pretending to be extremely unenthusiastic, with underlying shades of being put upon. "Let's go for that walk now."

Tamrissa agreed with the sort of insensitive burbling *she* was pretending to feel, but they only got to start for the door. They'd barely taken two steps when Warla appeared.

"Oh, dear, you're not going out, are you?" Warla asked at once, all but blocking the door. "It's going to rain any minute and you'll both end up soaked through."

"Better soaked than staying in this house a minute longer," Tamrissa replied after only a tiny hesitation, stiffening enough for Warla to notice. "That woman refuses to confine herself to her bedchamber, which means I'm not even free to walk through my own house without taking the chance of running into her. And with the men ready to snap at each other at any given moment, my nerves are almost shredded. We'll probably be back for lunch, unless it does rain and we're trapped somewhere."

Warla continued to protest, but Tamrissa simply led the way around her and out the door. Lorand followed without saying a word, more than relieved that he hadn't had to refuse the girl himself. Warla looked on the very brink of tears, and Lorand had always been helpless against women's tears.

Once outside, Lorand saw why Warla had been so worried. Clouds were dark and heavy in the sky, floating low overhead in a definitely threatening way. Tamrissa looked at them with a small shiver, then took Lorand's arm in an obviously possessive way.

"At least we should have time for me to show you off to my neighbors," she said, making no effort to keep her voice down. "One or two of them kept trying to introduce me to men after my husband died, as though they considered me incapable of finding a man for myself. This should show them."

She then pulled Lorand down the steps with her, which was a lucky thing for him. He'd almost laughed aloud at the excuse she'd come up with for their taking a "walk" even in the face of the coming storm. He continued to pretend reluctance, but once they were away from the house he let his grin show.

"How interesting that your neighbors live in another world," he murmured as they made their way down the drive. "Anyone who could believe even for a minute that you would have trouble finding a man . . . even our secret watchers might not believe it."

"But that part happens to be true," she protested softly, her cheeks coloring a bit. "I didn't have an immediate line of men waiting to propose, so two of my women neighbors decided that that was because I didn't know how to find them. It took me two invitations to dinner to understand what they were doing, and then I stopped accepting their invitations to dinner."

"Well, you can feel free to parade me past them whenever you like," he said with a chuckle. "In fact, you ought to take Mardimil and Ro past them as well. Then, the next time you see those women, you can casually mention the harem you're beginning."

"Lorand, stop it!" she hissed, clearly fighting to keep from laughing aloud. "If anyone sees us really enjoying ourselves, they'll know we were putting on an act earlier. Do you want to be thrown out of the residence for getting along too well?"

"It sounds ridiculous when you put it like that, but you're right," Lorand conceded, fighting his expression back into one of boredom. "I'll behave myself, at least until we're in the coach."

"I hope it's waiting where it's supposed to be," she said, deliberately making no effort to look through the hedges surrounding the drive. "If not, at least I hope it gets here before the rain does."

"We have almost an hour before the rain starts," Lorand told her, automatically checking everything around him again. "The trees and birds and small animals have an excellent rain sense, and that's what I'm getting from all of them. The rain is coming, but the length of time expected to pass until it does feels like just under an hour."

She accepted that with a nod, taking his word for it without question. Lorand remembered when a girl had doubted him once, and had ended up missing a fun time with their friends because she hadn't wanted to get her hair wet. It was impossible to picture Tamrissa doing something like that, not even when they probably *would* end up getting wet. It had been her idea to dress him in clothing that would not immediately mark him in some way. Both his practice outfits and his original country clothing would have made him stand out, but the maroon shirt and coal gray coat combined with his lighter gray practice trousers to make a perfectly ordinary outfit.

And ordinary was what he'd been warned to be. Meerk had stopped by the previous day to say that he'd found Hat, but he hadn't been prepared to offer any details. He said he'd be by this morning to call for Lorand, and hadn't been surprised when Lorand told him not to come to the door. There seemed to be more than one benefit in dealing with a man whose doings weren't always legal.

When they reached the end of the drive, Tamrissa firmly pulled him to the right. They'd decided the day before that if she turned possessive and he became reluctant, the testing authority watcher would be delighted to see them together. And they'd needed *something*, because she'd insisted on coming with him and he'd been glad she had. He had an obligation to find and help Hat if he could, but the time wasn't likely to be pleasant.

Just up the street a short way, a private coach stood waiting. He and Tamrissa pretended not to notice it until they got close enough to see Meerk inside, and then they hurriedly climbed in. Lorand had had his senses spread wide the entire time, and was relieved to find no human lurking in their vicinity and watching. The house watcher wasn't likely to have followed them outside when the rest of the group was still indoors, but that didn't mean the watcher couldn't have an outside confederate. . . .

"I wish this business was over and done with," Lorand said once he and Tamrissa were settled in the coach and it had begun to turn around. "I'm beginning to imagine spies behind every tree. Good morning, Dom Meerk. Are you ready yet to tell us where we're going?"

"You'll see soon enough," Meerk answered in his usual growl. He was a big man with a square face who was dressed slightly better today than usual, and he eyed Lorand in an odd way. "I don't need you tellin' me I'm crazy, which you'll prob'ly do until you see fer yerself. That's a whole lotta power you wus handlin' just now. You ain't thinkin' about pullin' a fast one?"

"The only fast one I'm pulling is on the people watching us," Lorand said, trying to reassure the man. "I have the feeling we're going somewhere public so they won't be fooled for long, but then they should have only half the story. As long as you don't volunteer any details for the other half, our business arrangement should work out just fine."

"I wouldn't give them nobles th' right time even fer gold," Meerk growled, the disgust heavy in his voice. "I done some checkin', and found out who wus standin' behind yer bunch. I thought maybe you din't know they wusn't on yur side, but now I c'n see you ain't *that* dumb. Not like some others I could mention."

The last of his words were muttered, and when Lorand tried to find out what he meant, Meerk simply shook his head and refused to elaborate. Lorand exchanged a glance with Tamrissa, who shrugged a little to offer the silent opinion that they'd just have to wait and see. Meerk's comment probably referred to Hat, and although the possibilities made Lorand nervous, there was no way to push for an explanation without starting a fight.

So he just sat back and watched the scenery from the coach window. They now traveled in a familiar direction, into the city and toward the business district. They'd gone this way to their first place of practice, and when they finally reached their destination it wasn't far beyond the practice buildings.

The stone edifice they stopped near had a large rendering of the Earth magic symbol, and broad slate steps led up to oversized double doors which stood open. A rather large number of people streamed up those steps, but none of them looked like members of the nobility. They were ordinary people, then, but what were they doing here?

"Come on," Meerk said, moving to the coach door and starting to get out. "It ain't far, an' you won't even hafta go in if you don't want."

Lorand got out and helped Tamrissa down, and then they followed Meerk up the broad slate steps. The husky man had stopped in front of a glass-covered placard near the open doors, and when they joined him Lorand felt shocked. The placard announced that a series of challenges for the position of High Practitioner in Earth magic would take place this morning, and a list of five names appeared under the heading of challengers. The second name on the list was Hattial Riven.

FOURTEEN

"That must be what he meant the last time he was at the house," Tamrissa said softly when she saw the name. "He insisted he was going to be taking the test again, but I don't understand why this would be happening. If he's only a Middle talent, how can he challenge for a High position?"

"He can do it if he's allowed—and encouraged—to do it," Lorand replied in a growl very much like Meerk's. "And a good reason for doing those things with him is that he can't possibly unseat the Seated High. You don't see my name on that list, do you? I'll bet everything I own that the other four challengers are also no stronger than Middles."

"An' prob'ly think they can do it, like Shorty did," Meerk added sourly. "Always knew them sons wus pullin' somethin' with these challenges, but never could figure out what. Now I know."

"And I've got to try to talk to Hat," Lorand decided aloud, reaching into his pouch for the two gold dins he'd prepared in advance. "You have my thanks for your help, Dom Meerk, and now you have the gold I promised you. You were right to think I would never believe this if you told me about it, but now I have to believe. Your part is over, but mine is just starting."

Lorand expected the husky man to take the gold and leave, but Meerk eyed him while weighing the gold in one hand, then he nodded in a way that said he'd made up his mind about something.

"You're okay, jobby," Meerk pronounced, putting the

coins into his own pouch. "Figured I'd walk away soon's I had the dins, but now I think I'll hang around fer a while. Wouldn't mind seein' what happens, even if Shorty *don't* talk t'ya. An' he prob'ly won't."

Lorand knew the man was almost certainly right, but he still had to try. There was a time when Hat *had* listened to reason, and if he'd sobered up, the time might come again. He nodded his thanks to Meerk, gave Tamrissa his arm, then led the way into the building.

Most of the people streaming inside were heading for a number of stairways on the right, and Lorand could see more people coming inside from an entrance on the opposite side of the building. Three closed doors to the left, at intervals along the wall, had guards standing beside them. Even as Lorand watched, a man and woman approached the door in the middle and a man alone went to the door on the far end. All three people were dressed slightly better than the ones going to the stairs, and the man at the middle door handed something to the guard before he and the woman were admitted.

"It looks like those who are willing to pay get the better viewing area," Lorand murmured to Tamrissa. "I have two more gold dins with me, but getting in can't cost *that* much. How do I ask for change?"

"Since it's probably a bribe rather than an admission charge, I have no idea," Tamrissa murmured back, her lovely eyes dancing with laughter. "I've never asked for change when bribing someone. Why don't you try showing the guard your bracelet instead? If it doesn't get us in, we can worry about getting change then."

Lorand glanced at his left wrist in surprise, having completely forgotten about his master's bracelet. It had almost cost him his life to earn it, but the object itself had been of no use whatsoever. That might not change, but at least it was worth a try. So he led Tamrissa over to the nearest door and then held out his wrist.

The guard did the first actual double take Lorand had ever seen. At first he glanced at the bracelet with complete disinterest, but then he jerked his head back to take a real look at it. The bracelet was made up of tiny replicas of the Earth magic symbol cast in silver, each circle attached to the ones on either side by even smaller links. Tamrissa's bracelet showed the symbol for Fire magic, of course, but hers wasn't given full scrutiny by the guard. The man's glance took in the presence of a bracelet on her wrist as well, and then he was opening the door with a nervous bow.

"Thank you," Lorand said with quiet dignity, fighting not to grin with boyish triumph. "And that gentleman is also with us."

After indicating Meerk with a nod, Lorand walked through the open door. The guard hadn't looked at all surprised that Meerk was with them, which probably meant he thought Meerk was their servant. Well, the mistaken impression wasn't likely to do any of them harm.

"Tamrissa, that was brilliant," Lorand whispered as he looked around at the comfortable chairs lined up in rows behind a low railing in the center of the room. More than a few of the chairs were occupied, but most stood empty. "How did you think of the idea?"

"There was a man using the door on the end, and he didn't pay anything," Tamrissa responded in a matching whisper. "The guard simply bowed and opened the door, so he probably recognized the man. That made me think certain people were allowed in without having to pay, and who better to fall into that category than a proven master of the aspect?"

Her cheeks were faintly pink with embarrassed excitement, which was one indication that she no longer touched the power. Last night her perfect skin hadn't colored at all no matter what she'd said, but this wasn't the time to remember last night. Tamrissa alone was a stunning beauty, but Tamrissa touching the power was all but irresistible. . . .

Lorand put that thought aside for later, since they were now approaching the chairs closest to the railing. Beyond the railing was a large square area, most of it taken up by a low dais, also in a square. Between the dais and the railing was a single line of chairs, which went all the way around the floor on three sides. The fourth side, the one directly opposite where they now stood, held a large thronelike seat with no other chairs on the floor behind its section of dais.

"Let's sit here," Tamrissa murmured, gesturing to three seats right near the railing. "The audience seems to be concentrated on this side, but not quite this close. I wonder if that means anything.''

"It probably means we can expect sloppy magic-handling," Lorand replied, following her to the seats. "If the challenger stands at this end and the Seated High throws something he can't handle, there could be considerable spill-lover. But if we're right about this contest, it shouldn't be anything *I* can't handle.''

She nodded to acknowledge that as she sat to Lorand's right, and Meerk, to the left, also nodded. Lorand had made sure to let Meerk hear the reassurance as well, and the man had accepted it as unquestioningly as Tamrissa. It was nice that the two of them accepted his word so readily, but the realization made Lorand faintly uneasy. If something should happen and he failed them. . . .

But failing people who were relying on him was out of the question for Lorand, so he pushed his doubts aside and occupied his mind with looking about a bit more. The second story was a gallery, and the section directly above where they sat was impossible to see. The rest of it, however, seemed much more populated than the ground floor area, and more people arrived up there all the time.

A number of uneventful minutes passed, giving Lorand more than enough time to grow impatient. Considering the number of people in the gallery the challenge should already have started, but the participants hadn't even appeared yet. Just as Lorand thought that, a door opened in the wall to the left, beyond the low railing. Five people dressed all in white, four men and a woman, filed through the door before it was closed again behind them. A scattering of applause came from the gallery, but the five people did no more than glance up at their audience.

"They all look terribly nervous," Tamrissa observed in a low voice as the five people came toward the seats right in front of the place they sat. "And that looks like your friend, although I can barely recognize him now that he's shaved and had a bath.''

The sarcasm wasn't as sharp as the words suggested, as Tamrissa was absolutely correct. Hat almost looked like his old self, and he even seemed to be sober. The small movements he made were very familiar and showed that Hat was nervous and trying to hide it. Lorand waited until the five people were almost directly in front of him, and then he stood up. That brought about the second double take of the day, when Hat glanced at him then looked back sharply.

"Lor, you came!" Hat exclaimed in a low voice, his face covered with a smile as he stepped closer. "I couldn't send you word about my great good luck, but hoped against hope that you would make it here anyway. I'm sorry you didn't qualify for this, but now we can say at least one of us did."

"What makes you think I didn't qualify?" Lorand asked with a frown. "But more importantly, how did *you* qualify? When you failed the first test, they told you to go home."

"But I didn't fail the first test," Hat replied with a short laugh, no longer smiling. "You're the one who failed, and you've been complaining about it ever since. Can't you even be happy for me *now*, Lor, when I'm about to win what we've dreamed about for years?"

For an instant Lorand was stunned, to hear Hat saying things that should have been *his* to say. It wasn't as if Hat were still drunk, so how could he believe—! The thought broke off as Lorand realized that Hat had been lied to in some way that had convinced him completely. He wouldn't have fought the lie, after all, not when he wanted so badly for it to be the truth. . . .

"Hat, listen to me," Lorand said quickly and earnestly, raising his left wrist. "This master's bracelet is proof that I *didn't* fail, not the first test or any of the ones following. They lied to you because you're meant to lose to the Seated High, who seems to prefer to face Middles rather than anyone stronger. You have to—"

"No, that isn't true!" Hat snapped, raising one hand as he turned his face away. "You're trying to ruin my chance, but I refuse to let you do it! I'm going to *win* this thing, and no one—not even you—is going to stop me!"

And with that he turned completely away, to walk to his place among the others and sit. He hadn't looked directly at Lorand again, but Lorand knew him well enough to detect a faint uncertainty in his bearing. That he meant to ignore the uncertainty was also clear, but at least it was there.

"Lorand, you'd better sit down now," Tamrissa said after touching his arm. "The officials in charge ought to be here any minute, and we know *they'll* believe you."

Yes, they certainly would. Lorand was reluctant to just leave things like that with Hat, but other than dragging the smaller man out bodily, there was nothing he could do to stop what was about to happen. Except maybe one thing. . . .

"What do you suppose they would do if I stood up and challenged their mighty High as soon as he appeared?" he asked Tamrissa in a murmur once he was seated again. "There are too many people here as witnesses for them to ignore the challenge, especially if I accuse them of rigging things by setting up a bunch of Middles. It would blow their little scheme wide open."

"Not really," Tamrissa responded with a sad smile. "Their first step would be to have you arrested and dragged away, and then they would explain that you were despondent over having failed to qualify for the challenge in the usual way. So you lied to yourself and made things up, caused a scene and forced them to restrain you, and all because you were disappointed. They would be sad during the announcement, and everyone would understand."

"Yes, they probably would," Lorand was forced to agree after taking a deep breath. "And I would be out of our group permanently as well. But there's got to be *something* I can do. I can't just sit here and watch Hat get knocked down and walked over."

"I agree that they're taking advantage of him, but don't make it sound as though he's entirely innocent," Tamrissa stated, disturbance in her lovely eyes. "If he'd gone home the way he should have, he wouldn't have been around to be taken advantage of. All this is his own fault, Lorand, and I refuse to see *you* lost trying to save him from his own stupidity. Again. Don't you think it's time to let him grow up and take what he's earned?"

Lorand wanted to protest that he wasn't keeping Hat from growing up, but the truth of the matter was that he—and most of their friends back home—usually had. No one had considered it right to let Hat be blamed for things, even when he was the only guilty one. He was the smallest among them, a bit younger than the average, and very "sensitive." Hat's mother had told them all about his sensitivity when they were quite young, and had asked for their help. . . .

Their help in standing between Hat and the reality of the world. He was the youngest child in his family, and for some reason his mother had been determined to let him get away with murder. Her pampering of him had always seemed harmless, but that was what had brought him to where he was today. It was the day Hat would finally grow up, and Lorand just hoped Hat would be able to survive it.

The next few minutes passed in brooding, and then the door to the left opened again. An official wearing the ancient robes of the Earth magic practitioner—all browns and greens and reds—entered slowly and with great dignity. Behind him came a man dressed all in white, the same robes but without the color. There were half a dozen others behind the man in white, but he was the one who held everyone's attention. And the people all around were getting to their feet, so Lorand and Tamrissa and Meerk did the same.

"Now isn't that strange," Tamrissa murmured, and Lorand turned his head to see that she stood frowning at the man in white. "I know it isn't the same person, but that man looks just like the noble who approached me after that supposed competition. He was the man who was there when I finally escaped from that very first test situation."

"Why—you're absolutely right!" Lorand exclaimed low. He'd had the impression that the man looked familiar, but hadn't been able to place him. "He *is* the one who was there after my own first test! Talk about your rigged challenges. They let him watch everyone who comes through, so he'll know who he does and doesn't want to face. That means some of these challengers may actually be potential Highs, but certainly the weakest available."

"That also means *we'd* probably be long thrown out if it weren't a twenty-fifth year," Tamrissa said after nodding her agreement. "Or at least we wouldn't be here. What does happen to those who qualify but are too strong to take a chance with?"

That was a question which had been asked before, but there was still no clear answer to it. Lorand joined everyone else in sitting down again once the man in white had taken his place on the thronelike chair, feeling dirtied by having accorded honors to a sneak-thief fraud. And the man's smug, self-satisfied expression suggested he really enjoyed the farce—which was only to be expected. . . .

"The Highest Practitioner in Earth magic bids you welcome to this challenge period," one of the entourage in colored robes announced from the center of the raised square, both arms held up for attention. "The Highest will defend his Seat from five mighty challengers, the first of whom may now approach and prepare himself."

A man in the midst of the challengers rose to his feet, then he stepped up to the edge of the dais. He had to wait along with everyone else while four large containers were brought in and positioned between him and the Seated High, and although the challenger stood quietly, it was impossible for Lorand to miss how nervous the man was. It was like watching a tightly coiled spring that was currently unmoving, but which might explode wildly in any direction without warning.

"What's in those containers?" Tamrissa asked in a whisper, possibly the same thing being asked in the murmur that undulated through the whole room.

"The two end ones are filled with soil, the second from the left has chunks of wood, and the one next to it on its right has iron ingots," Lorand answered at once, already having satisfied his own curiosity in the matter. "They're obviously props for the challenge, but I wonder how many of those five poor souls can do more than handle the materials."

"What more c'n *anybody* do but handle 'em?" Meerk asked in the same low tones, his expression peculiar. "An' how'd you know what was in them things? All *I* get's a lot of . . . smeared confusion."

"That means you haven't practiced with your ability often enough," Lorand told the man. "Practice lets you recognize the makeup of a lot of materials, separating them out one by one from the 'smear.' But as far as doing more than simply handling things goes, I'm very much afraid that that depends on how much strength you can bring to bear. We'll probably find out rather soon just how true that is."

Lorand nodded toward the dais, where the men who had brought in the containers were now filing out again. The challenger looked more tightly coiled than ever, but a faint and distant amusement played in the dark eyes of the Seated High. *He* knew which of them was stronger, and it was that sneering amusement which suddenly made up Lorand's mind for him. The results of that challenge might be completely predetermined, but everything happening before then was still subject to change without notice, so to speak.

"The challenge now begins," the robed man who had spoken earlier announced after stepping up to the side of the square. "Watch carefully and witness the talent and might of the victor, whomever he may turn out to be. The challenger is to begin."

If the way the challenger stiffened in shock was any indication, he hadn't been told that he was required to start things off. Just one more edge for the Seated High, another brick in the wall built against his opponents. Well, the challenger might be badly prepared, but Lorand wasn't in the same position.

The nervous man in white opened himself to the power and began to touch the contents of each container in a tentative way, obviously trying to figure out what to do first. That he hadn't considered the matter sooner couldn't possibly be his own fault, but Lorand found himself briefly startled. The man had more strength than a Middle would be expected to show, which had to mean he was one of the lesser potential Highs Lorand had theorized about. And that, in turn, probably meant the last challenger would be the same, only weaker, with the true Middles in the middle. Start and end the show properly, and the fools watching won't notice the sleight-of-hand in between.

It took the challenger a full minute to decide what to do, but then his determination firmed up his actions. He touched the soil in one of the containers with his ability, and sent a wide cascade of it toward the Seated·High. It wasn't clear to Lorand what the cascade was supposed to do, and that most likely meant the man had no real plan. He was probably tossing a handful of dirt in the face of the man he challenged, so to speak, in order to provoke the man into responding. Very often reacting to a response is easier—and less dangerous—than launching an all-out attack yourself.

The High Practitioner's expression never changed, which told Lorand that the man had to be ready to divert the soil around himself. The attack was slow and not in the least intense, so his response could, and probably would be, the same. The only thing the man wasn't counting on was Lorand, who hadn't had any trouble at all in deciding what to do first.

As the challenger threw the soil, Lorand slipped his own ability in behind the other man's. Quite a few people in the hall had opened themselves to the power in order to follow the confrontation in more detail, so Lorand's doing the same wasn't likely to make him stand out. And his hiding behind the challenger's ability, something he'd discovered how to do the night of the ball at the palace of the Five, would obscure things even more. So rather than simply observing, Lorand helped. Part of the cascade of soil sent at the Seated High was diverted from his waiting shield—right into his smallclothes.

To say the man was startled and distracted would be a masterful understatement. The gravelly soil entered his undergarments a good handful of seconds before the cascade reached him, bouncing around a bit against his privates before settling down. The no longer languid man yelped and jumped, and then the cascade hit him full in the face and upper body. His attention had been diverted from shielding just long enough to let the leisurely attack accomplish the most it possibly could.

Surprised laughter erupted all over the hall, and when the Seated High threw the dirt away from his face his rage was very easily seen. He also removed the gift in his underclothes, but despite the wielding of a respectable amount of power, he didn't seem able to rid himself of all the grit at once. It took a second, even more furious attempt before the final grains were removed, showing how sloppy the man had grown—assuming he hadn't always been that way. When your position is handed to you and then protected by gameplaying, it's undoubtedly natural just to let things slide.

The challenger had no idea why his attack had succeeded, and he certainly wasn't prepared when his opponent tried to retaliate. Surprise had diverted the challenger from any defensive plans he might have had, a lack the Seated High tried to take immediate advantage of. His talent freed the soil from both end containers and sent it toward the challenger, but not with the intent of dirtying his white clothing. The soil was still tightly compacted, and Lorand realized it was going to be used to bury and smother the challenger.

But that was something Lorand wasn't about to allow. His shield was in place around the challenger before the man had any idea about what was happening, so his ability to breathe went undisturbed. But so did his ability to be frightened, especially when he found himself unable to move the mass of soil away from him. A flash of terror reached Lorand through his link with the power, and then the man was shouting, "I yield! I yield!"

The Seated High was still too angry to drop the soil immediately, his inability to smother the challenger adding to all the rest. Lorand could feel the man's desire to destroy the pitiful specimen who had dared to insult him, and strangely enough there was nothing of suspicion showing. He should have wondered why someone strong enough to hold him off couldn't also force the soil away from himself, but apparently the man's anger was turning him stupid. And stubborn. The challenger kept trying to yield, but he refused to hear the man.

It took the intervention of the official in the colored robes before the Seated High turned the challenger loose. The official spoke to the High earnestly in a voice too low to overhear, probably telling the damn fool to control himself but in a nice, pleading way. After a moment or two the High let himself be persuaded, and the soil was returned to the two containers. The challenger looked ready to pass out from fright by then, and as soon as he was released he ran stumbling to the door he'd come in by and disappeared permanently.

"What's the name of this Seated High?" Lorand asked Meerk after a brief intermission was declared. "I don't remember seeing it on the placard announcing the challenge."

"I don't know his name, 'cause it ain't made public," Meerk responded in a soft rumble. "Don't know why, but it ain't."

"It's supposed to be because the office, and not the individual, is the important thing," Tamrissa supplied, leaning forward to add the soft comment. "None of the Seated Highs or their seconds are named, a point they usually make quite a to-do about. It's supposed to show how selfless and dedicated to the empire they all are."

"I'd be more inclined to believe that it's done to hide the fact that at least two of them are probably related—and nobles," Lorand said, his disgust with the situation rising again. "Not to mention how well it does in hiding just how long these superlative Highs have held their positions. This one shouldn't even be called an Adept, but I'll bet he's been the Seated High for more years than the general public realizes."

"You sayin' th' system's even more crooked than we thought?" Meerk asked, his expression filled with disturbance. "Considerin' what we thought, that'd be real hard, but—I c'n see fer m'self that he ain't nowhere near as strong as you. Why's he sittin' up there, then? No, never mind answerin'. He's sittin' there 'cause he's one of them there nobles."

"Exactly," Lorand agreed. "We found out for ourselves that the nobles have their own in most of the important jobs related to the testing procedure, and most of them don't have enough talent to 'light a stove or wet one down.' That's a really old saying, but in this case it fits all too well."

Meerk's face tightened with that, but he sat back rather than add anything else. Lorand exchanged a glance with Tamrissa, who shook her head sympathetically. They both knew how hard it is to lose illusions, even when the illusions aren't many or sacred. Disappointment always follows the loss, and it takes a while to adjust your thinking.

But it didn't take long before the Seated High was ready to continue. They'd given him something to drink along with a small snack, as though he'd really expended strength with what he'd done, and now he was properly refreshed. Hat was gestured to by the official, the gesture telling him to take his place on the dais, and Lorand watched his friend stand slowly. Hat wore an odd expression, as though he were disturbed about something, and he even went so far as to glance at Lorand. But then he seemed to get a better hold on himself, and simply walked to the proper place on the dais without any further delay.

Lorand had learned a lesson with the first challenger, and this time refrained from playing practical jokes. The first man had actually been stronger than Hat, but without Lorand's help he would have died. So Lorand stayed alert just to protect Hat from serious harm, and also stayed hidden behind Hat's ordinary Middle talent. Strangely enough, Hat seemed to calm down, just as though Lorand's hidden presence were something he was used to. That wasn't possible, of course, but. . . .

Suddenly Hat reached for the power, and then his ability was splintering some of the wood blocks and slicing small curls of metal from the iron ingots. Slicing metal like that should have been beyond him just as Lorand had believed it was beyond his own talent, but things were happening too fast for Lorand to stop and think about them. Once Hat had a good supply of splinters and curls, he began to throw them at the Seated High in an almost purely random way.

Which should have given the Seated High something of a problem. It was necessary to change the . . . nature of your ability's touch when different materials had to be handled, and first, of course, you had to know which material it was you'd be handling. By throwing the splinters and curls randomly, Hat obviously hoped to confuse his opponent enough that one or more of the missiles would hit, disconcerting the man enough to allow a more direct attack. Lorand and Hat used to wrestle with their talent regularly as boys, at least until Lorand began to win all the time. . . .

And at first the strategy of the attack seemed to work. The Seated High actually raised an arm along with his talent's shield, a sign that the man knew he might have trouble stopping the missiles with ability alone. Lorand was able to feel Hat's glee as the smaller man began to increase the speed of his attack. He really expected to win, Lorand realized, just as he'd often won as a child. Obviously he still didn't know that most of his early wins had been gifts from his friends.

And then it also became obvious that Hat's mother had neglected to tell the Seated High how sensitive and delicate her son was, and therefore should be allowed to win. The Seated High somehow *divided* his talent, setting up a screen with one section behind the other in front of him. The screen was invisible, of course, but to the eyes of Lorand's talent it was plain as day.

Just as the screen's purpose was. The first section of it stopped the wooden splinters and the second stopped the iron curls, but to the naked eye it looked as if both kinds of missiles were being stopped at once. Lorand felt Hat's shock at that, as if his friend were unable to perceive the double screen. Or maybe it was just that Hat considered the defense unfair, a variation he was unprepared for and which therefore shouldn't have been used on him.

The Seated High waited calmly behind his double shield until Hat used up all of his prepared store of missiles. When that happened Hat tried to prepare more, which was definitely a fool's move. The Seated High attacked the smaller man talent to talent, clearly knowing that Hat would be unable to match his strength. He hadn't gone up against the first challenger directly until he'd gotten angry, and the emotion had evidently added to his strength. Now the noble seemed dismissive: the small smile on his face made that perfectly clear.

And Hat, of course, wasn't able to resist the attack. He immediately tried to bring his full strength to the wrestling match, and he succeeded—but his full strength simply wasn't enough. Lorand noticed that he himself had automatically raised a shield of some sort between him and Hat, which made him realize that Hat had somehow tapped into *his* strength to begin with. It had to be something Hat had learned to do as a child, and something that Lorand, all unthinkingly, had learned to shield against.

But Lorand wasn't the only one who had learned to shield. He felt Hat reaching for the Seated High's strength, which caused the man to raise an immediate, conscious shield. The Seated High seemed to know all about the ability to borrow strength and calmly refused to permit it. Instead he bore down on Hat, forcing Hat's ability flat under the greater weight and strength of his own.

Lorand shifted in his seat with indecision, wondering if he ought to drop his own shield. Having Hat win to the position of Seated High wouldn't be the worst thing that could happen, but all it would really accomplish would be to cause trouble. He couldn't very well stay with Hat from now on, and the first time someone stronger challenged Hat for the Seat, Hat would lose. Better to let it happen now and get it over with, when he would be there to keep Hat from being too badly hurt.

The Seated High kept adding pressure until Hat dropped to his knees from the effort of defending himself. His breathing grew hard and ragged and sweat covered his face, and it quickly became clear that he couldn't continue. The small challenger finally raised a reluctant hand and gasped out, "I yield!"

This time the Seated High held his opponent in place only a moment before releasing his grip, and Hat dropped to all fours for a minute, doing nothing more than breathing with his head hanging low. After the minute Hat straightened and struggled to his feet, then glared at the Seated High.

"Okay, so you got me that time," he announced belligerently, just as he used to do as a boy. "Next time I'll be the one doing the getting, so let's go to it."

Murmurs of astonishment broke out all over the hall, and most of the people around the dais looked at Hat as if he were crazy. In point of fact he had to be crazy, since it was perfectly obvious that it was one try to a challenger. The Seated High ignored Hat completely while he reached for the refreshments being brought to him, leaving it to the robed official to gesture to the others in similar robes. Three of the men came up to Hat, one of them speaking to him quietly, but Hat gestured a dismissal of whatever he was being told and simply continued to stare at the Seated High.

The three robed men ended up having to carry Hat out. Hat shouted and fought and tried to stay where he was, and his agitation turned him so wild that it wasn't possible for the three to put him to sleep. Lorand considered helping them, then grudgingly decided to stay out of it. This time

Hat would have no choice but to accept the fact that he'd lost, and it would be no kindness to shelter him from the truth. He was finally being forced to admit that he was as guilty as Hat's mother of overprotection, and it was past time to cut the apron strings.

"I would appreciate it if you would do me a favor," Lorand said to Meerk in a murmur once Hat was carried out. "See if you can find out where Hat goes when they release him from here. He still needs to be able to go home, and I'll pay for his fare if I know he won't cash in the ticket to get permanently drunk again."

Meerk showed a faint smile and agreed with a nod, and then they sat back to watch the rest of the challenge. Leaving now would make them far too conspicuous, something they had no need of. Especially since Hat had been shouting about the whole thing being a setup and a cheat. They certainly didn't need to be linked with *that*, not when they had their own plans to get around the cheaters.

But Lorand couldn't shake the guilt he felt. He'd deliberately let down a friend, something he'd never done before. He seemed to have picked up new habits in Gan Garee, and only time would tell if the worst ones had managed to establish themselves too firmly to be shaken loose. . . .

FIFTEEN

We got back to the residence about an hour before lunch, with me talking at Lorand and him working manfully to ignore me. We'd stayed for the last three challenges, but could have left without missing anything. None of the three even came close to defeating the Seated High, and once we were back in the coach Lorand told me that only the last challenger had had anywhere near the talent to do it. But for some reason that one hadn't used all his talent, and it had seemed as though something were keeping him from it.

"But it wasn't a shield," Lorand had added as he leaned back on the coach seat. "I looked carefully to see if there *was* one, but there wasn't. I don't mind admitting that that bothers me."

It had bothered me as well, so much so that once Lorand "escaped" from me, I went to my own apartment and thought about it. It was always possible that the man had been drugged, but since he didn't act drugged they might have done something else to him. I sat in a chair and tried to imagine what that something could be until a servant came to announce that lunch was ready, at which point I gave up the useless line of thought. There was too much I didn't know, which made my thinking wasted effort.

But before leaving my apartment, I took a moment to remind myself how I was supposed to be feeling about the others. Jovvi had wrongfully accused me, Rion had been uncaring about my nervousness, Lorand had begun to avoid my company, and Vallant was the same hateful man he'd always been. I especially had to remind myself about that last point, since I'd caught Vallant staring at me once or twice. Half the time I wished I'd never told Lorand the truth about how I felt, and the other half . . . I rose quickly and left my apartment before thoughts about *that* made me forget about lunch.

When I stepped into the hall, it was to find that I'd been wise to restructure my emotions before coming out. The others were also leaving their bedchambers, and two servants were busily dusting and polishing in the midst of it all. There was no question that their work absorbed them completely, so they must have missed the very chill atmosphere that both Jovvi and I projected. The men were more aloof or standoffish, and we made a silent parade down to the dining room.

The meal was just as silent, despite Warla's appearance with an attempt to jolly everyone into a better mood. She began by bidding us all a good afternoon, and when I was the only one who returned the sentiment, her face fell.

"Please forgive me, dear people, for intruding during a time that must be filled with anxiety for you," she said with apology and compassion as she looked at us. "I merely came to say that word has been sent and your mentor will be here shortly after lunch, so some of the uncertainty is now gone. Not long after the meal, it will be my honor to share a residence with a real, true Blending!"

The delighted tone of her voice matched her ingenuous smile perfectly, showing she had no idea that she'd completely ruined my appetite. I wasn't sure if the others felt the same shock I had, since they seemed to be controlling their expressions in the same way I was attempting to do. Glances flickered around very briefly, and then Jovvi smiled faintly.

"It's lovely of you to say that, dear, but it's possible you may end up temporarily disappointed," she told Warla. "I understand that some groups don't Blend the first time they try, and maybe not even the second time. I'm sure we'll manage it eventually, but I won't be a bit surprised if it doesn't work the first time no matter what anyone tries."

"Oh, that *is* disappointing," Warla agreed sadly while the rest of us exchanged flickering glances again. Warla clearly thought that Jovvi was simply making an observation, but the rest of us were taking it as a very strong suggestion. No matter what anyone tried, it would be a good idea if we didn't manage to Blend on our first attempt. I agreed that it was a good idea, but it gave me something else to worry about: if we did Blend on the first try, would I be able to hide it? None of us had any idea what Blending would be like. . . .

Warla made some soothing and encouraging comments before she left, but what the exact words were I simply can't really remember. The thudding of my heart and the frantic flying of the butterflies in my stomach combined to make too much noise for me to hear much of anything. It even distracted me from the food being served, which meant I suddenly found myself eating from a plate I couldn't remember filling. But I *was* eating from it, which was an even bigger surprise. My appetite should have been long gone. . . .

I sighed before applying myself to the food again. Things were becoming so strange that another strangeness or two really made very little difference. I noticed that the others were eating their food with a distraction matching mine, so I didn't look at them again. Servants were walking in and out of the room, either bringing things or checking to see if anything was needed, and at least one of them had to be a spy for the testing authority. If that spy caught me looking for support from the others, he or she would know immediately that our disagreements weren't real.

So I finished my meal and drank an extra cup of tea without looking at anything but the pattern on the wallpaper. I had always hated that wallpaper, and had just about decided to have it replaced with something less expensive but in better taste when a servant entered to announce that we had a caller.

"A gentleman from the testing authority," the servant added, which should have eased our minds. It could have been one of the horde of people bedeviling us, like my father and his next choice of a husband for me. When I found myself trying to decide whether or not I would have *preferred* the caller to be my father, I knew exactly how frightened I was of what was coming.

"I'll greet the gentleman myself," I announced as I stood, forcing myself to ignore the fear. "And we'll all be in the library, so have someone bring us tea."

The servant bowed an acknowledgment and stood aside to let me walk out first, which I did. Behind me I was aware of the others rising and following, which helped quite a lot. If I'd had to face our caller all alone, I'm not sure I could have done it. Simply leading the way was hard enough, especially when I saw the man standing in the front hall. Tall and lean and dressed in the latest, most expensive fashion, his supercilious attitude proclaimed him to be a member of the nobility.

"Good afternoon, sir," I said in a voice that insisted on quivering, at the same time walking toward him at a slower pace than I usually used. "I'm Tamrissa Domon, the owner of this house. I take it you're here to . . . to. . . ."

"I'm here to teach you people about Blendings," he said crisply when I groped for the proper words, impatience sharp in his tone and expression. "The first lesson will obviously have to be about casting all doubt and uncertainty aside, which means my work is cut out for me. I'm Lord Carmad Lestrin, and now you will show me to the room I'll be doing my work in."

"Of course, sir, it's this way," I said, gesturing toward the library before beginning to lead the way to it. My voice was still a trifle unsteady, but now it was annoyance rather than fear causing the reaction. The man was as objectionable as the rest of the nobility seemed to be, but I had to swallow the annoyance at least until he showed us what we needed to know. After that . . . well, that remained to be seen.

Lord Carmad followed me into the library, and the others came in right behind him. He nodded when Lorand closed the door, then sat himself in a chair as if he were royalty rather than simply another member of the nobility.

"Yes, privacy is exactly what we want," he announced as he made himself comfortable in the chair. "From now on you will go to any lengths necessary to ensure your privacy, and moreover will discuss nothing of what you're about to be told if there's any chance of your being overheard. The law considers it a crime against the empire to speak of these matters to anyone not authorized to hear them, and even people like you will be arrested and put on trial if you fail to be properly discreet."

He paused to see what effect his announcement had had on us, but didn't have to search very hard. The others weren't as wide-eyed as I certainly was, but they were also far from being unaffected.

"I see you all appreciate the gravity of the situation," Lord Carmad said with a faint smile of approval as he crossed his legs. "That means we can begin immediately, which delights me no end. 'Soon begun, sooner done,' as they say, you know. Now, for these lessons and for your practice times, you will need to stand in the proper formation. You will also use the formation during the competition, but once a group performs together for a year or two, the formation is no longer necessary. We will begin by having your Fire magic user come forward."

I could feel everyone's eyes on me as I stood rooted to

the spot, back to being frightened rather than annoyed. I hadn't expected us to get into it quite that quickly, not without an hour of lecturing first. It took an incredible effort to finally move to a place directly in front of the seated man, and his faint smile changed subtly to a sneer.

"Why am I not surprised?" he said as he looked up at me, a comment I didn't understand at all. "Possibly because it was only to be expected. Well, they do like to do these things, so let's ignore it and continue. The next one we need is your Spirit magic user, standing precisely two feet behind Fire."

I heard Jovvi move to the place where she was supposed to be, and at the same time felt a wave of support and understanding coming from her. That made me feel a bit better, but I still would have liked to know what Lord Carmad had been talking about.

"Next in line we need Earth magic, behind Spirit and at the same distance from her as Spirit is from Fire," the noble went on. "That's right, stop right there. Now we need Water to Spirit's right and Air to her left, again, at the same distance that the others have already established. Yes, that's the way."

Lord Carmad examined the spacing from where he sat, not even bothering to stand. He'd made it sound as though the spacing were important, but apparently it wasn't important enough for him to bestir himself. He looked back and forth to either side of me for a moment, then nodded again.

"Yes, that's acceptable," he said, then paused at a knock at the door, bringing his gaze to me. "Do you know who that is?"

"It's probably the servant with the tea," I responded, remembering just in time to keep from saying I didn't know. "Do you want me to tell them to go away?"

"Not at all," he disagreed, showing that smile again. "You will all first step apart, and then you may tell them to come in. I already feel the need for a cup of tea, and will probably need one even more before we're done. Go on, now."

The gesture he used was suited for use with small children and servants who weren't very bright, but none of us

commented as we stepped out of the formation. Once that
was done I told the servant to come in, and happily it really
was the tea being brought. Lord Carmad finally got up, but
only to go to the service where it was put on the large table.
While he poured himself a cup I told the servant to pass
the word that we weren't to be disturbed for any reason,
which would hopefully take care of any further interrup-
tions. Now that we'd actually begun, I very much wanted
to get on with it.

Lord Carmad took his time getting the tea, and when he
turned back to us we were still standing in the places we'd
scattered to. I'd started to go back to my formation place,
but a short, surreptitious shake of Jovvi's head had kept me
from doing it. We weren't supposed to be all that eager, I
suddenly remembered, so being back in our formation
places would have looked suspicious.

"All right, try to remember where your places are and
get into them again," Lord Carmad said with annoyance
as he returned to his chair. "They told me you people
would probably be difficult, but it hadn't occurred to me
that your difficulty would be deliberate. Do try to bear the
strain of standing near one another, people. If you don't,
you'll *never* Blend."

We exchanged cold and distant glances to give his theory
of animosity support, then moved back into the formation.
The noble was settled into his chair again by then, and he
sipped his tea while checking our spacing. This time he
seemed to be looking for something to complain about, but
apparently he didn't find it.

"At least you seem to remember what you're told," he
muttered, crossing his legs before raising his voice back to
normal. "And now to continue. You will each open yourselves to the power, and grasp it firmly but lightly. Do I
need to explain what I mean by that?"

No one responded aloud, which answered his question
anyway. For myself I knew exactly what he meant, since
it was what I'd taken to doing during the times I felt I
needed to be more alert and whole. I was opened wide to
the power, but touched only the surface of it. It was like
kneeling beside a vast lake, one hand only just touching
the surface of the water. Plunging that hand and arm deep

was immediately possible, requiring no more than a tiny shift of position, which would make the touch firm rather than tenuous. I had no trouble following his instructions, but out of the blue I wondered what *his* aspect was.

"Do be certain that you're following my instructions about the lightness of your touch," Lord Carmad said after a moment. "Later on it won't matter in the least, but the first time of Blending is something of a shock to the system. A light touch will minimize that shock, a heavy touch increase it. Are you all properly prepared?"

I nodded in answer, at the same time silently reminding myself that I wasn't to show any reaction if we did manage to Blend. Remembering things and reacting properly was easier when I touched the power, and now most of my fear was gone as well. I was as ready as I ever would be, and had the distant but definite sense that the others were the same.

"Now, the next part of my instruction may sound too general, but it happens to be a necessity," Lord Carmad continued. "Others can only suggest the method of your Blending; you five alone can find the proper way to apply that method. Form a picture in your minds of a sphere rather than a flat circle, with Spirit in the center of the sphere. Spirit is the heart and balancing force of a Blending, sending out gossamer arms to the other four members. Those arms are as fragile as a spiderweb but as strong as woven steel, a contradiction that isn't a contradiction at all. Please try it now, Spirit."

For an instant nothing happened, and then I felt the oddest sense of being touched. It wasn't a physical touch, and wasn't even like being sent comfort or compassion. It was an insubstantial questing, a search for some sort of completion.

"And now the rest of you," Lord Carmad went on. "Spirit has sent out guiding supports, to lead you to her central balance point. You each occupy your own quadrant of the sphere, but must be linked to the center and to each other. First spread your insubstantial arms to Spirit, and once you've achieved connection, you'll then reach out to the first of the remaining three members. Do it now."

Lord Carmad's voice had grown to sound very small and

distant, as though I were floating away from it without moving from where I stood. What took all my attention was the sense of being reached out to, part of which was an urging to reach out myself. The urging had grown in strength during the last minute or so, quickly becoming a joyous demand for joining, and happily I complied. One segment of my talent reached for Jovvi, knowing exactly where she was, and found her easily. There was a . . . soft jolt of sorts when I touched her, and then—

If I could have gasped, I would have. The joining to Jovvi was a double one, me to her along one arm, her to me along the other. Then the joining changed, making it me-her-her-me along both arms. A merging rather than a joining, no seams or differences, and that's when *it* happened, making me want to gasp. Without effort or thought another three sets of double arms sprang into existence, linking me to the men as well. Their individual scents and tastes were in my mouth, merged and yet distinctive: the cool, slightly aloof taste of Rion, the gentle and humorous taste of Lorand, the strong and vital taste of Vallant. . . .

I felt as though I floated in the clouds somewhere, buoyed up on mighty wings of power. I still retained my individual sense of being, but I also felt myself to be an integral part of a WE. WE floated among the clouds in a beautiful blue sky, floating only because WE wished to. OUR strength was such that WE could have flown off in any direction, but WE didn't want to. Floating suited US at the moment, bringing a joy so great it was beyond description.

Don't say anything aloud, a part of the WE sent, the Jovvi part. Rion was the strongest taste in my mouth, but Jovvi was easy to recognize. *I think we've done it, but we don't want them to know*. The sending wasn't words, but something much clearer than words.

If we don't want them to know about it, we'd better break this connection, the Vallant segment of US sent with regret. *This is the best thing I've ever experienced, and we'll have to do it again once that noble leaves*.

The rest of US agreed with a joint sigh, and I did my part by pulling back from the merging. Suddenly I stood in the library again, Lord Carmad in the chair just a few feet in front of me, a sense of loss filling my mind. I'd only been part of the WE for a moment or two, and already being without it made me feel crippled.

". . . and now that you've all reached the heart of your Blending, you must reach out to the other segments of it," Lord Carmad was saying, his voice almost a droning. "Stretch first to the member on your right, then to the one beyond that, and lastly to the one on your left. If you can't maintain contact with all three remaining members at once, reach to them one at a time. Becoming familiar with each other is most important in this first instance, since that's the primary road to Blending."

I smiled to myself as I pretended to try doing as he said, knowing now that he hadn't noticed what we'd achieved a moment ago. If what I'd been part of wasn't Blending then nothing was, but the man continued to give us directions. If he knew, then he was wasting his breath, a pastime I doubted he indulged in often if ever.

"Just what exactly are we supposed to feel when this is done right?" Jovvi asked after another moment, her voice filled with vague annoyance. "I'm reaching out, but all I'm getting back is the impression of someone else reaching to me. More than one someone else, but how many and who I can't quite tell."

"But *that's* what you're supposed to feel," Lord Carmad said happily, brightening out of his droning doldrums. "It takes more than one effort to achieve a complete Blending, and the first step is always the same. Try to become more aware of who it is reaching for you, at the same time making an effort to strengthen the connection. You others make the same effort, and then we'll call it a day."

So we stood there pretending to reach to one another, in reality—for me, at least—fighting the urge to Blend a second time. I really wanted that sensation again, in the same way that I'd wanted a second taste of chocolate after the first. The desire seemed to have the capacity to become an obsession, which had to be considered a lucky thing under the circumstances. If we were going to win the ultimate competition, we'd need every bit of luck we could find.

Lord Carmad waited a full five minutes, then put aside his cup and stood.

"Time's up," he announced jovially, brushing at his coat sleeve. "Did the attempt bring you any progress?"

"Some," Jovvi answered with a frown I could see once I turned to her. "Right at the end there I could tell that four people were reaching toward me, and it was almost possible to distinguish one from the other. But I also had the impression that they were *just* reaching for me, not for each other."

"Once they connect to you, reaching out to each other will become much easier," the noble assured her, his tone the least bit distracted. "The important part is that they *are* reaching out to you, which means that a Blending is ultimately possible. If you were aware of only two or three of them, we'd all be wasting our time. Now, I want you people to practice reaching out as often as you have the strength to do it, and I'll be back tomorrow for another directed session."

I expected him to nod to us at the very least, but instead he dismissed us completely from his awareness. He strode to the door and left the way someone else would leave an empty room, but at least he did go. Lorand drifted to the door after him, opened it a crack, and peeked out. A brief moment later he closed the door again, then turned to us with a grin.

"He's gone," Lorand announced softly, sounding as relieved as I felt. "He's gone and he never noticed. Now let's try that again, but this time keep it going a lot longer."

I joined Rion and Vallant in offering immediate agreement, relief turning to exhilaration. We'd done it, we'd Blended, and even more, the testing authority didn't know!

Sixteen

Jovvi was filled with such excitement that she wanted to jump up and down like a small child, clapping her hands and laughing out loud. A good part of that feeling was her own, but much of it came from the inflow produced by the others. They'd shared the most incredible time, but before they repeated the experience there were things they had to talk about.

"We can't try again until we know it's safe," Jovvi reminded the others in a soft voice. "Can anyone else tell that we're about to have company?"

She nodded toward the closed door, beyond which she could perceive someone approaching slowly with the firm intent to be silent. The others all produced sounds or expressions of surprise which showed they *had* forgotten, only Lorand and Vallant also looking with their talent.

"There's a second one sneaking up to the windows outside," Lorand supplied, nodding toward the terrace doors. "I say sneaking because that's the only thing his or her pace can be."

"And believe it or not, there's one above us," Vallant added very softly. "From the mass, I'd guess it's a woman. Is she in one of the bedchambers?"

"No, she's probably in the upstairs linen closet," Tamma said with a frown, staring up at the ceiling. "And I've had more than enough of this. Now that we can, I'm putting a stop to it."

For a moment Jovvi felt just as surprised as the others at the way Tamma turned and marched toward the door.

117

There was no doubt or hesitation in the woman, an attitude produced by the fact that she still retained her hold on the power. Jovvi felt foolish for not having seen that at once, at the same time wondering whether or not to stop Tamma. They really shouldn't be doing anything to draw even more attention to themselves, but by then Tamma was already at the door and yanking it open.

"You!" she snapped at the male servant, who now tried desperately to pretend that he hadn't had his ear to the door. "I want every servant in the house lined up in the front hall in five minutes. Make sure you include the one lurking outside the terrace doors and the one in the upstairs linen closet. Now, run!"

The man jumped and took off as if he'd had his bottom singed, which, considering Tamma's mood, was more than possible. Rion, Lorand, and Vallant all looked at Jovvi with brows high, but all Jovvi could do was shrug. Tamma obviously had something definite in mind, but the details of what that was weren't clear. All they could do was wait to find out, but the wait shouldn't be a long one.

And it wasn't. No more than the specified five minutes could have passed before all the servants were gathered in the hall, most looking puzzled, the rest nervous. Jovvi now found it easy to tell which servants were being paid to spy on them, and as Tamma stalked over to stand in front of the group, Jovvi began to file faces in her memory.

"Is the entire staff here?" Tamma asked as she looked around. "I used to know everyone under this roof, but these days half of you are strangers."

"Yes, Dama, the entire staff is here," Weeks, the chief steward of the house, replied calmly. "Everyone but the gardeners, who rarely come into the house."

"Which means they don't need to be here now," Tamma said with a nod of agreement. "One of you can tell them what I'm about to say, just in case it applies to them. A number of you are being paid to watch and report on everything my associates and I do, but that's going to stop right now."

Murmurs and exclamations broke out in the group, a small bit of it surprise and disbelief, the rest protestations of innocence. Those who were guilty protested the loudest, of course, but Tamma simply held up a hand for silence.

"I haven't called you together to argue the point," she said once they'd quieted down. "It isn't an accusation we're dealing with, but fact, and I have no intention of dismissing the guilty parties. What I mean to do is a good deal worse."

That produced a round of muttering, but all Tamma did was smile.

"My associates and I have been told that what we're in the process of learning is highly confidential," she said, looking around at each member of the staff. "It's so confidential, in fact, that even we are subject to arrest and sentencing if we pass on any part of it to anyone else. If those of you now taking silver or gold continue with your spying activities, you won't be dismissed, you'll be reported to the authorities. Then you can tell a panel of judges how you accidentally found out what you weren't supposed to know even after you'd been warned. *They* probably won't consider it an accident, but that will be your problem. And if you think we can't tell when we're being spied on, guess again. Now you can go back to what you were doing—or most of you can."

Tamma turned then and walked back to Jovvi and the others, who had gathered just outside the library. The staff of servants stared after her in silence, many of them appalled, and then the group began to slowly break up. Jovvi watched them go for a moment then rejoined her own group, which was now back in the library.

"So how did I do?" Tamma asked with a laugh as Jovvi closed the door. "Did they believe me?"

"The ones who have been watching us did," Jovvi confirmed, that point having been what she'd been making sure of. "I think most of them have decided to give immediate notice, and so have one or two of the innocent but nervous ones. There were two, however, who felt nothing but frustration and a sense of being trapped."

"They're probably the ones spying on us for the testing authority," Tamma said with a thoughtful nod. "They don't have a choice about staying and watching, but if they happen to overhear the wrong thing their employers might not be able—or willing—to protect them. If we catch one or both in the wrong place, we'll have to test that by reporting them. This is too important for us to just let it go."

Jovvi felt the urge to argue that, but knowing Tamma was right kept her silent. It was the perfect time to change the subject, so after checking all around to be certain no one was listening, she did just that.

"That noble gave us a good deal more information than he realized," she said, gesturing to the others to join her as she went to find a seat. "One of the points is that we should now be beyond being separated as a group."

"Because of what he said about you being able to 'feel' all the rest of us," Rion agreed as he settled himself into a chair. "I caught that as well, and his certainty that we *would* eventually Blend. Was he really as pleased as he seemed, and as ignorant of what happened? I find it hard to believe he could have missed something that . . . intense."

"And yet, as far as I could tell, he did," Jovvi confirmed. "He was just as pleased on the inside as he appeared on the outside, maybe even more so. And now that you mention it I remember he was a *lot* more pleased, but I don't really understand why—"

Jovvi's words broke off when the knock came at the door, a firm, deliberate sound that couldn't possibly be considered part of sneaking or lurking. She got that intention clearly from the servant's mind, and then the man was opening the door and stepping inside.

"Please excuse the interruption, gentles, but there's a caller in the hall," the servant announced. "He said to tell you he's from the testing authority."

Jovvi exchanged startled glances with the others as Tamma directed that the caller was to be brought to them there. Why was there a second representative calling on them barely ten minutes after the first? The question fairly rang in each of five minds, making it unnecessary for any of them to voice it. They'd have their answer very quickly, but that didn't stop Jovvi from being disturbed.

"Lord Twimmal Royden of the testing authority," the servant announced, then stepped aside to let the caller enter. He was a fairly short man carrying far too much excess weight, and his bearded face was actually perspiring. He waddled past the servant, puffing as though he'd run for miles, and frantically gestured Lorand out of the chair Lord Carmad had been using. Lorand raised his brows but still got up, and the fat little man fairly collapsed into the seat.

"Tea . . . quickly . . ." Lord Twimmal whispered with effort, pulling out a large handkerchief to mop his face with. He seemed so close to the end that Tamma rose and got him a cup of tea, which he snatched out of her hands as soon as it reached him. He seemed to want to drain the cup, but had to settle for gulping it in between gasping for breath. It took a few minutes, but eventually the man was able to speak again.

"If I survive to reach home again, I will certainly have someone's head on a platter," he squeaked in what seemed to be a naturally high voice, complaining to the universe at large rather than speaking directly to them. "My carriage is currently being refitted, so I hired a carriage to take me around today. Two blocks from here the hired carriage lost a wheel, and in order to keep to my schedule I was forced to walk the rest of the way. I will most likely perish from the ordeal, but if I don't . . . Another cup of tea, my dear, if you will."

He raised the cup toward Tamma without looking at her, and after a very brief hesitation Tamma took it and turned back to the tea service. Jovvi was surprised that Tamma hadn't refused to play servant for the ridiculous little man, but when she returned with the refilled cup it became clear why she hadn't.

"Oh, Great Aspect, I think I've scalded my entire mouth!" the man exclaimed after taking a sip and then jerking the cup away. "Why must everything happen to *me*? It simply isn't fair, and I will certainly speak to someone about it."

"Why don't you speak to *us* now about what brings you here?" Vallant suggested, swallowing the same sort of laugh all of them were currently fighting. Obviously Tamma had warmed up the man's tea, a more satisfying response than refusing to be his servant.

"Well, why do you think I'm here?" Lord Twimmal countered pettishly while trying to cool the tea by blowing on it. "I did send word ahead of me, after all, although the way things have been going I won't be surprised if it never reached you. I'm here to teach the five of you how to Blend."

SEVENTEEN

Vallant felt the sense of shock which raced through the group, flaming high in all of them at the same time. He wasn't the only one to part his lips in preparation for asking how that could possibly be, but they all seemed to change their minds about speaking at the same time. Something stranger than usual was going on, but they'd learn more by listening than by talking.

"It so happens we did get that message," Jovvi said almost immediately, "but we became so immersed in our conversation about the servant problem that it slipped our minds. Do you need anything else before we can begin?"

"Three or four days to recuperate would be nice," Lord Twimmal replied with a sigh, obviously not joking. "That, however, is unfortunately out of the question, so we might as well begin with positioning you while my tea cools. The order you must stand in is Fire, Spirit, and Earth in a line, with Air and Water to left and right."

After saying that, the absurd fool went back to trying to cool his tea. The gleam in Tamrissa's eyes said she wasn't prepared to let that happen, which made Vallant want to grin all over again. When Tamrissa touched the power she *was* a different person, one who was beginning to really fascinate him. . . .

But this wasn't the time for thoughts about anything but what they were in the middle of. Tamrissa, Jovvi, and Lorand were lining up slowly and haphazardly to match the fat fool's offhand instructions, and that gave Vallant an idea.

122

He caught Rion's eye and gestured slightly with his head, silently suggesting that Rion move forward to stand beside Tamrissa just as Vallant was doing. They hadn't been told to flank their Spirit magic member, so there was no reason for them to do it.

"Oh, very good, very good," Lord Twimmal said distractedly with a wave of his fat hand when he finally noticed them. "I just don't understand why this tea refuses to cool off . . . Now, all five of you have to concentrate. Spirit magic will stretch out arms to each of you, and you're to do nothing to avoid the touch. Go ahead and try it."

"Do you mean stretch out my arms physically?" Jovvi asked with great innocence. "Since I only have two of my own, how can I touch all four of them at once? Or am I only supposed to touch them one or two at a time?"

"Why do all you people ask the same foolish questions?" the fat noble demanded in his girl's voice, back to being pettish. "Of course I don't mean stretch your arms out physically, why would I say such a thing? It's your talent you must use, which presumably you have in good quantity. Send it out toward your fellow group members, and touch them all at the same time."

Jovvi was silent for a moment, supposedly doing as she was told, but Vallant felt nothing from her—which might have been the best idea. His being still resonated with the memory of what they'd had so briefly, the desire for more of it gnawing like a giant hunger. If Jovvi had touched him even lightly, he would have been helpless to do anything but respond.

"All right, I've reached them," Jovvi said after the moment, her voice faintly strained. "It wasn't all that hard, just . . . awkward."

"Since this is your first attempt, that's only to be expected," Lord Twimmal commented, most of his attention still on the tea. "The next thing to be done involves all of you, and you must respond precisely at the same time. Each of you must touch the other four, in the same manner that Spirit touches you. Try it now."

Again there was a silence, during which Vallant did the same nothing as the others. The seated noble couldn't even be bothered to glance at them, being much too involved

with the mystery of his tea. Considering the fact that even
a Low talent in Fire magic could have done what Tamrissa
was doing, Vallant wondered what closet Twimmal could
have grown up in that he still didn't understand what was
happening.

"I'm having some trouble with this," Lorand said after
a short while, sounding a bit vexed. "I can reach our Spirit
magic member, but I'm having trouble reaching the others
at the same time."

"Yes, that's precisely my problem," Rion agreed, a faint
and distant amusement in his tone. "I'm able to reach
Spirit, but the others are a blur."

"Are all of you seeing it the same?" Twimmal asked,
finally looking up at them. "Is there someone who *can't*
reach Spirit?"

Tamrissa joined Vallant in assuring the fat fool that they
were able to reach Jovvi but not each other, and Twimmal
beamed and nodded, then began to struggle out of the chair.

"Then we've accomplished the first step toward Blending, and now I can be on my way," he said, breathing
heavily from the exertion of standing. "It's now certain that
you *will* be able to Blend, which was what I needed to
know. When I return tomorrow you may try again, but no
practicing on your own until you've Blended with me
watching. Now I can only hope that the carriage I sent for
when I arrived has gotten here. It always takes those people
so long to respond, and that no matter who you are. Horses
are so limited, and completely unimpressed with a man's
position in life. . . ."

The words trailed along behind him as he waddled to the
door and out into the hall, leaving the door open. He'd
abandoned his recalcitrant cup of tea in the same way, letting Vallant and the others know what category *they* were
in: inanimate and unimportant, good for only a single purpose. Once again Lorand ambled to the door, stood watching and listening for a moment, then came back to rejoin
them without shutting the door.

"His carriage isn't here yet, so he's demanding a 'snack'
in the dining room to help him survive the wait," Lorand
reported in a murmur. "Weeks is taking care of it, but until
the man leaves we need to see what's going on out there."

"We certainly do, because there's something very important we have to discuss," Jovvi agreed. She'd been frowning when Vallant had turned to look at her, but now she simply looked troubled. "It was his comment about carriages that triggered the memory, that and what went on at the trial yesterday. No wonder those men watching the trial were frustrated and annoyed. Lady Eltrina made a bad mistake using the trial in an attempt to damage my balance, because I found out something I wasn't supposed to know."

"What could you have found out about?" Vallant asked, taking his turn at frowning as he cast his mind back. "I was right there with you, and I don't remember learnin' about anythin' in particular."

"That's probably because you weren't suspicious to begin with," she replied. "I tend to distrust most situations, so I was. But let's sit down and I'll start from the beginning—and don't forget that we don't like each other all that much."

Vallant noticed that he wasn't alone in having needed the reminder, and that was more amusing than embarrassing. Many of his attitudes seemed to have been changed by that one brief moment of merging, at least as far as the others were concerned. Lorand and Rion were no longer Coll and Mardimil to him, and he was certain that they felt the same toward him. But just to be on the safe side they spread out a bit before sitting, then gave Jovvi their attention.

"Think back to that very first test we passed," she said, keeping her voice low and the words calm. "That was the one we also had to survive, and when we did we were then sent to this residence. Do any of you remember how long it took for the coach to arrive?"

"It took almost no time at all," Tamrissa answered, causing Vallant and the others to murmur their agreement. "I can remember being faintly surprised at that, but I was so pleased to be able to leave there that the thought became utterly unimportant. It still seems unimportant, but obviously you don't agree."

"You're right, I don't," Jovvi replied with a faint smile. "If you don't arrange for a coach or carriage to pick you up well in advance, you *always* have to wait for it to arrive. There was no sign of any coaches when I first got there for my test, so it couldn't have been just sitting there and waiting. It had to be sent for, and wouldn't have been arranged for in advance. If I hadn't managed to get myself out of that room, I would have had no need whatsoever for a coach.''

''Everything you've said goes for me as well,'' Rion put in, taking his turn at frowning. ''If I hadn't survived I would have had no need for a coach, and there were none in view when I reached the building. Even if the vehicle stood ready and waiting somewhere in the neighborhood, it would first have had to be summoned before it might arrive. The time delay involved wasn't even long enough for the summoning.''

''So what does that mean?'' Lorand asked while Vallant pushed away memories of how desperate he'd been to get out of that building. The speedy arrival of the coach had been too much of a blessing to be questioned. . . . ''If we're forced to assume that they had coaches hidden somewhere very close by, how does that fact become sinister?''

''The sinister part comes in when you realize that the coaches *weren't* hidden somewhere close by,'' Jovvi explained gently. ''I remember that glass of water I was given to drink once I'd escaped, odd-tasting water that was very refreshing and gave me back a small amount of strength with regard to my talent. It's funny, but I've never tasted water like that before or since, and I never got my strength back simply by taking a drink.''

''Puredan!'' Vallant blurted, finally having seen the point. ''We weren't given water, it was Puredan. No wonder a small amount of strength came back, and the coach seemed to get there in no time. We were full of that drug, so we had no idea how much time was passin'.''

The others interrupted to ask what Puredan was, so Jovvi explained while Vallant fumed. He'd been *drugged*, by damn, drugged like a criminal or slave! He'd been under the thumb of the testing authority all along without realizing it, thinking of himself as a free man when he was nothing of the sort!

''And we have no idea what they told us while we were under,'' Jovvi finished her explanation with. ''Any orders given us will be obeyed completely, and we won't even know we're obeying them. No wonder none of the 'smart gold' is being bet on a common Blending to win the competitions.''

"You know, I'll bet that that was what was done to the final challenger for the Seated High position in the Earth magic competition," Lorand said, a sense of revelation accompanying his anger. "I knew the man wasn't drugged, but *something* kept him from using his full ability. I think we all know now what that something was."

"But what we don't know is how to get rid of it," Tamrissa said, hot anger burning in her lovely eyes. "And we don't know how any buried orders are keyed, but you can bet those miserable testing authority people do. No wonder that noble was so casual when he talked about claiming me. He's the one who gave me the orders, so he has nothing at all to worry about."

"And as if this weren't enough, we also have that mystery confronting us," Rion pointed out. "Twimmal had no idea that anyone else had come to instruct us about Blending, most especially not someone who did a better job of it than he. Without that so-called Lord Carmad, we'd still be struggling and floundering in an effort to make sense of what we were being told. Now we have to wonder who the man was and why he made that effort to help us."

"And also if he gave the same help to any of the other groups," Jovvi added with a nod. "I can't imagine us being singled out for special treatment, but the possibility still remains. It would be nice if there was a group working against the nobility and specifically in favor of the common groups, one that could tell us all the things the testing authority is holding back on. I hope 'Lord Carmad' does come back tomorrow."

"If he does, it won't be at the same time," Tamrissa offered thoughtfully. "He would have come face to face with Twimmal if the fat little man's carriage hadn't broken down. He won't be able to count on luck like that a second time, not to mention the fact that we now know he isn't really from the testing authority. He'll have to know that we'll be asking questions about something other than Blending, and—Did anyone else notice that even he didn't describe the actual process accurately?"

"Yes, and *he* didn't even notice when we succeeded on the first try," Lorand said while everyone nodded or murmured in agreement. "Doesn't *anyone* know how this is really supposed to work?"

"How can they?" Vallant asked reasonably. "It's against the law even for people to do so little as use their talents together. Cooperatin' to the point of formin' a Blendin' means summary execution, and there hasn't been an execution in—how many years?"

"More than twenty," Rion supplied with a frown. "The law is one of the very few applied equally to the nobility as well as to commoners, and the last group executed was a noble one. They apparently paid quite a lot in gold to learn the process, bribing a minor official to research the matter in some obscure government records. The official disappeared as soon as he was paid, or he would have been executed as well. Which means we'll have to ask 'Lord Carmad' how *he* found out."

"I've always wondered why Blending is illegal for everyone but the Seated Five," Tamrissa mused. "I've heard it claimed that only High talents can Blend, so an illegal Blending would require the Five to stop them if they began to run amok. Now that it's just about certain the Seated Five were given their place rather than having to earn it, I'm not wondering any longer."

"I'm not sure it's only High talents who can Blend," Jovvi put in, looking thoughtful. "It's been reported more than once that places outside the empire have people who Blend all the time, and they're not solely High talents. If it comes to a choice between believing our government and believing ordinary people who have actually visited other places, I'll take the ordinary people."

"It's fairly clear we're going to have to *hope* it's true," Lorand said, his words heavy and his gaze troubled. "If we don't win the competitions, the empire will never allow us to stay together. We'll have to go elsewhere if we want to do that, immediately and without giving them warning. If we don't, we'll never see each other again."

"And they'll never let us remember what we're now learnin'," Vallant added in agreement, suddenly just as troubled. "They won't want people walkin' around who know how to Blend, and who might be unhappy enough to pass on what they know. Either they'll do somethin' to make us forget, or. . . ."

"Or they'll kill us," Jovvi finished calmly when he didn't. "That's been a very real possibility right from the beginning, starting with that first qualifying test. The idea of killing us doesn't bother them in the least, and if they have no other use for us they won't hesitate. It will be our job to see that they don't get the chance to do anything at all."

"Assuming we don't find a way to win after all," Lorand said in agreement after glancing toward the open door. "And it seems that our noble visitor's carriage has arrived. He should be gone in another minute or two, which will leave us free to do more than talk."

"I think we ought to wait until the middle of the night, when all the servants are asleep," Tamrissa said as Vallant's body began to tingle in anticipation of Blending again. "If there's a problem or someone comes calling, they'll have an excuse to walk in and see what we're doing. That fat little man said we're not supposed to practice without him, and if we do anyway the testing authority's spy will certainly report us."

"So we *had* best leave it for the middle of the night," Rion said in support, sounding as disappointed as Vallant felt. "I'd hoped there would be no further delay, but this one is unavoidable."

Arguing with the conclusion was impossible, especially when Weeks stopped in the doorway to announce that their visitor was finally gone. If they'd been doing more than just talking, the servant would certainly have noticed. But that left the rest of the day with nothing in particular to occupy them, so Vallant got up and ambled over to where Tamrissa now stood.

"This would be a nice time for a stroll through the garden," he murmured to her. "The private corners out there are badly in need of inspectin'."

"You're forgetting that they don't yet know we've Blended," she murmured back, the steadiness of her voice saying she continued to touch the power. "Until we're beyond the point where they can separate us, we have to keep on hating each other. After that, I'll arrange everything.''

Vallant stood with brows high as she walked away after sending him a brief, businesslike smile. He reluctantly had to agree that the time wasn't yet right, curse the luck, but as for the rest of it. . . . *She* would arrange everything? Just exactly what sort of woman was she becoming? As if Vallant didn't have enough to worry about. . . .

EIGHTEEN

Delin had just come back from the bathhouse and was dressing when a servant came to tell him that their expected visitor had arrived. He finished dressing in record time and went down to the sitting room, to find that only Kambil was there with their guest. Delin and Kambil had shared a late breakfast, but late or not, the others still hadn't come down.

"Ah, Delin, come and meet our mentor," Kambil said warmly as Delin entered the room. "Lord Idian Vomak, this is Lord Delin Moord, Earth magic."

"A pleasure, Lord Delin," Idian Vomak said with a smile. "Do pour yourself a cup of tea and join us."

Delin returned Lord Idian's smile and turned toward the tea service, but some of his excited eagerness had dimmed. Idian was rather an old man, with a seamed face, wrinkled hands, and streaked gray hair. He also appeared to be rather small in stature, but not small in the least where ego was concerned. Telling Delin to get a cup of tea in what was essentially his own home was overbearingly intrusive to say the least, and the worst sort of intrusion: fatherly. If there was one thing Delin couldn't abide. . . .

"We'll begin as soon as the rest of your group gets

here," Lord Idian went on, his tone warm and encouraging—and somehow not quite real. "I can see I should have sent word ahead as to what time I would be arriving, but it simply didn't occur to me. Tomorrow you'll know, so there won't be anything of a delay."

"Lord Idian tells me he expected Rigos to come along and introduce him," Kambil put in as Delin turned away from the service with a cup of tea in his hands. "Rigos, however, sent word that he was unavoidably detained, and would join Lord Idian tomorrow instead. When you arrived, I was in the process of wondering aloud if that scene with Bron might have had anything to do with Rigos's lack of attendance."

"That's an excellent question and possibly a very accurate surmise," Delin agreed, pleasantly surprised at the way Kambil had taken the opportunity to damage Rigos's reputation a bit more. "I don't mind saying I'm relieved the man isn't here, and apparently Bron and I aren't the only ones to feel that way. I went out to dinner last night and ran into some of the members of the other groups, and the majority of them feel exactly the same."

"Rather unfortunate in view of the man's innocence," Lord Idian commented with a sad headshake. "I was present during his questioning under Puredan, and there can't be any doubt. One simply doesn't lie with Puredan doing its work."

"But that's assuming the Puredan *was* doing its work," Delin said, repeating the idea he'd passed on the night before. "Everyone knows how powerful and wealthy Rigos's father is, a combination that might well have managed to substitute water for Puredan. Since no one else drank the liquid, how are we to know?"

"I'll admit I hadn't thought of that," Lord Idian granted with a frown, his sharp blue eyes appearing troubled. "It makes a significant difference, and even casts doubt on the testimony of that Earth magic practitioner who claimed Rigos spoke the truth. Oh, dear. This will surely complicate matters all the more."

"Complicate them in what way?" Kambil asked, to Delin's eye innocently curious. "Is it likely to affect our efforts at Blending?"

"Oh, no, the matter of complication lies elsewhere," Lord Idian replied with a chuckle, faint amusement which quickly left him. "In point of fact it lies with Ollon Capmar, the late Elfini's brother. He's been positively haunted and driven since her death, and when Rigos was cleared he was very . . . disturbed. It wasn't possible to argue the exoneration, and yet that left no one who might be accused of the crime. Now. . . ."

"Now the exoneration is less certain, so Lord Ollon might well become . . . agitated again," Kambil said with a nod, completing the thought. "It *is* unlikely the matter will affect those of us meant to compete, at least directly. Indirectly, however . . . it would be pleasant to have an Advisory agent who isn't likely to be snatched away from us again—or apt to have a public breakdown."

"You're referring, of course, to Lord Hiblit," Idian said with his own nod. "I wasn't present that night, but I'm told the scene was extremely disturbing. I've also heard that Hiblit's father is suffering socially, for being so heavy-handed with the boy that Hiblit lost all control. When these things become public, it's usually because the parent involved hasn't been sufficiently discreet."

"You know, a strange thought just occurred to me," Delin said slowly, drawing the attention of the others. "Hiblit was definitely odd when he first introduced himself, but he didn't seem unstable. Just how long before that . . . scene was Rigos released from custody?"

"Why, it was only that morning," Idian replied with a frown. "What are you suggesting?"

"I'm not quite sure," Delin admitted, a lie Idian certainly wasn't seeing behind. "It just seems strange that Rigos is released in the morning, and that evening his old position is suddenly vacated. I have no idea how something like that could be managed, but isn't it said that enough gold can buy anything anyone might want?"

Idian stared at him without speaking, but the deep disturbance in the man's eyes was a clear enough message. Delin had now managed to implicate Rigos in Hiblit's breakdown, a suggestion that would quickly begin to circulate. If the idea spread widely enough, they might be rid of the man much sooner than they could have hoped.

"Ah, here's the rest of your group," Idian said as he looked up, deliberately throwing off the dark mood. "Now we can begin."

"Before breakfast?" Selendi demanded, her usual surliness blurred by her not being completely awake. She and Homin and Bron stood in the doorway, all of them wearing wraps and looking half asleep. "I can't possibly do anything at all before breakfast."

"And neither can I," Bron agreed sourly, both of them ignoring—or not noticing—the way Homin had begun to step forward without argument. "Getting a man up this early is bad enough. Expecting him to function properly is completely unreasonable. We'll just step into the dining room and—"

"You'll do no such thing," Idian denied, the sudden steel in his voice turning him into a different person entirely. "You'll come in here and do as you're told, and tomorrow you will be fully dressed and waiting when I arrive. Appearing in nothing but wraps is inexcusable, an insult I refuse to tolerate. If you were taught nothing of proper manners until now, it's more than time you learned."

The man's tone and words were as familiar to Selendi and Bron as they were to Delin, coming as they did from a figure of authority very much like the Advisors—or their fathers. It wasn't possible to argue or disobey, and Delin had to exert quite a lot of self-control to keep from twitching the way Bron and Selendi did. Homin simply shrank into himself, as though he were just as guilty of trying to avoid his responsibilities. All three touched their wraps in some self-conscious way, and then quickly came forward to find places to sit.

"No, don't bother sitting down," Lord Idian said at once in the same inflexible tone. "In the beginning you will stand when practicing this exercise, as the symbolism will assist you in attaining the physical reality. And in a very real way Blending *is* physical, despite the linking of minds to achieve it. We'll begin with a straight line consisting of Fire, Spirit, and Earth, in that order, one behind the other with a distance of two feet between each of them."

Delin stood up a bare moment before Kambil did, the

two of them immediately walking over to join Bron. The Fire magic user seemed sullen but beyond the point of making objections, and the three of them were quickly in line.

"Now Air and Water will kindly add themselves to the arrangement beside Spirit, Air to the left and Water to the right," Lord Idian continued, invisible to Delin where he stood. Their mentor was still seated and apparently meant to stay that way. "Please be aware of the distance between you and Spirit, which should not exceed nor lessen the same two feet."

Delin watched Selendi and Homin position themselves, the pair using more care than with anything they'd done since arriving at the residence. It struck him then that he might have been too quick in his displeasure with Lord Idian, who now had them all behaving as efficiently as possible. Anything that helped his unruly group to become an actual, functioning Blending was beneficial, even if the man did remind him of his father.

"Now you must all open yourselves to the power, then close your eyes and use your minds," Lord Idian went on. "Spirit will reach out with his talent to touch all of you, and when you feel his touch you must attempt to return it. But don't anticipate. Wait until Spirit has reached you, and only then make your own attempt."

Delin had already closed his eyes, so he didn't know whether any of the others had nodded. It was perfectly clear that none of them had spoken, the others presumably as intent as he on what they were in the midst of. And their part was difficult, requiring as it did that they do nothing but wait for Kambil to act. That could well take—

A small gasp escaped Delin when he felt himself touched by a gossamer thread that could have been produced by no one but Kambil. It was the faintest trace at first, but then it strengthened to the point where there was absolutely no doubt. Kambil now touched him firmly, and that made it his place to return the touch.

Delin had rarely used as much concentration as he did now The power hummed all through his body as he reached toward Kambil, guided by the firm touch already established in his direction. The distance of his reach turned out to be longer than he'd expected, but after what could only have been seconds he actually came in contact with the Spirit magic user! The experience was incredible, more vital and electrifying than anything he'd ever done before, making him want to laugh like a madman. His dream was becoming a reality, one that went beyond even what he had envisioned.

The first thrill of contact didn't so much fade as settle down comfortably. The awareness of it remained, but Delin was able to . . . look around, so to speak. His senses now rode along the double contact between him and Kambil, a contact which allowed him to be aware of certain things. Like Homin's presence, somewhere to the right of both him and Kambil. The Water magic user also stood to the right, but the sense of him was somehow different. . . .

"All right, Spirit, by now you should be in contact with the others and they with you." Lord Idian's voice came to Delin clearly, but somehow from a long distance off. "You should be fully aware of them in the sphere the five of you have created, and each of them should be fully aware of you but only distantly aware of each other. You've reached that point, have you not?"

"Actually, no," Kambil said, a frown clear in his voice. "I've touched all four of them, but only Delin and Homin have managed to return the touch. Selendi and Bron are still half out of reach."

"It's not my fault," Selendi said at once, defensiveness strong in the words. "I just can't seem to *find* him, not when I'm still half asleep. It's simply too hard right now."

"It isn't my fault either," Bron added his own oar, the words as sullen as his expression undoubtedly was. "I know exactly where he is, but something is keeping me from reaching him. It isn't *my* fault if something does that."

"Indeed," Lord Idian commented dryly, clearly displeased. "It may well be that you're incompatible with the others. If so, there will be no Blending of your group, and you will be spectators at the competitions, not participants. You may all relax now."

Delin broke contact with Kambil immediately, before the surge of terror and rage he felt was able to travel up the connection between them. He'd *known* those fools would cause trouble, and the only surprise involved was that

Homin wasn't guilty as well. If they ruined this for him, he'd—

"Why don't you three go along to breakfast, and we'll continue this tomorrow," Lord Idian said to Selendi, Homin, and Bron. The man's voice was still commanding, but some of the sternness had faded. Selendi seemed almost in tears, and Homin cooed comfort at her as he guided her toward the door with an arm around her shoulders. Bron's sullenness had changed in some manner, as though fear now tinged his perpetual resentment, and he hesitated only a moment before following the two out. He hadn't made eye contact with anyone, and seemed determined to keep to that as long as possible.

"I believe I'll have to have a talk with those two," Kambil said once the three were gone. "I don't think Selendi was putting enough strength into her effort, but Bron—I still don't know what *his* problem is."

"It's likely the most common problem in groups such as yours," Lord Idian replied, now back to being warm and friendly. "Lord Bron apparently resents direction of any sort, and is used to turning stubborn in the presence of it. Once he thoroughly understands that no one will coax and wheedle him to try again if he fails, he may find it possible to push aside his habitual behavior. If not. . . ."

"If not, we'll *all* look like fools," Delin finished sourly, keeping the rest of his emotions well out of Idian's sight. "All my friends know what I'm in the middle of, and if we don't even make it to the competitions they'll never stop laughing. If Bron doesn't get over whatever it is keeping him from doing his part, I'll certainly throttle him."

"With Fire magic being as important as it is to a Blending, you might consider appealing to his vanity instead," Lord Idian said with a chuckle as he rose from his chair. "And as far as the girl goes, has either of you lain with her yet?"

Delin exchanged a glance with Kambil as they both shook their heads. Had they mistaken the proper time when that ought to be done?

"You, Lord Kambil, should do so at once, and you, Lord Delin, as soon afterward as practical," Lord Idian said, his nod telling them he wasn't surprised at their answer.

"Physical intimacy strengthens the bond of talent much more than you would believe, which means the others must lie with her as well. A pity you have only the one female, as two has proven itself optimal. Most of your . . . connections beyond the one with Spirit will need to go through the woman—unless two or more of you men have been intimate? No? A pity, but we all must work with what we have. Until tomorrow, gentles."

Lord Idian bowed very slightly and then left them, and Kambil went to the windows and moved the drape somewhat aside. He looked out for a very long moment, then finally turned back to Delin.

"He's gone," Kambil said as he returned to where Delin stood. "And he was quite right about what's ailing Bron, but he missed the most important part: Bron believes that a 'leader' ought to remain aloof from his 'followers,' mixing with them only when absolutely necessary and then not completely. It looks like our brilliant idea has backfired on us and singed our fingers."

"I knew it was a mistake encouraging him in that, I just knew it!" Delin spat, barely able to keep himself from laying the blame exactly where it belonged: on Kambil. "Now I'll have to do something about it, and pray it doesn't turn out to be too little and too late."

"Let me handle it," Kambil said, and his tone somehow calmed Delin's agitation a bit. "I think I can talk him out of that attitude, and he's already begun to talk himself out of the other. Not being pushed or argued with frightened him, since it made him realize that failure now will be no one's fault but his own. If you say anything to him at all, any failure will immediately become *your* fault."

"Won't the same thing happen with you?" Delin asked, cautiously relieved. "Logically speaking, it ought to."

"With me it isn't a matter of logic," Kambil replied with a smile. "I can keep Bron's fear from fading, for instance, and can encourage the idea of mixing with the rest of us. Being able to use his own emotions against him will keep me out of the position he puts everyone else into."

"I sincerely hope so," Delin commented, finding it only fitting that Kambil clean up his own mess. "And don't forget about Selendi. The two of them have to be ready by

tomorrow, sooner if possible. If we lose this opportunity
because of those two, I'll kill them with my bare hands.''

Kambil nodded with distraction and headed out of the
room, either not noticing or simply not commenting about
the fact that Delin hadn't been joking. He stood in the middle of the room, his eyes unblinking, his hands opening and
closing at his sides. No, he wasn't joking about killing
those useless fools, not joking in the least. . . .

NINETEEN

Kambil escorted Selendi into the dining room for dinner,
seating her beside Homin before going to take his own
place at the table. Homin snarled on the inside at Selendi's
satisfied little smile, but when she immediately lost interest
in Kambil in favor of himself, the snarl disappeared amid
delighted surprise. Kambil had assured Homin that he
would return Selendi with no harm done to their relationship, but Homin hadn't believed it. The small man also
hadn't been able to argue the necessity after it had been
explained to him, but he'd been certain that Selendi would
be lost to him afterward. Now that his fears had proven
groundless, what he felt toward Kambil was almost love.

Which was exactly what Kambil had been trying for. He
smiled to himself as he sat, but the amount of work he'd
done today left him only enough strength for a rather faint
private smile. First he'd had to explain to Homin why others needed to lie with the first woman who had ever taken
any sort of interest in Homin. Without his ability the effort
probably would have been wasted, and their group would
have broken up right then and there.

But his ability was more than just adequate, so Homin

had accepted the necessity. It would have been nice to reward himself with Selendi after that, but first he'd had to see to Bron. If he'd told Delin that letting Bron think of himself as their leader was a mistake, Delin would never have believed him. As it was the man now blamed *him* for using the flawed technique, since blaming himself was out of the question for Delin. Kambil had been able to see that clearly, not to mention how close Delin was to losing his grip on all pretense of normality and sanity.

So he'd volunteered to see to Bron, which had relieved Delin's mind. Delin hadn't been able to think of a way out of the trap, but Kambil had expected the problem and so was prepared. Working with Bron was like working with a stone wall already set in cement, but the man really had very little imagination. That made things much easier, and by the time Kambil had left him, Bron was eagerly looking forward to being "one of the very, very few." At their next attempt he would embrace the idea of Blending, both to elevate his social status and to keep from becoming a laughingstock.

Then it had become time to lie with Selendi, but not simply for the sake of the Blending or even purely for the pleasure. Selendi liked to be in control of when she bestowed her favors and was more than capable of refusing to cooperate just to exercise that control. Kambil had had to see to that part of it first, and then he'd had to set the right frame of mind for her for their next session. To say that her effort at Blending had been halfhearted would be to overstate the effort, but next time would be another story.

Only then had he been able to enjoy lying with her, using her warped need for acceptance and control to satisfy his own physical requirements. It had been a long, intense time of delightful exertion, and afterward they'd both fallen asleep. But not before Kambil had reinforced his work with her, bringing her to full compliance. He'd used the nap to regain a good part of the strength he'd expended, but the thought of going to bed—alone!—remained an attractive one.

And yet there was still Delin to consider. Kambil sipped from his wineglass as he watched the man saunter into the dining room, showing the world nothing but languid charm.

On the inside, however, there was a roiling, agitated mass of fear and determination and ruthlessness, all held in a precarious control that could be swept away at any moment. His mind filled with hatred and loathing when he glanced at Homin and Selendi, and the emotion eased only a very little when he nodded to Kambil before taking his seat.

"Bron's late *again*?" he asked in mock horror, pretending to tease about a subject which actually came close to setting him frothing at the mouth. "I can understand being late to dull and unimportant meetings, but when you start arriving late to meals you definitely have a problem."

"Bron had a visitor this afternoon, and they spent quite a lot of time in the bath house," Kambil supplied, pretending himself that the subject was nothing but idle conversation. "He began to dress as soon as she left, so he ought to be with us at any moment."

"That's a different story," Delin allowed, his mind grudgingly releasing some of the intensity of his hatred. "A man should never hurry a lady, especially not one who makes the effort to come to *him*. But we won't hold dinner, not when I'm as hungry as I am."

"Holding dinner won't be necessary," Bron's voice came, and then the man himself appeared to take his place at the table. "After my exertions of the past few hours, starving is a mild description of my condition. And I can't afford to be starving, not when I'll need all my strength for the next time we try to Blend. Next time it will work properly, I've promised myself that."

Delin returned Bron's smile, but Kambil could see that his mind was just short of being stunned. He'd never expected to hear that from Bron, and he turned uncomprehending eyes to Kambil.

"I suspect that Bron has come to realize just how few people are ever in our position," Kambil supplied in an offhand way. "Our social status will soar once we've managed to Blend, and we'll be saved from the ignominy of failure."

"And we'll have such marvelous control," Selendi put in, turning her face away from Homin to look at Delin, but continuing to hold Homin's hand. "Gaining control over ourselves is just the first step in controlling everything around us, so I can't wait until we try to Blend again. Bron and I will manage it the next time, just wait and see if we don't.''

Bron's smile of appreciation for her vote of confidence brought an answering smile from Selendi, and then she returned her attention to Homin. The proper balance was there in all three of them, and even Delin's stunned incredulity was turning to hopeful approval. Kambil's work was beginning to pay off, but then a ripple of disturbance went through Homin.

''It's just now occurred to me,'' the small, overweight man said, looking from Delin to Kambil and back again. ''A social position that very few can equal . . . the control we'll be able to exert once we've Blended . . . no one but the Five wields that kind of power, and the social position is one that *no one* can equal. I've never met or even heard about someone who was part of a challenging Blending twenty-five years ago. Can any of you say you have?''

Now it was three minds which were producing shock, with Homin's stunned realization not far behind. Obviously none of them had considered the point before, and in fact they found it almost impossible to accept.

''What you're suggesting just can't be,'' Delin protested, thrown off balance more than a little. ''They'd never do to us what they do to the peasants, not when we *matter*. They may separate challenging Blendings who fail, which is, after all, simple caution, but to do more than that—No one would stand for it.''

''How would they know?'' Kambil asked quietly, pleased that the others had finally reached a position of true understanding. ''If our friends heard we'd been rewarded for our efforts with extremely important positions in various parts of the governmental structure, how many of them would wonder why we didn't call on them to say goodbye before leaving? They'd decide we'd gotten to be much too important to bother with them again, and then they'd shrug and forget about us. Am I misdescribing the situation?''

''No,'' Delin grudged when the others remained silent. ''It's exactly what *I* would think if it happened to someone else. But what about our families? *They'd* expect to hear from us, and would certainly cause a stir if they didn't.''

"Now you've penetrated to the heart of the matter,"
Kambil agreed, trying to break it to them gently. "My father was very upset when he learned that I'd been drafted
to be part of a challenging Blending, but he refused to discuss why until just before we all left our homes to come
here. That was when he explained that he'd do the best he
could until the competitions, but so far he hadn't been able
to find a way to get me exempted from whatever they mean
to do with us afterward. All he'd managed to get was an
apology for the necessity of having to use me. I wouldn't
have been chosen if they'd had any choice, they said."

"Why not?" Bron asked, his tone absolutely flat.
"We've all been told what an honor and privilege this is.
Why would they have chosen someone else over you?"

"Because of two reasons," Kambil replied, leaking his
disgust over the subject so the others would know how he
saw it. "The first reason is that I get along with my father
and grandmother, and we're actually quite fond of each
other. The second is that I'm known for not getting into
. . . escapades, and several important people in the government have seriously considered taking me on as their chief
assistant. I had a . . . 'bright future' ahead of me, but they
weren't able to find anyone else strong enough in Spirit
magic."

The other four sat staring down at the table, and despite
the thick silence Kambil knew exactly what they were
thinking. None of them really got along with their families,
and if there wasn't out-and-out dislike between them, then
indifference was as good as it got. And as far as promising
futures went, there wasn't a single one among them. Even
Delin had been considered "too smooth to be trustworthy,"
a condemnation Kambil had heard from more than one
source. Most people seemed to believe that Delin would
immediately try to replace anyone foolish enough to take
him on as an assistant, which showed how astute even the
dull and unimaginative could sometimes be.

"Why couldn't they simply separate us?" Selendi asked,
her thoughts throbbing with pained disappointment. "I
mean, if we lost they wouldn't have to do anything else,
just keep us from ever getting together again."

"Keep us under guard for the rest of our lives?" Delin

asked, his tone less ridiculing than he would have wished. "Even if that were something *we* could live with, they would still have no guarantee that we'd never find a way around their precautions. It would be more than embarrassing for them if we got together, and their precious Seated Five turned out to be incapable of defeating us. No, they won't simply separate us."

"So you see that we, also, have no choice in the matter," Kambil summed up, now sending determination. "We *have* to Blend and we *have* to win, but not just for the unique position and its incredible amount of power. We have to do it to save our favorite necks, which no one else can do for us."

The others all stirred and began to absorb his determination, which they were able to do without interruption. No one had noticed yet that not a single servant had intruded on their privacy, something Kambil had made sure would be so before he began the conversation. Rigos's spy on the staff hadn't been easy to handle after all the rest of the work Kambil had done, but it had been necessary so he'd accomplished it anyway. All the servants were now waiting to be summoned, without the least thought about listening in.

"Well, if one or two of us didn't really want to win before, I think they've now changed their minds," Delin said after a moment, looking around at everyone else with an expression of grim satisfaction. "Before, winning could be looked at as simply saving face, but now it's the only thing that will save the rest of us as well. Do any of you believe otherwise?"

"Not anymore," Selendi surprised them by saying, anger and resentment strong in her mind. "I can see now that I never really believed we would win. I thought we would just perform in the competitions and then go back to our previous lives, but now I know that my previous life doesn't *want* me back. My father could have kept this from happening to me, but since he'll still have my sister he probably didn't even try. I want him to regret that, along with the way he never had any time for me once I reached the age of eleven. I *will* make him regret it."

"Along with my father," Homin agreed, his thoughts

more hardened than Kambil had ever seen them. "I can now remember at least two occasions when I overheard him saying I was an embarrassment to him. Once it was to an associate who was just as powerful as he was, and once it was to Elfini. After that was when she first began to . . . concentrate on me, but I couldn't bring myself to blame my father for the torment. Now I can, and suddenly I want to see him pay."

"For me it's my father and mother together," Bron said with his gaze on his empty plate, another surprise. "They always gave me everything I wanted, then seemed to blame *me* for wanting it in the first place. If there were things they didn't want me to have or do, why couldn't they have just said so? Why is it my fault that they could never refuse me anything? I want to ask them that, but if we don't win I'll never get the chance."

"And my father has spent my entire life trying to grind me under his heel," Delin put in, his gaze distracted and far away. "He's never been able to force me into accepting his authority without question the way everyone else does, and he resents that lack bitterly. He knows I've always been terrified of his punishments, but that's never been enough. He needs to be in complete control of everything, and I'm the one who kept that from happening. I swore a long time ago to *always* be the one, and winning is the only way I can keep that oath."

"Winning is also the only way I can ever see my grandmother again," Kambil said, feeling that closing the circle was extremely necessary. "She's always been my whole world, and would never understand if I disappeared without a word. I could never do that to her, not on purpose and not even involuntarily. I'll do anything I have to to avoid it, and I mean anything."

"So we're all agreed," Delin said with the first smile for his groupmates that wasn't forced or artificial. "We're going to do this, so I propose we get started right after dinner. Since we know what's supposed to be done, let's just go ahead and do it."

Everyone liked that idea, a fact Kambil checked on before reaching for the table bell that summoned the servants. Every one of them was prepared to do his or her best, and the resolve was strong enough to carry them along with it. If they were just able to Blend the first time, the greatest hurdle would then be behind them.

Dinner was a little less than perfect because of the forced delay in having it served, but no one seemed to mind. Everyone ate with better appetite than they had in a long while, and after dessert they retired to the sitting room with a large tea service. They were all prepared to keep at the practice until they finally achieved Blending, and once again the servants had been put into a state of complete forgetfulness where the five of them were concerned.

"All right, let's get into our positions," Delin said after Kambil had closed the door and joined them. "Bron first, Kambil second, me third, Homin to Kambil's right, Selendi to Kambil's left."

Everyone nodded and began to move, and actually checked their positions once they were in them. Kambil always found it amazing that the proper motivation was able to change a person completely, the proof of the contention now being right in front of his eyes. Bron and Selendi were totally different people, and Homin's slow change of character had now strengthened and intensified.

But it was Kambil's place to begin the exercise, so he put aside all extraneous thought and opened himself more widely to the power. The inrush of strength was both familiar and necessary, allowing him to extend invisible arms to his groupmates without the delaying drag of fatigue. He touched them all at the same time, and then—

And then was almost knocked over when all four of them responded immediately! Double lines of incredible strength held him to them and them to him, lines Kambil knew they were all aware of. And then the unexpected happened, when Homin also reached out to Selendi. Her instant touch in return spread to include the other two men, who also instantly returned the touch. And through her, in some way, all three men linked up with each other! There was almost a burst of light, soundless and extremely brief, but enough to illuminate the fact that everyone was now linked to everyone else.

We've done it! Delin's "voice" came through the link, exultant with delight and pleasure. *We've Blended, even though they probably thought we couldn't! So what do we do next?*

I don't know, Kambil admitted, aware of the way his frustrated annoyance reached the others immediately. *No one really knows how this works, so it's impossible to say. Let's make sure our ties are strong enough to return the next time, and then let it go.*

Kambil shared the disappointment which came from the others, but prudence had dictated his decision. When you don't know what you're doing, it's just as likely that you'll harm yourself as it is that you'll accomplish something positive. They'd come much too far to take a chance like that, not when their dream was almost in their grasp. Kambil checked his attachments to the others, decided that they couldn't possibly be stronger, and so withdrew his touch and let the Blending dissolve.

"I've never experienced anything like that in my entire life," Delin said then, his expression almost giddy. "I was myself at all times, but I was also each of *you.*"

"And I felt all the other connections go through *me,*" Selendi said with a faint frown. "The ones to Kambil and Homin were strongest, which means you were right, Kambil. I'll visit Delin and Bron tonight, so that tomorrow *all* the connections will be strong."

"And then we'll begin to be a force to be reckoned with," Homin said, giving Selendi a quick, encouraging hug. "Tomorrow our . . . mentor should be pleasantly surprised."

"When this happens for the first time in front of him, I think you mean," Delin corrected gently. "We don't want them knowing we're ambitious enough to have practiced, so we make sure not to mention it. And we especially make sure that Rigos doesn't find out."

"I've fixed it so that Rigos is less of a problem," Kambil pointed out, having found a place to sit as soon as he released the power. "I'm too tired to go into details right now, but Rigos's spy won't be telling him anything we don't want him to know."

"That will just make Rigos a small bit less dangerous," Delin disagreed, walking toward the tea service. "We need to be entirely rid of him, or he'll certainly find a way to ruin our intentions. But don't any of you worry about that. I'll find a way to dispose of him, just wait and see if I don't.''

The others nodded as they began to drift after Delin to the tea service, already discussing their own views of the experience so recently past. Kambil sat in his chair, trying to gather enough strength to go to bed, staring at Delin's turned back without expression. He had no idea of the details which Delin had in mind, but where Rigos was concerned, Delin needed to be watched carefully. If he messed things up and was caught, the rest of them would pay right along with him.

Which thought finally gave Kambil the ability to get to his feet. The sooner he got the rest he needed, the sooner he could be back on guard. Nothing could be allowed to ruin their plans, absolutely nothing. . . .

TWENTY

Jovvi saw Tamma heading out of the library, so she followed while pretending to be about her own business. Luckily it turned out to be the garden Tamma headed for, and none of the servants saw either of them go. Jovvi checked carefully for observers as she stepped outside, and when there were none to be found she hurried past the bath house and around to the far side of it. By then Tamma had seen her, of course, and hurried to join her when Jovvi gestured that she was to follow.

"What's wrong?" Tamma asked once they both stood safe from observation with the bath house between them and the main house. "Has something happened?"

"Not the way you mean it," Jovvi reassured her, adding

a bit of a smile. "There's just something you and I need to discuss, without the men around."

"That sounds almost ominous," Tamma replied with brows high. "I hadn't realized there were things they couldn't know about."

"There aren't," Jovvi said, still trying to find the best way to explain. "It's just that . . . I feel this is something . . . you and I need to . . . discuss first. Let me start by asking a question: when we Blended, did you perceive all the men in the same way? Or did the contact with any of them seem stronger than the others?"

"Now that you mention it, the contact with Rion was stronger than the ones with Lorand and Vallant," she responded slowly, her brow creased in thought. "I noticed it at the time, and then managed to forget. How did you know?"

"I knew because I perceived Rion and Lorand more strongly than Vallant," Jovvi answered, sending a trickle of calm toward Tamma. "I wasn't completely certain until you confirmed my guess, but now I'm sure of it: being intimate with the men increases the strength of our bond with them. The situation is logically sensible, but it puts us into what might be considered a . . . an uncomfortable position."

"Why?" Tamma asked, her head cocked slightly to one side. "If you've already lain with Lorand and Rion, you just have to do the same with— Oh. And I— Oh."

Her second "oh" was slightly higher than the first, showing she now saw the whole problem. It would be less of one if Tamma and Vallant had already lain together at least once, but that wouldn't have made the situation go away. Jovvi herself had lain with Lorand once, and her disturbance was still very much there.

"This whole thing is very confusing," Tamma complained, using one hand to rub at her forehead. "My feelings about Vallant are still scattered every which way, but knowing that you need to lie with him is somehow . . . upsetting. Do you feel the same about me lying with Lorand? I hadn't thought you would, but now I'm not quite sure."

"To be honest, I hate the idea of you lying with Lorand," Jovvi admitted, struggling to keep her balance.

"Considering my career as a courtesan the objection is absurd, but that doesn't mean it isn't there. The fact that he and I are having difficulties must be causing it, but the reason for it doesn't matter. If our Blending is to be as strong as possible, you and he have to lie together. Right now my main purpose in bringing up the matter is to ask if you'd rather lie with Vallant before I do."

"Which may or may not make it easier for me to accept the necessity," Tamma said with a nod, her gaze on the way her fingers twisted together. "It's really strange, but touching the power isn't helping me now at all. Which probably means that being attacked is easier to cope with than making this decision."

She looked up then with a wry expression, and Jovvi found herself replying with the same sort of smile. What Tamma had said was absolutely true, about attack being easier to accept and cope with. Allestine's trying to kidnap her hadn't been half this upsetting. . . .

"But I'm suddenly getting an idea," Tamma said, alertness bringing her head up. "This could be a golden opportunity, and I almost didn't see it. If Vallant lies with you first and then with me, his *returning* to me can only mean a true desire for involvement on his part. I know how marvelous you'll be for him, so his coming back to *me* will speak more clearly than any words he may use."

"Now, that's something I hadn't thought about," Jovvi said, her own brows having risen. "It's an excellent point, and I wish I had something like it."

"Jovvi, you don't *need* anything like it," Tamma said gently and slowly, as though she were explaining something to a child. "Your ability should tell you exactly how Lorand feels—if you aren't afraid to use it with him. You're not, are you?"

Jovvi's silence must surely have answered the question, telling Tamma just what Jovvi couldn't. There had been so much bitterness in Lorand the night of the costume ball at the palace that Jovvi hadn't been able to approach his emotions again.

"I don't know how much good it's done, but I *have* been arguing with him for you," Tamma offered, her expression now full of compassion. "He thinks he isn't good enough for you, but I won't let him tell me that. It's only his disappointment with himself talking, and once he's over that he should be over the rest as well."

"If only I hadn't said what I did," Jovvi responded with a sigh, feeling fractionally better. "When we can't be sure any of us will survive, I was a fool to talk about a secure future. But we all have our needs and fears, and that happens to be mine. If I had yours instead, I probably wouldn't have put my foot in it quite so deep."

"You probably wouldn't have put your foot in at all, or any other part of you, either," Tamma said with a grin that was very unlike her usual self. "But if it makes you feel better, I'll trade my problem for yours any day."

"Easier said than done," Jovvi told her with a laugh, now feeling a *lot* better. "We've discussed the point before, but you can't just tell someone to have a different problem. It would take—"

"Jovvi, what's wrong?" Tamma asked, obviously concerned over the way Jovvi's words had broken off so abruptly. "You look . . . strange."

"I *feel* strange," Jovvi replied, the original understatement of the ages. "I think I need to sit down, but if I do my mind will probably whirl me up into the air. That very odd thing Allestine said at the trial—I think I now know what it means."

"What odd thing did Allestine say?" Tamma asked, looking as though she were ready to catch Jovvi when she fell. Which wasn't that far-fetched an idea. . . .

"Allestine was asked why she hadn't left Gan Garee and returned to Rincammon," Jovvi explained. "Apparently she and the men had packed their possessions and they'd even paid their bill at the inn, but they were still here when the guardsmen went to arrest them. Allestine's answer to the question was something like, 'Oh, it isn't possible to leave, it just isn't.' "

"Why wasn't it possible?" Tamma asked, frowning over the same confusion Jovvi had felt. "It almost sounds as if someone had forced her to stay."

"Someone did," Jovvi told her heavily. "I'd just about forgotten the fact, but when I spoke to Allestine in the coach I used just those words. 'Don't even think about leaving because it isn't possible,' I told her, hoping she would do the exact opposite—and not realizing that I was fully in touch with the power at the time. It looks like there's at least one side to my ability that no one ever bothered to mention.''

"It's so unimportant, I can't imagine why they would,'' Tamma muttered, almost as stunned as Jovvi had been. "You told Allestine that leaving was impossible, and in spite of everything she obeyed you. The whole concept is so bizarre that I can't even imagine what you would use the ability for. Aside from making people your slaves, that is.''

"That's one thing I *won't* be using it for,'' Jovvi told her firmly, more determined about that than almost anything else in her life. "I'd rather die than make innocent people into slaves, people who would be helpless to stop me. But that idea you had just now, the one we discussed once before: you said people have trouble coping only with their own problems, not the problems of others. Assuming I got permission from Lorand and Vallant, what do you think would happen if I told each of them that he had the other's problem?''

"One of three things, probably,'' Tamma replied, her brows still high. "Number one, nothing at all would happen. Number two, they'd each have a problem they could handle. Number three, they'd each end up with two problems instead of one. Do you know for certain that number three can't possibly happen?''

"I'm barely certain what time of day it is,'' Jovvi said, not joking in the least. "This is going to take a lot of thought, a lot of discussion, and maybe even some experimenting. After all that I *might* try it, assuming Lorand and Vallant are willing.''

"Why don't you ask Vallant when you lie with him, and I'll do the same with Lorand?'' Tamma suggested, now much more calm and composed than Jovvi. "Once we get used to Blending, it might turn out to be totally unnecessary, but they still ought to know. And one of us should tell Rion what's going on.''

"I'll try to tell him,'' Jovvi decided. "It's easier for me

to know if anyone else is around. Are you . . . going directly to Lorand?''

''As soon as I get my nerve up,'' Tamma said with a sigh. ''It's one thing to ask a man to lie with you when you're angry and also don't intend to do it right away. Walking up to him and telling him the time is now is another matter entirely. Are . . . *you* going directly to Vallant?''

''Only if there's no opportunity to speak to Rion first,'' Jovvi said, then shook her head with a faint smile. ''We're a pair, aren't we? We've each told those men we want nothing to do with them, but now that another woman is about to lie with the man we want nothing to do with. . . .''

''Right,'' Tamma said sourly. ''But it's a good thing the other woman is you. If it ever turned out to be that floozy Vallant used to be involved with . . . Well, all I'll say is that if he ever gets together with a woman other than me, you can bet every din you have that it won't be her. I'll see you later.''

Jovvi nodded and watched Tamma walk away, then checked for other watchers before making her own way back to the house. As involved and complicated as their previous days had been, Jovvi had the definite feeling that they hadn't really seen anything yet.

TWENTY-ONE

The garden had been wet from the rain earlier today, and the sky had looked like it was preparing to rain on us a second time. I thought about the sky and rain as I walked back through the house, but for some reason it didn't help to distract me. What I had to say to Lorand hung in my mind like a burning missive from the Highest Aspect, an unignorable command to rush headlong into desperate danger and unknowable jeopardy.

Which was just plain silly. I shook my skirt a little as I walked, trying to get rid of the beads of moisture I'd picked up outside, telling myself silently but firmly that I was being ridiculous. Lorand wasn't a stranger off the street, after all, and Rion had shown me how pleasant lying with a man can be. On top of that it was necessary for our Blending, to make us the best we could possibly be. So why was I beginning to move so slowly, reluctant to peek into the library because Lorand might well be in there?

One of the answers to my question was that I'd released all but the faintest touch on the power. My memories relating to men still weren't the nicest it was possible to have, and the last thing I wanted to do was accidentally hurt Lorand if one of those memories got the better of me. The fact that that brought me back to my usual cowardly self couldn't be helped, except for the way I'd begun doing it: turning stubborn and refusing to back down.

So I took a deep breath, set my teeth firmly into a good chunk of stubbornness, and went to open the library door. The relief I felt when the room proved empty made me ashamed, but that didn't stop me from enjoying the relief for a short while. But it was a very short while, because empty downstairs rooms meant Lorand was probably in his bedchamber. The thought of that made me blush, which in turn made me even more disgusted with myself. I was supposed to be an adult, after all, not some silly, mouselike child. . . .

The wonderfully mature adult that was me found it necessary to peek into the dining room before it became absolutely certain that she had to go upstairs. I'd caught a glimpse of Jovvi earlier, going directly upstairs, but when I reached the upper hall there was no sign of her. *She* wasn't afraid to do what was necessary, I pointed out to myself sternly. *She* didn't stand around hoping some catastrophe would happen so that she'd have to change her plans.

The admonishment made me feel properly ashamed— until I remembered who she was being so efficient with.

That very strange feeling flared in me again, the one I'd thought I'd gotten so well under control, the one I really couldn't understand. I'd definitely decided to try to discourage anything deep from developing between Vallant and me so that he'd be safe, but the idea of him being with another woman made me feel . . . fluttery-bothered. There didn't seem to be any other way to describe the combined physical and emotional reaction, but the words were so inadequate. . . .

I suddenly awoke to the fact that I'd knocked on Lorand's bedchamber door. Part of me must have preferred the distraction of painful embarrassment to thinking about what would happen if Vallant discovered that he preferred Jovvi after all. The idea should have pleased me, especially since it was Jovvi rather than some strange woman I neither knew nor liked. But it didn't please me, not in the least. I'd never really had Vallant as anything but someone to argue with, and it could very well turn out that I never would. . . .

"Tamrissa?" I heard Lorand's voice say. "Did you want something?"

"I . . . need to speak to you," I replied, pushing away my previous thoughts with every ounce of strength I possessed. I'd been so distracted, I hadn't even seen Lorand open the door. "Do you mind if I come in?"

"No, not at all," he said, opening the door wider, then he added softly, "Only the five of us are upstairs right now, so your timing is perfect. What did you want to talk about?"

"Jovvi made a rather important discovery that you need to hear the details of," I said after turning back to him, taking the coward's way out, at least for the moment. "Let's sit down and I'll give you the details."

He'd closed the door by then, so he nodded with a smile and returned to the chair that had a book near it on the adjacent table. I'd already taken the second chair, so as soon as he was settled I described Jovvi's discovery of her talent to "tell" people things. Lorand listened with an amazed expression, and then he shook his head.

"If I didn't know better, I'd wonder why we weren't taught about any of this," he said after letting out a long breath. "The nobles try to keep every bit of useful information to themselves, which holds the rest of us under their thumbs.''

"It's always possible the nobles don't know about it either," I pointed out. "Many of them seem to be as ignorant as we are, but at least the five of us are learning. And this new ability just may be the answer to another of our problems, but you and Vallant have to decide about that. You two are the ones most directly involved, but you have to remember that any experiment could make things worse rather than better.''

"What sort of experiment are you talking about?'' Lorand asked, now appearing a good deal more intense. "If it's Vallant and me who are involved, it has to concern— Tell me what you mean.''

"Jovvi and I once agreed that it's much easier to solve someone else's problem than your own," I explained slowly, trying to find the best way to put it. "What we meant was that Vallant could overcome a worry about burnout easily, and you would have no trouble controlling an intolerance for enclosed spaces. It's possible that Jovvi could . . . get you two to exchange problems, but it's also possible it might not work.''

"But if it doesn't work, we won't be any worse off than we are right now," Lorand said, his whole being brightening with the possibility. "And if it does work . . . I'm for trying it as soon as possible.''

"It isn't necessarily true that you won't be any worse off," I put in, holding up a hand to slow the tide of his enthusiasm. "There's always the chance that you might end up with two problems instead of just one, and find them both equally unmanageable. Don't forget that Allestine stayed here in Gan Garee, despite the very real possibility that she would be arrested. If she hadn't been under a compulsion she might have gone home at least for a little while, just until she knew whether or not Jovvi preferred charges. Staying here was insane—but she did it anyway.''

"There's got to be a way around that, so we'll just have to look for it," he said with a smile, all but dismissing every word of caution I'd spoken. "This is something that *has* to be tried, and the sooner the better. You can tell Jovvi that if Vallant wants to wait while I go first, I don't mind in the least."

"I'll tell her, and I'm sure she'll be glad to discuss the details with you," I said, making sure I promised nothing. "In the meanwhile, we want to see if Blending again won't solve the two problems without any additional effort. For all we know it will, and then no one will have to take a chance."

"I hadn't thought of that," Lorand said, now looking surprised. "And you're right, we do need to try that first. I just wish we didn't have so long to wait until we'll be able to do it. When you knocked I was in the midst of thinking about taking a nap, to make sure I don't yawn in everyone's face and mind tonight."

"I have a different suggestion," I said, getting the words out before I could lose my nerve. "Do you remember agreeing to lie with me? Well, I thought that now would be a good time, because. . . ."

"Tamrissa, please," he interrupted, suddenly looking very upset. "You can't mean you expect me to lie with you *now*?"

"If it's a bad time I can come back later," I said, half relieved and half disappointed. "I certainly wouldn't want to intrude if you have something else that needs doing. We *are* friends, after all, so—"

"No, listen to me," he interrupted again much more gently, leaving his chair to crouch in front of mine before taking my hand. "Your face and voice say you think I'm rejecting you, but that couldn't be farther from the truth. You're a very beautiful, very desirable woman and I feel honored that you would consider lying with me, but I agreed to your request before I had that talk with Vallant. Now that I have, everything's changed."

"What could possibly have changed?" I asked, completely at a loss. "And what does your conversation with Vallant have to do with me or us? You're really not making any sense, Lorand."

"I had the horrible feeling I wasn't," he muttered, almost looking desperate, and then he forced a smile. "Let me see if I can explain what I mean, and then if you have any questions I'll try to answer them. All right?"

I nodded because that was what he clearly wanted me to do, not because I knew what was happening. Or why Lorand had suddenly turned so strange. . . .

"Men seem to have a . . . different way of looking at things than women do," he began slowly and haltingly. "I suppose I've always known that, but being here with you and Jovvi has really brought the point home. The difference we're discussing now is the one about a man and a woman lying together when another man has . . . involved himself with caring deeply about the woman. If a man knows that another man feels that way, he'd be a cad and worse to lie with the woman anyway. Are you following me?"

This time I shook my head, not daring to say a word. Whatever was making Lorand so unintelligible might be catching, and keeping silent could be the only defense against it.

"Still not following me," he muttered, apparently fighting not to become even more upset. "All right, look, I'm just going to say it straight out, without giving you any detailed explanations. If you still don't understand, you'll simply have to take my word for it. Tamrissa, I would love to lie with you, but if I do it will cause Vallant a lot of pain. He's as crazy about you as I am about Jovvi, and your lying with me instead of him will hurt him very much. It may not make sense to you, but you have my word that it's the truth."

For an instant I *didn't* understand, but then I remembered how the idea of Jovvi lying with Vallant made me feel. It wasn't what I consider pain, but hurt was a fairly good description. The idea hurt me, in a way that had never happened before.

"I think it's beginning to make sense," I admitted after a moment, which brought an immediate look of relief to his face. "But I would advise you not to be so happy about it. This makes for another very large problem."

"Which is?" he asked, now eyeing me warily. "I have the feeling I'd be better off *not* knowing, but I still have to ask."

"Well, Jovvi and I discovered that intimacy with a man makes the Blending bond stronger," I said, glad that he was still holding my hand. "If we want to have the best

Blending possible, she and I have to lie with every one of you men. But if it's going to cause hurt and difficulty among us, I don't know *what* we'll do.''

"Are you two absolutely sure about that?" he asked, his look of relief gone again. When I nodded he said, "How right you are about it being a problem. I can see that Vallant, Rion, and I will have to talk, but I refuse to try to guess about how it will turn out. I'm not feeling any too broadminded myself right about now. . . ."

His attention drifted off at the same time his words did, and I made no effort to call him back. Very frankly, I was too busy thinking about Jovvi and Vallant. I was sure she'd had better luck than I, but what I wasn't sure about was how I felt about it. Even my sense of language was becoming tangled, confronted as it was by the picture of Jovvi and Vallant together. I wanted Jovvi to be successful, but I didn't want her to succeed. But she had to succeed . . . even though I didn't want her to. . . .

TWENTY-TWO

Jovvi saw Tamma dawdling around, but she went upstairs rather than stopping to encourage the girl. The horde of servants trying to watch them were out of sight, but not quite out of hearing range. Any casually exchanged words would be overheard, and if they weren't properly argumentative . . . Better to just let things be, and allow Tamma to work them out for herself.

Not to mention the fact that Jovvi didn't *want* Tamma to hurry in finding Lorand. Just because something is necessary doesn't mean it also has to be pleasant. Those words of wisdom made Jovvi sigh as she stopped in front of Vallant's door. If she and Lorand hadn't had that problem between them, she wouldn't have thought twice about the necessity. Sharing a man's body didn't necessarily also mean sharing his love, at least not the kind of love that had nothing to do with the physical sort. But the awful uncertainty caused by her own stupidity was now twisting everything out of normal shape and size. . . .

Jovvi quickly knocked on Vallant's door, before her rampaging thoughts took her to Lorand's door instead. He answered sooner than he might have, as he'd been on his feet rather than sitting or lying down.

"Well, this is a pleasant surprise," Vallant said with a smile when he saw her, then the smile disappeared as he stepped back to allow her entrance to the room. "Is somethin' wrong?"

"Not really," she replied with the best smile possible as she accepted his wordless invitation to enter. "There are some things we need to talk about, and there's a decision you'll have to make."

"A decision," he echoed, staring at her calmly as his mind raced. "That sounds almost portentous, so I'll need a cup of tea to fortify me while I listen. There's a second cup if you'd like some yourself."

"There's always a second cup when you ask for an individual tea service," Jovvi grumbled as she joined him in walking to the tray. "Is that a command not to drink alone, do you think, or a snide slap to tell us they know we never do? I've been wondering ever since I got to this house."

"It's probably for use in case your first cup gets too clogged with tea leaves," Vallant answered, doing an excellent job of hiding his surprise. "In any event, I'll wash your cup after you leave, since these days I *ought* to be drinkin' alone. Are you sure nothin' is wrong?"

"What I'm sure about is that the testing authority used the wrong thing to ruin my balance," Jovvi answered ruefully, his continuing calm helping her to find her lost control. "If they'd wanted to do a really effective job, they should have used the topic *I've* found. But that's beside the point. What isn't is Allestine's trial, which you were there for. Did anything about it strike you as really odd, more than the rest of it?"

"I'm glad you qualified that," he said, waiting until she had her tea poured and sweetened, and then following her to the chairs. "There wasn't anythin' about that trial that wasn't odd, so findin' one item in the bunch is almost impossible—at least for me. Which thing were *you* thinkin' about?"

"It was what Allestine said when she was asked why she hadn't left Gan Garee," Jovvi replied, sitting in the chair Vallant had gestured her to. "She said something like, 'It isn't possible to leave,' and I remember that her response bothered me at the time. Somehow the words sounded familiar, and a little while ago I realized why. I'm the one who told her that."

"*You* did?" His frown was clear as he settled himself in the chair, just as clear as the confusion in his mind. "Jovvi, are you sure? People are always sayin' somethin' like that, and not because someone else has said it first. This whole trial business has been hard on you, I know, but—"

"No, Vallant, really," Jovvi interrupted, tenderly amused with how genuinely concerned he was. "I'm not trying to find more things to blame myself for. What I'm trying to tell you is that when I was in the coach with Allestine and had opened fully to the power in order to control Ark and Bar, I told Allestine that leaving would not be possible. I was trying to frighten her into believing I meant to report the incident to the authorities, and never even stopped to consider how much power was then flowing through me."

"Power," Vallant said, now looking startled. "Of course. I also missed that, and probably everyone else did, too. You told her to do somethin' while you were filled with the power, and she couldn't even disobey to avoid bein' arrested. I've never heard of someone with Spirit magic doin' that, and it's fairly obvious you haven't either."

"Someone has to know about it, but clearly not someone who's in the habit of sharing information." Jovvi was annoyed at that, but brushed the emotion aside. "And if that wasn't revelation enough, Tamma and I have once or twice thrown an idea around that now seems possible rather than ridiculous. She and I agreed that solving and handling other people's problems is always easier than coping with your own. Do you agree with that?''

''Certainly,'' Vallant granted at once. ''Problems are always easier to handle when you're not emotionally involved. So where is *that* leadin' us?''

''To the possible solving of your and Lorand's problems,'' Jovvi said with a faint smile, very aware of the leap of hope inside the man. ''But first I need to have some idea about what caused your problem in the first place—if you know. Lorand told me about a girl at school burning out when he was very young, and the picture of her sitting mindless in the rain has always stayed with him. But what about you?''

''It . . . started after that swimmin' incident, I suppose,'' Vallant replied after a very long hesitation. ''I don't usually talk about it, and even try not to remember. I was about eight or nine, and decided that followin' my older brothers when they went explorin' in the underwater caves of our cove would be fun. I couldn't let them know about it, you understand, or they would have told Daddy and he would have ordered me to stay home.''

Jovvi nodded silently while Vallant gulped some tea, understanding only too well. Telling a bright, adventurous, outgoing child not to do something dangerous almost always brought about tragedy. Why people didn't simply teach the child to do that something properly, with supervision, was beyond Jovvi. Was it nothing more than stubbornness? A need to feel superior about something? Possibly a matter of laziness? Most street children learned not to take unnecessary chances, but that was because they had no families. Could there be circumstances where a family was more of a burden than a blessing?

''I remember how beautiful the day was,'' Vallant continued, drawing Jovvi out of her own thoughts. ''Hot almost to sweatin', but not in the water. That was just perfect, cool and refreshin' and all-around delightful. I'd grown up swimmin' in those waters, and felt more at home in them than in our back garden.

''Followin' my brothers was easy, and they never even knew I was there. I saw them swim up to the rock formation that held the caves, then dive under. The caves were a short way down, you see, and there were a lot of them. That meant I didn't have to pick the same cave my brothers did, especially since I'd brought my own lantern wrapped in waxed burlap. I wasn't too young to keep the water away from the lantern with my ability, but I wanted to make doubly sure. I did everythin' right—except for pickin' the wrong cave.''

''What made it wrong?'' Jovvi asked gently as he gulped tea again. ''Was it too deep?''

''Actually, it wasn't deep enough,'' he replied with a headshake, just short of looking haggard. ''It was also small, which didn't bother me at all to begin with. I lit my lantern and began to look around, noticin' the signs on the cave walls that it filled completely with water at regular times. It had enough air for me to breathe right then, so what was the sense in worryin' about later? And then there was a small earth tremor, nothin' that didn't happen from time to time—except this one shook loose a boulder from the rock above, and it settled to the ledge right in front of the entrance to the cave.''

''Oh, no,'' Jovvi gasped, suddenly feeling what he had, all those years ago. ''And you weren't able to move it?''

''Not with every ounce of strength in my body,'' he agreed heavily, his gaze apparently involved with studying that old, painful scene. ''I was only a boy, after all, and even usin' Water magic just made the boulder quiver some. I was trapped, with no way of tellin' anybody where I was. And then, after some time passed, the tide started comin' in. The cave began to fill slowly with water, on its way to makin' more marks on the walls and ceilin'. And there wasn't as much fresh air for breathin' as there'd been to start with. . . .''

''For goodness' sake, Vallant, tell me how you got out of there!'' Jovvi demanded, more disturbed than she'd expected to be. ''I can feel just how horrible it was, how confining and terrifying . . . Did your brothers know you'd followed them after all?''

''No, it turned out to be my younger brother who saved me,'' he replied with a wan smile. ''He knew what I was plannin' to do, but he didn't say a word until I didn't show up for dinner. That was when he told Daddy all about it, and Daddy and my older brothers came rushin' back to search for me. They brought underwater flares, which was lucky. My lantern had gone out, and there were so many caves they didn't know where to start lookin'. But I caught a glimpse of one of the flares, and used my ability to start a whirlpool in front of the cave I was trapped in. They got the boulder moved and I was finally able to get out.''

"And you've been paying for a child's mistake ever since," Jovvi summed up, fighting off a chill. "Being trapped like that . . . I'll have to think about it for a while, but I believe I'm getting an idea to add to the one Tamma and I discussed. That one concerned helping you and Lorand to trade problems, since each of you should be able to cope with the other's. I still think we ought to do that, even if my idea on how to solve your problem completely actually works."

"How to solve—! Jovvi, do you really think you can?" Vallant's surge of hope had returned, much stronger than it had been earlier. "Gettin' rid of it would mean bein' free again! But I don't understand why you would want Lorand and me to switch problems if our original ones were cured. What would be the point?"

"The testing authority is the point," Jovvi reminded him. "Even if I do manage to help you two to cure yourselves—which is by no means certain—we can probably count on the testing authority to try to ruin our Blending. One way would be to strike at you and Lorand through your vulnerabilities, which could end up wrecking whatever you two accomplish in the way of a cure. But if we put a different problem in front of your eyes, it might work as a shield against whatever those people try. Are you following me?"

"Not even from a distance," he answered with a small, honest laugh. "And I was just rememberin' somethin' Lorand once said, about his bein' afraid you girls were smarter than us. It's a good thing he was only jokin' about bein' afraid, because I'm beginnin' to think you *are* smarter than us. How about givin' a poor, dumb man an explanation usin' the kind of small and easy words he can understand?"

"You, my poor, dumb man, will have to wait for your explanation until I get the thing figured out so that my superior self can understand it first.'' Jovvi chuckled as she said that, knowing that Vallant had been gently teasing her. Self-confidence was no part of his problem, and the only thing he felt threatened by was small, tight spaces. ''In the meanwhile, we can put off that decision I told you earlier that you would have to make. In its place I'll need a different decision from you—assuming you're amenable to the suggestion.''

''Have I ever mentioned that I like mysteries only up to a certain point?'' he replied, confusion raising his brows again. ''Nothin' you just said made the least sense, and this time I *know* it isn't me.''

''I must be spending too much time with Tamma,'' Jovvi muttered, realizing he was absolutely right. ''That habit of hers of talking all around a subject must be catching . . . What I meant to say was, I'd like to know if you'd be willing to lie with me. If so, we can see to it right now— unless there's something more important that you need to do?''

Jovvi automatically added her best smile, the one no man had ever been able to resist. Vallant's inner reactions matched the ones those other men had experienced, which made his immediate headshake completely incongruous.

''It pains me to say it, love, but I won't be doin' that,'' he told her, the decision firm and unshakable. ''You've come to mean a lot to me, but I won't take the chance of hurtin' Tamrissa again and maybe drivin' her away permanently. Besides, I know how Lorand feels about you, and that no matter what he said. If he found out that you and I were lyin' together, he'd be hurt for sure.''

''Then that means we now have another problem,'' Jovvi said, partially delighted that Vallant's decision was based on what Tamma might think. ''I knew from the first that you were a gentleman, but personal preferences really don't enter into it. Tamma and I have discussed it, and she and I agree that being intimate with you men makes for a stronger bond in the Blending. While I'm here talking to you, she's gone to say the same to Lorand.''

''Gone to ask him to lie with her?'' Vallant demanded, immediately getting to his feet at the urging of a monstrous jolt of jealousy. Then calm seemed to descend again, and he sat himself back in the chair. "No, there's no need to go rushin' over there. I know Lorand, and I haven't the least doubt that he's refusin' Tamrissa the same way I'm refusin' you. Rion may not have enough life experience to understand somethin' like this, but Lorand does."

"I wish I understood it," Jovvi said, staring at him. "Doesn't it make a difference that the . . . *sacrifice* would be for our Blending? And isn't it the woman who's supposed to be shy and reluctant?"

"Nobody said anythin' about shyness and reluctance," Vallant returned, clearly amused by her annoyance. "It has to do with a gentleman's honor, which usually involves men. You may not understand it, but I'm afraid you'll have to accept it."

"I'm not in the habit of accepting silliness," Jovvi said, suddenly rising to her feet. "If Lorand is indulging in the same thing the way you claim he is, Tamma and I need to give you both a good talking to. Right now, so I'll appreciate it if you come along."

And with that Jovvi marched toward the door, set on getting that nonsense straightened out. Her attitudes had just changed radically, but that was something she could worry about later. As she opened the door, she realized she was supposed to have spoken to Rion first, only she'd forgotten. Ah, well, he'd probably hear the small war she was about to start, and would certainly come running. . . .

TWENTY-THREE

Delin sat his horse in the darkness, his inner senses stretched in all directions, his outer senses concentrating on the house that was visible through the trees. Lamplight spilled out into the night from two of the first-floor windows, and even as Delin watched, one of them went dark. That meant his wait would soon be over, but for once he was in no hurry. His thoughts were still too pleasant for him to want to abandon them.

A smile creased his face again, the same smile that had been visiting him since he and the others had managed to Blend. Only hours earlier he had almost been ready to give up all hope, having failed to realize just how effective his leadership really was. He hadn't known that his people would try their utmost for him, but they had. They knew how much success meant to him, and had gone ahead and made it happen.

Delin's horse shifted restlessly, and he patted it to let it know that it would indeed be allowed to return to its stall and its sleep in just a short while. Most of those back at the residence had been either ready for bed or already asleep when Delin had left, especially Kambil. The Spirit magic user had really produced results, making Delin wonder if he hadn't misjudged Kambil. He still disliked the man to a certain extent, but dislike can be overlooked in the presence of gratifying results.

Even if the basic reason for the results is frightening beyond ordinary comprehension. Delin felt the clutch of terror again, just as he had when he and the others had come face to face with the truth: they were all doomed if they didn't win the competitions. They would not be separated, or even exiled to various remote parts of the empire. At best they would be killed out of hand, at worst they would have their memories destroyed, their *selves* wiped out before they were put to lifelong menial labor.

It continued to be hard for Delin to believe that *he* could be treated so, but that didn't mean he *dis*believed. It was absolutely typical of the way the powerless and socially unacceptable were treated, which two categories he and the others certainly fell into. It was their fathers who were too well situated to be brushed aside, but their fathers had stepped out of the way so that the Advisors might do as they pleased. Another thing that was hardly unexpected, but a shock nonetheless.

But shock tends to fade and behind it rage flows in, hot and burning and demanding the soothing of revenge. It was almost laughable that they'd all underestimated him so badly, actually thinking he would stand still and let himself be erased. That wasn't going to happen, and when he took the Fivefold Throne they would all learn the truth the hard and painful way. The Advisors were talentless nothings who manipulated the empire through their various weak-willed Blendings, a situation that was about to come to an abrupt halt.

Delin was caught up in his thoughts, but not so deeply that he failed to see the lamp which had appeared at the recently darkened window. The lamp was moved back and forth three times before it receded again to restore the darkness, the signal Delin had been waiting for. He patted his horse again before dismounting, tied his reins to a tree, then headed for the house on foot.

By the time he reached it, the back door was no longer locked for the night. Relana waited just inside with the lamp, and once Delin had closed the door softly behind him, she smiled and led the way back to her private sitting room. That door, too, had to be closed quietly, and only then was Delin able to take Relana in his arms and give her a proper kiss hello. It would never do if they were discovered by her husband, which might have happened if they'd dallied in the hall.

"He's already snoring," Relana said after the kiss ended, apparently having shared his thoughts about her husband. "Would you like to make love to me again in the room right next to his?"

"All in good time, my lovely," Delin replied with a soft laugh. "I've never failed you yet, I think, nor do I plan to. But before we get to the main reason for my visit, I believe you have things to tell me?"

"Oh, my dear, I certainly do," she agreed enthusiastically, taking his hand to lead him to a couch where they both might sit. Relana enjoyed passing along gossip at least as much as she enjoyed lying with younger men, possibly even more.

"You really should have been there," Relana continued after they were seated, her right hand casually touching his left thigh. "Kilia's guest list usually includes just everyone, of course, but no one expected Ollon to show up last night—or that Rigos boy. Rigos has always adored Kilia's parties, though, and after being forced to miss one or two of them, he seemed almost desperate. I was there early and saw him arrive.''

Delin nodded his encouragement as his left hand slid to the opening in the top of her wrap. He'd run into Relana the night before when he'd gone out to dinner, and she'd mentioned intending to go to Kilia's latest late-night party. He'd bemoaned the fact that he was unable to attend, and she'd promised to tell him about everything that had happened when she saw him tonight. It wasn't the first time he'd asked that, so she suspected nothing—including the fact that it was Delin's hasty and anonymous note to Ollon which had brought him to the party.

"My dear, you would never believe how strange those two have grown since Elfini's death," Relana continued, her smile appearing as she pretended to feel nothing of his hand on her breast. "To see Ollon, one would think Elfini had been the love of his life rather than simply his sister. And Rigos tells just everyone how thoroughly he was cleared of guilt in the murder, as though anyone would risk angering his father by speaking up in disbelief.''

"Are you saying there was *unspoken* disbelief?" Delin interrupted to ask, the words deliberately casual. The point was an important one, but it would never do for him to show it.

"Well, of course there was unspoken disbelief," Relana answered with a laugh as she squirmed a bit under his hand. "You must realize, my dear, just how powerful and wealthy Rigos's dear father is. It's possible to do anything with enough gold and influence, including having your son cleared of a murder charge. Everyone knows that, so I'm surprised that you don't.''

Delin tried to look contrite as he nodded again, privately delighted that Relana had—typically!—forgotten where she'd first heard that. By now everyone she knew had been told the same, but not by Delin or anyone in his group.

"Well, as I said, we were all surprised when Ollon appeared," she went on. "We thought he had finally come to his senses and was prepared to enjoy the party, but he ignored everyone and marched straight over to Rigos. And he looked absolutely awful, wearing rumpled clothing and needing a shave, just like a commoner. He's also lost weight and doesn't seem to have slept much, and the alcohol on his breath is enough to make one ill."

"How did Rigos look?" Delin put in casually. "Especially after Lord Ollon appeared in front of him?"

"Well, the boy actually looked a bit drawn," Relana decided after a moment, turning some so that Delin's right hand might slide into her wrap above her thighs. "He strolled in as usual when he arrived, but something that was part of the usual seemed to be missing. When Ollon appeared in front of him, he blanched and actually looked close to fainting. By then there wasn't a sound in the entire room, so everyone was able to hear every word of their exchange.

" 'Are you enjoying the party?' Ollon asked him in a very flat, emotionless voice. 'Elfini loved to attend parties, and probably would have been here tonight— Except that she can't be here because she's dead.'

" 'Not by my hand,' Rigos protested faintly, still as pale as milk. 'I give you my word that I had nothing to do with her death. I've been cleared of the charge, cleared twice! Why won't you believe me?'

" 'It's not me who disbelieves,' Ollon returned, still speaking emotionlessly. 'Elfini keeps coming to me in my dreams, demanding to know why her murderer hasn't been punished yet. She's the one who doubts your highly valued word, since your father's wealth and power don't impress the dead. You murdered her, but everyone is letting you get away with it.'

"That was when Rigos began to cry, sounding like a heartbroken child. He sank down to the floor and just sat there crying, and after a moment some of the men took Ollon aside, while others got Rigos up on his feet and out of the room. Rigos kept saying, 'I didn't, I didn't' in the most pitiful way, as though he knew no one believed him but still felt it necessary to make the denial. Once he was gone Ollon simply left, not even nodding to his own wife where she stood with her friends. She was terribly embarrassed, of course, and had to work very hard to keep the scene from ruining her evening."

"My goodness, I am sorry I missed it," Delin murmured, shifting a bit so that her meager but nicely wielded Air magic might stroke his privates in the proper way. "It must have completely made Lady Kilia's party. After all that, surely nothing else of any interest happened?"

"Only Ildemar's usual performance once he drank too much," Relana murmured in answer, leaning a bit closer to Delin. "He began to cry just as Rigos had, mourning the fact that the poor boy might be innocent after all, but no one would ever believe him. Leave it to Ildemar to weep over the plight of a murderer. . . . Have I ever told you how aroused I become when you listen to me rather than order me to silence?"

"Any man who refuses to listen to your lovely voice is a fool," Delin assured her, exultation adding to his own arousal. He would have given almost anything if he could have seen Rigos groveling on the ground, begging for a belief that would never be granted him. Delin's anonymous note to Lord Ollon had pointed out how easily a guilty man might be exonerated, and the accusation had sent Ollon to confront his sister's murderer.

But that wasn't quite enough. It made a marvelous basis for what had to happen next, but in and of itself it was largely innocuous. Rigos was beaten down but not totally crushed, and that's what he had to be: totally crushed. Delin's father had pointed Rigos out too often as the better man for Delin to be satisfied with anything less. As though having secured an appointment really made Rigos the better man. Delin would show them, he'd show them all. . . .

"Oh, my dear!" Relana moaned, and Delin returned to an awareness of her to discover that his fingers had clamped tight to her nipple. His right hand also pinched her tender womanflesh, and surprisingly, her response was faster and stronger than usual. Relana, it seemed, enjoyed being given pain, a key to her inner being which had eluded him until now. She'd enjoyed lying with him, but tended to enjoy each of her lovers right up until the time she told them not to bother coming back.

"I think you've been something of a naughty girl," Delin murmured, doing nothing to ease his grip on her. "For that reason we're going to have to punish you, to teach you not to be so much of a tramp. And you *are* a tramp, aren't you?''

"Ohhh, yes," she moaned, her eyes now closed as her body shuddered faintly with delight. "And I do need to be punished, so that I'll learn to be a good girl."

"That decision is mine, not yours," Delin told her softly but coldly, overriding the urge to tighten his grip. "You will be punished in the manner *I* choose, with what level of severity *I* decide on. Go now and fetch a leather strap, as well as a cloth to stuff in your mouth. It would be a pity if we were interrupted because you made too much noise."

She nodded jerkily but without hesitation, and all but jumped to her feet when he released her. She rushed over to a beautifully made cabinet, opened it and rummaged inside, then stumbled back to the couch with a length of cloth in one hand and a broad razor strop in the other.

"No, don't sit down again," Delin ordered easily. "Give me the strop, put the cloth in your mouth, and then remove that wrap."

She wasted no time doing as he'd said, not even when it came to removing her wrap. She'd never let him see her naked body before, and it was no wonder. Her figure was still quite good under clothing, but once bared it was obvious that she'd borne children and was no longer a young woman. She whimpered as he examined every inch of her body with his gaze, turned to let him see the back of her when he gestured for her to do so, then tried to gasp when he grabbed her without warning and pulled her across his lap.

"You'll find this lesson rather painful, but it's for your own good," Delin said as he put one hand in the middle of her back and raised the strop in the other. "When the punishment is done you will serve me with your body, and I expect to hear nothing about how tender you are. If I do, you'll become even more tender. Do you understand me?"

She nodded spasmodically, then jumped at the first stroke of the strop. The heavy leather left a beautiful band of red behind it, and after another four strokes the red band had covered her entire bottom. That was when she really began to squirm and tried to protect herself with her right hand, but Delin captured the hand in his own left and continued with the punishment. In point of truth it should have been her back that he strapped, giving her what all women deserved, but first he needed to establish his dominance over her. Once he had he would find it possible to do anything he pleased to her, just as he did with the sluts in the pleasure parlors.

The woman writhed and whimpered and squirmed every time the strop cracked across her blazing red bottom, a clear signal of just how deeply in need she was. If he entered her now she would explode like a volcano, Delin knew, but that wasn't going to be happening yet. He had something else to do once he left Relana, but that appointment was hours away. He would stay here and amuse himself with this slut until it was time to leave, a stroke of luck he hadn't been counting on. Relana usually eased him out the door once he had satisfied her. . . .

Delin chuckled to himself as he applied yet another "stroke of luck," enjoying himself quite a bit. But not as much as he would enjoy himself later, after he left the woman. Yes, that was what he really looked forward to, the ultimate delight which would settle his problems with Rigos permanently. . . .

Twenty-four

Delin's horse tried to turn in the direction of the residence when he mounted, and Delin was almost sorry that he had to disappoint the beast. He told the horse softly that his next stop would be a much shorter one, and then they would go straight home. He himself needed to be up early in the morning, so the additional stop couldn't be anything *but* short.

Which was a real shame, Delin thought with regret as he moved through the stillness of the night. It would have been pleasant to take as much time as he had with Relana, but morning was only a few hours away. He had to be asleep in his bed at the residence before then, and yet he also needed to do a good, thorough job. Pleasure was the only thing available to be sacrificed, at least extended pleasure was. Just seeing to the chore would be pleasant in itself, that and a consideration of the results which would obtain.

The stillness all around worked to remind Delin not to whistle, and the height of his good mood needed that reminder. Relana was well on the way to being entirely under his control, his worst enemy would soon be in a position from which no one would be able to save him, and his group had already managed to Blend. Life had changed from a living nightmare to a living dream, and he didn't even mind having had to be careful not to cause Relana any lasting damage. There had to be a way to keep things working well, and if so, he meant to find it.

It was a fairly long ride to his destination, but once again his previous preparation stood him in good stead. He'd made it his business to learn where every powerful man in the government lived, and Ollon Capmar was certainly no exception. With Lord Ollon as deeply involved in the competitions as he was, his house was one of the first Delin had learned about. The man was more involved with the peasants than with anyone of decent social standing, but oddly enough that seemed to increase his importance rather than lessen it.

Or had increased his importance until now. Delin smiled as he thought about the only thing that would increase Lord Ollon's importance after today: the fact that he would be Rigos's second victim, directly after his unfortunate sister. The scene Relana had described in such glorious detail was even better than what Delin had hoped for when he'd sent that anonymous note to Lord Ollon about the party. Rigos now had every reason in the world to kill Lord Ollon, and with Delin's help he would do just that.

Lord Ollon's house looked as dark as any other from a distance, but once Delin had reached it he was able to see lamplight coming from one of the side windows. It was actually a terrace door which spilled faint light out into the inky darkness, with what looked to be a private garden surrounding it on the outside. Deep shadow suggested a hedge separating it from the area at the front of the house, and Delin realized that it could well be Lord Ollon's study.

Moving silently to the terrace door gave Delin the opportunity to review his plan. He could see it all now, just exactly as it would be. He would step up to the door, look inside to be certain that Lord Ollon was alone, and then he would open the door and enter.

"Who are you?" Lord Ollon would demand as he looked around from his chair, his eyes smudged darkly from lack of sleep and heavy drinking. "What do you mean by simply walking into my house?"

"I've come to help you with your search, Lord Ollon," Delin would say with a smile as he closed the door behind him. "You've been looking for your sister's murderer, and you believe you've found him in Rigos. I'm here to tell you that Rigos is entirely innocent."

"Be damned if he is," Lord Ollon would mutter, refusing to turn loose what he considered his prey. "And how would *you* know anyway? No one could know that for certain unless—"

"Exactly," Delin would beam as Lord Ollon guessed the truth. "No one would know that for certain unless he were the *real* murderer. Which I am."

Lord Ollon's obsession would then send him into a rage, and he would rise and throw himself at Delin in attack. But Delin would be expecting that, of course, and would paralyze the man in midmotion. Then he would stroll behind the helplessly raging fool, slip the knotted cord he'd brought along around the man's neck, and strangle him to death. Just at the end he would release the man from paralysis so that he might be properly positioned near his desk. With Rigos as small as he was, it would have to seem that he had caught Lord Ollon unawares from behind. Then he would remove all traces of himself from the room and substitute traces of Rigos, and the thing would be done.

Delin blinked back to awareness to realize that he'd reached the terrace doors, and now simply stood staring.

He really had to do something about these episodes he kept going through, these times of blacking out without realizing it. Once he and the others had won the Throne, he'd have to find a physician strong enough to do him some good. But for now, an important chore was waiting.

Stepping closer to the door let him peer inside, and immediate disappointment stabbed at him. Lord Ollon wasn't seated at his desk, although the lamp on the desk was lit. Had the man gone to bed after having forgotten to turn down the lamp, or had he simply gone to relieve a call of nature? It made a big difference in what Delin himself would do, so he had to—

All thoughts and plans ended abruptly when Delin noticed what he really should have seen immediately: the dark, unmoving, lumpish pile of something on the floor beside the desk. An instant's staring told Delin exactly what it was: Lord Ollon's body, precisely where *he* had meant to leave it. That little daydream he'd just had—could that have been reality instead, distorted by another episode?

Extreme disgust filled Delin as he realized that that was precisely what it must be. He hadn't daydreamed the exchange with Lord Ollon; it had really happened. His initial confusion lay in believing he hadn't yet done the deed, but obviously he had. He was even able to see the ends of the knotted cord now, dangling down the back of the corpse. And corpse it was, something he could tell even from where he stood.

"Which means I won't go back in and ruin my previous work," Delin muttered, a decision he would be firm on despite his really wanting to get closer to his handiwork. Better to leave now, and practice looking surprised when someone eventually told him about the murder. And about Rigos's arrest, of course. This time even Rigos's father would be helpless to do anything to save his son.

But as Delin made his way back to his horse, he became even more determined to do something about his problem. After all, how many people did one have to murder before one was allowed the pleasure of actually experiencing the act . . . ?

TWENTY-FIVE

Rion answered the knock at his door to find Jovvi and Vallant standing there. His surprise must have been rather evident, as Jovvi smiled just a bit as she shook her head.

"No, we haven't moved up the time we'll be Blending," she told him softly. "We seem to have a different problem, and although it doesn't involve you directly, you really should be there while we discuss it. As one of us, you—"

"Why doesn't the problem involve him directly?" Vallant interrupted to ask, looking at Jovvi with the same puzzlement Rion himself felt. "The same thing would go for him, wouldn't it?"

"What same thing?" Rion asked, trying to make sense of the scene. "And what problem are we discussing?"

"Please!" Jovvi temporized, holding up both hands. "This isn't the place to discuss the matter. Let's just go to Lorand's bedchamber, and then all your questions can be answered."

Although Rion's curiosity was beginning to grow somewhat intense, he agreed that that wasn't the place to discuss anything at all. One or more of the servants could appear at any moment, which did make it wisest for them to retire to Lorand's bedchamber. Rion therefore stepped out of his own and closed the door, then followed the others to Lorand's door.

A single knock brought Lorand, who added his own surprised expression as the three of them entered. Tamrissa was already there, and although she seemed momentarily

176

startled to see them all, another, more difficult to define expression dominated her visible emotions.

"I think we've both run up against the same brick wall," Jovvi said to Tamrissa, who raised her brows before nodding. "Yes, I can see that Vallant was right, so we all need to talk."

"May I ask *now* what we're to talk about?" Rion put in, trying not to allow annoyance to take him over. "I was unaware of any problem involving a brick wall, and would like to know why I, among the rest of you, am uninvolved."

"You're uninvolved because you seem to be more reasonable than Lorand and Vallant," Jovvi said dryly after exchanging a glance with Tamrissa. "Tamma and I have discovered that during Blending, we have a stronger bond with any man we've lain with. Because of that we decided we needed to lie with *all* you men, but Lorand and Vallant have been . . . reluctant to cooperate. It seems there's some sort of code of honor involved. . . ."

Lorand and Vallant both began to speak at once then, a combination of protest over unfair accusation and a defense of a perfectly reasonable stance. Rion, however, had the sudden impression that he might have made a large social faux pas, and not having realized it at the time was possibly not enough of an excuse. For that reason he quietly went to a chair and sat, leaving the others to sort the matter out among themselves.

"But this whole thing is ridiculous," Tamrissa protested after the men had run down a bit. "How can anyone feel hurt because of a necessity? Even if you don't happen to like the need, that doesn't stop it from *being* necessary."

"And it really isn't a personal matter," Jovvi added, clearly working to sound calm and reasonable. "Being intimate with someone isn't a betrayal of someone else, not when the someone else is aware of what's happening and is cooperating with a like necessity. You do see that, don't you?"

"I'm not seein' much of anythin' beyond the picture of another man lyin' with the woman who means so much to me," Vallant put in, his expression disturbed. "Not to mention me doin' the same with a woman who means that much to another man. It just isn't *right* to do that to a friend, and Lorand is a good deal more than a friend.''

"As Vallant is to me," Lorand agreed with a nod while the ladies seemed to be fighting expressions of exasperation. "I can't imagine ever betraying him like that, even if betrayal isn't the proper word under the circumstances. I— wait a minute. Why are we just talking about Vallant and me? Shouldn't we be including Rion?''

"That's a good question," Vallant agreed, his expression showing his own startlement. "As soon as Lorand said it, I wondered again why Rion was told that this doesn't concern him. I can't see how it *doesn't* concern him."

The questions were mostly being put to Jovvi, who had exchanged another glance with Tamrissa before beginning to show an extremely neutral expression. Tamrissa immediately adopted the same expression, which left Rion as the last to decide on his appearance. This turned out to be rather difficult for Rion, as he had no true idea about how he *should* feel. Had he betrayed Lorand and Vallant? If so, he would not be terribly pleased with himself. Jovvi began to speak, but Lorand interrupted before she produced the first word.

"And now that *I* think about it, there's another question that hasn't been asked," Lorand said, dividing his stare between Jovvi and Tamrissa. "How did you two discover this . . . closer bond between you and men you had lain with? As far as I know, the only ones in this group who have lain together are Jovvi and myself."

By then Vallant had added his own stare, which was also directed at the women. Tamrissa now looked more uncomfortable and faintly distressed rather than expressionless, and she studied her hands where they twisted together a bit at her waist. Jovvi's calm seemed to have thinned somewhat, and for the most part her gaze avoided Lorand's. Rion would have enjoyed staying out of the situation, but doing that at Tamrissa and Jovvi's expense was simply beyond him.

"I'm . . . afraid I'm to blame," Rion said, breaking that very awkward silence. "I really had no idea anyone would object, so I—"

"No, it wasn't your fault," Jovvi interrupted at once, speaking to Rion first and then giving Lorand a defiant look. "The whole thing was *my* idea, which was completely within my rights. No one else had any interest in me, so—"

"And it was also *my* idea," Tamrissa rushed to add, the blush on her cheeks weakening the firmness of her tone. "I asked Rion a favor, and he was good enough to—"

"You actually went so far as to take advantage of Rion?" Lorand demanded of Jovvi in apparent outrage. "A man with such a small amount of life experience is worse than a fish in a barrel, but you speared him anyway. I never thought I'd say this, Jovvi, but I'm really disappointed in you."

"You leave her alone!" Tamrissa said, clearly trying for a snap in her voice, but achieving a trembling instead as she put an arm about Jovvi's shoulders. "She isn't the only one who did it, and she wasn't even first. And not only isn't Rion as innocent as you seem to think, he also doesn't have all these . . . ridiculous objections that you two do. He makes a woman feel *appreciated*, not unreasonably intrusive."

Jovvi hadn't seemed prepared to defend herself, and Tamrissa's defense came as something of a surprise. Lorand and Vallant exchanged a glance before each of them looked briefly toward Rion, and once again Rion had no idea how to respond. It had been shocking enough that the ladies had been blamed for the incidents rather than himself; now, with comparisons being made. . . .

"Are you sayin' you'd . . . rather lie with Rion than with me?" Vallant asked Tamrissa, sounding more vulnerable and hurt than he had the other night in the coach. "If that's what your choice is then I can't argue it, but—"

"Oh, for goodness' sake!" Tamrissa interrupted, actually sounding annoyed as she looked at Vallant. "Don't you understand that I was saving you for last because—"

Her words ended abruptly as color flooded her cheeks, but Vallant began to glow as if strong sunlight shone on him.

"Because after lyin' with me you don't expect to want any other man?" he suggested, moving closer to her. "That's just what *I* had in mind, and I mean to work real hard gettin' it done. I don't want to own you, Tammakins. I mean to make you want to own *me*."

Tamrissa blushed again as she looked up at Vallant, his

grin obviously adding to her discomfort. But Rion noticed that she didn't look away again, nor did she seem to want to.

"This meeting has turned out to be more involved than when we Blended," Lorand said with a sigh, his gaze on Jovvi. "I didn't really mean it when I said I was disappointed, love. Or maybe I meant I was disappointed in myself. I shouldn't have made you feel that no one wanted you, because the truth is that I want you more than anything in the world. If only I were good enough for you. . . ."

"Don't say that!" Jovvi interrupted sharply, a plea rather than a command. She had left Tamrissa's side and now stood in front of Lorand. "Your thinking that is *my* fault, and I just can't bear it. I never dreamed that a man could be as wonderful as you, and if you speak about yourself that way again, I'll . . . I'll . . ."

The threat trailed off unspoken, and they stood there gazing at one another. Just as Tamrissa and Vallant stood doing the same. Rion sighed very softly, then rose and silently left the room. He was truly delighted that his groupmates seemed to have worked out their difficulties, but being among them was a bit on the painful side. If only Naran were there. . . .

Rion headed downstairs rather than return to his empty bedchamber, in no mood for being alone but somehow also in no mood for company. But he made sure to move slowly and idly, as he knew that a servant now seemed to be on the way to the stairs. The human body displaced a certain amount of air, and he'd discovered that he could use his awareness of that to judge if anyone was near or approaching. The four people upstairs needed no distractions, but he could certainly use one.

And sure enough, the servant had crossed half the hall by the time he reached the bottom of the stairs. It happened to be the servant who had sought him out the night Naran had come by to tell him where she would be, and when the man saw him he changed his direction from the stairs to Rion himself.

"Ah, Lord Rion, how fortunate," the man said with a smile. "I was just coming to look for you. That young lady from the other night is at the door again."

Rion could barely believe his ears, but he lost no time in doubting the marvelous coincidence. He immediately followed the servant to the side door used primarily by servants and tradespeople, tipped the man, then opened the door to see the most beautiful face in the universe.

"Oh, my lord, how quickly you came," Naran said breathlessly, seeming a bit startled at his sudden appearance. "I would not have disturbed you here again, but I feared that you would search for me at the same house and I'm no longer there. I haven't as yet found anything permanent, but as soon as I do I'll be certain to let you know where I am."

"I live for the moment," Rion said as he reached out and drew her into his arms. "I worried so about you since the other night—I returned to the house shortly after I left it, and found you gone."

"Oh, if I'd known you would return, I would have stayed despite the warning," she said, looking up at him in just the way that Tamrissa and Jovvi had looked up at Vallant and Lorand. "As soon as you were gone, a friend came to say that I might have been found. Men searched the neighborhood, and they could well have been *his* men."

"They were in the pay of my mother's agent," Rion said, feeling the frown he now wore. "I'd believed I'd avoided them, but it turned out I hadn't. But who is this person who might be searching for you? You've said nothing about another man."

"He isn't a man, he's a beast," Naran replied with a small shudder, fear showing briefly in her gaze. "I . . . had business with him some time ago, and he was very abusive. After that I refused to see him again, a decision he refused to accept. He's a very powerful man, but fortunately for me he can't come after me openly. He's forced to have his agents skulk about, which has allowed me to stay one or two steps ahead of him."

"Running like a common criminal," Rion said, fighting to keep the fury suddenly filling him from exploding in all directions. "Well, that's all over with now. You're to gather your things together and return here during the small hours of the morning. There's certainly enough room in this house for you, and my friends will help to hide your pres-

ence. And if that . . . beast discovers where you are, he'll
have me to deal with.''

"But my lord, how can I impose that way?'' she ob-
jected, upset clear in her lovely eyes. "Your friends might
not be willing to shelter a stranger, and that man is really
very rich and powerful. To put you in his path would be
to put you in terrible danger.''

"The danger will be his to fear, not mine,'' Rion said
so flatly that she gave another delicate shudder. "Perhaps
the matter has failed to take your attention, dear lady, but
you are no longer alone in the world. Will you return here
tonight?''

She struggled for a moment with indecision, her hands
flat to his chest while he held her close, and then, reluctantly, she nodded.

"I loathe the idea of putting my troubles on your shoulders, but I truly have no other choice,'' she admitted. "He's
managed to find me everywhere else I went, and I've now
run out of refuges. But when I return, I shan't come to the
door. If your friends dislike the idea of my being here, you
need only fail to come out and find my carriage. I swear
I'll understand, and will let you know where I've gone once
I find another place.''

"There will be no need of that,'' Rion assured her. "I
will come out at the stroke of three, and fully expect to
find you waiting. If you are not, I fear there will be words
between us.''

"I can't allow there to be words between us, so it seems
I must be here,'' she said with the smile which always
melted his essence. "I love you very much, my beloved
lord.''

"And I you, my precious lady,'' Rion murmured before
sharing a kiss with her. When the kiss had ended she
slipped from his arms and disappeared, and rather than follow, Rion slowly closed the door. He'd caused his mother's
watchers to fear him, but actually giving them something
to report might be too much of a temptation. Besides, he
needed to discuss the matter with the others as quickly as
possible.

Rion walked back toward the front hall, intending to return directly upstairs. His plans were abruptly changed,

however, when that same servant appeared for the second time.

"Ah, how fortunate that I needn't interrupt you, sir," the man said at once. "It seems you have another caller, this time at the front door. Another lady, but this one is a good deal older than the first."

Rion stood rooted to the spot, as this second caller could only be his mother.

TWENTY-SIX

It took a moment for Rion to absorb the news, and then he noticed something odd: the idea of seeing his mother again was distasteful and made him uneasy, but the panic he'd previously felt at the thought of confronting her was absent. Her visit was hardly likely to leave him untouched, but it would certainly not be as disturbing as her last one.

"Did you admit her to the house?" he suddenly found himself asking the servant, his voice calm and unconcerned. "Her last visit here was scarcely so pleasant that any sort of deference would be due her."

"In point of fact, sir, we're not permitted to admit anyone to the house," the man replied politely. "This is an official residence, and as such is considered a shelter for those talents who reside here. Inasmuch as you gentlemen and ladies will participate in the competitions, we on the staff consider it our privileged duty to protect you from any distractions."

"A pity not everyone on the staff feels the same, but you have my thanks nevertheless," Rion told him, managing to keep his smile to a minimum. "Let's go and see how the lady takes to being kept waiting like a tradesman."

The servant bowed and led the way to the front door, which he opened when Rion was properly positioned to block easy access. The visitor did turn out to be his mother, and when she caught sight of Rion she exploded.

"So there you are!" she choked out in accusation, as though Rion had been deliberately hiding. "Have you any idea how these peasants have dared to treat me? My health is so fragile that I shall certainly take to my bed as soon as I return home, but now I must sit down for a time. Show me to your apartment, and then order the servants to—"

"No, Mother, you aren't coming inside," Rion said calmly when both her words and her attempted advance into the house ended rather abruptly. She'd expected Rion to give ground as he'd always done before, but this time he'd stood firm.

"Clarion, what have they done to my darling boy?" she wailed, clearly on the verge of falling to tears. "You've *never* behaved so abominably, and I'm going straight to the palace to speak to the Five. They'll have you taken out of here, and then—"

"None of that will work either, Mother," Rion interrupted, forcing himself to pretended calm. On the inside it was all he could do not to react the way he always had, flinching and immediately giving in to her desires. "Your crying won't accomplish a thing as far as I'm concerned, and even the Five have no power over one of their possible successors. If they ordered me taken out of here, the people of this city would riot over the deliberate ruining of a common challenging Blending. And for the hundredth time, my name is now Rion."

"And what will your name be when you and your little peasant friends lose the competitions?" she asked, dropping the pretense of illness and tears to stare up at him with steel in her gaze. "It will certainly be 'mud,' just as theirs will be, and you will also be just as penniless. At that point no one will care in the least when I have you brought to me, and you will spend *years* doing penance for your present insolence. One way or another you will return to me, Clarion, but please don't be foolish enough to expect the time to be as pleasant as it was. You will pay for this nonsense many times over, and will certainly end up wishing you had never indulged in it. For this you have my word.''

And with that she turned with her head high and marched toward her waiting carriage. Rion was able to keep all expression from his face, but once again his insides roiled like a volcano. The anticipatory gloating in her voice had made him ill, knowing as he did that she usually got exactly what she wanted. Right now what *he* wanted and needed was to be with his own, so he left the closing of the front door to the servant, hurried upstairs, and knocked on Lorand's door. The babble of conversation inside ceased rather abruptly, and it was Lorand himself who opened the door.

"Rion, where did you run off to?" Lorand asked as he stepped back to let him enter. "We really could have used a referee."

"Again?" Rion asked in surprise as he looked around. "When I left, all you four seemed to need was privacy."

"That didn't last long, because admitting the truth changed nothing," Jovvi replied, staring at him with a frown. "But first you'll have to tell us what's bothering *you*. That agitation inside your head is threatening to knock me over."

"That part of it is fairly simple to explain," Rion answered, going back to the chair he'd left and collapsing into it. "Mother came calling again, but the servant who came to fetch me pointed out that this is an official residence. No one who might disturb us has to be admitted, so I didn't let her in."

"Good for you," Vallant said with a grin. "I'll bet she's still hatin' bein' left standin' on the doorstep."

"As a matter of fact, it made her tell me exactly what she plans to do once she has me back under her thumb," Rion agreed, wishing he were up to a grin himself. "She doesn't seem to understand that I'd rather starve to death in the streets than let her control me again, but that isn't why I disturbed your . . . discussion. It so happens I need to ask a favor."

"As long as it doesn't involve Lorand and me lyin' with you, there shouldn't be a problem," Vallant said, making the others—and Rion himself—chuckle. "What did you have in mind?"

"I had another caller before Mother," Rion responded,

distantly able to feel the support coming from all four of them. ''Naran came to tell me she was no longer at the house where we met the last time. Some friend of hers saw Mother's people searching the neighborhood trying to locate me, and thought they'd been sent by the man trying to find Naran. Apparently he's rather powerful and wants her, but since she wants nothing to do with *him* she's been forced to keep moving around.''

''So now you know why she disappeared that night,'' Jovvi said, looking oddly relieved. ''And why she hasn't told you where her permanent house is. She doesn't have one.''

''Nor, it seems, does she have any temporary refuge left,'' Rion said with a nod. ''She was in the process of looking about for one when she came here, stopping by only to make certain that I don't return to that house in search of her. I—intruded on the privacy of the rest of you by saying that we would hide her here, in the residence. It should be the one place the powerful man searching for her won't find her.''

''Well, I should hope you did tell her we'd hide her,'' Tamrissa said immediately, sounding indignant. ''No woman should have to do as a man wants just because he's powerful and she isn't. There are enough empty bedchambers that she can have her pick, and we'll find *some* way to make certain she doesn't starve.''

''I think *I'll* be able to help with that,'' Jovvi said, her attitude sweetly assuring. ''I couldn't think of a decent way to practice that ability I discovered of telling people what to do, but using it to keep your Naran from starving is a good enough cause. One servant and the cook should suffice, and no one else ought to know anything about it.''

''And having Rion's lady here ought to keep *him* occupied,'' Lorand added rather dryly. ''That will make one less thing for Vallant and me to worry about.''

That comment caused another round of general laughter, which warmed Rion through and through. These people were his and he was one of them, a fact which weakened his mother's threats all the way down to being negligible. With their support he could do and be anything, even a free, independent man. He was about to say just that when a knock at the door interrupted him.

"Please excuse the intrusion, gentles," the servant said when Lorand opened the door, the same servant who had advised Rion about his callers. "It pains me to disturb your group efforts, but there's someone at the door for both Dama Domon and Dom Ro. A gentleman for Dama Domon, and a lady for Dom Ro."

"You're mistaken," Vallant told the servant while Tamrissa paled a bit. "If they're the people I'm thinkin' about, they're neither gentleman *nor* lady. Tell them we'll be down in a minute."

The servant bowed and went to do as he'd been told, and Lorand closed the door before grimacing.

"Has someone declared this an official visiting day without telling us?" he asked. "If so, Jovvi and I are at something of a disadvantage."

"In my case, happily," Jovvi returned before looking at Tamrissa and Vallant. "Why don't you two take care of your visitors, and Lorand and I will make plans with Rion about Naran. Later we can get together again and fill each other in, and then get back to our original argument."

Tamrissa and Vallant both showed brief but odd expressions before agreeing, then they moved toward the door. Rion knew he would have to ask about what he'd missed, but truthfully he felt very reluctant to do so. It seemed there were definite benefits in being "innocent," at least as far as certain subjects went. . . .

TWENTY-SEVEN

As I left Lorand's bedchamber with Vallant, I wondered if there would ever come a time when I didn't feel a chill at hearing that my father had come calling. All brave words and thoughts aside, I would have enjoyed standing behind Vallant before the door was opened. But then I remembered that *that* woman would also be there, and made the fastest, firmest decision of my life. Using the power to stiffen my backbone and resolve might not be the same as learning to do it without help, but sometimes it's downright idiotic to refuse whatever help you can get.

"I wonder what Mirra wants *this* time," Vallant muttered as he put a hand to my elbow at the stairs. "And she's here with your father rather than with her own. She's got to be up to somethin', but not somethin' to do *us* any good."

"She can be up to anything she pleases," I replied, relaxing as the strength of the power flowed through me. "She and my father both. I don't really care *what* they want, and I'm not letting them in. If Rion can leave his mother on the doorstep, we should be able to do at least as much."

"You're touchin' the power, aren't you?" he asked very softly, his glance something I could feel. "Are you sure that's wise?"

"I have no idea if it's wise," I replied just as softly. "All I know is that it's better than letting my father get the upper hand. He's had too many years of making things go his own way for me to worry about playing fair. If he decides he wants fair play after all, he can go and bother someone else.''

Vallant stayed silent after that, but I sensed that he still felt . . . uneasy, I suppose you could say. His disturbance seemed to center more around worry for me than anything else, which was really nice but nothing which had to distract me. My father was here, and I couldn't wait until he met the new me.

The servant who had come to Lorand's room stood waiting by the front door, obviously ready to open it. He was another of the group I didn't know, but somehow seemed a bit more pleasant than the others—and also somehow less afraid. He smiled as we approached, waited until we were positioned properly to block the door, then opened it.

"Well, it's certainly about time!" the girl Mirra huffed, my father looking outraged beside her. "Leavin' us just standin' here—! You'll regret this, Vallant, by my oath you surely will."

She tried to charge inside then, expecting me to shrink out of her way, and when I continued to stand my ground, her two-step advance came to an abrupt halt. Petty outrage flashed across her overblown features, and my father frowned his disapproval.

"Tamrissa, you will immediately step out of the way and allow us to come in," my father ordered, the sternness in his tone demanding instant obedience. "There are serious matters to be discussed among us, and we have no intention of conducting that discussion while standing here like beggars."

"Then you might as well leave, because you aren't coming in," I told him flatly, ignoring the distant memory of my heart pounding whenever he'd spoken to me like that before. "If you have something to say, you can do it right here. Personally, I won't mind if you take your trollop and turn and leave."

"Trollop?" Mirra screeched as my father's frown deepened. "You steal the affections of the man I was engaged to marry, and then have the nerve to call *me* a trollop? Well, we'll just see who's callin' who what when we get to court!"

"Goin' to court would be a waste of time," Vallant put

in, his voice sounding as cool and calm as mine. "Here in Gan Garee the matter would be your word against mine, with any objective witnesses all the way back home. Unless they like throwin' away court time here, they won't spend even a minute listenin'."

"They'll do more than listen with *my* suit added to that of the young lady's family," my father disagreed at once, his sleek smile very familiar. "Her parents are at this moment seeing about sueing you for breaching the marriage agreement, and I'm sueing you for alienating my daughter's affections. Her own marriage was all arranged until *you* came along, and the court can reinstate that arrangement. *Now* do you think we might come in and sit down to talk?"

"No, we don't," I answered while Vallant hesitated, wiping away both Mirra's smugness and my father's sleek smile at the same time. "You're trying very hard to forget that we're full participants in the upcoming competitions, but no one else wants to forget. One of our group was recently challenged in court, her word against the other woman's. That other woman was given Puredan—which doesn't let you lie—and afterward was sentenced to five years in the deep mines. If you'd like the same for yourselves, just go ahead and continue with those suits."

Mentioning the kidnapping charge that was also involved didn't seem the thing to do right now, so I continued to omit it—and for the first time in my life saw my father's overwhelming self-confidence actually falter. Mirra had gone pale briefly, disbelief clearly fighting with forced nose-rubbing in an unpalatable truth, but my father looked shocked and shaken. I usually tried to defend myself against his attacks, but this time I'd counterattacked without the least hesitation. The action seemed to have frightened him, and his gaze and expression turned earnest.

"Tamrissa, I really hate this difficulty that's between us," he said, his tone half coaxing and half pleading. "I don't *want* to take you or the young man to court, but you've left me with very little choice. If we can sit down and talk quietly, you'll discover that all I need from you right now is a simple agreement to discuss your marriage to Dom Hallasser once this competitions nonsense is behind you. That isn't so much to ask, and it will allow me to leave you in peace until that time comes.''

"That sick beast must be putting an incredible amount of pressure on you," I commented, thanking whatever Higher Aspect there was for my having decided to touch the power. "You really expect me to agree to that just to get rid of you, supposedly not realizing that the agreement—which you probably have in writing—will bind me into a situation which doesn't hold me even loosely at the moment. It's really too bad that your plans are being ruined, Father, but it's none of my concern. Just as the horror of the life you condemned me to was none of yours."

"You ungrateful little slut!" he growled, a definite pallor to his skin now. "I made that arrangement for *your* sake, to give you someone with enough gold to support you properly for the rest of your life. If this is the thanks I get, I'll obviously have to take you to court after all.''

"And so will I!" Mirra piped up, a spoiled-brat look on her face. "I'm not losin' the man I love without a fight, especially since they won't be sendin' *me* anywhere. No man with eyes will *ever* do anythin' ugly to a woman like me.''

"The woman involved in that other matter Tamrissa mentioned was a retired courtesan," Vallant commented, sounding as unimpressed as I had. "She hadn't been retired all that long so she was still beautiful and desirable, and her residence for courtesans had made her wealthy. But havin' beauty and gold didn't help her, any more than it will be helpin' you two. You go ahead and do what you need to, but don't blame us if your game turns around and bites you.''

"And don't come back here again," I added, really enjoying the expressions of frustrated fury they both wore. "Next time we won't even come to the door.''

Vallant joined me in stepping out of the way, and the servant who had opened the door promptly closed it again in the faces of our visitors.

"That was nicely timed," I said to the servant, feeling absolutely marvelous. "What's your name?''

"Hovan, Dama," he replied with a bow. "It has been

my privilege to serve in this residence for, alas, only a short while.''

"Well, we're glad to have you, Hovan," I said with a smile. "Did you hear what I told those two? Yes, of course you did. Please let all the other servants know that if either of them returns, Dom Ro and I won't be available."

Hovan bowed his agreement to that and left, letting Vallant and me go back to the stairs. I'd had the feeling that Vallant was watching me, and as we began to ascend, he cleared his throat a bit.

"We made a really good team there, I thought," he commented softly. "Why don't we continue bein' a good team in your bedchamber—or in mine. Goin' back to that argument doesn't make much sense."

"It makes perfect sense," I disagreed, paying more attention to not tripping on my skirts than to how much I wanted to take his suggestion. "If things work out the way we both expect, we *really* won't want to change partners once we lie together. Better that we see to the matter now, to keep from *having* to do it later."

"I think I like you better when you aren't touchin' the power," he grumbled, his hand still firmly under my elbow. "You don't argue as well that way, even if you do argue as much. Are you tellin' me that you and I won't be lyin' together until you and Lorand and Jovvi and I do?"

"Now that you mention it, yes," I confirmed, ignoring the flutter of worry in my middle. "And there's really no reason for you to keep resisting. For all we know, you'll find that you enjoy lying with Jovvi better than you do with me."

"*You* may not know it, but *I* do," he disagreed immediately, using his hand on my elbow to move me away from the head of the stairs, where someone below would be able to see us. "What I feel for you goes beyond my desire to lie with you, which you'll discover when we do finally get to it."

And with that he pulled me close and kissed me, refusing to let me say another word. I would have expected to be frightened by such treatment, but so much yearning flared inside me that there wasn't enough room for fear. My hands spread out against the broadness of his back as I joined him eagerly in the kiss, and for a time the world faded and disappeared from around us. Only he and I were left in the universe, and I discovered that I also wanted more of him than just his body.

It wasn't at all long enough before he ended the kiss, grinning down at me when I tried to hold onto his lips with my own.

"This isn't the safest place to be doin' this," he murmured, his arms still around me. "Let's go to your bedchamber and continue the discussion there."

"You did that on purpose, so I refuse," I mumbled, hating to have to insist but using the power to let me do it. "You're a horrible, miserable man, and I won't forget how you tortured me."

"And I won't forget how much I hate havin' you touch the power," he countered in a grumble, finally releasing me. "You're a mean, stubborn woman, and you plus the power is more than I can stand up against."

"Then you agree?" I asked, relief and regret battling inside me. "You'll tell Lorand it's all right to lie with me, and then you'll lie with Jovvi?"

"Only if Lorand agrees as well," he corrected, stubbornness appearing in those light blue eyes. "I still won't go behind another man's back, especially if the other man is Lorand."

"Men!" I muttered, pushing aside the, feeling that I still wasted my time. Half the battle *was* won; now we had only the other half.

"And women right back at you," Vallant said as I started toward Lorand's bedchamber. "We can talk about that later, when it's *our* turn."

I tried to ignore what I felt from that comment, but my hand still tried to quiver when I raised it to knock on Lorand's door.

TWENTY-EIGHT

". . . and she'll be here at three in the morning," Rion said, looking as though he were just short of fretting. "I can bring her things into the house alone, so—"

"You won't be doing it alone," Lorand interrupted, not about to let Rion worry over the picayune. "Vallant and I will help, while Jovvi makes sure no one sees any of us."

"There has to be a way to do that that I don't know about yet," Jovvi said, her gaze turned inward. "I've been thinking about it, and simply commanding people to do things can't be all there is. Somehow I feel that I should be able to do quite a bit more, things most people don't even know are possible. And so should the rest of you."

Her attention had returned from the distance and now divided itself between Lorand and Rion. Rion looked faintly vexed and troubled, and Lorand knew just how he felt.

"I've often had that same impression," Lorand said, going to the foot of his bed to sit. "That the few things I'm able to do that others can't are just a tiny bit of what I *should* be able to do. From your expression, Rion, I'd say you felt the same."

"And it's extremely frustrating," Rion agreed. "It's as though I were a sculptor, able to turn clay or stone into any shape I wished—but was unable to picture any of those shapes. A lack of imagination, perhaps, to resolve a blur into solidity."

"Maybe that's something we can do for each other,"

Jovvi mused as she studied Rion. "For instance, it's occurred to me that solidified air can hide what someone behind it is doing if the air is also opaqued, but the area of blankness itself would be noticed. Is it at all possible to . . . to . . . superimpose a reflection of the innocent scene *behind* the activity, and hide it in that way? I know I'm not being clear in explaining what I mean, but—"

"No, as a matter of fact you're being extremely clear," Rion interrupted, apparently taken with the idea. "If the block of air properly reflects the nonactivity behind the activity, the activity itself should be invisible. And I can almost see how that would be done . . . although normal background sounds would be absent, and someone watching might notice an occasional slip or lapse. . . ."

"Normal background sounds would be in my province," Lorand said with his own surprise, suddenly knowing it was so. "Persuading crickets to play their song isn't difficult, and even birds can be Persuaded to ignore your presence."

"And having the occasional slip ignored would be mine to do," Jovvi added, her satisfaction so thick that Lorand was able to feel it with seven or eight feet between them. "I don't have to speak to someone or even be very near them to make them doubt what they just saw, or feel too lazy to investigate what was probably their imagination. If we all work together, I'm sure we can accomplish it easily."

"And the more we do it, the easier it will be," Lorand said in agreement, then had another thought. "You know, it just came to me that working together in such a way would be almost effortless if we were Blended, but that would cover just the three of us. Where would Tamrissa and Vallant fit in?"

"I think I know the answer to that," Jovvi said as Rion looked puzzled again. "I've been thinking about it ever since that noble told Rion that Tamma was the most important one among us. Considering the fact that a Blending links through the Spirit magic talent, he shouldn't have put the matter that way. Then I realized that linking was only the very first step for a Blending. Once it's formed, it needs to be able to function in a combative situation . . . like attacking and defending. . . ."

"Now I see it," Lorand jumped in, beating Rion to it by

no more than a breath. "Tamrissa is meant to attack a challenging group, and Vallant's part is to defend us from a similar attack. Do they really go that far during a competition?"

"Obviously they must," Rion said when Jovvi hesitated. "The things we did to gain our masteries hinted at that, but Tamrissa isn't the only one who needs to be able to attack. My own part can fall into the same category, but possibly not to begin with. Once Tamrissa gets their attention and softens them up, so to speak, then my ability to take away the air they breathe would come into play."

"Or you would taint their air somehow," Jovvi added. "While making sure the same doesn't happen to our air. And Lorand would attack the ground they stood on, while defending our own ground. Vallant can add or take moisture from the air around them while keeping an eye on our own, and even Tamma will have to help to defend us while she attacks. My own part, I think, will be to coordinate the efforts, keep us all calm and assured, and possibly try to rattle our opponents at the same time. I wonder how much of that they'll teach us before the competitions begin."

"Teach us?" Lorand said with a snort. "They probably won't even mention the possibilities. Like the fact that I can affect more than the ground our opponents stand on. The various demands of their bodies can be emphasized or glossed over, depending on which would be more effective. I may even be able to change their perceptions of what's going on around them, especially if I have the help of Spirit magic."

"And I may be able to do more as well," Rion said, again looking thoughtful. "As we've discussed, more may be done with air than simply taking it away or retaining it. But the point which interests me most at this moment is: how much of this information will be given to most of our opponents? If one of the noble groups has been chosen to be the next Seated Five, will any of the other four be given more help than just what they need to prevail over the common Blendings?"

"That's a very good question, but you're probably in the best position to answer it," Lorand returned. "If, as you once said, their own people can't be trusted to cooperate with the decision about who will win, *would* they tell them any more than necessary?''

"Certainly not,'' Rion answered with a wry smile. "Put like that, which is really the only way *to* put it, our opponents won't know any more than we do—and probably less. I should have seen that myself, but this business with Naran has been very distracting.''

"There's one exception to what you just said, and we'd better keep it in mind,'' Jovvi put in, her forefinger tapping her lips. "Only four out of the five groups won't know any more than we do. The fifth, the chosen Blending, will probably be fully trained. What I'd like to know is who's supposed to face them first. That group won't have a prayer of winning.''

"Logic suggests that the strongest of the common Blendings will face them first,'' Rion said, shifting a bit in his chair. "That arrangement would have the benefit of eliminating the greatest threat first, which would also work toward protecting the other noble groups.''

"And since we shouldn't be considered the strongest, we ought to be relatively safe,'' Lorand said, also looking toward Jovvi. "At least that seems a fairly decent working theory.''

"Only if we aren't missing some point we don't know about,'' Jovvi replied, apparently troubled. "I don't trust those people at all, so I'll feel much better if we don't assume even the least, smallest thing. Which means we'll have to do quite a bit of practicing, both individually and as a Blending.''

Lorand joined Rion in nodding his agreement, but the chance to add to what had already been said was lost when a knock came at the door. Lorand went to open it, and discovered that Tamrissa and Vallant were back.

"We're happy to report that our visitors are gone,'' Tamrissa said after she and Vallant had entered. "We followed Rion's example and didn't let them in, and also told the servants that we're to be unavailable if they come back.''

"Which doesn't mean they won't be plottin' and plannin','' Vallant added with a grimace. "I think we'll need some extra protection, like Blendin' in front of that fat fool tomorrow. After that we ought to be harder targets, at least until the competitions are over.''

"I've been thinking the same thing," Jovvi said as Lorand went to reclaim his seat at the end of his bed. "If the rest of you agree, we might even be able to make additional use of the effort—assuming Lord Twimmal knows more than he's willing to tell us.''

"That's a good idea," Rion agreed as Tamrissa matched Lorand's sudden amusement. "The chances of Twimmal knowing anything worthwhile are minimal, but even the smallest crumb will give us more than we have at the moment.''

"And speaking of more than we have at the moment, Vallant has agreed to be reasonable," Tamrissa said, giving a brief glance to the man she referred to. "At least he's being partially reasonable, since he still insists on making his agreement conditional on getting the same from Lorand. Now it's up to you, Lorand. Do we make our Blending more effective, or do we go ahead as we are and work under a handicap?''

Lorand gave her a sharp glance, but there was really no need. Tamrissa alone would never have spoken like that, so that meant she currently touched the power. Why she'd felt it necessary to do that he didn't know, but more importantly he wasn't sure how he should answer.

"Before Lorand responds to that, I'd like to say something," Jovvi put in, apparently surprising the others as much as she did Lorand. "Everyone has been talking about needs and desires and restrictions in relation to all of us lying together, so I'd like to add a requirement of my own. I'll lie with Vallant only on the condition that tonight I'll be able to spend the night with Lorand. If that turns out to be too much to ask, we'll just have to manage with the bonds we've already established.''

Lorand joined the others in staring at Jovvi, and her return stare seemed defiant enough—if you failed to notice the faint suggestion of trembling beneath it all. Lorand studied her for a very long moment, and then had to show the smile which had grown inside him.

"I've always suspected there might be a benefit in being surrounded by demanding women," he said, unable to take his eyes from Jovvi's face. "Now, at last, I believe I've found that benefit. In other words, with everyone else willing, how can I refuse?"

The others all made some comment or other, but Jovvi simply returned his stare with the shyest smile he'd ever seen her show. Lorand hadn't intended going near her again until and unless he found a solution to his problem, but he couldn't stand to see her in pain from thinking she'd caused the rift between them. He would spend the night with her and gently explain the truth in a way she would have to believe, and then they'd be able to go their own ways until he became the kind of man she so much deserved.

"If we're goin' to do this, let's do it right now," Vallant said, breaking the spell which had held Lorand's gaze to Jovvi's. "There's plenty of time until dinner, and after dinner I mean to nap. We have a lot to do tonight, and after it's done I don't expect to be sleepin' alone either. Rion will have our new resident ghost, so everybody ought to be happy."

"We won't know that for certain until tomorrow morning," Tamrissa put in blandly, proving she hadn't yet released the power. "But as far as right now goes, I agree with Vallant. Once we have this behind us, we'll no longer need to spend hours talking about it."

"I believe my own role has suddenly become lookout," Rion said, rising from his chair. "I'll watch for the air displacement which usually means the approach of a human being, and head off any servant who means to search out one of you. Are we agreed that none of us is going to be available to visitors until further notice?"

"I'd better be the only exception to that," Lorand said as he also stood. "I've promised to pay my friend Hat's coach fare home, so he or that man Meerk ought to be stopping by. If one of them does, make arrangements for him to come back after dinner."

"That won't be difficult," Rion agreed with a nod. "I'll simply pretend that I'm maliciously intruding in your affairs by seeing a visitor meant for you. May I see to anyone else's affairs?"

"I'd say we've come to the time where we'll all be seein' to our own affairs," Vallant told him dryly, holding out his arm to Jovvi while most of them chuckled. "I'm at your service, dear lady."

"Yes, you are, aren't you?" Jovvi returned with a mischievous smile, walking over to take the offered arm. "If you don't mind, we'll go to my bedchamber. Later, of course, you'll want to make other arrangements."

There was another general round of chuckling, during which Rion, Jovvi, and Vallant left the room. When the door closed behind them Lorand became aware of Tamrissa, who hadn't joined in the last bit of amusement. She stood staring down at her hands, which suggested something to Lorand.

"This is just a guess, mind, but I think I ought to be thanking you for releasing the power," he said softly. "If I'm right about that, please don't be worried. I intend to make very certain that you have pleasure and not pain."

"That wasn't what I was worrying about, but I still appreciate what you said," she replied with a wan smile. "And you're right, I did release the power. How did you know?"

"I suppose I'm learning to recognize your two selves and tell them apart," Lorand hedged, preferring to say nothing about *how* he knew. "Would you like to sit down and talk for a while before we . . . do our duty? The distant practicality of it all must be hard on you."

"Actually, that isn't at all the hard part," she disagreed with a better smile. "I'm more nervous than I expected to be, but I really do believe that you won't hurt me. And no, I'd rather not sit down and talk first. I think I'm more in need of being held in the arms of a friend."

"I've just been struck by insight," Lorand said as he studied her, his sudden guess feeling more right by the second. "You're worried about Vallant being with Jovvi, aren't you? Is that because you know something I don't?"

"No, it's because I have no confidence at all in happy endings," she replied with a sigh, back to looking miserable. "Not to mention having almost no confidence in myself. What if he decides that he *is* happier lying with Jovvi than with me? You'll have nothing to worry about, not with Jovvi being as crazy about you as she is, but what will *I* do? It's too late to forget about him. . . ."

By then she was staring down at her twisting fingers again, and Lorand found it difficult to know what to say. Telling her she had nothing to worry about would be futile, as she had obviously not gotten what he had from their brief time of Blending. The link between him and Vallant and Rion had shown him the kind of men his Blending brothers were, men just like himself. Vallant was no more casual or indecisive than he was, not in the least likely to tell a woman untruths just to get her to lie with him. And lying with a woman wasn't the most important part of a relationship. . . .

"Tamrissa, we're going to have to find you a hobby," he said at last with his own sigh. "The one you have now is just about guaranteed to make trouble for you and everyone else, so I'll appreciate it if you consider giving it up."

"Lorand, what are you talking about?" she asked, now looking and sounding completely bewildered. "I don't have a hobby."

"Of course you do," he disagreed with a wry smile. "It's called 'borrowing trouble.' You can't know that Vallant will prefer Jovvi to you, but here you are, worrying about it anyway. And not only worrying about it, but making yourself miserable over something that might never happen. Have you ever considered knitting or sewing? If you choose sewing and put as much effort into it as you do worrying, we'll never have to have our clothes made by outsiders again."

The look she gave him then was rather odd, since she obviously struggled between laughter and indignation. After a moment the laughter won, and she shook her head ruefully.

"You, Lorand Coll, are terrible, but something tells me I'm worse," she said. "Worrying about something that hasn't happened yet *is* rather silly, especially when you can't do anything about it. And considering what we're about to do, I should be paying *some* attention to you. Will you . . . kiss me?"

"With pleasure," Lorand responded, meaning every word as he stepped closer to take her in his arms. His heart and essence belonged to Jovvi, but his feelings for Tamrissa went well beyond fondness. He shared a bond with her and more, mostly what people usually called friendship, although the word was pitifully inadequate. There was love of a sort between him and the small, beautiful woman in his arms, but a comfortable love rather than a romantic one.

So the kiss he began was warm and tender, coaxing her shyness into joining his effort. Her arms stole gingerly around him, the touch on his back hesitant, and it seemed that he now knew what it would be like to hold and kiss a doe. Wide-eyed with nervousness, ready to run at the first frightening event, trembling very faintly with anxiety over what she was about to do. . . . He would have to be exquisitely careful and gentle to keep her from bolting. . . .

And so he was. He began by having her help him take his clothing off, which made taking her own things off a bit easier. They alternated one item each, and her blush was bright even before they were bare. At the last she seemed to be forcing herself not to clutch her clothing to her, a battle she may have won only through sheer stubbornness. In order to distract her Lorand lifted her onto his bed and quickly followed, then began to kiss her all over while he touched her lightly here and there with his talent.

Her response took a moment or so to appear, but once it did she matched his mounting passion perfectly. Her kisses were hot as she stroked his body, and very quickly it felt to Lorand as though his blood were on fire. The flaming boil forced him to more frenzied activity, which in turn brought him to the point of no longer being able to keep from entering her. Being gentle as he did so proved horribly difficult, but for her sake he accomplished it.

And again her response was a bit hesitant, but then she moaned in pleasure and began to join him wholeheartedly. He slowly increased the speed and intensity of his thrusting until they both tried frenziedly to fuse their flesh, her intense pleasure merging with and increasing his own. It was mindlessness that they quickly slipped into, so it wasn't possible for Lorand to know how long it took before he exploded in the ultimate ecstasy. Tamrissa had found her own ecstasy more than once, he knew, and after giving her a final kiss he lay beside her on the bed and tried to catch his breath.

"That was . . . really very nice," she said tentatively at last, obviously having difficulty thinking of the proper thing to say. Her tone accomplished what her words hadn't, however, which he found instantly amusing. "Lorand, why are you laughing?"

"I'm laughing because that wasn't 'really very nice,' " he explained, turning on his side to look at her fondly. "It was absolutely marvelous, and I suspect that your talent had something to do with it. Where did you learn to set a man's blood on fire like that?"

"Lorand, stop," she protested with a delightful blush that also seemed to be delighted. "I did no such thing."

"You most certainly did," he disagreed firmly, brushing a damp strand of her hair aside. "Didn't Rion mention it? I'd say it's a good thing that I feel the way I do about Jovvi, otherwise Vallant would have company in courting you. You're a very special woman, Tamrissa, and I feel more honored than ever to be considered your friend."

"You're more than just a friend, Lorand, and always will be," she replied as she took his hand and squeezed it, a light sheen of tears in her lovely eyes as she smiled. "If the two years of my marriage was the price I had to pay in order to have you and Rion and Jovvi and Vallant, I'd be willing to pay it a second time just to make all this possible. And now I think it's time for me to dress and leave."

He agreed with a nod and his own smile, exchanged a final kiss before she arose, then leaned back and closed his eyes to give her privacy for dressing. And to give himself a chance to think about later tonight, when Jovvi would be beside him in his bed. He very much wanted simply to hold her, and dream about a time when he would be free of his problem. Then he would give every man in the world a run for his gold in courting her. . . .

TWENTY-NINE

Vallant followed Jovvi to her bedchamber, exchanging a wordless glance with Rion when the other man made for his own bedchamber. And he couldn't help noticing how odd it was to associate with Rion at a time like that. No suggestive winks or grins, no self-conscious embarrassment, nothing but an attitude that said nothing at all unusual or different was about to happen. From all it was possible to tell by Rion, Vallant might be on the way to having a pleasant chat with Jovvi.

"What are you thinking about?" Jovvi asked curiously as he closed the door behind himself. "Your face is wearing the strangest expression."

"I was just thinkin' that strange is a really good word for some of the things Rion does," he replied, running a hand through his hair. "But strange good instead of strange bad . . . And I ought to say that you didn't do badly yourself. You got Lorand to do exactly as you wanted without touchin' him even a little with your talent."

"You seem to be sure I didn't touch him because you're sure of *me*, and I thank you for that," she said with a dimple-filled smile. "Touching him with my ability wouldn't have been fair, but I was almost ready to do it anyway if that trick hadn't worked. And to tell the truth, it wasn't completely a trick. I'm just about desperate enough to do exactly as I said I would. Because of my big mouth."

"You couldn't help it any more than Lorand can help feelin' as he does," Vallant said, moving closer to put a hand under her chin. "Neither one of you is to blame, so stop thinkin' about what was and start thinkin' about what will be. But not everythin' that will be."

The last of his words was something of a mutter, and he turned away to keep his expression from betraying him. With anyone else the effort would have worked, but Jovvi tended to look at people with more than her eyes.

"It's bothering you that Tamma stayed behind with Lorand," she stated, just as though he'd said the words first himself. "You aren't jealous, just . . . bothered. Is there anything I can do to help?"

"You can move the day along faster so that it's bedtime tonight," he replied with a faint snort of self-ridicule. "I need it to be that time so I'll know if she really will be sleepin' beside me. Right now I keep expectin' somethin' to come along and make it impossible."

"When I say I know exactly how you feel, please believe I mean it in every sense of the words," she agreed with a sigh. "I won't believe that Lorand is back beside me until it actually happens, and waiting for it to happen is killing me. You . . . don't really mind that we'll be lying together, do you? I know you agreed to go along with the necessity, but I also know you still have certain reservations."

"None of which has anythin' to do with you," he assured her at once, turning back to touch her cheek gently. "I keep flinchin' at the thought of Tamrissa turnin' her back on me because of this, even though she was the one who forced me into it. A man would be crazy not to want to lie with you, Jovvi, and my craziness runs in another direction entirely. Would you like to begin?"

"No, I think I'd rather continue to stand here torturing myself with doubts," she said, then laughed aloud at whatever his expression must have looked like. "No, Vallant, I'm just joking. I would very much like to begin now."

She came into his arms with a smile then, and began to raise his interest with a kind of coaxing-teasing combination that he'd never experienced before. It felt perfectly natural and real, as though his mere presence excited her passions, and his response grew faster and more intense. He felt tempted to think that it was just her expertise as a courtesan at work, but something told him it was much more than that. His feelings for Jovvi were surpassed only by his feelings for Tamrissa, and he suspected she felt the same about him in relation to Lorand.

Their kissing quickly progressed to caressing, and then they began to rid themselves of their clothes. Jovvi was an extremely beautiful woman, and Vallant hadn't been lying about how desirable he considered her. She aroused him completely in a very short time, and once they were entirely unclothed he did the same for her. When she was fully ready for him he entered her, and the pleasure was long lasting and very intense.

Afterward she lay with her cheek on his chest, her satiety a full match to his own satisfaction. They spent a few moments regaining their breath, and then she chuckled.

"I hadn't realized sooner just how odd this is," she replied when he made a sound of inquiry. "I've spent years as a very popular courtesan, but not once in all that time did I come across a man as . . . all-around satisfying as you and Rion and Lorand. Nothing for years, and then three at once. I'd like to know what I did to attract such marvelous luck. If I can figure it out, I'll certainly continue doing it."

"Odd may not be a strong enough word," Vallant said slowly as he digested the idea. "Tamrissa started out as a woman who cringed even if her *hand* was touched by a man, but she's already lain with Rion, is in the process of lyin' with Lorand, and apparently intends to lie with me at *some* time. Lorand and I are so deeply into this thing that I doubt he can think about other women any more than I can. And Rion . . . goin' from bein' a virgin to bein' the first among us to lie with both of you . . . and the fact that Lorand and I were more concerned about his well-bein' than jealous of him . . . No, odd is definitely not a strong enough word."

"You're absolutely right," Jovvi said with a frown, having straightened to sitting so that she might look at him. "My first thought was that the Blending had caused it, but that can't be true because much of that happened before we Blended. So what did cause it?"

"You're askin' if somethin' brought us together and is now keepin' us together," he responded, having no doubt that that was what her question actually meant. "All I can say is that I wish I knew, at least as much as I want to know the answers to the rest of our questions. Maybe we'll find out before this is all over."

"Somehow I have the feeling that we need to know *this* answer as soon as possible," Jovvi replied as she ran both hands through her hair. "Not that our needing it will bring the answer on magical wings. I think I'm getting very tired of discovering mysteries we can't yet solve, and I'm no longer in the mood to just lie here oozing satisfaction. What I need is a bath, and maybe even a bit of a swim. Please feel free to stay as long as you like, even if it means still being here when I get back. I won't mind."

The smile she sent him before rising to begin dressing was a mischievous one, a teasing between friends rather than between lovers. Vallant chuckled as he lay there watching her, knowing that under other circumstances she would have taken his complete attention.

But under the current circumstances, his mind slipped past her to center on Tamrissa again. It wasn't that Tamrissa was more beautiful than Jovvi, because both women were equally beautiful each in her own way. It was just that there was . . . more to Tamrissa in some way, something inside her that called out to him in some way. It wasn't possible to define the attraction in any other sense, at least not in words.

Thoughts, however, were another matter. Vallant put his hands behind his head and thought about Tamrissa, how she would look lying beside him, how she would feel in his arms, how soft her lips had been during that too-brief kiss. Being with her would be ecstasy beyond description— if nothing happened to stop it. . . .

Jovvi had grabbed up a wrap before leaving her bed-chamber, and was so intent on getting to the bath house that she almost collided with Tamma in the front hall. The other woman had just hurried out of the library with a book and a wrap cradled in her left arm, apparently at least as distracted as Jovvi felt. They both nearly greeted one another with smiles, remembering only at the last minute that they were supposed to be in the middle of feuding.

"You'd better learn to watch where you're going," Jovvi said as quickly as possible, now aware that two people, both out of sight, were watching and listening. "If you don't, you might actually end up bruised."

"If I end up bruised, I won't be the only one," Tamma returned defiantly, but with a quiver in her voice. "And I *was* watching where I was going, which happens to be in the direction of the bath house. If you're heading in the same direction, you'll just have to wait."

"I'm not in the mood to wait," Jovvi drawled, looking Tamma up and down in the most insulting way possible. "It's rather easy to tell that you need a bath more than I do, but you're still the one who will have to wait."

"I refuse to wait," Tamma spat, the trembling in her voice showing that she now forced herself to respond like that. "This is still my house, and I'm tired of everyone trying to push me around. I'm going to the bath house to soak and read, and don't intend to let anyone stop me!"

"And I'm going to wash and swim, and don't intend to let anyone stop *me*," Jovvi returned with matching defiance. "Just stay out of my way, and we may both end up surviving."

Jovvi ignored Tamma's gasp of outrage and marched off toward the back of the house, pretending to be unaware of the way Tamma followed immediately with shaky determination. The two unseen watchers were amused, one of them only faintly with a good bit of impatience behind the ridiculing laughter. Both, however, had decided against following, small nodes of cautious fear causing the decisions.

It took Jovvi only a couple of minutes to reach the bath house, with Tamma hurrying along only a few small steps behind. She walked inside with senses extended in all directions, but their privacy was actually complete—at least for the moment. For that reason she waited until the door was closed again, then she turned to Tamma with a grin.

"If we manage to survive this mess, I may one day audition for a part in a play," she said softly. "We're no longer under observation, so we can forget about clawing and pulling hair. How did your . . . relaxation go?"

"Definitely not in the direction of relaxation," Tamma replied with a laugh despite her immediate blush. "Lorand is a love, but I know you already know that. How did . . . your time go?''

"Vallant and I spent a ridiculous amount of time bewailing the fact that you and Lorand were together," Jovvi answered frankly with a wry smile. "After that we enjoyed lying together, but once the enjoyment was over our thoughts returned to you two. If you think he's any less anxious now to spend the night with you, you're in for something of a very big surprise.''

"What I think is that he may end up disappointed," Tamma admitted ruefully, studying the wrap and book that she held. "I won't let that stop me from lying with him, though, because I have to know for certain. Jovvi . . . do you think it's possible that I . . . 'set a man's blood on fire'? Lorand said I did, and I'm not sure whether or not he was joking.''

"Well, of course, why didn't I think of that before?" Jovvi said, definitely annoyed with herself as she led the way toward the benches. "It isn't only your beauty and air of innocence that attracts all those men, it's also the fact that your aspect is Fire. Allestine's aspect is Fire, and it served her so well that she was able to open her own residence.''

"Jovvi, I have no idea what you're talking about," Tamma protested as she followed. "Are you saying that Lorand *wasn't* joking?''

"Of course he wasn't joking," Jovvi replied, turning after setting down her wrap and beginning to undress. "I tend to forget that those who are unfamiliar with courtesans are usually just as unfamiliar with certain truths. The two most desirable aspects for courtesans are Spirit and Fire, with Spirit being slightly better because of our ability to adjust emotions. Fire can't do any adjusting, but you don't really need to. That sense of 'setting the blood aflame' makes a courtesan with Fire magic more than ordinarily popular.''

Tamma now stood with her mouth open, the wrap and book held by her left arm apparently forgotten. Her mind felt stunned, which convinced Jovvi not to show her vast amusement.

"If I'm not mistaken, Vallant knows as little about that as you do," Jovvi said in place of chuckling. "That means he isn't very likely to know what's in store for him, which in turn means he ought to be more than a little impressed. Are you still worried that he might be disappointed instead?''

"Yes, but not as much as I was," Tamma said with a short, breathless laugh. "Oh, Jovvi, I wish I knew how to make it happen on purpose! Did Allestine learn to control the ability?"

"I don't think she ever knew that control is possible," Jovvi replied, tossing her underthings on top of the pile of her clothes. "Most courtesans simply *let* it happen, but I met one once, just before I joined Allestine's residence, who had learned to *make* it happen. She was really sweet and told me all about the life, except for being part of a residence. She wasn't, and was all but rolling in gold and influence. Most of her patrons were from the nobility, and none of them dared to hurt her because of what the others would do if deprived of her services. Controlling the ability was her way of staying safe.''

"I wonder how strong she was," Tamma mused as she rid herself of the wrap and book and began to remove her clothing. "Maybe you have to have a certain strength before you *can* establish control, but what about touching the power? Will a full grip on it help you with control, or do nothing more than add to the strength of the ability?''

"A full grip on the power could well leave you with a pile of ash instead of a living man," Jovvi warned as she slowly entered the beautifully warm water. "I don't know enough about it to give you advice, but using caution is always a good idea when trying something new. You want Vallant impressed, not carbonized.''

Tamma didn't answer in words, but Jovvi couldn't have missed her shudder from a mile away. That picture, at least, should make the girl cautious, which was all anyone could ask. Jovvi submerged herself briefly but completely, pushed back her sopping wet hair, then began to swim back and forth a bit. She had her own anxieties to work off, at least for the time being.

Tamma had already finished washing when Jovvi decided she'd had enough of swimming, so Jovvi did her own washing quickly and then took the headrest next to

Tamma's. She'd been watching with her ability to make sure they remained unobserved, and since they still had their privacy she decided to mention an important point that hadn't yet been discussed with Tamma.

"I know you're busy thinking about Vallant, but there's something we need to talk about," she said, drawing Tamma from what was more than half daydream. "What makes the subject easier to discuss is the fact that you're a different person when you fully touch the power."

"I know *I* see me differently, but I hadn't realized that the rest of you would find seeing the same so easy," Tamma replied. "What was it that you wanted to discuss?"

"It has to do with your ... purpose in the Blending," Jovvi responded carefully, trying to find the best way to put it. "I'm sure you know how much more ... aggressive your power-enhanced personality is, and I think there's a very good reason for it. You're most likely the one who will ... lead and direct our Blending in attack during the competitions."

"Attack?" she echoed with raised brows, her emotions suddenly turning uncertain. "I know they had me doing attacklike things in order to qualify for my mastery, but no one ever said it would be part of the competitions. Are you sure that that's what we'll have to do?"

"Nothing else makes any sense," Jovvi replied as casually as possible, trying to calm Tamma. "And of course they never said anything about it. The last thing they want is for us to be fully prepared, but it isn't something *you* have to worry about. Your other self will be in charge during the time, and it's for her to worry—if you think she will."

"No, I don't expect that she will," Tamma replied with a faint smile. "I'm slowly learning to be like that when I'm *not* touching the power, but I've something of a long way to go. She *likes* the idea of starting a fight, while I still try my best to avoid one. Hopefully I'll make a bit more progress by the time the competitions begin."

"Well, don't make too much progress," Jovvi said, surprising Tamma again. "It has just now come to me that your ... easily observed reluctance to fight is probably the reason you're in this group. They can't be pleased with how strong we are individually, so the fact that the member of our group who is supposed to be most aggressive isn't that at all must be reassuring to them. If they find out what you're like when you touch the power, they may decide to break us up.''

"They could use the excuse that we haven't yet Blended, which is the truth as far as they know it," Tamma said, sitting up at the urging of the disturbance inside her. "That means we have to make it official tomorrow, so they won't have that particular excuse. And now I think I know what that so-called Lord Carmad meant when he commented about me."

"What comment was that?" Jovvi asked with a frown, searching her memory. "I can't seem to remember one."

"When he called me forward first and I went to stand in front of him, I was nearly petrified with fright," Tamma explained. "Only a blind man could have missed how I felt, and he sneered out something about how my reaction was to be expected, considering the way the testing authority liked to do things. *He* knew I was supposed to be aggressive, and his sneer was for the fact that I wasn't."

"So now we can wonder why he sneered," Jovvi said thoughtfully. "We've already decided that he was there to give us the help that Twimmal wouldn't or couldn't, so why would he be cynically amused to think our Blending was crippled even before it formed?"

"Maybe . . . maybe some organization of commoners sent him, to give the common Blendings a better chance against the nobility," Tamma suggested hesitantly. "If he was supposed to visit all the common groups, he could have been disappointed that his help would be wasted on us."

"And that produced the cynical reaction," Jovvi agreed with a nod. "Yes, that's perfectly possible, even if none of us has ever heard about such an organization. They would have to keep their existence extremely secret, or the nobility would root them out and destroy them. That ought to mean he probably won't be back."

"If he does come back, I'm going to make sure he doesn't see the other side of me," Tamma said, this time surprising Jovvi. "I've learned a certain cynicism of my own from my father, which tells me that one visit from the man means he's on our side, but two will mean he's working for our enemies. They would *expect* us to decide that Carmad is on our side, from the way he helped us. Then, when he reappears, we let him in on any secrets we may be hiding from the authority.''

"You know, that makes more sense than I like to think about, and I'm surprised I didn't come up with it myself,'' Jovvi decided aloud. "As suspicious as I usually am I should have, but the way he was almost caught by Twimmal distracted me. Even if he comes back in two days rather than tomorrow, we'd better stick with our suspicions. Not knowing our secrets won't harm him even if he does happen to be on our side, but the reverse could certainly harm *us*."

"I'm tempted to feel that not telling him will keep him from sharing what we need to know if he is on our side,'' Tamma fretted, still not relaxing back in the water. "That doesn't necessarily hold true, but it's certainly a possibility. If he does come back, do you think we can use the Blending to find out the truth?''

"Since I could probably do that part of it myself, I don't see why not,'' Jovvi replied with only a short hesitation. "I really hate the idea of taking advantage with my ability, but if the man's a secret enemy, he doesn't deserve to be treated fairly. And if he's a friend, he ought to understand the reason for our caution.''

"What I really hate is living like this,'' Tamma said, finally sinking back to the headrest. "All this intrigue and doubt, lying and being spied on, sneaking around and pretending all the time . . . Sometimes I wish the competitions would start tomorrow, just to put all the rest of it behind us.''

Jovvi made a sound which suggested commiseration, but in full truth she didn't agree. The longer it took for the competitions to begin, the better their chance of winning. Which probably meant the competitions were scheduled to begin any day now. They still hadn't been given that unimportant little detail, a lack which suggested that the announcement was meant to come as a shock. Anything to throw them off balance. . . .

A sigh escaped Jovvi, showing how weary she herself

had become of the game they were caught up in. But their futures and possibly even their lives were at stake, so weariness was a luxury she couldn't afford. Vallant meant to meet with the small ex-groom Pagin Holter, Jovvi knew, so she had to remember to tell Vallant that they needed to ask about "Lord Carmad." And to pass on a warning, just in case the man really was an enemy.

The warm water was deliciously relaxing, but Jovvi's mind found it impossible to rest. Now that she'd laid the groundwork with Tamma, it ought to be easier to break the news to the girl that she was considered to be the most important one among them. And after they all saw what their Blending was capable of, she might have to work with Lorand and Vallant on their problems. And with Rion's lady in the house, would it be harder for the man to concentrate? And come to think of it, could his Naran be one of the enemy herself?

All those questions and problems threatened to make Jovvi's head spin, but she firmly resisted the inclination. Their first chore would be to see about Naran, and Rion had to know in advance what they intended. Honesty was one of the most important things they owed each other, but how was she supposed to broach that delicate a subject? What words could she possibly use to keep from breaking their group completely apart . . . ?

THIRTY

When my mind refused to stop fretting, I gave up on the idea of soaking and left the bath. Jovvi was so deep in thought that she didn't seem to see me, so I used a bit of the power to heat all the moisture from my body and hair, got into my wrap and picked up my clothes and book, and left the bath house. Actually I pretended to run out of the bath house, also pretending that I'd been driven out of it by a sharp-tongued enemy.

For that reason I reached my apartment rather quickly, wondering all the while if anyone had seen my playacting. Not that it really mattered. It was just something to think about to keep me from thinking about Vallant. For all intents and purposes I'd promised to spend most of the night with him, and the conflict in my emotions was driving me insane.

I looked at the book I'd chosen to distract me from my thoughts while I soaked, and was forced to admit that it wouldn't have done the job any more than it was currently doing. The conflict bothering me was that I really wanted to become involved with Vallant, but because of the danger to him couldn't allow an involvement to develop. In the face of that, no book ever written could have distracted me.

Ignoring the sitting room, I carried my burdens through to the bedchamber and disposed of them properly. I was very much in the mood to drop everything in a heap and then turn my back on the heap, but that would have been too much like running away from my problems. Turning your back and forgetting about things is easy—until the giant pile of problems you've built topples down on your head.

So I put the book on a table and the dirty clothes with the rest of my things that needed washing, then lay down on my bed to think about my problem with Vallant. The plan I'd come up with, to let my power-enhanced self annoy him to the point of making him walk away, might not work, but it was the only thing I could think of. That was probably because I didn't want to think of anything else, not when it would end any relationship even before it began.

But ending things was in Vallant's best interests, so I knew I'd just have to keep trying. If only thoughts of being with him didn't distract me so badly. . . . I turned over onto my back to push those personal thoughts away, but they refused to go. Platinum blond hair and pale blue eyes above a devilish grin forced their way in front of my mind's eye, then drew me along into the realm of marvelous daydreams.

Time disappeared to nothing in that realm, and the next thing I knew there was a knock at my bedchamber door. A maid called through the door that dinner was almost ready to be served, and then the shaped cluster of warmth that represented her body heat quickly retreated. She hadn't been sent for so she hadn't come in, undoubtedly a result of the lecture I'd given earlier. I forced myself to sitting and then up off the bed, glad of the privacy. Unless you were very firm, I'd discovered, some servants took over and ran things to suit themselves.

My thoughts seemed rather disjointed as I dressed and brushed my hair, and leaving my apartment didn't help much to clear things up. I had no trouble remembering how I was supposed to behave with the others, but everything beyond that felt far too complex even to consider briefly. For that reason I sent my glares to everyone as I took my place at the table, received their glares in return, then paid attention to nothing but my food.

Everyone else was just as silent during the meal, and afterward we each took our own private chilly silence back to our bedchambers or apartment. Once there I sent for a tea service, waited for it to be brought, then told the servant not to try to collect it again until tomorrow. I deliberately gave the man the impression that I would probably be reading until the wee hours, but as soon as he left I headed straight for bed. I'd finally figured out that sleep was what I needed, especially since we were scheduled to Blend again as well as help Rion and his Naran. When I woke up I would need the tea, much more than I needed it right now.

As it happened, when I woke up it was to remember a strange, disturbing dream. I'd been standing in a large, indistinct room, completely surrounded by a lot of men. To my relief the men were ignoring me, and then suddenly, without warning, a flow of flames began to leak out of me at several points. In frantic fright I began to try to stop the leaks, but stopping one simply started the leak in another place.

I'd been trying, of course, to keep the leaks from the notice of the surrounding men, but they'd seen them instantly and then I was no longer being ignored. They all began to advance on me, and as I started to run in the only direction possible, I glimpsed Vallant behind one bunch of them. He gestured in an effort to get me to run in his direction, at the same trying to fight his way through the horde, but there were too many of them. He couldn't reach me and I couldn't reach him, and so I ran across the marble floor, the sound of pursuing footsteps coming right behind. . . .

And then that sound came again, only now I was awake enough to realize that it was knocking rather than footsteps. I looked at the door, trying to discern the shape of the person out there knocking, to see if I'd yet learned to tell man from woman. But there was no shape of heat outside my door, which meant either that the person knocking was dead, or the door knocked by itself.

I shivered at both thoughts, still too groggy with sleep to know fantasy from reality, and then the knock came a third time. Gentle and impersonal, it seemed almost light-hearted, and a glance at the clock suddenly suggested a third possible source for the sound: it was two o'clock in the morning, and if Rion had wanted everyone to be awake, he could have solidified a bit of air to knock with.

The relief of that realization made me want to stretch out again, but then the knock came for the fourth time. For a moment I wondered why he hadn't stopped now that I was definitely awake, and then I understood that he didn't know he'd succeeded. It was up to me to find a way to tell him, so I thought for another moment and then smiled. It felt as though I were in the midst of playing a child's game, and I'd just figured out how to make someone else "it."

Looking in the direction of where Rion's bedchamber lay, I took a firmer grip on the power and . . . rode it, so to speak, into the room. In the same way that I would have surrounded a feather I meant to burn, protecting everything around the feather, I chose a small volume of air in the room. The power let me know that the volume contained nothing but air, so I set a small but very bright flame to burning. I kept the flame alight until the time for a fifth knock was well past, and then, knowing Rion had gotten my message, let it go out.

Which left me with nothing but the memory of that dream as I got up to wash my face. The idea of flame leaking out of me like water was ridiculous, but it hadn't felt ridiculous in the dream, it had been terrifying. I hadn't been able to make it stop, and all those men had been drawn to me because of it. . . .

I poured water from the pitcher into the basin, then wet my hands and pressed the wetness to my face. I'd really have to remember to thank Jovvi for telling me what she had about women with Fire magic, as it had done a marvelous job in adding to my store of subjects for nightmares. And that business about Vallant trying to reach me and not being able to . . . I'd been left with the impression that the crowd was about to trample him, but I'd been awakened before I was forced to stand there and watch it happen. . . .

The cool water felt soothing against my skin, but did nothing to ease the fevered jumble in my mind. Part of me, the part still touching the power, was furious over the idea of Vallant being trampled. It wanted to lash out with fire in all directions to protect him, burning to ash anyone who didn't back off. The rest of me, however, the larger and more basic part of ME, wept at the thought that I might not be able to help keep him from being trampled. It was the old story of my lack of self-assurance, but that didn't change the fact that I could well contribute to Vallant's death.

And that was a thought I simply couldn't live with. I now knew the probable reason all those men wanted me, but my knowing about it didn't change things. Those rich and powerful men would continue to want me, and if Vallant got in their way they would simply brush him aside—even if the brushing killed him. That left me no choice but to discourage a relationship between us, doing my best to make the plan actually work.

I'd dried off on a towel and was brushing my hair when another knock came at my door, but this time someone actually stood on the other side. I opened the door to find Jovvi, who gave me a warm smile.

"It came to me that the best place for us to gather is your sitting room," she said softly. "I've already checked, and the servants are all asleep—although one of them was at a peephole. The peephole gives a fairly good view of the hall outside our doors, and it's so low down and hidden in a corner that I never noticed it. The man watching through it was only somewhat sleepy, but I had surprisingly little trouble overcoming that. Now that I've found that out I'll have to watch myself to be sure I don't begin taking advantage of everyone, but is it all right for us to gather here in your apartment?''

I nodded my agreement, trying not to frown at the flood of words she'd sent at me. Jovvi didn't usually ramble like that, and somehow she seemed more excited than calm. For a moment the change was puzzling, and then I realized that the time was drawing nearer to when she would be with Lorand again. I watched her hurry back across my sitting room, probably on the way to let the men know where to come, and silently wished her all possible happiness with Lorand. It would be nice to know that at least someone was happy. . . .

Jovvi was back rather quickly, and she seemed to have gotten control of herself again. In point of fact she now looked a bit worried, so I asked her if something was wrong.

"It's not exactly *wrong*," she replied, a bit of vexation moving through her expression. "It's more a matter of making sure there *isn't* anything wrong, but broaching the subject will be very awkward. Lorand and Vallant should be here in a minute, so let's wait until they arrive before I go into details."

"What about Rion?" I started to ask, but that was when Lorand slipped into the room, followed an instant later by Vallant. They also seemed to be looking for Rion, which made Jovvi shake her head.

"No, he isn't late because I haven't called him yet," she said, answering everyone's first question at once. "I needed to talk to the rest of you before I did, because we have a delicate problem to solve. We're about to sneak his Naran into the house and hide her—but how do we know that she isn't working for the testing authority?"

The question stopped me in my tracks, so to speak, because it was such a good one. We were half killing ourselves pretending we weren't getting along, but all our efforts would be out the window once we cooperated to sneak the woman in.

"I was about to say that Rion would know, but that isn't true," Lorand commented with a sigh. "Rion has no experience with women, and he's absolutely crazy about Naran. So what do we do?"

"We have to find out for certain, but not behind Rion's back," Jovvi said, looking briefly at each of us. "First we have to tell him what we're about to do, and that's the part I'm having trouble with. What words can I possibly use that won't upset him?"

"The sort of words you're looking for don't exist," I said when the men simply shook their heads. "He *is* going to get upset, but maybe I can make it a little easier. If you'll go and get him, I'll give it a try."

Jovvi hesitated very briefly before nodding and heading out of the room, so I went over to the tea service. Warming a cup of tea would take next to no effort, and I happened to need it.

"You're touchin' the power again, aren't you?" Vallant said from behind me, the words somehow overly neutral. "Do you really think you need protection when you're with no one but us?"

"I had to use the power to reply to Rion's wake-up knock, and just didn't happen to let go," I responded without looking at him. "It doesn't mean anything beyond the fact that I'm too lazy to keep touching and releasing the power, but if it really bothers you all that much, just say so. I won't mind calming your worry by putting aside my strength."

I turned with my teacup to look at him then, making certain my expression showed nothing but blandness. At the moment he seemed to be struggling not to frown, and before he was able to say anything at all, Jovvi reappeared, followed by Rion.

"I'm pleased that you're all awake and ready," Rion said with a grin once he closed the door. "I wasn't able to sleep, so I thought I would help out those of you who could. I hope I didn't startle any of you too badly."

"Your staying out of the hall to do the waking was worth being startled," Jovvi replied with a smile. "One of our watchers had set himself up where he has a view of our rooms, but he didn't seem curious or disturbed enough to have noticed the knocking. He's asleep now, so for the moment we needn't worry about him.''

"But there's something we do have to worry about, or at least I do,'' I put in, saying the words before his very evident happiness made them even more difficult. ''I hope you can forgive me for this, Rion, but my life until now has taught me not to trust anyone or anything. When your own parents betray you . . . Do you know how hard it was for me to really trust all of *you*?''

"I think I have a small idea,'' he replied, the happiness having disappeared. ''Are you trying to say you've changed your mind about wanting Naran in the house?''

"I'm trying to say that I won't mind having her here at all—once I'm certain she's actually the person she seems to be.'' Again I had to speak quickly, to keep the sight of tragedy in his gaze from silencing me. ''Jovvi and I were talking about that Lord Carmad, and we realized there's even a chance that *he* works for the testing authority. We simply can't afford to trust anyone at all, Rion, not until we're completely certain about them.''

"I *am* certain about Naran, but I realize that it isn't possible for the rest of you to be the same,'' he said, apparently fighting to keep a certain stiffness out of his tone. ''So what are we to do about her? Keep her living in the street until we're certain she's no threat, or shall we torture the truth out of her?''

"Personally, I'd rather just question her with Lorand and myself being alert for evasions and half truths,'' Jovvi said, looking at Rion with sympathetic diffidence. ''You don't . . . *really* think we'd harm her, do you? Rion. . . .''

"No, Jovvi, of course I don't think that,'' Rion said hastily, responding to the air of painful disappointment which Jovvi exuded like an odor. ''I didn't mean to hurt your feelings, but this is all so very important to me. You four and she comprise the very fabric of my existence, and to think there might be a reason for your not getting along. . . .''

"The only possible reason would be if she were lying to you and leading you on for her own purposes,'' Jovvi said rather more firmly when it was clear that Rion couldn't go on. "In that event she would be the enemy of all of us, but if she isn't an enemy then she's your beloved—and because of that, also one of us. Doubt will harm all our relationships, Rion, so we owe it to ourselves—and to Naran—to find out for certain."

"You're right, of course," Rion agreed, his voice now almost toneless with tragedy. "I love her so deeply that it never occurred to me to doubt the reason for her attraction, but now . . . My love remains the same, but the boring insect of doubt now eats away at the heart of that love. . . ."

"So we'll just have to kill the doubt with truth," Jovvi said briskly. "I think we ought to use our Blending to get Naran into the house if we can, but I'm somewhat nervous about using it to question her. We don't yet know what we're doing with it—not to mention what we might be capable of—and the last thing we'd want to do is hurt the girl. What do the rest of you think?"

"I think we need to find out what we're capable of, and that as quickly as possible," Lorand mused. "I agree that it would hardly be wise to experiment on Naran, but the longer we delay learning about our Blending, the more of a disadvantage we're at."

"But we can't simply plunge ahead without knowin' where we're goin'," Vallant pointed out. "A seaman learns how unwise that is when his vessel is torn apart on hidden reefs. Isn't there some way we can get charts tellin' us which way clear sailin' lies? Somebody has to know."

"The only ones who know aren't likely to tell us," I reminded him. "Unless we can figure out a way to kidnap one of the present Seated Five and force him or her to talk, we're just going to have to manage this on our own."

"Kidnappin'," Vallant mused, those very light eyes directly on me. "Now that's an idea . . ."

"But not a very practical one," Rion said, clearly forcing himself to participate. "Each member of the Blending is always surrounded by guards when they come out of the palace, and when they're inside the guards are on the grounds and three deep in the halls. It's a marvelous idea, but as I said, not very practical."

"And there's no guarantee that the members of the present Five actually know what we're searching for," Jovvi suggested. "If our suspicions are true and they were chosen for their place rather than having won it, they might know almost as little as we do. Why don't we Blend again, and then see if we can make any headway?"

The idea of that perked us all up, and as I put my cup of tea aside before starting to move into my assigned place, I had to suppress a surge of eager excitement. I very much wanted to Blend again, but even beyond that, time was passing. In just a little while we'd know the truth about Naran after we'd practiced as a Blending, and then it would be time to go to bed again. . . .

THIRTY-ONE

Lorand followed behind Jovvi as Jovvi lined up behind Tamrissa, each of them being very careful of his or her spacing. Vallant and Rion were also doing the same, and the air of excitement among them was almost thick enough to touch.

"One of the things we have to find out about is just how necessary this formation is," Jovvi said when everyone was in place. "I have the strangest feeling about it, but that's for later. Right now I'm about to close my eyes, touch the power lightly, and reach out to the rest of you."

Lorand closed his own eyes and opened a bit to the power, and then Jovvi's touch was there. He returned it almost automatically, at the same time reaching to the others, and in the next instant they'd Blended again. It all happened so fast that it was breathtaking, but one . . . layer, so to speak, of Lorand's mind remained capable of a cool assessment. To that layer it was clear that his connections to the other men through Jovvi were solid and complete, as was his connection to Tamrissa and, through her, to Rion. But his bond to Vallant through Tamrissa was definitely weaker than all the others, which proved that the ladies had been right about intimacy.

I apologize for having made a fuss earlier about lying with Jovvi, the Vallant part of their Blended entity sent to everyone else. *I wasn't able to feel a difference the first time we Blended, but now there's no doubt. My bond to Lorand and Rion is much stronger through Jovvi, which means we still aren't entirely complete.*

But by tomorrow we will be, Tamrissa put in while Lorand felt amusement over the lack of Vallant's usual drawl in his thoughts. *Right now, though, I just want to fly again.*

Lorand thought that that was a very fine way to describe the soaring sensation he felt. It *was* like flying, although when he paid stricter attention he noticed that at most they were floating somewhere above where they'd formerly stood. And where the others still stood. He could see them there in front of him, spread out just the way they were supposed to be, an odd winking glow about each of them—

I've just noticed that I'm looking at everyone, but I haven't opened my eyes, Lorand told the others, the solidness of their presence all around him cushioning the shock of his discovery. *Are the rest of you doing the same? Does anyone have his or her eyes open?*

First unified agreement came, followed immediately by amazement. They *were* all able to see around them, but none of them had opened their eyes.

I wonder just how far this ability extends, the Tamrissa part of them mused. *Do you think we'd be able to float outside, for instance, without going there physically?*

I, for one, would enjoy trying, the Rion part of them agreed at once. *The outer air calls to me as never before.*

I sense a danger in doing that, their Jovvi part put in just as quickly before Lorand might add his own agreement. *I suggest that we move our awareness only a short distance from our bodies, and then see what there is to observe.*

Jovvi's sense of caution now filled Lorand just as Tamrissa's eagerness had a moment ago. He joined the others in agreeing to the suggestion, then agreed to a trial distance of approximately five feet. Once the agreement was complete their combined awareness floated over to the windows, where it paused to look around again.

This is delightful, but really strange, their Tamrissa part sent, her enjoyment not simply clear, but shared. *I feel very free, but I'm also aware of a ... line of sorts linking me to my body. It would be possible to disconnect the line, but for some reason that doesn't feel like the right thing to do.*

That ... line seems to be the extension of your consciousness, their Jovvi part sent, along with a sense of struggle related to understanding. *I recognize my own easily enough, but wasn't able to see the part about disconnecting until you mentioned it. Can you feel what I get about that?*

Even as the thought came, Lorand felt a strong sense of alarm. Just as Tamrissa had shared the knowledge about disconnecting, Jovvi now shared the feeling that disconnection would be certain death. Her hold on her own "line" was extremely secure, as Lorand's became as soon as he was aware of the need.

Disconnecting would be to sever ourselves from our bodies, their Vallant part sent, putting into mind words what Lorand now knew to be the truth. *After that we would float away completely, losing all touch with the way back. After a while our bodies would die, and then so would our minds. How do I know all that?*

You know it because I do, the Jovvi part responded. *Once the question came up, the answer became perfectly clear. It's too bad that all our questions can't be answered like this, but I suspect that this one relates to my talent. Now that we've all strengthened our ties to our bodies, what shall we do next?*

Lorand considered her question as he looked around, finding the sight of his unmoving body vaguely amusing. People spoke about being in two places at once, but no one he knew had ever actually accomplished it. Then he noticed something odd which immediately became three odd things, so he decided to ask about them.

Why am I seeing those strange patterns in the air? he put. *They also seem to be inside our bodies, but only in tiny bits and pieces. But now I see one of those patterns spread widely through us, along with something like a reddish smudge. What is all that?*

The others seemed to exclaim and chuckle both at the same time, a conglomeration of reactions mixed up like differently colored swirls of paint. It took Lorand's mind a long moment to separate the swirls, but once it did he had his answer: he now saw things the way his Blendingmates did when they touched the power. He saw Rion's sense of air patterns and Vallant's sense of water, in the air and in their bodies. The reddish smudge was body heat, the contribution of Tamrissa's talent. There were currently no emotions to be sensed in the bodies they'd left behind, but Lorand suddenly understood that their mental rapport was through Jovvi's talent.

It feels so odd to know the exact composition of the furniture and decorations in this room, Rion sent with a delighted chuckle. *I'd had no idea that different materials had very different . . . vibrations.*

Or that the composition of each material supplied the details of how it might best be taken apart, Tamrissa added with her own enjoyment. *We're actually seeing the world with all five of the talents.*

I have the feeling we can do better, Jovvi mused into the general sense of delight. *It seems as if our Blending should be a single entity without individual parts, rather than the partial sharing we're now accomplishing. Let's all lean into it a bit more, and then see what happens.*

Lorand knew exactly what she meant and shared the need to find out more about their situation. The others felt the same, he could tell, so all of them . . . moved closer at precisely the same time. There was a moment of disorientation, and then—

And then the WE become ONE. One Blended mind made up of five talents, a true single entity without awareness of division. The entity checked the individual lines to its separate bodies, found them secure, and so turned its attention to what lay beyond the windows it floated near. Curiosity became motion, and floating through the wall proved not difficult in the least.

Outside the world was filled with life, but much of it slept in the wraparound darkness. The entity noted all that life in passing as it floated around toward the front of the house. It knew it could have moved a good deal faster than it was doing, but caution continued to prevail. It was wiser to walk before trying to run, to float slowly before flying with the wind. And the wind was there as an awareness rather than as a sensation, as was the heat and cold of temperature. The entity knew all there was to know about those things, but felt neither heat nor cold nor buffeting. The entity realized that was most likely due to the lack of a body, which was currently a fortunate lack.

And then the entity's attention was taken by the sense of awareness coming from four separate sources. It had floated to the front of the house and down the drive, and now hovered close to the street. To the left of the drive and on the opposite side of the street was a coach containing two of the awarenesses. Both were male and both were bored, despite the game of cards they played. Every few minutes one or the other looked out the window, to eye with suspicion something that stood to the right of the drive.

The something was a carriage which contained the other two awarenesses, one male and one female. The male awareness sat patiently and almost without thought on the carriage's driver's seat, and the female huddled inside with her thoughts in turmoil. Worry threaded through every aspect of the turmoil, increasing both when she looked down the street to the coach, and when she glanced toward the house the entity had come from.

Naran, the entity thought, and spears of love combined with many varied visions flashed for a brief instant through its awareness. *And she's early*.

The entity realized that the Naran awareness *was* early, and also that she raised up now and again to search the street behind her carriage. She was definitely aware of being observed, and seemed to be dreading the arrival of some nameless horror. The entity felt her inward shiver, and abruptly decided on a course of action.

The first part of that was to return to the awarenesses in the coach and put them to sleep. Part of the entity felt surprise at how easily that was accomplished. But the surprise was short lived and vanished quickly, especially when the same was done to the carriage driver.

And then it was the woman Naran that the entity touched, sending her into a state of floating much like its own. The contact was difficult to maintain, however, so relevant questions had to be put rather quickly.

Are you working in any way for the testing authority or the Advisors? the entity inquired.

"No, I would never work for those people," the woman answered dreamily in a whisper. "They're stupid as well as corrupt, and have no idea that they're destroying themselves along with us."

What are your true feelings about Rion? the entity put next, ignoring the faint reluctance it felt to hear that answer.

"He is the love of my life, and I was born to be his other half," came the response, accompanied by a smile. "I would happily do anything for him, even accede to his insistence and put him in danger. If that pig should ever try to harm him because of me, I would certainly find a way to kill the beast. He can't know what I know, after all. . . ."

Her words trailed off, and the frown she'd grown changed to a faint smile. She was under a compulsion to speak the truth, and even beyond that the entity knew for certain that she voiced no lie. There were no other questions that needed to be put at the moment, so the entity broke its connection to her with a great deal of relief, then put her to sleep as it had the others. Then the entity began the next phase of its plan. It moved back quickly to the house, caused the front door to unlock, then used hardened air to open the door. Once that was done it was possible to move the woman's belongings out of the carriage, all of it borne along either on hardened air or solidly frozen water. It was necessary to take the belongings up to the second floor the long and difficult way, and once they were deposited in an empty bedchamber, another discovery was made.

The awareness in the house which had been watching the

hall before it was coaxed into sleep had awakened, and now sat frightened and stunned at having seen what appeared to be luggage moving itself. The entity touched the mind of that awareness, whispered the command to forget what it had already seen or might see in the future, then left the awareness more solidly asleep than it had been.

After opening the door to the sitting room where its bodies stood, the entity returned to the carriage much more quickly than it had come. It was now time to move the woman herself, and the entity discovered that it was able to take strength from more than one source to form a bed of solidified air to carry her on. But not all the strength available was used for that purpose. One definite segment of the entity was on guard against attack and prepared to launch an attack of its own, and the augmented strength of that segment was not to be diverted.

What remained, however, was more than enough. The woman was borne carefully into the house and up to the second floor, where she was deposited gently on a couch. After that the entity had only to visit the awarenesses in the coach and order them to forget what they'd seen, then rouse the carriage driver and send him on his way. He, too, was commanded to forget, both the woman who had been in his carriage and the place he'd taken her. With that final chore completed the entity returned to the house, relocked the front door, closed the sitting room door, and—

"Oof!" Lorand breathed as he suddenly found himself back in his body. His muscles seemed to ache everywhere, his hands felt shaky, he was close to exhaustion, and he had the impression that he'd returned just in time. He tottered to a chair and dropped into it, aware that the others were doing the same, and tried to think about what had happened.

Of all the incredible experiences! If Rion's Naran hadn't been there on the couch, fast asleep, Lorand might have begun to wonder if he hadn't been imagining things . . . and come to that, there was one last thing he had to do. . . .

THIRTY-TWO

"I think we made it back just in time," I heard Jovvi say in a strengthless voice as I tried to pull myself together in the chair I'd fallen into. "It didn't seem like it at the time, but we must have pushed ourselves too far."

"I feel just as I did after that very first test we were put through," Rion panted from where he lay on the carpeting. "I haven't even the strength to find a proper place to sit."

"And I feel like I've been liftin' bales of steel all by myself," Vallant contributed from where he sprawled on a couch next to Jovvi. "Physically drained as well as almost strengthless in talent. Not exactly the same as it's been until now."

"Lorand hasn't said anything," I pointed out, "but I think that's because he isn't in any condition to. All of you agree, and I find that odd. I'm tired as well, not to mention how my legs and back hurt, but I'm not nearly that close to exhaustion."

"I think that's because your strength wasn't drawn on fully," Jovvi forced herself to say. "I remember a thought about not tapping our defense and attack capability and thereby weakening it. Does anyone else remember the same?"

The men made sounds of agreement, and I added my own because now I did remember. I was the one who guarded us, so my strength wasn't taken. I felt a twinge of nervousness over that, but before I could mention it someone else spoke up.

"What's happened to me?" a female voice asked in confusion. "Where have I been taken? What—my lord!"

I'd looked over to see Naran sitting up on the couch she'd been put on, fright paling her skin. She'd been looking around wildly, but when she saw Rion lying on the floor, she struggled off the couch in a welter of skirts and hurried over to kneel beside him.

"Fear not, my love, we've merely brought you into the house," Rion said with weak reassurance as she lifted his head to her lap. "I apologize for the method used, as we had no intention of behaving so. It merely . . . happened."

"That's completely unimportant," Naran said firmly, stroking his face and hair. "What isn't unimportant is how you fare. Why do you lie here on the floor, looking pale as bleached linen? How have you been hurt?"

"I'm not hurt, Naran, simply exhausted." Rion even managed a smile, although a faint one. "We're all exhausted, but please don't ask for details. It's not something we're able to speak about at this time."

She made a sound of concern and held him even more tightly, but that wasn't doing any good for anything but his morale. What he and the others needed was some tangible assistance, so I got myself out of the chair and went over to the tea service. As usual two cups had been provided, so I quickly finished the tea I'd poured earlier, then filled both cups. It took very little effort to warm the tea enough to dissolve sugar in it, and then I carried one of the cups to Naran.

"Help him drink every drop of this while I give the other to Jovvi, and then we'll do the same for Lorand and Vallant," I told her. "If we don't help them to get some strength back, we'll have to carry them all to bed."

Rather than ask any silly questions about who I was and what I was talking about, she simply nodded in a businesslike way and took the cup. That left me free to go over to Jovvi, and by the time I'd helped her drink the tea, Naran had finished with Rion. It amused me that she'd taken the trouble to replace her lap with a pillow from the couch she'd awakened on, and Rion looked perfectly comfortable stretched out on the floor.

"I'm adding extra sugar to go along with the stimulant of the tea itself," I explained as I joined Naran at the service. "The effects won't last long, but hopefully long enough to get them moving. You'll have to put that cup down, or the sudden heat might cause you to drop it.''

''A heat that could very well touch my fingers as well as the tea,'' she agreed with a smile, putting the cup down. ''I remember when my grandmother did that to me once, when I was a very little girl. It upset her for days that she'd accidentally hurt me, even though I got over the minor singeing in just a few minutes.''

I smiled my thanks without correcting her, wondering if she hadn't seen my master's bracelet or simply didn't know what it was. People with a Low talent in Fire magic usually had very little control, as control took practice and Low talents rarely bothered. I'd never burned anyone by accident in my life, but if I were the group's protection, I might have to do it on purpose. . . .

''That's Lorand over there,'' I said with a gesture once the two cups of tea were ready. ''Rion and Jovvi are already beginning to stir, so let's get the last of them. I'm Tamrissa, by the way.''

She acknowledged that with a shy smile and a nod, obviously knowing I already knew her name, and started toward Lorand. I took my own cup over to Vallant, who opened his eyes when I sat down next to him.

''It's almost worth feelin' like this to have you sit this close,'' he murmured, those very light eyes filled with amusement. ''I can't remember you ever doin' it before.''

''I never helped make you half dead before,'' I countered weakly, wishing it were possible to learn how not to blush. ''Stop talking silliness and drink this.''

His grin was brief but very amused, and the way he kept those eyes on my face while he drank served to divert me from chilling thoughts of having to burn people on purpose. Instead I was pulled into thoughts of what he and I would soon be sharing, and a shiver of a different sort coursed through me.

''Your excellent idea seems to be working, Tamma,'' Jovvi said just as Vallant was finishing the last of the tea. ''I think I actually have enough strength now to get the blood flowing in my veins again.''

I glanced over to see that she'd straightened where she sat, and the color had come back to her face. Rion was now climbing slowly to his feet, but only to move to the couch where Naran had been, where he sat heavily. He, too, looked better, and his smile improved him even more when Naran finished helping Lorand and went to sit beside him.

"I'd say we learned an important lesson just now," Jovvi went on. "We ignored the signal telling us we were over-doing it, and almost caused ourselves serious damage. Next time we'll have to—"

"Signal?" I interrupted, finding myself lost. "I don't remember anything like a signal, so you'll have to explain what you're talking about."

"I don't remember a signal, either," Rion put in with a frown, his arm about Naran's shoulders. "Were Tamrissa and I the only ones excluded?"

"You can add me to the list," Lorand said from the chair he still sprawled in. "I wasn't aware of anything that could be considered a signal."

"And me," Vallant agreed. "Nothin' like a signal reached me."

"Then the fault was mine alone," Jovvi said with a frown from her place to my left. "I assumed everyone felt the same, but apparently I'm the one who's supposed to watch over our well-being. Even as a small part of what we were I could feel the strain, the growing demand that we stop and go back. Next time I'll know enough to let the awareness spread, so . . . WE can know everything that's happening."

"I wish *I* knew what was happening, but I think I'm afraid to ask," Naran offered in a small voice. "You're all so close, I can feel that like some tangible, solid presence. Am I intruding here? If I am, I'll be more than willing to leave again. . . ."

"After what we went through to get you in here?" Lorand asked immediately with a sound of ridicule while Rion showed sudden worry. "If you decided to leave now, I'd probably break down and cry."

"And I'd be cryin' with you for sure," Vallant said at once as he straightened up on the couch beside me. "But we men are the delicate, sensitive sort. I've got to warn you that our ladies won't be cryin'."

"Stop trying to frighten her, Vallant," Jovvi said with

amusement before moving her gaze to Naran. "Tamma and I aren't the steel hard monsters he's suggesting we are, but even more importantly we understand how you feel. We all are closer than any group you've ever known, but you have to remember that Rion is one of us. As important as you are to him, that's almost as important as you are to us. We don't regret the effort we put into bringing you inside, we just wish we'd been more cautious in expending our strength."

"I've just realized something," Naran said slowly, her expression odd. "I should have seen it sooner, of course, but you simply don't expect— That identification Rion wore when he and I first met . . . I barely glanced at it, but obviously I should have looked closer. You're all members of one of the challenging Blendings, aren't you? You might even become the next Seated Five. Oh, my goodness—!"

"Naran, please don't tell me that it makes a difference in how you feel!" Rion said miserably, flinching at the awed look in her eyes. "We're the same people we were when you and I last met, so please don't begin to think that anything has changed."

"But of course it's changed," she denied, now gazing at him longingly. "You're so very important, and I'm completely insignificant. I'd hoped our time together would be longer, but once you've won the competitions you'll be much too busy to bother with me. I don't mind that, I really don't, not when we'll have each other from now until then. Just . . . when do the competitions begin?"

"We haven't been told that yet," Rion replied with a sigh of relief, pulling her close again. "For a moment of dread I was certain you meant to say you feared me, but happily we've been spared that. You simply believe I mean to toss you aside, and time will disprove that more thoroughly than words. But do please note that our winning is by no means guaranteed. Instead of joining us in the palace of the Five, you may well have to join us when we run for our lives."

"Oh, but of course you'll win," she said quickly, putting a gentle hand to his face. "Don't let that worry you even for a moment. . . . I'm . . . really certain, so please don't feel disturbed. It gives me pain to see your face creased with frown lines.''

And then she began to massage his face slowly and gently with her fingers, a fierce look of dedicated concentration on her own face. With the crisis over I tried to exchange a glance with Jovvi, but Jovvi seemed wrapped up in private thoughts. Or in the midst of drifting off to sleep, which was more than possible.

''Now seems to be the time to send all of you back to where you belong,'' I announced as I stood. ''We have to be as rested as possible when our visitor—or visitors—arrive tomorrow—I mean, later today. Oh, you all know what I mean.''

''What you mean is that you're almost as tired and befuddled as we are,'' Lorand replied as he pushed himself to his feet. ''May I have the honor of walking you to your door, Dama Hafford?''

''Only if you expect me sleep at my door,'' Jovvi answered dryly as she took the hand Lorand extended to help her off the couch. ''I seriously doubt that I can make it all the way to my bed by myself.''

''Then I would be a cad if I left you at the door,'' he said, looking down into her eyes. ''Perish the thought that I would ever be a cad.''

Jovvi sent a smile to match the one he now showed, and they moved together toward the door to the hall. By now Rion and Naran were also up and moving, his arm around her shoulders as he pretended to lean on her. I say ''pretended'' because she could no more have really supported him than Jovvi or I could have. Naran didn't seem to know that, though, or maybe she had higher expectations of her physical strength. As they moved out into the hall, I heard her urge him in a whisper to lean on her as heavily as he needed to.

''That was nicely done,'' Vallant said, and when I turned from closing the door behind those who had left, I saw that he'd managed to stand. ''Now let's help each other to your bed.''

That stupid blush flamed in my cheeks again, but I had no intention of letting anything interfere with the time I'd so been looking forward to. I approached him slowly and offered my hand, and his bigger one swallowed it up. But gently and softly, like a cotton net over a butterfly. And then I was actually leading him to my bedchamber, just as I'd dreamed about a hundred times.

We paused near the bed to share a brief kiss, and it quickly became very obvious that standing up was far from easy for him. So I suggested that he disrobe while I used the comfort facility, and then he could do the same before we settled down. He agreed with a smile before giving me another fleeting kiss, then began to move around to the side of the bed. At the last instant I grabbed a wrap to take into the comfort facility with me, to keep from having to walk naked to the bed. I still didn't feel quite up to that, and knew I would probably blush more than enough without adding to the situation.

I would swear it never took me longer to undress in my life, although objectively speaking it probably wasn't any longer than usual. It was just that all objectivity was well out of my reach, displaced by wild impatience and anticipation. If I hadn't been so nervously intense I would have been able to forget about emptying my bladder, but that choice wasn't possible. So I waited the months and years it took to relieve myself, rinsed my hands and pulled the wrap on, then *finally* hurried back to the bed.

"Vallant, it's your turn," I said softly, climbing onto the bed next to him. He lay on his back under the quilts with his eyes closed, but that broad, magnificent chest was fully exposed. Resting while he was able was a marvelous idea, but the time for rest was over. "Vallant, when you get back I'll be right here waiting for you."

I put my hand to his bare shoulder, expecting those very blue eyes to open with a smile, but nothing happened. No smile and no eyes opening, which quickly began to upset me.

"Vallant, please don't tease," I asked, shaking his shoulder a bit. "You have no idea how long I've been waiting. . . . Please stop pretending to be asleep."

The shoulder under my hand barely moved to the shaking, and the rest of him didn't move at all. Instead I noticed how deep and slow his breathing was, adding to the image of a man lost to exhausted sleep. He wasn't teasing and he wasn't pretending; he'd really fallen asleep.

I sat back on my side of the bed, bitterly staring at a wall. After all that waiting and anticipating, I now had a dead body sharing my bed. In another moment or two I would replace the wrap with a nightgown, turn down all the lamps in the apartment, then lie down to sleep myself, but first. . . .

First I had to decide between crying my eyes out and smashing everything breakable within reach. . . .

THIRTY-THREE

Despite a late night, Delin rose earlier than usual. He sat at his writing desk for a short while, then searched out his carriage driver in the servants' quarters. Giving the man the sealed envelope he'd prepared and saying it was to be delivered to Timbal was all that was necessary. His driver had done the same more than once before, and had learned long ago not to ask impertinent questions.

The servants were just setting out the breakfast buffet when Delin entered the dining room, so he took a cup of tea to the table to wait for them to finish. The note he'd sent to Timbal, instructing the sleazy little man to see to the anonymous delivery of the letter accompanying his note, would be obeyed without delay—and without the unauthorized opening of the letter. Delin had used the little guttersnipe for years to see to errands he didn't care to be associated with, and he'd long ago taught the man what would happen if he pried too deeply into the affairs of his betters.

So Delin wasn't concerned over the possibility of his

letter being seen by the wrong eyes, but that didn't mean he was *un*concerned. The letter contained the triggering phrase that would be used against the first peasants who were to face Adriari and her group, the peasants who had been in blue and silver the night of the ball at the palace. He'd originally meant to send them the triggering phrase almost as soon as he'd discovered it, then he'd found himself with second thoughts.

Second thoughts had led to third, mostly suspicion over how wise that course of action really was. The peasants would be freed of almost all restraint, and the information his own group had about them might prove insufficient when it became time to face them. He'd decided to think about it a bit more, but then his exultation had gotten the better of him. Between the Blending they'd managed yesterday and the elimination of his greatest enemy, Delin had recklessly ignored all thoughts of caution and had sent the letter.

"Which I don't really regret doing, despite feeling uneasy," he muttered to his cup of tea. The servants were no longer in the room, so he was able to speak to whatever he pleased. "You can't keep making decisions then changing your mind, not if you intend to retain the leadership of those around you, so I won't change my mind. I just wish I were filled with fewer misgivings. . . ."

"Well, good morning," a voice came, and Delin looked up to see an almost unrecognizably bright-eyed Bron entering the room. "I expected to be first in for breakfast this morning, but you've beaten me to it. Even though you haven't actually taken any breakfast yet."

Bron's good mood and gentle humor were almost as shocking as his appearance at that time of the morning. Not only wasn't the Fire magic user sullen, he was actually dressed in clothing rather than a wrap. Delin sipped his tea, wondering if it were possible for one to nearly burn one's tongue on hot tea in a dream, and then the situation was made even worse.

"Good morning, good morning," Homin sang out as he and Selendi entered hand in hand, both of them looking just as wide awake as Bron did. "We decided we wanted to know what breakfast tastes like when it hasn't been kept warm for hours.''

Predictably, Selendi laughed at that, but unexpectedly so did Bron. That went even further to convince Delin that he was dreaming, but the absence of one of their number kept the dream scene from being complete.

"If this were real, Kambil would have shown up before you three," Delin pointed out, then had to ignore their renewed laughter. "I'm perfectly serious. Since Kambil isn't here, I must be dreaming."

"A servant told me that Kambil left instructions not to be disturbed until twenty minutes before Lord Idian is due," Bron supplied with a chuckle as he filled a plate. "He was really tired last night, and obviously wants to restore his strength before we Blend for Lord Idian. For the first time."

That last was added so blandly that Delin was amazed all over again. *Bron*, being circumspect? Obviously Delin had underestimated his own leadership abilities; he now knew himself to be extraordinary, considering the changes in Bron, Homin, and Selendi. They were all following him and learning, so the least he could do was follow them for once.

"I can see it's time that I ate as well," he said, rising and walking to the place behind Homin, who had urged Selendi to the buffet ahead of him. "It will never do if I faltered during our efforts, simply because my mind was on a rare beefsteak and whipped potatoes instead of on business. Is the bacon underdone or overdone?"

Bron assured him that the bacon was just perfect, and so it turned out to be. Delin discovered a rather large appetite, probably stemming from the exertions of the night, and happily took care of it. The meal was punctuated with occasional light and pleasant conversation, and afterward they took additional tea in the large sitting room. Rather than despising the company of his groupmates as he had done in the past, Delin found himself actually enjoying the time. At long last they were a unified group, undoubtedly thanks to the Blending they'd managed.

It was nearly time for Lord Idian to arrive when Kambil

appeared. The big man still looked faintly tired, but his smile of greeting was full of warmth.

"If I didn't know better, I'd think I was dreaming," he announced as he headed toward the tea service. "Everyone here and ready before me? Definitely a dream."

Even Delin had to laugh at that, so similar was the comment to what he'd been thinking and saying earlier.

"Delin said almost the same exact thing," Selendi commented as she watched Kambil pour a cup of tea. "Is that all you're going to have for breakfast? If you like, I'll have the cook throw something together for you."

"I had a plate brought up by the servant who woke me, and I ate while I dressed," Kambil said, then turned with his teacup in his hands and a wider smile on his face. "But I appreciate the thought, and thank you for the offer."

"Well, we do have to look after one another now," she responded, for all the world like a shy, virgin schoolgirl. "And I like looking after Homin so well that I thought I might try branching out. 'Mama Selendi' has a certain ring to it. . . ."

That time everyone laughed, Selendi first among them. The closeness and warmth reached to a part of Delin which had never stopped wanting something like this: membership in a group which was his while he was theirs. No wonder the Advisors limited the number of people who knew how to Blend. If something like this ever became available to everyone, who would bother to fight for governmental positions and social standing?

"Lords and Lady, Lord Idian," a servant announced, and then Idian was nodding a greeting and making his way to the chair he'd used yesterday. Once he'd seated himself, he looked around at them.

"I bid you a good morning, young gentlefolk," he said in a mildly firm voice. "As you are all here and properly attired, we may begin at once. Take your formation places, please."

At another time Delin might have felt insult over being treated with such abruptness, but this morning was a special time. They would Blend "for the first time" in front of Idian, and thereafter would be free to do the same again at any time they pleased. Bron stepped forward briskly to establish the mark they would all measure from, and Kambil left his cup of tea to line up next. Delin brought up the rear as Selendi and Homin placed themselves to either side of Kambil, and then they were ready.

"At last you show a proper amount of enthusiasm," Lord Idian commented with dry satisfaction. "If it continues, you may actually manage to make it work. Spirit magic begins by reaching out to everyone else, and everyone else must attempt to return the touch."

This time Kambil's touch came instantly, and Delin returned it in just the same way. Once connected, Delin saw that the others had done the same, and so he reached out in three additional directions. . . .

"I take it from the young lady's gasp that you've been successful," Lord Idian said, more than simply commenting as he leaned forward a bit. "Are we discussing just the first attachment to Spirit, or have you accomplished Blending?"

"We have become one," Delin said, and only then discovered that the others spoke at the same time he did. "What would you have us do next?"

"I would have you withdraw from the Blending, and that immediately," Lord Idian replied, his tone having sharpened. "There are cautions you have not yet been given, and you must have this information before you begin experimentation. Withdraw, I say, and then find yourself seats."

The WE Delin was a part of wanted nothing to do with separation, but one part of the WE was extremely tired and shaky. Some of that unsteadiness came from him, Delin knew, and possibly even all of it. It was unthinkable that he might damage that glorious WE, so he withdrew instead back to the chill loneliness he'd known for all of his life.

"Excellent," Lord Idian said as their formation relaxed and they all took deep breaths. "You are to be congratulated, young friends, for achieving what many considered well beyond you. Please take seats now, for there are things you must be told."

Kambil was the least bit unsteady as he returned for the teacup he'd abandoned before going to a chair, and Delin knew exactly how he felt. The Blending had been in existence for mere seconds, but drained was a mild way of describing his condition. So he, too, poured a cup of tea, and carried it to a chair he didn't quite fall into.

"To begin with, young friends, you must know that Blending is extremely draining on the systems of those involved," Lord Idian began once Delin was seated. "If one or more of you have not had a proper amount of rest, the strength of the others will be used to activate and maintain the Blending, leaving little or nothing to be used to other purpose. To come to the formation less than fully rested and adequately fed is to waste everyone's time and effort."

No one actually looked at Delin when they heard that, but they didn't have to. Delin hid his shame behind the pretense of sipping at his tea, his resolve to do better in the future solidifying to the strength of a vow.

"When you first begin to practice, you must keep the sessions short and be extremely vigilant," Lord Idian continued. "Although you won't believe it at the time, the judgment of a Blending cannot be relied on. Ideas will come to your joint minds, but to follow through on them will be to put yourselves in extreme danger. I will provide a list of proper exercises, which will more than prepare you for the competitions. And there's one final thing."

He paused to look around at them, his gaze resting on each of their faces. Suspicion had flared in Delin's weary mind, but it had been many years since his true feelings could be read in his expression.

"There will come a time of temptation which you must resist at all cost," Lord Idian pronounced as he continued to look from one to the other of them. "Once you become used to Blending, you will eventually feel the urge to . . . go even farther. What this farther point is I couldn't tell you, nor can anyone else who has reached for it. It somehow . . . *draws* the members of a Blending in deep, and at some point refuses to release them again. They end up . . . unmoving and unfeeling, trapped in a vortex outside their bodies. If you ignore this advice, on your heads be it."

Delin frowned at such callous disregard for their well-being, watching poor Selendi shudder against a worried-looking Homin. Bron and Kambil seemed just as disturbed, and the group reaction made Lord Idian nod in satisfaction.

"It relieves me to see all of you taking my caution so

seriously," he said, obviously gathering himself to stand. "There are stories about a Blending from the last competitions, whose members ignored the warning. I shudder every time I think about them, and fervently hope that nothing of the same occurs *this* time. . . . I'll have the list of exercises sent over a bit later, and tomorrow I will watch you perform one or two of them. Until tomorrow, then."

By that time Lord Idian was on his feet, but Kambil spoke up before the man might depart.

"It was surprising to see you without Rigos again, but somehow not entirely unexpected," Kambil put gently with the hint of pain in his voice. "Do things . . . continue to go badly for him? I've known him for years, and I almost feel as though I've . . . betrayed him in some way."

"At the moment, young Lord Rigos is in the process of betraying himself," Lord Idian returned stiffly. "I waited for his arrival this morning and finally was forced to leave alone. Neither Rigos nor any explanation or excuse has thus far reached me, which puts me very much out of patience with the young fool. If I should fail to hear from him by tonight, tomorrow morning I shall demand that he be replaced."

With that Lord Idian turned and left, marching out as though going to Rigos's hanging. Delin felt a wave of enjoyment sweep through him at the thought of Rigos cooperating with his own destruction, and that despite the stab of disappointment which he also felt. Lord Ollon's body should have already been discovered . . . unless the madman had found a reason to dismiss all his servants. . . .

"Thank you," Delin heard Kambil say, and he looked up to see a servant in the doorway who bowed briefly before disappearing. "He was asked to tell me when Lord Idian's carriage pulled away, which apparently it now has. Would anyone like to comment on what we were told?"

"The idea of that . . . vortex really frightens me," Selendi said simply and openly. "It may be because I sensed . . . *something* beyond our Blended state, and was tempted for a moment to find out what it was."

"I felt the same something, and also the same temptation," Bron put in thoughtfully. "I don't remember noticing it yesterday, but today it was perfectly clear."

"And I can make it three," Homin said in agreement, equally sobered. "Not yesterday, but definitely today. What about you and Delin, Kambil?"

Delin nodded to show that it had also been the same for him, though more vaguely than definitely. His weariness had apparently cut into his strength rather severely, he thought, and then Kambil confirmed the surmise.

"I'm still too tired to be at my sharpest, so I only just noticed what the rest of you felt so clearly," he said. "But believe it or not, the discovery isn't what interests me most. I do happen to have enough strength left to know that Lord Idian was lying through his teeth."

Delin exclaimed aloud along with the others, his suspicions flaring again like a beacon. He'd *known* there was something wrong with what they were being told, he'd known it for certain!

"I suppose they were counting on me being too distracted by having Blended for the first time to pay full attention to our mentor," Kambil went on. "And they also think we haven't noticed that something yet, so they're poisoning our minds against it before we do. There's no danger of a 'vortex,' and there are no chilling stories handed down from the last competitions. The only truth he spoke was about how draining Blending is, and that we all need to be well rested."

"I'll bet Adriari's group isn't being told any fairy tales," Bron growled, clearly verbalizing what all the rest of them thought. "They're obviously trying to keep us limited in what we can do, to be certain we don't become a real threat to their plans."

"Isn't it a shame that they haven't succeeded?" Homin said with an edge to his voice that Delin had never heard before. "I'm absolutely crushed on their behalf, and incidentally can't wait to see that list of 'permissible' exercises."

"I got the impression of limitation rather than exercise," Kambil said after sipping at his tea, "which means you're right to be suspicious, Homin. They need us to perform in the competitions, but they don't want us to become too strong or effective. It's a very fine line that they're walking, and we should be able to slip by while their attention is on where they put their feet.''

''Am I mistaken, or was Lord Idian really surprised when we Blended for him?'' Delin asked through a haze of fury. ''He said something about people not believing we could do it . . . Worthless little nothings actually doubting *us* . . . !''

''I discovered yesterday that the other groups—not counting Adriari's, of course—Blended on the first try,'' Kambil said gently. ''I didn't pass on the information because I didn't care to put additional pressure on everyone, and also because I felt convinced that we, too, would be successful. I don't know what they would have done if we hadn't managed it . . . Possibly sent us in anyway, under orders to *pretend*.''

''Not managing to Blend wouldn't have saved us,'' Selendi said, as serious as Homin had been. ''As long as we had the details about *how* to Blend buried somewhere in our heads, we'd still be a threat to the Advisors. Not to mention still being unwanted by our families. No, winning the competitions is still the only thing we can do.''

Delin was tempted to feel stunned again that *Selendi* had actually said that, but pride pushed forward too strongly. He'd done it, he'd really gotten through to his groupmates, and from now on everything would work out perfectly.

''Which means we need to begin real practicing,'' Kambil said after draining his cup and then putting it aside. ''I'd love to begin at once, but common sense insists that I get more rest first. I'm going back to bed, and I strongly suggest that any of you who feels the least weariness should follow my example. By this afternoon, I'll be completely ready to go again.''

''I, for one, intend to follow your example,'' Delin said as he put his own cup aside and stood. ''Breakfast helped a bit, but my sleep was disturbed last night by all sorts of dreams. By this afternoon I, too, intend to be ready to go.''

''I'm going to make it three,'' Bron announced as he stood and stretched. ''I had a good night's sleep and felt fine when I first got up, but now the early hour must be getting to me. A nap sounds like a really good idea.''

Homin and Selendi said they weren't terribly tired, but if everyone else was going back to bed, they would do the same. Delin marveled at their unity as they all left the sitting room together, that brand new warmth touching him again. Everything would have been perfect . . . if only Lord Ollon's body had been found, and Rigos was arrested for the second and final time. . . .

THIRTY-FOUR

Lady Eltrina Razas had been enjoying herself thoroughly, until the knock came at the bedchamber door. It was the deferential knock of a servant, so she ignored it and told her current toy to continue with what he'd been doing. The dear boy had *such* knowing hands and mouth, not to mention the fact that he'd been completely ready for her for quite some time. . . .

"Rot!" Eltrina snarled when the knock came again, this time more insistent. "They're supposed to go away if I don't answer the first time. I'm not going to dismiss whoever it is, I'm going to have them drawn and quartered!"

The beautiful young man chuckled as she kissed his desire before getting out of bed, but chuckling wasn't what Eltrina felt like doing. She hadn't been joking about the drawing and quartering, and she barely had the patience to pull on a wrap before going to the door. But she was about to find out who was to blame for this intrusion, so she yanked open the door and—

"Please excuse the disturbance, my lady, but Advisory representatives are downstairs demanding to see you," Shorten, her husband's majordomo, said as quickly as possible. "I tried to tell them that the hour was much too early, but they refused to be put off."

"Give me just a moment, Shorten," Eltrina said quietly

before closing the door again. She had no idea what was going on, but when Advisory representatives "demanded" to see someone, that someone obliged or was immediately arrested. It was really bothersome, but going downstairs was preferable to being arrested.

"I'll be back in just a few minutes, so don't you go away," Eltrina said to the beautiful boy as she found a decorous nightgown to put on under the wrap. "Spend the time thinking about what you'll do next, and if I find I like it I'll buy you a present you'll adore."

The boy nodded with eagerness in his lovely eyes, so Eltrina slipped on a pair of mules and went back to the door. Shorten stood waiting patiently just outside, and when she appeared he led the way downstairs to her husband's study. Her husband wasn't in it, of course, since he was currently away on a business trip, but the two strange men who failed to rise from where they sat reminded her strongly of him.

"Lady Eltrina?" one of the two said, looking up from the papers he studied. "I'm Lord Anglard Nobin, and the Advisors speak through my voice."

"Funny, but I could have sworn that the Advisors had voices of their own," Eltrina replied dryly, strolling over to sit in a chair opposite the man. "I don't know why you're here, Lord Anglard, but you'll get a lot more accomplished if you come to the point. Wasting time with vague and childish threats is . . . a waste of time."

"Getting straight to the point suits me as well," Lord Anglard agreed without showing anything even vaguely resembling a smile. "You began as the assistant of Lord Ollon Capmar, became his mistress in a very short time, then took over his responsibilities when he . . . suffered a personal tragedy. When was the last time you lay with him? Was that also the last time you recall speaking to him?"

"The last time I spoke to him was after the . . . tragedy," Eltrina snapped, feeling the heat which had risen to her face. "That was when he asked me to take over his duties until he felt able to return to work. The rest of what you said is disgusting, and I refuse to comment on malicious rumor."

"Your prestige rose quite a bit when Lord Ollon was

incapacitated, didn't it, Lady Eltrina?'' Anglard pursued in the same cold tone. ''It was a situation you were hoping for, and one you might even have been willing to arrange. That rumor you mentioned has it that you were more than willing to make Lord Ollon's absence permanent.''

''I don't have to sit here and be insulted,'' Eltrina said as she rose from the chair, the heat in her face having turned chill. ''I don't know what you're accusing me of, and seriously doubt if *you* know. I—''

''Sit down, Lady Eltrina,'' Anglard ordered in a voice of steel. ''You will either speak to us here, or in your cell once you're arrested. Our forbearance is for your husband's position, and is merely a matter of courtesy. If you force me to it, that courtesy will be forgotten.''

Eltrina hesitated only a moment before obeying, her mind sick and wild with conjecture. How much did they really know, and how much were they simply guessing at? She *had* intended to have Ollon murdered, but since she hadn't actually gotten around to it, how much could they do to her?

''Your aspect of talent is Earth magic, I'm told,'' Anglard went on in the same chill, distant way. ''Just how strong does that talent happen to be, Lady Eltrina? Middle strength, surely, or possibly even more?''

''Are you insane?'' Eltrina whispered, no longer able to control her own voice or emotions. ''I was declared a Low talent, just like one-fifth of the rest of the people in the empire, but what can that possibly have to do with anything else? Why are you doing this to me?''

''Show me your talent, Lady Eltrina,'' Anglard commanded, ignoring her plea entirely. ''Open yourself to the power and touch me with your talent.''

Eltrina's head spun even more wildly, but very frankly she was too frightened to refuse. Everyone involved in a career played stab-in-the-back, and the only hard-and-fast rule was, Don't Get Caught. If she'd really been caught, the only thing that might possibly save her was full cooperation.

So she opened her mind to the power, and reached out gingerly to touch Anglard. She gasped when she finally accomplished it, as Anglard was stronger than anyone she had ever met.

"Yes, a Low talent beyond all doubt," Anglard said, but not to her. He spoke to the other man, who until now hadn't said a word.

"And her guilt seemed to be over plans she'd made, not over something she'd actually done," the second man broke his silence to agree. "She was a good possibility, but now we'll need to look elsewhere."

"What are you talking about?" Eltrina demanded wildly when Anglard nodded and began to gather up his papers. "What's going on here?"

"You no longer need to be disturbed, Lady Eltrina," Anglard said as he rose to his feet. "You were one of our main suspects, but now you've been cleared. And, by the way, congratulations on your advancement."

"Advancement?" Eltrina echoed, barely able to keep control of herself. "What advancement?"

"Why, to the position of permanently replacing Lord Ollon," Anglard said as he and the other man walked toward the door. "I'm certain it will be yours, now that Lord Ollon is dead."

Dead! Eltrina slumped back in stunned shock as the two men walked out without saying anything else. Ollon was dead, but . . . if *she* hadn't done it, then who had?

"Now I'm feeling marvelous," Delin announced as he joined everyone in the sitting room. "I've slept for hours and I feel like a new man."

"I'm sorry, Delin, but Kambil has already claimed the new man title," Bron informed him with a grin while everyone else chuckled. "I'm beginning to think that you two have the same person writing your passing comments for you, and whichever of you arrives first gets to speak them first."

"Say, I never thought of that," Delin returned, much too pleased to let some innocent banter disturb him. "Hiring someone to write my comments, I mean. It would certainly save me the effort of having to do it myself, and then I'd be able to avoid the fate of sounding like Kambil's echo."

"If you find someone, do let me know what his name

is, won't you, old man?'' Kambil drawled, turning away
from the tea service with a freshly poured cup. ''Just to
satisfy my curiosity, of course.''

Kambil's words had been so thickly coated with innocence that everyone began to laugh really hard, including
Delin. It was no longer possible to be angry or impatient
with those wonderful people, not since they'd Blended.
They were now part of each other, and everything said was
simply said in fun. Delin not only knew that, he was end-
lessly thankful for it.

''Hmmm. I wonder if the rest of us should also be curious,'' Bron said after a moment, glancing to Homin and
Selendi. ''That way we could say the words with them, and
correct any mistakes they might make. . . .''

That set them off again, and Delin laughed till the tears
ran down his face. Never in his life had he enjoyed himself
so much, not even when he—

''Pardon the intrusion, gentles!'' a voice said rather
loudly, as though it had tried to say the same before. Delin
joined the others in turning to the doorway, and was startled
to see Lord Idian behind the almost-shouting servant.

''You'll have to excuse this unscheduled visit, but there's
a very important reason for it,'' Idian said as he made his
way forward, gesturing at the servant to leave. ''Something
extremely upsetting has happened, and I've been asked to
inform all my people.''

Delin disliked the way Idian said ''my people'' but had
no intention of making an issue of it. This was probably
the announcement he'd been waiting for, and he intended
to enjoy every word of it.

''I know you all have reason to remember the source of
the scandal Rigos became embroiled in,'' Idian said as he
sat heavily in the same chair he'd used earlier. ''The life
which was lost belonged to your stepmother, Lord Homin,
and I'm afraid I'm now the bearer of further ill tidings.
Your late stepmother's brother, Lord Ollon Capmar, has
also been murdered.''

Delin joined everyone else as they gasped or made some
other show of surprise, and then Bron spoke up.

''You see?'' he said, looking around at everyone. ''I
knew that doing it once meant it was only a matter of time

before it was done again. They'd better have already arrested Rigos, and this time they'd better *keep* him locked up."

"Considering the fact that Rigos and Ollon made a scene at a party last night, they did indeed go to arrest him," Idian agreed as he continued to look from one to the other of them. "The major problem arising there is that they found him to be beyond arrest. After leaving orders with the servants that he wasn't to be disturbed under any circumstances, he apparently then proceeded to take his own life."

This time there was a deep, shocked silence in which Delin fully participated. Rigos had found a way to escape from the horror Delin had planned for him, and it just wasn't *fair*!

"Young Rigos apparently left a letter for his father," Idian continued after a moment. "In it he asked forgiveness for his cowardice, but he could no longer bear the accusations. Had he been guilty he could have easily accepted the blame, but as it was . . . he felt that his life was no longer worth living, as proving the truth to everyone would be impossible."

"He . . . could have been lying," Bron tried hesitantly, the words more a hope than a certainty. "He could have intended to *seem* to kill himself, but expected to be stopped or saved. Afterward people would have believed—"

"Lord Bron, he went to the bath house, entered the water, and opened his wrists with a razor," Idian interrupted to supply. "After the orders he'd given about not being disturbed, he had no hope of interruption. Special investigators were called as soon as he was found, and they determined that it would have been impossible for him to have killed Lord Ollon. Rigos was, beyond doubt, already dead when Ollon was killed."

"But . . . that would mean he really was innocent, and someone else committed both murders," Bron whispered, his face pale. "He was innocent all along, and I said—"

His words ended abruptly, but Delin almost didn't notice. A great chill had formed inside him, centering around a suddenly growing fear. He'd left traces to prove that Rigos had killed Ollon, but with Rigos dead first, those traces would prove something else entirely. . . .

"Are you all right, Lord Delin?" Idian said, breaking into Delin's thoughts. "You appear to be even more pale than Lord Bron."

"I feel more pale," Delin said, automatically responding in a way to cover himself. "I knew Rigos since we were boys together, but instead of supporting him I joined the ranks of his accusers. Now I feel as though it were my hand which ended his life, rather than his own."

"I think we were all equally guilty in that particular area," Kambil put in quietly, sending Delin a look of support. "We believed the rumor rather than the truth, and tragedy followed. If it were only possible to take back those words and actions. . . ."

He, too, let his words trail off, turning away to bow his head. Delin walked to a chair and sat, almost too numb to notice how Selendi cried against a Homin who seemed deeply touched by tragedy. None of them was taking the supposedly marvelous news at all well, and Lord Idian stirred before rising to his feet.

"Here's that list of exercises I promised you," he said quietly, removing a folded sheet of paper from his coat and placing it on a nearby table. "You won't feel much like practicing for a while, but when you do, follow the instructions carefully. I'll see all of you again tomorrow."

Lord Idian took one last look at the five people, then he left the room. A servant stood near the front door, so in another moment Idian was outside and climbing into his carriage. His driver already had his instructions, which meant that Idian's carriage left the residence's drive but not to take him home. When he reached the carriage waiting just out of sight up the street, Idian's carriage stopped.

"Well?" Lord Anglard asked in the same cold and emotionless voice he'd used since Idian had first met him. "Was it one of them?"

"I'm tempted to say no, but something is keeping me from being completely certain," Idian replied. "They've all changed radically since they Blended, and they're very difficult to read."

"How difficult can it be?" Lord Fortner Oplis asked, surprising Idian. "Your talent in Spirit magic is easily as strong as my own, and I'd be able to tell without any trouble."

"You say that only because you haven't yet come in contact with High talents, my friend," Idian rejoined dryly. "You and I are strong Middles, but these people soar way above us. I've been able to feel the mountain of strength inside Kambil since the first moment I entered that residence, and the rest of them aren't that far—if at all—behind."

"But Delin Moord is the one you were supposed to be looking at the most carefully," Anglard pointed out. "He's the one with Earth magic, so he's the only one who could have accomplished what was done. *He* doesn't have a mountain of Spirit magic inside him, so what did you learn?"

"He was really stunned when he heard about Rigos," Idian replied, remembering that clearly. "I didn't understand why so I asked a question, and the answer I was given made sense. He's an odd sort, the kind of man who looks forward gleefully to hearing bad news about other people. He expected to enjoy whatever tragedy I'd come to announce, so his shock was deeper than it would have been ordinarily."

"And you don't see anything suspicious in his being ready to enjoy the news of tragedy?" Anglard demanded. "If I'd been there—"

"If you'd been there, you'd have gotten nothing more than what he cared to give you," Idian interrupted to say slowly and carefully. "Try to understand that these people are a *lot* stronger than you, just as you're stronger than those with Low talent. Your presence would have put the guilty on guard, something we tried to avoid by having *me* break the news."

"So what has our very clever strategy accomplished?" Anglard demanded. "This is the last of the four residences, and we're no closer to an answer than we were. I've half a mind to revisit each of them personally, only with Puredan rather than you as my companion."

"If you did that, the Advisors would skin your 'half a

mind' along with the rest of you,'' Idian returned, really beginning to be annoyed. ''Get it through your head that these people have to be available to compete in a short while, even if one of them does happen to be guilty of two murders and bringing about a suicide. After they've served their purpose, no one will care *what* you do with them— as long as your guilty party isn't a member of Lady Adriari's group.''

''Every member of her group can be accounted for at an all-night party,'' Anglard replied, gesturing a dismissal. ''They were all in plain view at the time Ollon was killed, especially her Earth magic member. No, it has to be one of these other four, who *won't* be protected by having won the Fivefold Throne. How long must I wait?''

''Now that this last group has Blended, I can answer that question,'' Idian said, still vaguely annoyed. ''We wouldn't have waited more than another day or so, but they finally managed to make waiting unnecessary. The first day of the competitions will be exactly seven days from today.''

''And as soon as the last of it is over, I can have the last of them,'' Anglard said with satisfaction. ''But the first group should be available rather quickly. Will that be a matter of chance, or has everything been worked out?''

''Leaving things to chance is never a good idea,'' Idian told him, wondering how an Advisory representative could possibly be so innocent. Then he outlined exactly what was planned. . . .

THIRTY-FIVE

Jovvi had just finished filling her breakfast plate and was turning away from the buffet when Tamma walked in. The girl didn't even nod to her, which surprised Jovvi until she remembered that they still weren't supposed to be getting along. Ordinarily Jovvi wouldn't have forgotten, but having already taken care of the problem had made her dismiss it automatically.

"We don't have to worry about what we say any longer," she told Tamma with a smile. "When I woke up I felt strong and refreshed, so I had a brief chat with every servant on the staff. It finally came through to me that our lives are at stake here, so my worrying about taking advantage with my ability is not just silly, it's downright stupid. From now on we won't be taking any chances at all, because no matter what we say or do, all the servants will see and hear is bickering and discord."

"That's nice," Tamma answered, walking past Jovvi to the buffet without saying anything else. It was as though Jovvi had announced that the day would be sunny and pleasant, not at all the reaction Tamma should have given.

"Are you all right?" Jovvi asked, just stopping herself from reaching to Tamma with her ability. "You sounded as though you didn't hear a word I said."

"I heard you, I still think it's nice, and no, I'm not all right," Tamma replied without turning. "How did your night lying beside Lorand go?"

"It went the same for both of us," Jovvi answered ruefully. "We undressed and got into bed, put our heads on the pillows—and then I was asleep. I'd feel awful for Lorand, but I have the definite impression that the same happened to him."

"I'm sure it did," Tamma commented, still not turning. "All four of you were so completely exhausted. . . ."

"Oh, no!" Jovvi exclaimed, finally understanding. "You *weren't* as tired, but Vallant was. Weren't you able to wake him?"

"I now know what it's like to spend the night with a dead body," Tamma replied, no longer filling the plate she'd taken. "And I think that someone is trying to tell me something, like that I'm a fool to believe I'll ever get together with Vallant. Something has kept it from happening every time, and I'm really tired of finding nothing but frustration."

"Tamma, it's nothing but a run of awful coincidence," Jovvi said, trying to sound as reassuring and certain as possible. "No one is telling you anything but that our circumstances are far from usual, so what you need to do is have patience. Everything will work out, just wait and see if it doesn't."

"Of course it will," Tamma said, back to filling her plate. "I'm sure you're right, and I'm just being foolish."

"You're saying the proper words, but you don't sound convinced," Jovvi pointed out, trying not to share the heavy sense of frustration coming from Tamma. "If you look at this right, it's really kind of funny. . . ."

"Well, now we know what the real problem is," Tamma said glumly, finally leaving the buffet with her plate. "I have no sense of humor. Can we talk about something else?"

Jovvi felt the definite urge to close her eyes, after which she would give herself a good talking to. Not only hadn't she helped Tamma, she seemed to have managed to make things worse. She might have done better not getting up this morning. . . .

"Good morning, ladies," Rion said neutrally as he entered the dining room, then he added in a whisper, "And what a truly marvelous morning it is."

Jovvi explained again about their being able to speak freely as she took her place at the table, then added, "Why is the morning so marvelous, Rion?" Anything that might divert Tamma from the glumness of her thoughts would be worth listening to.

"It's marvelous because of . . . our guest," Rion replied, obviously trying to be circumspect. "We were able to merge our essences before I simply *had* to sleep, and then when I awoke this morning—"

The clatter of Tamma's eating utensils hitting her plate interrupted Rion, and Jovvi felt like groaning. This was not only getting out of hand, it was progressing from ridiculous to absurd.

"Have I said something wrong?" Rion asked diffidently from where he stood at the buffet. "If I've distressed you ladies in any way—"

"No, no, Rion, it isn't your fault," Jovvi quickly assured him. "It's just that Tamma has gotten this really silly idea—"

"Silly?" Tamma interrupted in turn, her voice just short of being shrill. "*Rion* managed to stay awake, so why is it silly for me to have expected Vallant to do the same? Obviously Rion cares more about Naran than Vallant does about me, and that vague someone was perfectly right. Vallant and I just aren't meant to be together."

Jovvi could feel Tamma's need to hurry out of the room, but she must have remembered that Vallant might still be in her apartment. So instead of running she began to eat again, deliberately seeing to at least one of her body's hungers.

"I'm considering taking a vow of silence," Rion murmured as he sat in his place at the table to Jovvi's right. "A pity I didn't consider it earlier."

"You had no way of knowing, so it wasn't your fault," Jovvi murmured back with a smile. "I'm tempted to go looking for a stick to beat Vallant over the head with, but this wasn't really his fault either. If only Tamma had just a *little* bit more self confidence. . . . She should be laughing about it all, not thinking it's the end of the world. . . ."

That was when Lorand walked in, giving Jovvi a wry smile on his way to the buffet. Jovvi's first urge was to tell him that it was all right to speak freely, but right now speaking freely could prove to be more dangerous and damaging than when half the servants were listening to every word. It was hard to imagine anything that might make Tamma feel worse, but Jovvi was confident that somehow someone would manage it.

"Silly of me," Rion muttered in apparent annoyance, then he rose from his seat to return to the buffet with his plate. He seemed to have forgotten to take something, but when he got over there Jovvi became aware of him whispering to Lorand. He must have been passing on everything Jovvi hadn't been able to, as well as cautioning Lorand against foot-in-mouth disease. That wonderful man! Right now Jovvi loved him more than anyone but Lorand.

Rion returned to the table first, and a pair of moments later Lorand took his place to Tamma's left. Tamma had apparently missed seeing Rion speaking to him, as she turned to him after he was seated.

"Jovvi says it's all right for us to say anything we like," she informed him with very little enthusiasm. "I don't know why she didn't tell you as soon as you walked in, so you might ask her. At least she's still speaking to you."

"Why shouldn't she be speaking to me?" Lorand asked cautiously, sending Jovvi a glance filled with a plea for help. "Is there someone she's decided *not* to speak to?"

"Of course not," Tamma responded, shifting her gaze back to her plate of food. "Jovvi always talks to everyone, probably even if she hates them. I suppose it's a good way to be, but it isn't *my* way. I seem to be more into . . . brooding and blaming, I suppose you would call it. And I don't want to talk about it."

Once again she went back to eating, and when Lorand looked at Jovvi and parted his lips, Jovvi quickly shook her head. Tamma was working herself deeper and deeper into despondency, the hatred she'd spoken of partially self-hatred. Her reactions to what had happened—or, more accurately, to what *hadn't* happened—were completely out of proportion to the importance of the incident, but there might be a reason for that. She was a woman who had been taught not to hope, and she'd managed to overcome that harsh and heartless lesson. If she'd gotten to the point of hoping *too* hard, her disappointment would certainly be completely out of proportion to what others considered normal. If only she could be shown how farcical it really was. . . .

"Oh, oh," Rion murmured, and Jovvi looked up to see Vallant in the doorway. His arrival was hardly unexpected, so for an instant she wondered at Rion's comment—until she realized that Vallant was grinning. Very obviously *he* saw how funny the situation was, which made Jovvi groan all over again.

"You really will have to tell Vallant how upset you are," Jovvi said to Tamma as fast as she could get the words out. "He probably thinks the joke's on him, and doesn't realize that you don't consider it a joke."

"I can't tell him because I'm not speaking to him," Tamma disagreed, a different cast now showing up in her thoughts. "I've decided my mistake was in listening to him in the first place, so I'm not listening either. None of this will affect the Blending, of course, just our lives outside the Blending."

"You consider it fair to blame a man for something that wasn't his fault?" Jovvi asked, relieved to see that Vallant had lost his grin. "If he'd deliberately made the decision to fall asleep, then I'd have to agree with everything you've said. But speaking from personal experience, he had no choice at all in the matter. Complete exhaustion does that to people."

"*Rion* had a choice in the matter," Tamma countered with growing annoyance, and Jovvi was able to feel Rion flinch inwardly. "If one man can do it, so can a second— unless the second isn't quite as interested in doing it as he's been claiming. If something's been trying this hard to tell me not to get involved, it's about time I started to listen."

Vallant's brows had risen as his expression turned thoughtful, and then he stepped back out of the doorway and out of sight. Jovvi could tell that he'd gotten an idea, and she could only hope it was a good one. Things were getting worse by the minute, and if Tamma's growing annoyance progressed to full anger . . . Jovvi didn't even want to think about it.

A full minute went by, and then Vallant suddenly strode into the room. His thoughts were calm and under careful control, but outwardly he looked furious.

"Jovvi, I'm not pickin' up any trace of people close enough to overhear us," he said curtly as he stalked closer to the table. "Does that mean I can do some open talkin' for a couple of minutes?"

"Yes, you certainly can," Jovvi responded cautiously. "As a matter of fact—"

"Good, because I've got somethin' to say," Vallant interrupted to growl. "I don't know how they're doin' it, but it looks like the testin' authority is workin' on me. We've got to find out what they're doin' and stop it, because I don't *ever* want that happenin' again."

"What sort of thing are you talking about, Vallant?" Jovvi asked in sudden but hidden delight. It looked like the idea he'd gotten *was* a good one, as even Tamma had been startled by his vehemence.

"It started when I went to bed this mornin'," he said, his words continuing cold and hard. "Sure, I was tired, but not tired enough to forget that I was waitin' for the most wonderful woman in the world. One minute I was picturin' holdin' her in my arms, and the next I was wakin' up all alone in her bedchamber. Whatever was affectin' me didn't even let me hear her get up and dress, which ought to prove the point. And when I find out who's doin' it. . . ."

The deadliness in his voice couldn't be missed, and Jovvi felt Tamma shiver inwardly. Her thoughts were badly confused, but she didn't seem to be actively disbelieving.

"In the meantime, there's no way I can apologize to the woman who means everythin' to me," Vallant continued after a brief pause, touching Tamma's shoulder lightly for an instant. "She's been given the worst insult a man can give a woman, and until I've avenged her honor I won't even be able to bring myself to speak to her. . . . Bein' too ashamed is somethin' I'm just not used to, and somethin' I don't mean to *get* used to. . . ."

His words choked off as he paused again in what was very obviously deep embarrassment, and then he turned and walked to the buffet. Jovvi felt Lorand and Rion fighting to control their expressions, just as she was having to do with her own. Vallant's performance had been marvelous, and Tamma sat staring down at her plate in utter confusion. The temptation was there to help Tamma toward full belief, but Jovvi firmly resisted it. Meddling now with anything but words could only make things worse instead of better.

"It never occurred to me that the testing authority could or would do something like that, but it sounds like them," Jovvi mused instead. "I don't know how they'd accomplish it, but why they'd bother is much easier. Anything they can do to disrupt us is completely to their benefit."

"But of course you know how they would do it," Lorand put in, speaking as solemnly as Jovvi had. "Just the way I did it last night, or rather, this morning. Anyone with enough strength in Earth magic could do the same, and if the victim started out tired to begin with, it would not even take that much strength."

"Yes, I do remember now," Jovvi agreed, not really having forgotten. She'd wanted the point stressed for Tamma, and Lorand, the love, had obliged. "Obviously I should have been more alert, so this is definitely my fault. It was just that I was so exhausted. . . ."

"No, love, the fault wasn't yours alone," Lorand disagreed at once. "I was also too exhausted, otherwise I would have been able to detect Earth magic being used. We'll have to work together to make sure this doesn't happen again."

Jovvi nodded with a smile, more than aware of the fact that Rion had kept quiet throughout all of the previous conversations. He'd apparently made good on his decision to take a vow of silence, which was really very wise of him. And then, suddenly, Tamma rose from the table and left the dining room without a word. Jovvi followed her with her mind until Tamma reached her apartment, and then she released the line with a sigh.

"All right, she's out of hearing range," Jovvi told the others, who were all staring at her. "She hasn't yet made up her mind to believe what she heard, but guilt is making her reexamine her decisions. She may have been blaming Vallant for something someone else did deliberately, and the unfairness of that is very painful for her. But the idea of trusting and believing again is also painful, so she'll need some time to resolve the conflict."

"I didn't much like doin' that to her, but I didn't have any other choice," Vallant said as he brought his plate to the table and sat to Lorand's left. "My fallin' asleep this mornin' was actually *her* fault, for stayin' in the facility so long. I waited and waited, fightin' to stay awake, then finally lost the fight. But if I'd pointed that out, she would have accused me of makin' excuses.''

"And she probably would have dismissed my saying that Naran didn't leave my side," Rion put in glumly. "I really do owe you an apology, Vallant, for having such a big mouth. I had no idea why discussing one's pleasure was a subject to be avoided in polite conversation, but now I believe I've learned the reason."

"If we weren't part of each other, Rion, Vallant would probably join me in murdering you," Lorand said dryly. "I know you're not aware of it, but a man keeps silent about his pleasure for more than a single reason. How would *you* feel if Vallant and I casually told Naran about various esoteric techniques he and I know but you haven't learned to perform yet? If she then expected you to know about them as well...."

"I would end feeling inadequate, and also contemplating murder," Rion finished with a sigh. "If it weren't too late, I believe I would seriously consider living a solitary existence again. There's so much to *know* when one associates with other people."

"Don't worry, Rion, you'll pick it all up in no time," Jovvi assured him as she patted his hand. "In the meantime, just be careful about what you say to Tamma. She's still the most vulnerable one among us, and needs to be protected from things the rest of us don't even notice. She's doing really well with turning herself around, but she's still not ready to laugh off frustrating accidents."

"You're absolutely right, of course," Lorand agreed with a frown, "but that picture of her is so different from the one we see in the Blending. I can remember feeling part of myself on guard this morning, and that part was as hard as steel and completely ready to attack or defend. *She* was that part, and not a single corner of her usual problems showed."

"I don't remember seein' my problem or yours, either," Vallant pointed out. "I was too busy to notice at the time, but I remember usin' all the power I needed to get the job done, and didn't feel crowded or closed in at any time. I'm hopin' that means what I think it does. . . .''

"And I'm hoping the same," Lorand agreed, moving his gaze to Jovvi. "What do you think, love? Are we just fooling ourselves, or does being part of the Blending really free us from our problems?"

"Give me a minute to remember back," Jovvi said, feeling extremely stupid. "I can't believe I didn't think to check before this . . . Yes, you're absolutely right. I felt nothing of problems while I did what needed to be done—except for the awareness that I might be stretching things too far. How about you, Rion? Did you notice anything the rest of us missed?"

"Not at the time, but I seem to have noticed something now," Rion replied slowly. "I remember saying I felt as exhausted as I did after that very first test, but that can't be true. After only a few hours of sleep, I feel completely restored. That didn't happen the first time."

Jovvi joined the others in voicing startled agreement, then said, "That's another thing I missed, and I wonder how much more there is. I'll have to— Wait, there's someone coming."

It wasn't really necessary to break off all conversation and pretend to be alone in the room, but Jovvi did it anyway. It was good practice for all of them, against a time when they would be among people who weren't under her control. A glance showed that the men withdrew into their own worlds just as she had, and then a servant entered from the hall.

"Pardon the intrusion, gentles, but there's a caller at the door for Dom Coll," the man announced. "Shall I inform him that Dom Coll is still at breakfast?"

"No, I'll see him now," Lorand answered at once, putting his napkin to his lips before tossing it aside and rising. "You can lead the way."

The servant bowed and did so, and Jovvi felt Lorand's hope as he followed. Wasn't Lorand waiting to hear something from or about that friend of his . . . ?

THIRTY-SIX

Lorand followed the servant to the front door, hoping it would be Hat he found standing on the step. The delay in hearing from his friend had worried Lorand, but so much had been going on in his own life that he hadn't been able to think of a way to follow up on his request to Meerk. Hat could have been anywhere in the city—

"Mornin', Dom Coll," Lorand heard as soon as the servant opened the door, but it wasn't Hat speaking the words. Meerk was back, once again looking semi-respectable, but also looking somewhat disturbed.

"Good morning, Dom Meerk," Lorand replied politely, very aware of the servant only a step or two away. "Have you had any luck finding that produce I asked you to locate?"

"Sorry t' say I ain't," Meerk answered, suddenly sounding as though he wasn't very bright. "I been lookin' all over th' city, but I ain't found none yet."

"Isn't that strange, Dom Meerk?" Lorand pursued, now understanding the man's disturbance. "I did see some in that warehouse my coach passed, so they must have taken it to *some* shop for sale. Weren't you able to locate the warehouse either?"

"Now, I found *that* easy enough," Meerk replied, swiping at his nose with one hand. "They wouldn' let me in t' look around, tho, so I kinda hung out waitin' fer th' stuff t' come t' me. I waited a real long time, but I never did see none a' it."

"It's possible that what I saw was a special order for one household," Lorand mused, just speaking the words while he thought furiously. Hat never came out of the building where the challenge had taken place? That wasn't very likely, not when there was an easier answer.

"You know, I just had an idea," Lorand said after a short pause. "Maybe the produce I saw was taken out of a different door in the warehouse while you were watching just the one. If it was and someone working in the warehouse saw it being taken out, they just might know where it was taken *to*. Here's some silver. If you have to buy the information, do it."

"Yeah, I like that there idear," Meerk agreed, pretending to brighten. As he took the three silver dins, he added, "I'll go askin' around, an' if I find sumthin' out I'll come back."

"Just make sure you don't accidentally offend anyone," Lorand cautioned, knowing Meerk would understand what he meant. "That special produce is grown only on the farms near where I used to live and I miss having some of it, but not so much that I want to see you get into trouble trying to locate it. If it looks like something like that might happen, come back and discuss it with me first."

"Sure, sure, don't you worry none," Meerk agreed breezily, but his almost imperceptible nod said he understood and agreed. He would try to bribe someone in the building to find out where Hat was, but if it looked like something might go wrong he'd back off and return to report.

Meerk turned and began to leave, so Lorand left the servant to close the door and returned to the dining room. Jovvi, Rion, and Vallant were still at the table, so he reclaimed his seat and reached for the pitcher of tea.

"The man who was supposed to find my friend Hat hasn't been able to locate him," Lorand reported, knowing the others were waiting to hear about what had happened. "I find that very strange, since they should have thrown him back out into the street after he served his purpose. Unless—"

"Unless what?" Jovvi asked anxiously, probably having felt the jolt in his middle that he'd suddenly been hit with.

"Unless he kept yelling about the competition being a put up job," Lorand answered slowly, deep illness causing him to stop abruptly in the pouring of the fresh cup of tea. "I . . . tried to tell him before the challenge started that he was being used, but he didn't believe me until after he was defeated. Then he made such a scene that they had to carry him out."

"That doesn't sound good," Vallant confirmed, disturbance clear in his eyes. "They don't want people talkin' about their dirty little games, and our lives aren't worth much to them. If your friend refused to keep quiet . . . Are you thinkin' he didn't have sense enough to close his mouth in time?"

"That's exactly what I'm thinking," Lorand admitted, deciding that he didn't want another cup of tea after all. "Hat's never been very bright about certain things, and knowing when to keep quiet is one of them. If they've hurt him. . . ."

No one added anything when he let the words trail off, but they were probably thinking the same as he: even if they'd killed Hat, there was nothing any of them could do about it now. Their winning the competitions would be another story, but for right now they were helpless.

"Pardon the intrusion, gentles, but you have another caller," that same servant announced from the doorway. "This one, however, is the lord from the testing authority, and he requests the presence of all of you. Dama Domon has already been sent for, and the lord awaits you in the library."

"Please tell him we'll be there in a moment," Jovvi said to the man, then continued in a soft voice once he'd bowed and left, "I wonder which one it is? If it's Twimmal we have to Blend for him, but something tells me we shouldn't go all the way. What do the rest of you think?"

"I agree completely," Rion put in at once, echoing Lorand's thoughts. "What we accomplished is well beyond anything described to us until now, and there's a possibility they may not even know about it. And if they do, there's very little sense in telling them we're capable of it."

"That's the way I see it," Vallant added with a nod which Lorand matched. "We play it safe and easy, and save questionin' the man until tomorrow or the next day. Gettin' him under our control might leave marks that show to anybody able to see them, so we ought to let him report our success first."

"And we better remember to check for those marks when we do touch him," Lorand said, forcing back his worry about Hat. Until he reached a position where he might do something. . . . "If we can find them first, it might be possible to disguise them in some way. But what about Tamrissa? Does she know what we intend to do?"

"Yes, but someone ought to tell her about the rest of it," Jovvi said as she rose. "Rion, see if you can pretend to be lecturing her pompously."

"That shouldn't be difficult," Rion said with a faint smile as the rest of them stood as well. "As long as I stay with that one subject, I shouldn't cause *too* much damage."

Lorand joined Vallant in chuckling at that, but Jovvi was too busy hurrying out of the dining room to notice. The three of them followed her, and when they reached the front hall they discovered the reason for Jovvi's hurry. Tamrissa was coming down the stairs, and if they'd delayed even a moment longer, they might have missed the chance to speak to her before she reached the library.

Lorand watched Rion stride over to her and begin his pompous lecture, and after an instant of being startled, Tamrissa played along by looking bored but cornered. As this went on they all continued in the direction of the library, and opening the door finally answered Jovvi's first question: the portly Lord Twimmal sat in his favorite chair, sipping a cup of tea which behaved better than the last one he'd had there.

"You must know at once that your behavior is completely unacceptable," the man said as soon as he saw them, heavy annoyance in his too-high voice. "When I arrive I expect you to be waiting for me, so that we may begin at once. My time is much too valuable to be wasted in waiting for *you*."

"Possibly we can make *our* time just as valuable," Jovvi said hastily, probably knowing that Lorand—and maybe the others as well—was about to reply in a much less . . . neutral way. "We've discussed the matter among us, and we've decided to put personal animosities aside so that we can Blend."

"Very commendable, I'm sure," Twimmal commented dryly, obviously unimpressed. "Now all you have to do is perform in accordance with your decision. Would you care to take your places in the formation and make the effort?"

The fool of a man was too dense to notice the heavy anger coming from all of them, something Lorand had no trouble feeling for himself. He also felt the urge to do something outrageous to the man—like making him lose control of his bowels for a moment—but instead followed the others into the proper formation. First they needed to establish themselves as truly important in the governmental scheme of things, and then there would be time for some of life's little pleasures.

"Oh, by the way," Twimmal added negligently, "Air and Water should be standing more to either side of Spirit. I thought there was something wrong with your formation yesterday, but I was simply too distressed to realize what."

Lorand had seen that Rion and Vallant had taken their places to either side of Tamrissa, just as they had yesterday. When Twimmal corrected them there was another general flow of anger, this one a bit stronger than the last. If positioning was as important as they'd been told, the fool's "distress" could have kept them from Blending.

But they weren't there to play the what-if game, so Lorand opened himself to the power and simply waited for Jovvi's touch. When it came he returned it, and then all of them were Blended again. That same sense of excitement and delight also returned, as well as a strong sense that the world was finally right again. He breathed out his satisfaction while at the same time keeping himself from sinking more deeply into the meld, and Twimmal looked up sharply.

"Two or three of you sighed at the same time," he observed, almost in accusation. "Does that mean you've actually managed to do it? Are you Blended?"

"Yes, we've Blended," Lorand said, only faintly surprised that all of the others spoke at precisely the same time using exactly the same words. They were, after all, almost completely a single entity.

"Excellent," Twimmal commented, just in passing and as if by rote. "You've done your duty and have certainly made your peers proud. Now you must dissolve the Blending at once. There are cautions you must hear, and instructions you're to be given.''

Let's find out what he's talking about, the Vallant portion of their Blending suggested, which made good sense. They would certainly be Blending again later, and right now they needed to know what Twimmal could tell them. Lorand withdrew himself from the meld just as the others did the same, and then he also joined them in finding places to sit where they could all see Twimmal easily.

''You all are certainly to be congratulated, but from now on you must be very careful,'' the fool said pompously as he looked around at them. ''There is a terrible danger awaiting the unwary, something described to me as a mind vortex. I'm told that the second time you Blend you'll become aware of its call, but you must ignore and resist it. Those who don't will surely become enmeshed, and shortly after that will be unable to pull free again. Your minds will be trapped while your bodies remain unmoving, and shortly thereafter you will all die.''

''I don't think I'd enjoy that much,'' Tamrissa said with a frown that didn't look at all real, apparently having decided to play less-than-bright. ''Will we really be caught right away? Even if you step into mud, you can always pull your foot out again.''

''You can pull your foot out again, child, only if you haven't advanced too far *into* the mud,'' Twimmal replied, seemingly taking the comment perfectly seriously. ''If you're right near the edge of the mud puddle you can play at stepping in and out, but one of those times you can step out too far. Once that happens there's no going back, because dry land is out of your reach.''

''So you're saying we should ignore the pull from the very first time we feel it,'' Jovvi put in, sounding thoughtful. ''That's good to know. Is there anything else we have to be careful of?''

''You must remember not to stay Blended too long, nor should you Blend more than twice a day at most,'' Twimmal replied with a nod. ''The condition is actually rather bad for your health and general well-being, and if you indulge too often you may not have the strength to compete.

The most effective exercises have been written down for you in the form of instructions. . . ."

Twimmal began to pat at his pockets, obviously looking for something. It took him a moment to locate the something in an inner pocket, the item turning out to be a small sheaf of folded papers. He removed one sheet from the sheaf before returning the rest to his pocket, then put the sheet on the table near his hand.

"You're to practice these exercises once a day, and at other times you're to rest, relax, and enjoy yourselves," he said then. "Ten gold dins will be delivered to each of you, and you're to spend them on new clothes, fine meals, and enjoyable entertainments. When you go out you need not go as a group, as what one of you finds amusing may not be to the taste of the others. After the competitions there will be another twenty gold for each of you, so spend the first ten with an open hand."

"Are you saying that if we win the competition, all we'll get is another twenty gold dins?" Tamrissa asked with her nose wrinkled. "Goodness, somehow I thought it would be much more than that."

"Ah . . . yes, you're quite right, child," Twimmal said as he struggled to his feet. "If you win the competitions you will certainly get a good deal more than that. I will be by later tomorrow, so that you'll be able to practice once before I arrive. I'll expect a report when I do arrive, not a demonstration."

With that said he headed for the door, actually opened it by himself, and waddled out. Since he didn't close the door again it was possible to see him going toward the front door, and a moment later he was gone. The servant who let him out also disappeared quickly, so Lorand was able to look at everyone else and grimace.

"Oh, yes, dear children, if the impossible should somehow come about and you win, you'll certainly get more than twenty gold dins. But no one really expects the impossible, so why bother even discussing it?"

"The man really is almost a true idiot," Jovvi said while everyone else made sounds of agreement. "He forgot that we aren't supposed to know we'd be losing, but that's the least of it. Taking him over to find out what he knows has become unnecessary, because we already know what he knows.''

''I have no trouble believing it,'' Rion commented dryly. ''The more I see of his sort, the happier I am that I no longer need to associate with them. But what exactly do we know?''

''There's no doubt that he believed everything he told us,'' Jovvi answered, sounding faintly annoyed. ''That 'mind vortex' nonsense was presented to him as fact, and he passed it on in the same way. They probably did it like that so *we* would believe it too, and refrain from experimenting.''

''Why experiment when you can be out havin' a good time?'' Vallant asked sourly. ''They'll be givin' us all that gold, after all, and to waste it would be a cryin' shame. I wonder if they're encouragin' their noble groups to carouse instead of practice.''

''With most of the noble groups, they probably *are* doing the same,'' Jovvi said as she rose and walked to the table holding the sheet of paper which Twimmal had left. She picked up the sheet and glanced at it, then shook her head. '' 'Practice one,' '' she quoted. '' 'Immediately after Blending, the Air magic member is to manipulate a volume of air to form a solid stairway. As soon as this is accomplished, the Blending is to be ended.' ''

''When it gets to be my turn to practice, will I actually be permitted to light the logs in a fireplace, or must I touch only the match?'' Tamrissa asked with a snort. ''And since we'll supposedly be Blended, why is the Air magic member supposed to do anything? Why isn't it the Blending performing the practice?''

''Obviously because they don't want us to *be* a Blending, just *pretend* to be one,'' Jovvi answered with her own sound of ridicule. ''We're on our own as far as figuring out what to do goes, but we can take advantage of the freedom they're pressing on us to contact the other common Blendings. Maybe one of them will discover something we miss—''

Jovvi's words broke off abruptly as she turned her head to look at the open door, and when Lorand did the same he saw the servant approaching. It was the friendly servant who had been calling them to the door when visitors arrived, and he entered the room and stopped before Jovvi to bow.

"Please excuse the interruption, Dama, but this arrived for you while you were closeted with your noble visitor," he said, holding out an envelope. "It's addressed to the Spirit magic member of your group, which I'm told is you."

"Thank you," Jovvi said, taking the envelope. The servant bowed again as she opened it and took out its contents, and he really was a good servant. By the time she looked up from the page, he had already left the room.

"I don't know where this comes from, but if it's the truth it's the most important gift we could have been given," she told them all slowly. "I've been cautioned not to look at the second page of the letter immediately, because it's supposed to contain the phrase we've all been keyed to respond to. If we can find someone we trust, they can use the keying phrase to free us from it for good!"

THIRTY-SEVEN

"What?" everyone demanded at once and in different ways, almost giving Jovvi a headache with their surprise and shock.

"Yes, I know exactly how you feel because I feel the same," Jovvi threw into the cauldron of comments, repeating it two or three times until they had actually heard the words. "I have no idea who sent this because it isn't signed, and it isn't possible to know if it's a trick until we try it. But we can't try it until we have someone here we can trust."

"Why should that be?" Vallant demanded. "If we've got the keyin' phrase, we can just use it on each other and neutralize it. If it isn't the right phrase, nothin' will happen."

"That's what I would have thought, but the letter says differently," Jovvi replied with a disturbed shake of her head. "It says that our simply seeing the phrase will trigger it, and then we'll just stand there and wait for orders. If those orders don't come from the one who triggered us. . . ."

"We'll just stand and wait forever," Tamma finished when Jovvi didn't. "I hate the idea that those miserable people can have this kind of power over us, and I want to see an end to it. Who can we trust enough to test the phrase with?"

"That's easily answered," Rion put in, his anger just as great as Tamma's. "I have someone upstairs whom I'd trust with my life, so I'm obviously the one to try this. Once I'm freed, the rest of you can be freed also."

"I wonder if it's possible to resist a command like that when we're Blended," Lorand commented while everyone thought about Rion's offer. "It's too bad we can't afford to do research on the point . . . but I agree with Rion. Right now Naran is the only one we can be sure of."

"Because of the questions we put to her last night," Jovvi said with a slow nod. "I'd almost forgotten about that, but now that I've been reminded I also agree. Does anyone disagree?"

Jovvi looked from Tamma to Vallant and back again, but both of them shook their heads to show they had no objection to the idea. Apparently they also remembered the questioning, and even Tamma, still obviously touching the power and exhibiting a stronger than usual mind-set, couldn't find fault with the idea.

"That settles it, then," Rion said with a satisfied smile as he rose. "I'll caution Naran to be alert in case there's a trap of some sort involved, but if there isn't I'll return a free man in just a few minutes."

"If it is the keyin' phrase, see if she can order you to resist somethin' like this in the future," Vallant suggested as Jovvi handed Rion the letter. "It may not work, but it shouldn't hurt to try."

"That's an excellent idea," Rion said as he glanced through the letter. "And in case anyone is interested, I would guess that this fascinating missive comes from a member of the nobility. Not only is the paper above average in quality, the phrasing used in the letter itself suggests an upper-class education. That causes me to be suspicious in an automatic fashion, but it also makes inarguable sense. Who better than a member of the nobility to manage access to information of this sort?"

"The answer is no one, so you're undoubtedly right," Jovvi decided with her own slow nod. "The next question, however, has to be: what noble do we know who would do something like this for us? The names on that particular list have to be incredibly few in number."

"Maybe it was done by that noble who all but announced that he meant to claim me," Tamma suggested in a droll tone. "He's suddenly discovered that he's fallen madly in love with me, and chose this as the best way to impress me."

"Maybe it was done by Eltrina Razas," Lorand countered after making a small sound of ridicule. "She's suddenly discovered that she's fallen madly in love with one of *us*, and so wants to make sure that her beloved wins the competitions."

"And maybe this was done for someone else's benefit rather than ours," Jovvi said, the idea coming rather suddenly. "The only way that would make sense is if someone knows *we're* scheduled to face the chosen noble Blending first and wants us to get rid of them for them. Then the way would be clear for *them* to become the chosen Blending, without having to defeat the others themselves."

"But that would mean they believe themselves able to defeat *us*," Rion pointed out as everyone frowned. "Do they know themselves to be that much stronger, or have they some unmentioned secret that will allow them to get the upper hand regardless of relative strength?"

"I hope they're countin' on bein' stronger," Vallant put in with an exasperated headshake. "If they found out the keyin' phrase they probably also got to those test results—

the ones where we all held back some. If they're expectin' to be stronger, they could be in for a nasty shock.''

''Unless it's something else they're counting on, like our 'secret' problems,'' Lorand suggested slowly. ''Those problems are without doubt part of our records, including the fact that our Fire magic member isn't very aggressive. And don't forget that our Air magic member doesn't really fit in, because he's a noble with no experience in mixing with anyone, not to mention commoners.''

''I'd say they're definitely in for a shock where our Fire magic member's aggressiveness is concerned,'' Tamma stated, all but showing the reflection of flames in her eyes. ''How we're associating with our Air magic member is another story, though, since we all go out of our way to avoid him. If that's all we have to worry about we'll do fine, but I really don't trust those people. They could be planning something we haven't thought of.''

''If they are, I hope the one doing the planning is the same one who wrote the letter,'' Lorand said, an odd expressionless expression on his face. ''His not signing the letter suggests that he's trying to hide his identity, but he made no effort to disguise or remove his trace from it. If he walked in right now, I'd know him immediately.''

''That's not in the least surprising,'' Rion said while Jovvi—and the others—made sounds of incredulous disbelief. ''The noble mind set dismisses everyone it considers beneath it, and commoners certainly fall into that category. Why bother to do more than exclude a signature, when it's lower life forms one is dealing with?''

''Put like that, it makes perfect sense,'' Jovvi agreed without the least hesitation. ''They intend to use us for their own purposes, then brush us out of their way. Let's see if we can't make that brushing a lot harder to do than they expect it to be.''

Rion nodded with determination and headed for the door, and once he was gone Jovvi sat back with a sigh. As if things weren't complicated enough, they now had to wonder if there weren't some hidden trap in the information provided. They *ought* to have the answer to that fairly quickly, but considering all the negative ways they might get it. . . .

". . . been thinking about the situation, and I've made up my mind," Jovvi suddenly heard Tamma say, and looked up to see that she spoke to Vallant. "You and I still have to lie together in order to make the Blending as strong as possible, but that will be as far as it goes. Becoming involved with someone leads to nothing but trouble, so I've decided not to do it."

"Just like that?" Vallant countered, his sudden distress painfully clear to Jovvi. "You've decided against gettin' involved, so you've just turned off all your feelin's for me? Well, I don't think you can, so don't expect me to try the same."

"But of course I can do it," Tamma replied with a faint smile. "Making decisions and carrying through on them is much easier when I'm touching the power, so I'll just have to keep touching the power for a while. After that I'll have accepted the situation, so I'll be able to let things go back to normal."

"If your definition of normal doesn't include me, I won't be acceptin' it," Vallant stated flatly, stubbornness now flowing out of him. "I said I wasn't goin' to be changin' my mind about you again, and I wasn't lyin'. If any mind gets changed, it's goin' to be yours."

"And I refuse to change my mind," Tamma told him calmly, but with growing anger beneath. "What do you imagine you can do about it?"

"That's somethin' you'll have to wait to find out," Vallant said, then he deliberately turned away from the very clear danger in her stare. "I don't think touchin' the power so much is terribly good for you, but I won't argue with. you when you are. We'll each do what we have to, and then we'll see."

"Yes, I do think we will," Tamma murmured, still clearly determined. But beneath the determination Jovvi could detect . . . *something* that didn't quite fit. Hopefully, it would be enough to keep real trouble from developing, Jovvi thought as she exchanged a worried glance with Lorand. If it wasn't. . . .

Jovvi sighed again as she got up to ring for a larger tea service. Why couldn't something *easy* happen for once, like being in the middle of a tornado, or having the ground open up and swallow them . . . ?

Rion hurried upstairs and to Naran's door, where he stopped to knock. She appeared almost immediately, and smiled that beautiful smile when she saw him.

"Oh, my lord, I'm very glad it's you," she said, stepping aside to give him room to enter. "It's been very disconcerting this morning, beginning almost as soon as you left. Someone would knock and I would answer the door, and the person knocking would turn out to be a servant. But the servant would walk right past me as though I were invisible, even if they brought a tray of food or came to pick up the empty dishes."

"Now we know what instructions Jovvi gave them," Rion said with a chuckle after sharing a brief kiss with her. "To them you *are* invisible, although I'd be curious to know how they regard your emptied tray. I'll certainly try to remember to ask, but right now there's something I must ask of *you*."

Naran raised her dark and lovely brows, so Rion explained about the orders he and the others were certain they'd been given after passing their very first test. That necessitated an explanation about Puredan, which made Naran angry.

"How vile of them to do something like that, but how typical of the truly incompetent," she declaimed. "They're unable to keep their places fairly through their own efforts, so they've found a way to cheat. How can I help?"

"By using the keying phrase to be found in this letter," Rion replied, handing her the folded sheets of paper. "None of us can so much as read the words without being affected, but the same won't be true of you. Once the phrase has me in its power, you're to order me not to respond to it ever again, nor to anything of the same sort. Then you must attempt to return me to normal."

"*Attempt* to return you to normal," Naran echoed, her full agreement and willingness coming to an abrupt halt. "Are you saying I might not be able to accomplish that? Whyever not?"

"We suspect there might be traps of some sort," Rion

admitted reluctantly as he took her hand. "If there are, they can have been placed there when the original key was implanted in our minds, or they might be woven into the phrase somehow by the one who sent it. We have no way of knowing, but the risk must be taken. Without freedom from their control, our lives are forfeit in any event."

"Unfortunately, that's perfectly true," Naran murmured, her thoughts clearly turned inward. "They might well have planned for the possibility of your learning the key, and have done something to negate that accomplishment. Let me think for a moment . . ."

Rion failed to see what there was to think about, but still made no attempt to interrupt. Naran would always have whatever was in his power to provide, so giving a handful or two of minutes was hardly to be considered a burden. He would, in truth, have waited as long as necessary, but after no more than a rather long moment, Naran smiled again.

"No, I've decided that the original nobles are much too arrogant to believe that anyone—especially commoners— would learn what they'd done," she announced. "As for whomever sent this letter, I'm convinced they haven't the ability or knowledge to incorporate a trap. That means using the phrase will be perfectly safe, so let's get it done."

Rion was too relieved to see her worry disappear to complain—or explain—about making decisions based on little or no real information. The experiment had to be attempted in any event, so her lack of distress could only be a benefit. She pulled him to a couch where they both sat down, and then she released his hand so that she might open and read the letter.

"All right, I believe I'm ready," she said after having finished the page—and then turned to the next. "I'm going to speak these words, and then I'm going to give you the first and last commands I ever mean to."

Rion began to chuckle, but the next instant he seemed to have forgotten what it was that he'd found amusing. And Naran simply sat there looking at him, which wasn't the way things were supposed to have gone.

"I'm waiting for you to begin, my love," he prompted gently, wondering if she were nervous and unsure after all.

"Please don't be upset, as I'm certain you were right to say that everything will go perfectly."

"Everything *has* gone perfectly, my love," she corrected gently with a tiny smile of amusement. "I've not only already begun, I've also finished."

"Without my being aware of it?" Rion asked in startlement. "Surely that isn't—"

He'd been about to say it wasn't possible, but it was true that he also recalled nothing from the time the key was set. He hadn't realized there would be absolutely no memory at all of this time left to him, and that lack added to the anger he felt toward those he'd once considered his own.

"Allow me to prove the matter to you," Naran said with gentle understanding as she took his hand. "The keying phrase is, 'Now is the time for all commoners to come to the aid of the empire.'"

"Commoners, indeed," Rion growled, close to being furious. "Common is as common does, which makes *them* as common as dirt. They— Wait a moment. I not only heard that, I didn't react to it! It *did* work!"

"If you begin to doubt my word, my love, it will greatly distress me," Naran said teasingly with a laugh. "The greatest danger, as I saw it, was in releasing you from the compulsion to obey before giving you instructions about reawakening. So I saw to the instructions first, and *then* released you. With another man I might have . . . added to the instructions, but with you there was simply no need. You already give me everything I now or ever will want."

"And willingly," he reminded her with a grin, then shared a kiss with the woman who meant the world to him. "I must tell the others that the danger is past, or will be once we have you command them as well. I'll return in just a few moments."

After another brief but delightful kiss, Rion hurried back downstairs. As Naran had obviously put a good deal of thought into the matter, he meant to suggest that she be the one to free the others as she'd freed him. He strode to the library and walked right in, but slowed at the sight of the others clustered in the middle of the room, all of them looking at something which Jovvi held. The girl Warla stood not far from them, and Warla's face, at least, shone with delighted excitement.

"Ah, there you are, Lord Rion," she exclaimed when she saw him. "Do come and see what was left for us, duplicates of which have been posted all over the city."

"What is it?" Rion asked, aware of a much different reaction than delight coming from the others.

"Why, it's a placard announcing the official scheduling of the first competitions," Warla replied as Jovvi silently turned the placard to allow him to see it. "Isn't it wonderful, sir? The time is nearly here!"

However enthusiastic the girl was, Rion's feelings were more like those of his Blendingmates—which undoubtedly included a queasiness in the pit of the stomach. Without any prior warning, the competitions were scheduled to begin less than seven full days from that very moment.

THIRTY-EIGHT

Delin stirred in satisfaction after he and the others broke apart, but the satisfaction covered nothing more than the facility they'd gained when Blended. Leaving behind the single entity they became when Blended was always difficult, forcing him, as it did, to return to his solitary, limited existence. The one thing it didn't seem possible to do when Blended was drink a cup of tea, something Delin suddenly felt a great need for.

"That was really very good," Kambil said as Delin headed for the tea service. "We're getting faster and stronger every time we practice, and there's still four days left before the first of the competitions. By the time the big day arrives, we should be completely ready."

"I still say they should have given us more warning about that," Bron put in, not for the first time. "Finding out about it only when the placards came out telling everyone . . . they really don't give a damn about us. If one of us had panicked. . . ."

"It would have weakened our Blending," Homin finished when Bron's words just trailed off. "Weakening us is the name of their game, since we aren't their chosen pets. You can bet Adriari's group had more warning."

"Adriari's group has also probably had more practice," Selendi added thoughtfully. "They must have had her and the others Blend as soon as they were chosen, and what you can also bet on is that they aren't wasting their time with useless exercises. Or should I say deliberately wrong exercises? If we'd gone along with them, we'd still be Blended individuals rather than a single entity."

The others made sounds of agreement, and Delin moved out of the way with his tea so that Bron might reach the service—and so that Delin might examine his groupmates. The changes in them still amazed him, despite the fact that nothing less should have been expected to develop from his leadership. They'd all become able human beings, and it was no longer necessary to cater to Bron's ego by pretending *he* was their leader. The only one Delin still had some small reservations about was Kambil. . . .

"I've been thinking about this," Kambil now announced from where he still stood in the middle of the room, "and I've decided that we simply don't know as much as we should. Some of the things we've learned to do we discovered by accident, a procedure we can't continue to rely on. If our opponents have one more lucky accident than we do, they could conceivably defeat us."

"So where do you suggest we get that information?" Delin put evenly despite his sudden annoyance. "I've already gone through the files pertaining to everyone participating in the competitions, and there's nothing more there."

"Which is why we now need to look elsewhere, but not in a file," Kambil fretted, looking down at the carpeting. "We need the kind of information no one will want written down, so it will be only something people know. What I can't figure out is who is the most likely person to know it."

"My dear friend, the answer to that couldn't possibly be more obvious," Delin told him with a chuckle, suddenly feeling marvelous again. "Our own Lord Idian is certainly one of the inner circle, and if he lacks the specific information, he'll still know in whose skull it resides. Since he'll be here in just a short while, we'll just have to ask him."

"We can't do that," Bron said calmly, instantly denting Delin's good mood. "His superiors have to know what we're capable of even if by some chance he doesn't, so they'll probably be alert for signs of tampering. If we leave those signs in him and discover they can't be erased, we'll be telling everyone just what they shouldn't know."

"We'll be much better off finding someone high enough up that they won't be monitored," Selendi proposed. "Signs of tampering won't matter if no one thinks to look for them, but we'll still have to be careful in general. We don't want to run into any part of that very widespread investigation of the murders."

"They're really determined to find out who's behind it all," Homin put in while Delin's indignation dissolved into chills. "Everyone is furious over having accused an innocent man, thereby being the direct cause of *his* death. They're dead set on finding out who used them as a murder weapon, and when they do. . . ."

"And when they do, I'd hate to be the one," Kambil agreed with his own shudder. "If they don't make the most horrible example of him imaginable, the sun will probably fail to rise the next day. But that doesn't tell us who we ought to question. Choosing one of the Advisors, for instance, would probably be a waste of time, because he would be too high up. Details would be known by his subordinate, but just which one. . . ."

Delin's attention withdrew from the discussion, his mind still clanging over that phrase Kambil had used: the most horrible example imaginable. That was what would happen to *him* if he were caught, and all for such an unimportant little to-do. But of course *they* didn't consider it unimportant, not when they were the ones he'd made fools of. They would even the score in blood and agony, *his* blood and agony. . . .

Small beads of sweat sprang out on Delin's forehead, the same sweat that arose anytime he thought about the matter. He also felt that terrible sense of shock again that he'd first experienced when he'd learned that Rigos was dead, too soon, unfortunately, for people to still be in doubt about his guilt. Leave it to Rigos to ruin Delin's plans even in death. . . .

". . . so that's what we'll do," Delin heard Kambil say. "It makes the most sense, but we'll have to cover our tracks carefully. We'll pretend we're going out to party, we'll find a group to join, and after making sure they all believe we're still there, we'll go about our business. If we pay attention to the details, we won't have a problem."

The others all added their sober agreement, which meant Delin would feel like a fool if he asked about what they were agreeing to. He'd either have to wait and see, or get Kambil aside a bit later and question the man. Delin's dislike of Kambil flared again, almost to the point of hatred. Kambil now acted as though *he* were their leader, a usurpation Delin refused to allow. He might need the Spirit magic user now, but once they'd won the Fivefold Throne. . . .

A moment later Lord Idian appeared, but the man stayed only long enough to take the report on their "progress." Kambil dutifully gave Idian what he wanted to hear, and once the man left again the group broke up. Delin searched discreetly for Kambil without finding the man, nor did he appear at lunch. A servant told Delin that Kambil was napping, and had left instructions not to be disturbed. That meant Delin had no choice but to wait, and so after lunch he took his own nap.

They all got together to go out to dinner, during which they pretended to boisterous good cheer. Delin pretended along with everyone else, and soon was feeling almost as good as those around them thought he did. A good number of party invitations came their way from other diners, but they accepted only the one where the most people were likely to appear. Kambil did the accepting, and that, too, rubbed Delin the wrong way.

The party was alive with music and laughter, but Delin had scant time to enjoy himself. Homin had quietly reminded him that it was his responsibility to keep them all sober no matter how much they drank, and he also had to do the same for himself. Delin was ready to feel put-upon until Selendi whispered, "I thank any Higher Aspect that you're here, Delin. We certainly couldn't do this without you."

The truth of that soothed Delin so much that he *was* able to enjoy himself, and that despite his chore. The five of them were scattered all over the large ballroom, but Delin still had no trouble keeping track of his people—and keeping them free of the effects of alcohol. The negligible effort interfered not at all with Delin's usual lies to the women who interested him, and he was in the midst of that when he felt Kambil's touch.

Responding to the touch had become so automatic that it was done before Delin had time to think about it. Then three additional connections sprang into being, and despite the lack of a proper formation, the five of them were Blended.

It's gotten good and late, so this might be the best time for us to move, the Kambil part of them sent. *What do you think, Delin?*

Yes, this is definitely a good time, Delin agreed, his ego soothed by having been deferred to. *If we affect only the ones in our immediate vicinities and those in the fringes, the matter will appear much more natural. People on the other side of the room can't be expected to be aware of our presence or absence.*

Complete agreement came from the others, so they all moved one step higher into that state of being where they were a single entity. The entity reached out to the people near its five separate locations, ordering them to remember its individual presence even once those individuals were gone. Then the entity searched out and touched with forgetfulness all those who would have to be passed on the way out of the room, and the chore was done. Those who saw them leave and later return would never remember the times.

And then Delin was himself again, which he needed to

be in order to leave. He parted his lips to excuse himself from the presence of the ladies he'd been speaking with, then nearly laughed aloud. The ladies were still speaking to—and apparently hearing—him, but a "him" supposedly standing a foot and a half to the left of his actual position. The foolish sluts looked and simpered at empty air, which meant he was free to simply walk away.

One by one the others joined him in the outer hall, but they didn't go toward the front door. They made their way to a side door instead, slipped out without notice, moved through the shadows of the lawn to the street, where a coach unfamiliar to Delin waited. The driver sat and stared as though in a trance, and Kambil climbed up to join the man while the others entered the coach.

The trip wasn't all that long, and when they reached their destination Delin finally realized who they would be questioning. High Lord Embisson Ruhl lived on the estate just ahead, and their coach pulled into the drive but stopped well before reaching the house. No one had been around to see them enter the grounds, and later no one would see them leave.

"Lord Embisson ought to be able to tell us everything we need to know," Delin murmured, realizing that the choice must have somehow been influenced by him. "He's in charge of everything to do with the competitions, but never comes near any of the participants."

"We ought to know in just a few minutes," Kambil said as he opened the coach door and climbed inside to sit on the floor. "We all know what has to be done, and we'll do it as soon as Delin tells us it's safe to begin."

They all looked at Delin then, who preened for a very short time before checking all about. He was absolutely essential to the group, and the gratifying part was that they all knew it. Not a single consciousness of the human variety was aware of their presence, so he nodded regally, giving his permission to begin.

And begin they did. So swiftly were they Blended and then melded, that the Delin individual would have gasped. But the Delin individual was no more, not while the entity was awake and functioning. It drifted away from the five bodies which had spawned it, floating easily toward the house where its objective could be found.

Walls were no barrier to the entity, but being unfamiliar with the quarry's trace slowed it down. More people were awake and moving about than the entity had expected to find, and it finally gathered that some sort of private party was in the process of being enjoyed. That made things both harder and easier, as the quarry was with the party attendees, and therefore not alone.

But being in the midst of a crowd was no protection for the quarry, as a single, light touch convinced him that he needed to relieve himself. The entity floated along after him as he left the room, deflecting some rather powerful probes that came in its direction. Some of those at the party obviously had stronger than average ability, but none was strong enough to penetrate to the entity's presence.

Lord Embisson led the way to the largest privacy facility the entity had ever seen, one that was, happily, *not* meant for the use of the party attendees. Lord Embisson's thoughts reflected the concepts of personal property and complete privacy, and so it turned out to be. No one was in the room, and so it would be unnecessary to send the man elsewhere.

Stand and respond to the questions put to you the entity commanded with another touch. *You will answer fully, and speak only the truth. Afterward, you will forget.*

"I will answer fully and truthfully, and afterward I will forget," the aged man agreed easily, otherwise unmoving and unblinking. "What would you like to know?"

What secrets concerning Blending are there in your possession? the entity put first. *And what evaluation has been made about the various noble Blendings? Are any of them a match to the Blending chosen by the Advisors?*

"All information about Blending is closely restricted," Lord Embisson answered at once. "It's worth a man's life to learn even one fact too many, and there are no exceptions made. I enjoy life far too much to want to see it ended over some bit of lore I have no use for in the first place."

And the rest? the entity prompted. Disappointment tried to touch it, but it was far too occupied to allow that.

"The four noble Blendings in my province are primarily all the same," Lord Embisson continued, his tone unexcited. "They have all managed to Blend, which is just as well for them, as we would have used them in any event. They're all pretending to do their assigned exercises, but most of them are lying about it. They're basically too lazy and stupid to do anything *but* pretend and strut, but that's hardly unexpected. As far as the chosen Blending goes, I know nothing about it, nor do I care to. Those who are dealing with it most closely won't survive the end of the competitions by even a full day. I'm one of the very few old enough to remember that, so I haven't even made the effort to find out who the soon-to-be-doomed are. After all, why bother?"

The entity considered that very briefly, then found itself agreeing. Although completely unhelpful, the attitude was entirely reasonable. Wise men learned to avoid what was dangerous to know, and wasted no time on those slated to die. So it touched the man again, returning him to normal, then floated out of the house and back toward the coach. This time its floating was faster, however, as one of the party guests could conceivably choose to leave at any moment.

When the entity reached the coach it became five individuals again, one of whom, Bron to be precise, reached up and rapped against the coach roof. Delin watched him do it, only faintly surprised when the coach began to move again, then could no longer hold back his anger.

"Of all the stupid wastes of time!" he snarled, glancing longest at Kambil, who was wholly responsible for the fiasco. "If that man knows nothing, no one within our reach will be any different. All this effort to learn absolutely nothing!"

"We did learn one thing," Kambil had the nerve to disagree, shifting uncomfortably where he continued to sit on the coach floor. "We found out that no one suspects what we're up to, at least not yet. I caught an echo of surprise from Idian today, and didn't understand it until just a moment ago. We've been behaving much too well for the 'lazy, stupid, and useless' people we're supposed to be, and Idian has noticed. Tomorrow we'll all have an excuse for

sleeping late and missing our appointment, and I think we
ought to make use of it.''

The others all agreed immediately, and despite Delin's
outrage and anger, he was forced to add his own agreement.
The rest of them seemed pleased to hear that awful opinion
being voiced about them, not one of them taking it as the
mortal insult it really was. To them it was protective col-
oration, but to Delin it was completely unforgivable, almost
as bad as what Rigos had done. . . .

That thought calmed Delin, and let him lean back in his
seat with a smile. Rigos had done his worst, but still no
longer lived. It was necessary to remember that, and remember as well that Embisson was simply a man. He, too,
might die, especially if his death served to divert suspicion
from Delin where the previous deaths were concerned. . . .

THIRTY-NINE

Vallant strolled along the path in the park, pretending to be
out doing nothing more than enjoying a pretty day. He'd
been told that there was a lake in the middle of the park
where models of sailing ships were raced, and that was
supposed to be his ultimate destination. He'd complained
about missing the sea, and so had been sent to watch the
model racing. In reality, however, he was there for an entirely different reason.

There weren't many people in the park around him, and
those few didn't seem to notice when Vallant left the path
for the privacy of a thick stand of bushes. He stood for
several long moments making sure of that, and only at the
end of the time did he leave his watchpost and head deeper
into the shrubbery. The presence of the lake was like a

bright beacon for him, but another, brighter beacon had been flashing ever since he'd entered the park.

Finding that second, deliberate beacon wasn't difficult at all, especially since Vallant knew what it looked like on the outside. Pagin Holter was a small, energetic man who'd been a groom before passing that first test, and all through the rest of the tests he and Vallant hadn't had any trouble matching one another. Now he waited in the midst of another thick patch of shrubbery, using the power to pulse his talent like a flashing light every minute or two.

For the second time, Vallant paused to take a good look around. It was just as possible that Holter might have been followed, so Vallant used his ability to check for lurkers. There were none in evidence near either of them, so he continued on to where Holter stood waiting.

"Knew you wus here when you started checkin' around th' first time," Holter said in greeting with a grin, putting out his hand. "Won't never fergit whut yer inside voice sounds like."

"And I'd know yours in the middle of thousands," Vallant agreed with his own grin, taking the offered hand. "We can't afford to be found talkin', so let's get right down to it. How is it goin' with your group?"

"Never thought it would happen, but we made it all th' way t' Blendin'," Holter replied with a shake of his head. "Thet there fat noble din't do nothin' t' help, 'cept tellin' us about how t' stand. Thet there's th' key, looks like, standin' in th' right place."

"We found that it only has to be done the first few times," Vallant told him, gesturing the smaller man along to a sunny patch of grass where they might sit. "After that just the touchin' alone starts the Blendin', and then you all decide if you want the surface kind or the full meld."

"You folks been goin' fer thet vortex thing?" Holter asked, looking surprised as he settled himself on the grass opposite Vallant. "We been stayin' away frum it, figurin' thet there's th' reason folks ain't supposta Blend. Losin' group after group wouldn' do th' empire a whole lotta good."

"That sounds like Eskin Drowd talkin'," Vallant guessed with disgust. "The man's a coward, remember, so he'd be sure to come up with a good excuse to avoid takin' a chance. That vortex business is a lie, put out by the nobles to keep us from bein' really effective. If you go into the competitions only surface Blended, you'll lose right away.''

"Damn thet Drowd anyways," Holter spat as he echoed Vallant's disgust. "He keeps pickin' away at me, tryin' t' git me riled crazy, an' th' others 'r scared t' face up t' 'im. Been thinkin' I oughta do sumthin' t' slap 'im down, an' now it looks like I ain't gotta choice. His partyin' an' carousin's been hurtin' th' group anyways. . . .''

"Have you found out where the other three groups are?" Vallant asked when Holter's voice trailed off. "There's things everybody needs to know, and not just that vortex lie."

"So happens I did, but there ain't three more groups, they's four," Holter replied, surprising Vallant. "Th' last group's kept real close t' their residence, an' don't seem t' know th' competitions is comin' in four days. I figured they ain't gonna be a part a it lessen somethin' happens t' one a th' rest a us."

"I can't really tell you what to do, but I have a suggestion," Vallant said slowly. "Drowd won't do your group much good even if you force him into line, because he just isn't strong enough. If it were me, I'd get the Earth magic talent from that extra group, and try usin' him or her in the Blendin'. There's only four days left and it might not work anyway, but it's better than continuin' to carry a loser like Drowd."

"It's funny you sayin' thet," Holter mused, studying Vallant in an odd way. "Th' woman who's Earth magic in thet there extra group wus parta ours, b'fore they put Drowd in. Her an' th' Air magic talent, a decent guy we all liked. Now we got Drowd an' sum bimbo who keeps tellin' ever'body how t' talk 'n' act. She's kinda like thet there Beldara Lant, on'y 'bout everythin' 'stead a jest Fire magic. An' I gotta tell ya: I seen thet Lant gal agin."

"Where?" Vallant asked. "It's been so long since Tamrissa left her behind that I forgot all about her."

"Sum a us went t' see th' challenges fer Seated High in Fire magic," Holter replied. "Our Fire magic talent's a real nice little gal, an' she wanned comp'ny t' go see 'em. Me an' Jerst, th' Spirit magic talent, went along, an' there wus Beldara Lant, one a th' challengers.''

"Don't tell me," Vallant said dryly. "She marched out expectin' to win, but was beaten with very little effort. Lorand's friend Hat, who's no more than a strong Middle, ended up as one of the props in the Earth magic farce. Most of Beldara's strength was pure opinion, which made her another perfect prop. And that reminds me: you and the others have to know that we were all drugged after that very first test. As it stands now, you'll obey anybody who keys you with the right words."

"I don't believe thet," Holter said, but his stunned expression said he certainly did believe. "How . . . whut. . . .''

"That water they gave us to drink wasn't water," Vallant said, answering the question Holter wasn't quite able to put. "We figured it out and worried about it, then we got the luckiest break yet: one of the noble groups is hopin' we'll take out their strongest competition, so they sent us the keyin' phrase. We tried it usin' somebody who wasn't keyed, and now it doesn't work on us anymore. If you like, I can do the same for you."

"Damned straight I like," Holter agreed at once, his expression having turned grim. "Never been a slave b'fore, so I ain't gonna start bein' one now. You go ahead an' do 'er."

"My pleasure," Vallant told him with a smile. " 'Now is the time for all commoners to come to the aid of the empire.' ''

Holter immediately froze where he sat, a breathing statue of flesh. He waited for his instructions, Vallant knew, so he very carefully gave them.

"These are the last commands you'll be required to obey," he began, remembering what Naran had told him. "After the last of them you'll return to yourself, behavin' as you usually do. First, you'll never respond to those keyin' words again. Second, you'll never respond to any other keyin' words either. And last, you're to return to the way you usually are."

Repeating the same command twice was probably unnecessary, but Vallant agreed with Naran that it was better to be safe than sorry. Holter blinked at him, no longer under the phrase's control, and then the small man frowned.

"Well, whut's takin' s' long?" he demanded. "Go on ahead an' do 'er."

"It's already done," Vallant told him with a grin, remembering that he'd reacted in exactly the same way. "Now you'll have to learn the keyin' phrase, so you'll be able to free everybody else."

Holter had no trouble learning the keying phrase, and then Vallant gave him the wording he needed to use to free others. The small man memorized that as well, and then they were able to move on to the other topics which needed discussing: the fact that full Blending was very draining the first time, but got easier each time it was done; the fact that the Blending bond grew stronger if the male and female members of the group lay together; and the fact that a full Blending was capable of doing a lot more than anyone realized.

"But you're goin' to have to find out what those things are by yourselves, because we don't have all the answers yet," Vallant finished up. "Oh, and let's agree now that if they want us to eat or drink anythin' at the competitions, we all refuse. If they try makin' us stay anywhere but at our residences, we all refuse. If we give those lowlives any chance at us at all, we'll deserve anythin' that happens."

"I hear thet," Holter agreed, deeply thoughtful. "They ain't gonna turn loose a th' Throne easy atall, so we gotta force 'em. . . . I hope you don't mind me askin', but how's it goin' with you 'n Tamrissa? After whut you said 'bout stronger bonds 'n all . . . Last I saw, you two were fixin' t' start a war. . . ."

"I'd really rather not talk about that," Vallant growled, suddenly back to feeling the way he had for the last three days. "She claims she knows we have to lie together, but every time I see her she says somethin' that gets me so mad I can't see straight. I keep wantin' to give her a good shakin', but she keeps a touch on the power most of the time. If I try shakin' her into rememberin' what we really feel for each other, it could turn into a battle of our talents. That means I don't know *what* to do. . . ."

Holter's expression of confusion prompted Vallant to tell the other man about what had gone on between him and

Tamrissa since Holter left the residence. For someone who didn't want to talk about something, Vallant realized that he left nothing out. But he *needed* to talk about it, and not to the others in his group. They were more than willing to help, but so far their suggestions had done no more good than his own few ideas.

". . . so she's probably waitin' for the last night before the competitions," Vallant finally summed up. "She's afraid of gettin' involved with me, and nothin' any of us say to her changes her mind. That's one true mule of a woman, and when she's touchin' the power there's no arguin' with her."

"An' she's always touchin' th' power," Holter said, nodding his understanding. "Doin' thet ain't hurtin' her 'r makin' her real tired? I'd prob'ly be flat dead frum touchin' it all th' time."

"Me, too," Vallant agreed glumly. "But she seems to be fine, no trouble at—"

"You get a idea?" Holter asked when Vallant's words stopped dead. "Sure hope so, 'cause it sounds like you need one bad."

"Yes, it so happens I did get an idea," Vallant agreed as he began to rise. "It isn't terribly fair, but you know that old sayin' about everythin' bein' fair in love and war. This is both, so it ought to do just fine. You know how to reach me, Holter, and I'll enjoy knowin' how things go."

"They'll be goin' lots better now, thanks t' you," Holter said as he also rose, holding out his hand again. "You an' th' rest take care now, an' good luck with thet idea."

"I'll probably need it," Vallant muttered as he shook hands with Holter again. "It'll be a while before I can try it, but I'll probably need the time to do some convincin'. Keep your eyes open goin' back, to find out if anybody tried followin' you."

Holter said something about not seeing anybody, so Vallant asked if the man had searched with his ability as well as his eyes. It turned out that he hadn't, so Vallant described how to do it before they parted to go their separate ways. Holter gave him the oddest look before he walked off, but Vallant didn't have the time to wonder what it meant. He had to marshal the strongest arguments he could find to get the help he needed against Tamrissa, and *then. . . .*

FORTY

"Who was at the door?" Jovvi asked when I returned to the library and reclaimed my chair. "The servant called him a stranger."

"Let's just say he was a stranger personally but not actually," I replied as I picked up my teacup again. "He was an assessor sent by my father, to appraise the value of *his* house before the sale. The man was a self-important fool, and demanded to be let in to do his job."

"I should have gone to the door with you," Jovvi commented while Lorand looked pained. "Entertainment of that sort always interests me. So what did you tell him?"

"I told him that this house belongs to me, not to my father, despite my father's repeated attempts to steal it," I said after sipping at my rewarmed tea. "I also told him that I've asked the court to do something about my father, because his continual nonsense is distracting me from the competitions I'll be entering in four days' time. I added that if I ever saw that man or anyone from his firm again, I'd include *their* names in my plea to the court."

"No wonder he began to radiate waves of fear," Jovvi said with a laugh. "He probably wasn't told that this is an official residence, otherwise he would never have come here. How did you think of that part about going to court against your father?"

"I thought of it because that's what I did this morning," I answered comfortably. "Just defending never wins any battles, you also have to counterattack. After giving the court the details of what my father has done to me so far, I asked the sitting panel if there was any way they could help me. They all seemed angry and upset, and quickly assured me that there was quite a lot that they could do. I can't wait to find out what they have in mind.''

"I hope it's something that teaches him a good lesson," Lorand put in, sounding rather unforgiving. "He's deliberately trying to distract you so that we won't be at our best in the competitions. Is he really so uninformed that he doesn't know what will happen if we lose, or does he expect his gold to buy you back under his thumb?"

"I have the feeling he's too desperate to think straight," I said, considering the point. "That man Odrin Hallasser—I now remember people mentioning his name, but not in any friendly or everyday businesslike manner. Most seemed to be afraid of him, and I got the impression that they did quite a lot to stay out of his way. My father's oversized ego led him to make a deal with the man, and now he's having trouble keeping his end of the bargain. Dear, sweet Dom Hallasser may even have begun to threaten him.''

"It would hardly surprise me," Jovvi agreed, also looking thoughtful. "I remember how I reacted to that man, and thought then that your father was a fool for getting involved with him. I just . . . wonder if going to court was the wisest thing to do. When things become official, I become very uncomfortable. . . .''

"What choice did I have?" I asked as Lorand reached over to touch her shoulder gently in support. They weren't sitting together, but I was certain they *were* spending nights together. Not that I envied them in any manner at all, or Rion and Naran either. Becoming involved was a foolish thing to do, and I was perfectly delighted that I hadn't done the same.

"She really did have no other choice," Lorand assured Jovvi in support of what I'd said. "The visitor she just had proves her father has no intention of stopping his harassment, and at the very least it was annoying and distracting. The court will hopefully keep us from being bothered again.''

"Yes, I know you're both right," Jovvi admitted with a sigh. "The only other choice we had was to visit the man as a Blending, and people would have noticed his abrupt change in behavior. If the wrong someone noticed, it could have—''

Her words broke off abruptly, undoubtedly because of what sounded like a riot coming from the front hall. A woman's voice rose shrilly above a man's, and then the two combatants appeared in the doorway I'd left open. The man was the servant currently attending to the front door, and the woman was my mother.

"Forgive me, Dama, but she forced her way past me," the servant, Hovan, apologized with fluster. "Shall I call for assistance in putting her out again?"

"You horrible, unnatural child!" my mother shrilled as I shook my head and gestured to Hovan that it was all right for him to leave. His former opponent stalked into the room and planted herself in front of me, her chin rising to regal height. "You will come with me this minute, and tell the court that you lied about whatever you told them! Do you hear me? Get to your feet at once!"

"You really should stop screaming, Mother," I suggested calmly, ignoring the strong urge to do exactly as she said. "It makes you sound like a fishwife and is extremely unbecoming. Would you like to calm down and tell me what's happened?"

"You know perfectly well what's happened," she growled, her face flushed with sudden embarrassment, the change in tone undoubtedly meant to push me off balance. "Guardsmen came to the house and arrested your father, informing me that he would be held until after those ridiculous competitions are over. At that time he will be given a trial, and fined heavily if found guilty. Don't try to deny that this is *your* doing!"

"Considering how browbeaten my sisters are, of course I'm the one responsible," I agreed pleasantly. "I thought about Father's various friends on the bench, and decided I would be foolish to simply wait until he arranged for our disagreement to come up before *them*. 'He who strikes first strikes best,' Father always says, and he certainly is right."

"Your outrageous display of cheek is making me extremely angry, Tamrissa," she said, the growl still in her tone. "When your father proves his innocence he will return and see to your punishment, so you'd better move quickly, young lady. If you make them release him now, your punishment will be a good deal milder.''

''I find it amazing that at one time I would have responded to that by doing just as you said,'' I commented, forcing away all awareness of my lesser self's worry. ''Now, of course, I know it for the nonsense it is, as nothing I told the court was untrue. If Father denies the charges they'll make him testify under that drug that forces people to tell the truth, and then he'll support what *I* said. After the judges show how angry perjury makes them, I doubt he'll be in a position to punish anyone.''

''I have no idea what's come over you, but I want it to stop this minute,'' she said sharply, sounding just as she had for all the years of my growing up. ''This disagreement is a family matter, and family matters are to be kept private. Go and do what you must to have your father released, and then we'll all sit down and discuss whatever happens to be bothering you. Your father has never been concerned about anything but what's best for you, and—''

''Oh, please, Mother!'' I interrupted, fighting to hold my temper. ''All you're doing is repeating the same self-serving lies I've heard my entire life. You and Father don't care about anyone but yourselves, so you have no right to complain now that you're receiving that kind of treatment rather than giving it. I'm sick of the both of you, and I want you out of my house. Now!''

I'd stood up by then, holding my mother's gaze as I'd never before been able to do. She stared back at me with fury and hatred, blaming me for having learned to be so much like my parents, then drew herself up as she looked away.

''You'll regret this, girl, you have my word that you'll regret this,'' she stated very softly, then turned and walked out. I waited until she left the room before sitting down again, and that was when Jovvi and Lorand left their own chairs. Lorand walked to the door to make sure my mother actually left the house, and Jovvi came over to me.

''It's all right, you did perfectly well,'' she said soothingly, putting an arm around my shoulders. ''You aren't letting yourself feel all those tearing emotions, but that doesn't mean they aren't there. She did her best to twist you around in an effort to keep her husband from having to pay for what he's done, and she's shocked that this time it didn't work. The two of them don't ever expect to have to pay for what they do to others, which is one of the reasons they're so uncaring. Whatever happens to your father will be *his* fault, not yours for refusing to be his victim again.''

''Understanding that intellectually isn't quite the same as understanding it emotionally,'' I said, fighting not to be overwhelmed by those tearing emotions Jovvi had mentioned. ''If I weren't still touching the power, I'd probably be running after her and begging for forgiveness. Forgive me for not letting you turn my life into a horror again, Mother. Forgive me for not letting you do as you please with me, Father. I have to be insane, Jovvi, or I would never feel like this.''

''It isn't insanity,'' Jovvi told me with a hug and a sigh. ''It's part of everyone's nature to want to please their parents, so that those parents will love them. If doing the wrong thing brings that love, we do the wrong thing and consider it right. You've broken out of the pattern, but staying out will take all the strength you have.''

''She's gone, and I think it's time we talked about something else,'' Lorand said, coming over to crouch beside my chair and put a gentle hand to my face. ''I don't think you ladies know that I managed to speak privately to Meerk this morning.''

''I certainly didn't,'' Jovvi said as I shook my head to agree with her. ''Has he found your friend Hat yet?''

''He can't even find a trace of him, and it's begun to drive him wild,'' Lorand replied with heavy disappointment in his voice. ''No one knows anything and no one has seen anything, not even for silver. The challengers were brought to the building and afterward were taken away again, just as they always are. Where they came from and where they were taken, no one knows or cares.''

''That doesn't sound good at all,'' I said, gratefully taking Lorand's problem in place of my own. ''If your friend had been turned loose after the challenge, Meerk would have been able to find him even if he promptly got drunk again. What bothers me most is the way he began to shout about the challenge being nothing but a show. If he refused to stop saying that, they might have refused to release him."

"I've already thought of that, and so did Meerk," Lorand said with a headshake. "That's why he tried to find *any* of the challengers, thinking it would be easier to locate four than one. He's had everyone he knows out and looking, but there isn't a trace of the other four either."

"Which means either that they're dead, or the government has found another use for them," Jovvi said, putting a hand to Lorand's arm. "I know what you're feeling, my dear, but denying the probable truth doesn't change it. There's nothing we can do about it now, but if we win the competitions. . . ."

"Yes, I know," Lorand agreed heavily. "I've been telling myself the same thing, but that hasn't stopped me from wanting to become furious. And Meerk has decided not to give up. Somewhere in this city is someone who knows what became of those people, and he's determined to find that someone. I have the feeling that Meerk is more than he appears to be, but how much more and precisely what, I simply don't know."

"What *I* know is that I'm suddenly in the mood for a soak in the bath house," Jovvi said as Lorand straightened up. "I'm also in the mood for company, but not male company. That means you, Tamma, so let's go."

I tried to refuse her very unsubtle invitation, but she pulled me out of the chair and dragged me along with her. Part of me wanted to be alone, but another part shivered at the idea of being alone with my thoughts. So I let myself be bullied into going along, and the time was unbelievably peaceful. Jovvi and I soaked in silence, but her presence made me know that I'd never be alone again—and that there were people who really did love me. I didn't have to become a victim again to be loved, and that knowledge was true freedom.

After bathing I stayed in my apartment until dinner, mostly to keep from running into Vallant. I'd been trying my best to annoy the life out of him, but it was becoming harder and harder to do. Most of me wanted to do something other than annoy him, despite what I'd learned about the pain of becoming involved. I did have to lie with him, that went without saying, but if I could just put the time off long enough. . . . The first day of the competitions would certainly be insane enough to distract me from anything that might have happened the night before.

At the last moment I decided to take dinner in my apartment. My insides still felt bruised from the confrontation I'd had with my mother, which meant I was in no condition to argue with Vallant the way I'd been doing. If I saw him I was more likely to ask him to hold me, and that would ruin every one of my very sensible plans. It's ridiculous that weakness so often overcomes common sense, and I couldn't help wondering if it were just me. . . .

I expected Jovvi and Lorand to come by after dinner, to tell me what Vallant had learned from Pagin Holter if for no other reason. By the time it occurred to me that he might not have learned anything, I'd already begun to yawn. I'd had an upsetting day and was in need of a good night's sleep, which would give me the strength to hold my own during the next morning's practice. We'd taken to testing our limits, and that required more than a little effort.

The yawning began to get out of hand while I undressed, so I wasn't surprised when I fell asleep immediately after getting into bed. I seemed to sleep only for a short while before I began to dream, and at first I felt surprised to know that I dreamt. Then the surprise went away, replaced with the idea that it was all perfectly normal.

In my dream I sat up against my pillows in bed, having already relit one of the room's lamps with my talent. The door to my bedchamber opened and Vallant came in, wearing a wrap and the sort of stare he'd been giving me for the last few days. When he saw me watching him, he grinned faintly.

"If you're waitin' for me to start performin' immediately, you're in for a small disappointment," he said as he circled to the other side of the bed. "I don't believe in performin' alone, and in any event prefer to take my time."

"What are you doing in my dream?" I asked, watching as he reached to the tie of his wrap. I had to admit that I really wanted to see his body again, and since this was a dream there was no reason why I shouldn't.

"I'm here because you want me here," he replied, pausing before opening his wrap. "If for some reason that doesn't happen to be true, I'll leave again at once."

"No, I don't want you to leave," I decided after a moment. "I don't ever really want you to leave, but I simply can't cope with the ups and downs that go into a relationship. There are so many uncertainties, so many times when all you can do is hope for the best . . . I'm not very good at hoping."

"That's why you need *me*," he said with a tender expression, taking off the wrap and tossing it aside before getting into bed. "I've got lots of experience with hopin', so I can do it for the both of us. Why don't you try it and see if you like it?"

His arms were around me by then, and I discovered that being held was a lot better than simply looking at his marvelous body. He was so broad and strong, and yet so gentle and tender at the same time. I felt absolutely no fear of him, and for that, at least in part, I had Rion and Lorand to thank. It would have killed me if I'd flinched away from Vallant's touch . . . not when he meant so much to me. . . .

"I've been waitin' a long time to give you my physical love, but it's goin' to have to wait a bit longer," Vallant murmured as I held to him tightly, my cheek against the warmth of his chest. "Holdin' you in my arms like this feels too good for me to want to rush it. You don't mind, do you?"

My lips already curved in a smile from his offer to do my hoping for me, and now the curve deepened at the thought that I might mind being held like something very precious and dear. I shook my head in answer to his question, unwilling to intrude on my enjoyment with words, and he made a sound of satisfied acknowledgment. We would do no more than hold each other for a while, letting everything else wait.

I expected the wait to be a long one, or even that he might suddenly dissolve back into dreamstuff, but neither thing happened. Instead my desire for him began to increase, heating my blood so quickly that it startled me. It hadn't been like this with Rion or Lorand, neither the speed nor the intensity of the feelings, and for a moment I didn't know what to do. Then what to do became obvious, and I raised my face and moved my lips toward his.

His response came so quickly, it was as though we were linked as a Blending entity again. Two minds merged into one, a single thought, a single intention, a single desire. His lips demanded mine as furiously as mine demanded his, and the fire in my blood leaped to his flesh and through it to ignite his own blood. My hands caressed the broad hardness of his back, and his moved around and under my nightgown to explore me thoroughly.

Once again I was the one to cut the preliminaries short. I pulled out of his arms for a moment in order to rid myself of the nightgown, and then I returned to press my body directly against his. His hands came to my face and then his lips had mine again, and I couldn't keep from burying my fists in his long platinum mane. I wanted him desperately, needed him terribly, and the sounds coming from deep in his throat said he felt the same.

Insanity gripped us after that, but not so far that I failed to notice when he moved above me. It was the moment I'd been hungering for, but he suddenly turned cautious and overly careful! I snarled a curse at all men for being either too uncaring or too solicitous, and arched up high to capture him quickly. When I locked my legs about him he seemed startled, but only for an instant. After that the insanity had him again, and I was able to forget about everything but pleasure.

Even after having lain with Rion and Lorand, I had no idea that pleasure could be so intense. We both flamed with it, on my part again and again, on his part, twice. After his first release I thought with disappointment that we were done, but he quickly showed me that I was in error. Happily in error, deliciously wrong, and we continued on and on until our strength was completely spent.

Afterward we lay side by side for quite a while, gasping to regain the breath we'd lost in so wonderful a way. Vallant held my hand as though we were innocent sweethearts, and finally he raised the hand to his lips.

"I can honestly say that I've never had such an incredible experience," he murmured, then kissed the hand again. "It worried me that you were touchin' the power, but at some point I found that I was touchin' it as well. Maybe that was what helped to get me through it alive—or mostly alive.''

He chuckled before kissing my hand again, but I felt puzzled. He was right about the experience having been incredible, but an awful lot of things didn't make sense.

"But it isn't possible to touch the power when you're asleep," I protested. "And why are you still here? Most dreams fall apart just before you can enjoy them, or at the very least right afterward. And why does it all seem so real?"

"Why do you keep talkin' about a dream?" he asked, turning to face me and raising up on one elbow. "I expected you to argue and fight when I just walked in, but I wanted you so badly that I had to take the chance. And I did give you the opportunity to tell me to leave, if you'll recall. Did you think I was lyin' when I said I would?"

"No," I replied, suddenly thinking furiously despite my shock. "It's just . . . Did you decide on this visit privately, or did you tell the others you were going to try it?"

"I had to tell them," he responded with a small shrug. "If a riot started, they had to know why and be prepared to keep it as private as possible. Why do you ask?"

"Because now I know why I thought this was all a dream," I said, more than a little annoyed. "Jovvi and Lorand obviously decided to help you, so first thing tomorrow I'm going to have to murder them. I'd do it now, but I haven't the strength to move."

"Was it really *that* terrible for you?" he asked, and the pain in those very light eyes echoed in the middle of my breast. "If I'd known you would feel like that—"

"Don't be an idiot," I interrupted, putting my hand to his face. "I'm going to murder them because it wasn't terrible at all, quite the opposite. It was even better than I'd thought it would be, but how am I supposed to forget about you now? How can I spend even one more night refusing to lie beside you?"

"The answer is you can't," he said, the pain now replaced with loving delight as his arms went around me. "But you haven't lost anythin', you've gained someone to share strength with. Why not try it for a while before decidin' whether or not you like it?''

"As if I still had the choice," I muttered as I snuggled closer to him. "I'm still going to murder them, but maybe not *first* thing tomorrow. I may let them live until second or third thing. Do you have the strength to put out that lamp?"

"Only just," he acknowledged, and then the steady flame abruptly winked out. It was nice not having to bother myself, but not nearly as nice as getting ready to sleep in the arms of the man I cared so much about. Jovvi and Lorand had had no right to interfere with my decision about Vallant, but maybe after I thought about it for a while I might not murder them at all. . . .

FORTY-ONE

Lord Idian Vomak listened to the group's latest description of how their last practice session had gone, pretending to be interested and attentive. In truth his thoughts kept trying to veer away, distracted by much more important matters. The Advisors were far from happy that they would have to wait until after the competitions before they would have a culprit to blame for three deaths, and they'd taken to making everyone's life miserable. Happily, though, it would not be for much longer. . . .

"Lord Idian?" he heard, and blinked back to the realization that Kambil spoke to him. "Is that result satisfactory, sir?"

"Completely satisfactory," he replied with a brief smile, although he had no true idea what he'd been told. "In any event, you must agree that it has to be satisfactory, as tomorrow is the first day of the competitions. Are you all prepared? Beginning to be nervous? If you are, I assure you that it's quite natural.''

"I think we're all just bundles of raw nerves," Delin Moord commented, possibly even telling the truth. "The only time we're not is when we're Blended. Is that true of the others as well?"

"I really don't know, as I haven't spoken to them about it as yet," Idian replied, fighting not to show his opinion of Moord. In general the man seemed too . . . sleek to be capable of murder, but Idian had been forced to believe that he might very well be the one. . . . "And at the moment we have other things to discuss, things which are more pressing."

"About tomorrow?" Lady Selendi asked with thinly veiled excitement. "I've been thinking about it for days, and I've finally decided what to wear. It's—"

"Excuse me," Idian interrupted, "but what you wear is decreed by tradition, not decided individually. Each of you will compete in a white, hooded robe, just as your opponents will. Members of Blendings dress alike to stress the fact that they are in reality one being, and everyone wears white to show that everyone has an equal chance to win to the highest place. That is tradition, and we see no reason to alter it."

The five young people exchanged glances and shrugs, as if to say that the silliness wasn't worth arguing about. The matter was more ridiculous than silly, but there was no need for Idian to mention something they all knew.

"The coaches will come for you tomorrow morning," Idian continued, "but not particularly early. The first competition will begin at noon, and although you need to be there well ahead of time, it's nonsensical to keep you sitting around for hours. Do not, however, use the opportunity of a less than early beginning to practice, as that will wear you out and leave you easy prey for your opponents. You must make as good a showing as possible, to keep your failure from reflecting on the rest of us as a group."

They barely blinked at that, which Idian found extremely satisfying. If they'd penetrated the lies they'd been told and had realized the truth, they would have reacted in some way to what he'd just said. The lack of reaction meant they were still under control, just the way they were supposed to be.

"Assuming you're successful against your opponents tomorrow, you will be returned here for the night," Idian went on. "The second competitions are scheduled for the second day, of course, but only four of the five remaining Blendings will compete in it. On the third day there will be two Blendings competing, and on the fourth day our new Seated Five will be decided on. By then there will be near hysteria in the city, and we'll all do well to avoid the crowds completely."

"What if we're not successful against our opponents?" Kambil interrupted to ask, the question casual and almost one in passing. "Will we go somewhere other than here?"

"Yes, actually, you will," Idian responded, annoyed that the point hadn't been bypassed as he'd hoped it would be. "You'll go instead to the temporary headquarters established by my superiors, where you will each give a detailed description of your individual view of what Blending has been like. While you're about this your possessions will be packed by the servants, and will arrive at your various permanent places of residence not long after you do. Are there any other questions?"

Once again the five glanced at one another, and a second series of shrugs was his reply. They had no other questions, and so it was time for him to leave.

"I'll see you all tomorrow, then," he said as he moved himself to his feet. "I mean to be there to wish all of my people good luck."

The smiles and nods they gave in answer were perfectly polite and correct, so Idian was able to dismiss the group from his thoughts as soon as he left the house. One or two of the others would give him a good deal more trouble, and he certainly wasn't looking forward to it. . . .

"He's gone," Kambil came back to report, reclaiming his chair among them. "And as far as I could tell, he noticed nothing at all."

"That's a considerable relief," Delin said, speaking for himself and probably for the others as well. "We took a rather large risk, and on the eve of the most important day of our lives. If he'd noticed our little trick, it could have been all over for us."

"How could he have noticed what he never consciously saw?" Kambil asked, keeping his tone reasonable and reassuring. "Our Blending projected an illusion for him, the details of which he himself supplied. In it he went through the routine he expected to, and received only the most ordinary reactions from us. We did ask a single mildly annoying question, but one he had no trouble responding to. After that he simply left, remembering nothing of the real question and answer period."

"But I remember it," Bron said, sounding sober and bleak. "If we lose tomorrow we'll be sent somewhere to— 'describe our experiences as part of a Blending.' An interesting euphemism for being quickly put out of the way, which is what will really happen. What lovely, grateful people they are."

"Don't forget that they'll take us on separately," Homin pointed out with disgust in his voice. "We're expected to be almost useless as a Blending, but they're still frightened enough of us that they won't face us as a group. It makes me sick to think that I used to consider myself one of them."

"The only thing we're one of now is this group," Selendi said fiercely, looking around at each of them. "They don't expect us to be one of the winning Blendings, but they're in for a very big surprise. We're going to be the only winning Blending when the competitions are over, and then we'll see who gets sent where."

"We certainly will," Kambil agreed, blocking out Delin's usual vague dissatisfaction. "We'll have a very large house to clean, but it's well past time that it was done."

"And I know just where we'll start," Delin put in, finally finding something to agree about. "Once we win, I'll tell the rest of you all about it. . . ."

"Yes, that's truly marvelous," Lord Twimmal said to the group of peasants, pretending he cared how their latest practice had gone. "But we do have other things to discuss, and I would prefer to get to them without any further delay."

"Of course," the female Spirit magic user said with a smile. "Please do go on."

The woman was rather attractive for a peasant, as was the other one, the Fire magic user. Twimmal wouldn't have minded keeping either of them for a while once their usefulness to the empire was over, but the matter would have been more trouble than it was worth. Powerful men had already expressed an interest in the girl of Fire, and as far as the other one went, Twimmal knew his wife would never understand. . . .

"As you know, tomorrow is the big day," Twimmal continued after clearing his throat. "The first of the competitions will be held, so I'm afraid there won't be any partying permitted this evening. You must all get your sleep tonight so that you'll have sufficient strength tomorrow."

Two of the male peasants made sounds of disappointment, and the third looked extremely annoyed. They'd all undoubtedly been spending gold like water, and now disliked the idea of stopping. Well, that was just too bad about them. They'd had their pay, and now it was time that they worked for it.

"What sort of thing will be involved in the competitions?" the Spirit magic female asked. "I mean, will we and our opponents both be trying to do the same thing, or will we be competing directly against each other?"

"My dear girl, do I look old enough to have attended the last twenty-fifth year competitions?" Twimmal countered in annoyance over being interrupted. "I have no more idea of what will be done than you, which, I understand, is the way my superiors want it. May I continue now?"

Her nod looked properly chastened, so Twimmal felt considerably better.

"Tomorrow morning, the coaches will be here for you rather early," he said, picking up his dropped thread of thought. "Everyone wants to be completely certain that you're prepared to do as you must, and you will also require a short time to change your clothing. Traditionally, everyone in these things competes wearing white hooded robes, therefore you will wear the same."

Twimmal was certain one of them would interrupt again, but his earlier rebuke of the Spirit magic female had undoubtedly impressed the rest into keeping silent. That result was more than gratifying, as it allowed him to wind things up.

"I'll be attending the festivities tomorrow along with Lady Eltrina, so I'll see you all then," Twimmal said as he began to struggle out of the chair. "Enjoy the rest of today, but do practice as much as possible. In fact, if you're able to rise early enough to practice in the morning, by all means do so. It can only sharpen you for the actual event."

And with that, the last of it, said, Twimmal made his escape. These peasant places always stank of filth and squalor, which usually made him quite ill after he visited them. He kept the illness from taking him over until he was home, of course, but then he was forced to empty himself. Thank whatever Higher Aspect there was that the torment was nearly over. And the next time his wife and her father banded together to insist that he accept an appointment, he would be much more firm in refusing it. . . .

". . . and his carriage is leaving the drive now," Rion heard Jovvi say. "He's obviously not going to be coming back, so now we can talk."

"A point of interest has occurred to me," Rion said, looking around at his groupmates where they sat. "The Advisors prefer to have as few people as possible knowing about Blending, but Twimmal is one of those who has learned the method of accomplishing it. His knowledge is sloppy and skimpy to be sure, but it's knowledge nevertheless. What do you suppose will be done with the fat fool now that his usefulness is at an end?"

"That's an excellent point," Jovvi said with a startled expression. "It hadn't occurred to me that they would be quite so ruthless with their own, but they must be using this opportunity to cull their ranks. Pick the ones they most want to be rid of, have them learn what no one is supposed to know, and then dispose of them. Two birds with a single stone."

"More than two," Lorand pointed out. "They also want to be rid of any possible competition for their chosen Blending, so they also dispose of all challengers. And since you didn't initiate the Blending while Twimmal was here,

I'm assuming we were right to believe that he knows little or nothing.''

"He was all but reciting by rote," Jovvi confirmed with a nod. "They told him what to say and he said it, and then he left. He simply isn't bright enough to wonder about any of it."

"But we are," Tamrissa put in, looking annoyed. "Go ahead and practice in the morning, he said. Are we supposed to still have no idea how draining Blending can be? Even after they mentioned the point? With everything else being equal, if we practiced and our opponents didn't, they'd start out immediately with an edge."

"But all other things aren't equal," Jovvi reminded her with amused satisfaction. "We've built our Blending strength up to the point where we actually could practice and not lose much if anything, so that's one less worry. We *won't* do it, of course, but we could. Now let's talk about the things we do have to worry about, like how the other groups are doing. Vallant? You got back just before Twimmal arrived, so please tell us now what you learned."

"I learned that Holter is doin' better than fine arrangin' things," Vallant said as Rion joined the others in giving him their full attention. This was rather important. . . . "He told me that four of the five competin' Blendin's are now free of that drugged state, but we can forget about the fifth. They were too busy enjoyin' themselves to want to hear about anythin' that might help."

"The ten gold dins apiece were obviously too much for them," Lorand said with a sad shake of his head. "It's really too bad, but I consider us lucky for losing only one of the five."

"We're luckier than that," Vallant told him, leaning forward a bit. "As usual, Holter thought of somethin' the rest of us missed. Before gettin' rid of the drugged orders from the fourth group, he thought to ask if they'd already been *given* any orders. They weren't told much, but it's somethin' we all need to know about: how to respond properly when the time comes that we *are* given orders."

"Bless that brainy little man," Jovvi said with a wide and delighted smile. "We'll certainly have to pretend to be accepting their orders, but without being able to give the proper response we would have been wasting our time. What's the right way to do it?''

''We're supposed to say, 'At your command, my lord,' '' Vallant replied, his expression twisting into one of disgust. ''That will tell them they're doin' it right, so they don't have to worry. It's goin' to take somethin' for me to say that, but I mean to make the effort. Seein' their faces afterward will make it all worthwhile.''

''Yes, it certainly will,'' Rion agreed, forcing his scandalized feelings well away from himself. ''And afterward I mean to do more than simply look at them.''

''I'll join you in that,'' Vallant agreed with grim anticipation, then he continued, ''and Holter had more good news. The two people moved out of his residence and put in that extra Blendin' were happy to sneak back, and the five of them Blended without any trouble at all. They've been spendin' their time practicin' like crazy, and at the last minute they intend to substitute those two for the woman with Air magic they can't abide, and our old friend Drowd.''

''And it's unlikely anyone will notice,'' Tamrissa said, obviously tickled by the idea. ''If Drowd is still drinking and carousing the way Pagin said he was, even *he* probably won't notice. But isn't it strange that they were able to Blend with two different people after Blending the first time with others? For some reason I thought that that wasn't possible.''

''I think we're all learnin' that things are possible which aren't supposed to be,'' Vallant said to her, his smile tender and personal. Rion was delighted to see her return it impishly, as though they shared some private memory. The last few days had been *so* much better, now that the two were together as they were obviously meant to be. And, happily, it seemed Tamrissa had no idea that the help Lorand and Jovvi had given Vallant had been all Vallant's idea. . . .

''I agree with Tamma,'' Jovvi said, clearly swallowing a smile over the way Vallant had been sidetracked. ''None of the officials tomorrow is likely to notice the substitution, and the residence officials won't be able to tell them about it until it's too late. What about our suggestions concerning accepting any hospitality from them?''

"Holter said everyone agrees with us completely," Vallant replied after tearing his gaze away from Tamrissa. "Those of us who win tomorrow will insist on returnin' to their various residences. If they try to insist that we stay somewhere else, we tell them we won't compete in the followin' contests. Since they *have* to hold public challenges, they shouldn't have any choice but to agree."

"I hope you mentioned that they may try force," Jovvi said, obviously concerned about the issue. "At that point they'll be desperate to get us back under control, and might not be willing to give in without an argument."

"I did mention it, but someone else had thought of it first," Vallant said with a nod. "That means the others have already agreed: if they force us to it, we Blend against them. It's doubtful they know what that means, but if they push us they'll surely be findin' out."

"What about the flasks for water and tea we suggested they buy?" Lorand asked. "And that special oiled wrap for sandwiches? If we keep the things with us at all times, we'll be able to know that they aren't tampered with."

"Holter liked the idea, and he had another suggestion," Vallant replied. "Before we eat or drink even from our supply, our Earth magic member ought to check everythin' over. Holter and I could both put tainted water in a flask without ever comin' near it, so it would be foolish to think *they* couldn't."

"He's right again, so I'll be sure to remember," Lorand agreed. "It looks like we really are lucky to be working with the others on this. Did you get a chance to ask Holter if Twimmal was the only instructor he and his group saw? We haven't seen or heard a thing about that so-called Lord Carmad since the day he was here."

"I did, and Holter knew nothin' about another instructor," Vallant returned, now looking disturbed. "He didn't believe any of the others had been visited either, so we still have a mystery on our hands. Who was he, and why was he here?"

"And how did he find out the way to make a Blending?" Jovvi added with her own disturbance. "Considering how close the government is with the secret, that's the biggest mystery of all. Is there anything we can do to get even one or two of the answers?''

"Short of finding the man and questioning him?" Tamrissa said with a very unladylike snort. "I don't see what, and even that isn't practical. It's too bad we didn't know enough to grab him on the spot."

"Yes, it is," Jovvi said slowly, "but there's something even more important that we ought to talk about now. I try not to pry so I haven't been sure, but—Tamma, are you still touching the power?"

"Well . . . what if I am?" Tamrissa replied, a faint uneasiness behind the confidence which Rion had noticed but hadn't really *seen*. "It isn't doing me or anyone else any harm, so why shouldn't I? It isn't as if anyone can regret not seeing what I'm like when I'm not touching it. . . ."

"How do you know it isn't doing you any harm?" Jovvi countered gently with a good deal of concern. "With as little as we know about using our abilities . . . Tamma—*can* you release the touch?"

The last was asked as though Jovvi had had a sudden revelation, and at first Rion found himself joining the other men in producing sounds of protestation. Jovvi's guess couldn't possibly be right, but then Rion saw Tamrissa's expression.

"I . . . can't retain the touch when I fall asleep, but as soon as I wake up again it's . . . there," Tamrissa admitted slowly and reluctantly. "I don't know what it means or even if it really does mean something, but I can't seem to control it. It's something you all ought to know, even though I can't find the condition doing me any harm. I'm not exhausted all the time or even compulsively active. . . ."

"Maybe we can use the Blendin' to find out," Vallant said when her words trailed off. He'd left his chair to crouch beside hers and take her hand, his expression one of confident support. "I feel like a fool for not noticin' sooner, but don't you worry, love. We'll all help you take care of it."

"We certainly will," Jovvi said briskly as she rose from her chair, dispelling the air of worry which had settled over all of them. "But right now we all have things to do, including finalizing our party arrangements for dinner. We may all be going to bed early, but first we're entitled to a pre-victory celebration. Rion, please remind Naran, and tell her that her presence is all arranged for.''

Rion nodded agreement as he also stood, able to feel good about that at least. The others had taken to Naran almost as strongly as he had, and although they couldn't risk having her constantly among them, Jovvi had gone out of her way to arrange occasions which Naran could attend. If only this last one proved not to be the actual last. . . .

And if only Rion could be certain that Tamrissa really would be all right. . . .

FORTY-TWO

The coaches came for us after breakfast the next morning, and we separated the way we used to: Vallant, Rion, and Lorand in one, Jovvi and me in the other. We'd toned down our ''feuding'' to merely being a bit standoffish, something we decided the authorities would be able to accept without suspicion. We weren't in the mood to give them the full act which we'd come close to perfecting, not with the case of nerves we'd all developed.

''I'm actually glad that we're going this early,'' Jovvi said, as our coach began to follow the men's down the drive. ''If we'd had to do our waiting here, I would probably have ended up flat and useless. I can refuse to receive the emotions of anyone I choose—except for you four.''

''I wonder why we're starting out *this* early,'' I said, trying to ignore the knot my insides had become. ''The placard said that the festivities begin at noon, which means that once we get there we'll have more than two hours to wait—the exact amount of time depending on how long this trip turns out to be. Why do they need more than two hours to hand us robes and tell us to lose?"

"They may also intend to do something to make the wait more unsettling or uncomfortable," Jovvi suggested with a shrug. "We can't put even the smallest dirty trick past them, since they're obviously believers in the saying, 'Something worth doing is worth overdoing.' And speaking of doing, how are *you* managing? Did you have any luck working with Vallant to release your hold on the power?"

"No, and it's beginning to be annoying," I said, finally the least bit distracted. "We should have realized even before we tried that Blending wasn't likely to help, because when we Blend we all touch the power. Lorand said that hilsom powder would certainly do the job, because that's what they use on people who go insane and won't release the power. But the effects of hilsom powder hang on for a while, so I can't afford to try it until after the competitions. Oh, well, being permanently attached doesn't seem to be harming me in any way. . . ."

"I thought of one way in which you're being harmed," Jovvi responded, apparently also distracted. "You were only just beginning to learn self-confidence, how not to let yourself be taken advantage of. Am I wrong in believing that you aren't really learning those things any longer?"

"But now I don't need them," I pointed out with the puzzlement I felt. "I have all the confidence and assurance I need, without having to fight for it every inch of the way. How can that be bad?"

"Considering the circumstances, I suppose it can't," she replied with a sigh and a faint smile. "We'll just have to wait to see what happens after the competitions. But no matter what else might be uncertain, at least our relationships with the men have improved."

"The problem between you and Lorand was easy, because Blending solved it," I reminded her. "Lorand and Vallant feel nothing of their previous fears and difficulties when we're all Blended, so it's stopped being something to worry about. And as far as Vallant and I go . . . the Blending bond increased a good deal more than I expected it to."

"I think we were all surprised," Jovvi said as she narrowed her eyes at me. "What surprises me now, though, is what you're *not* saying. There isn't any trouble between you and Vallant?"

"Trouble? No." My smile must have been on the strange side, considering what my feelings were. "He's blissfully happy, and I'm simply waiting for it all to end. I can't seem to get rid of the feeling that it will, and soon. It's made me cautious."

"About committing yourself to the relationship," she said with a nod of understanding. "He's very deeply committed, but you're only pretending to be. When did you intend to tell him?"

"It won't be for *me* to say anything," I told her with a mirthless smile. "It won't even be my idea. One day soon it will just be over, and then I'll have the choice of staying with him in my memories, or forgetting about him completely. I haven't yet decided which I'll do."

"Tamma . . . can you think about the possibility that your basic lack of confidence is making you believe all that?" she suggested gently, comfort flowing from her mind. "It can just as easily be a fear-induced misconception as a true premonition, maybe even more easily. Will you at least consider the possibility?"

"Sure," I agreed without hesitation, but only to make her feel better. There wasn't any real possibility of my being wrong, and I knew it even if she didn't.

We rode in silence after that, watching the city disappear after a while as we took one of the roads leading to the amphitheater. I'd never been out to it myself before, but everyone in the city knew approximately where it was. It was used only once in twenty-five years, for the Blending competitions, and was supposed to be almost four hundred years old. The government maintained it in between those times, and very often schoolchildren were taken out to see it.

Today there were more than schoolchildren heading for it. It was already a beautiful day, which probably encouraged everyone to get a nice early start, so our fairly rapid progress quickly slowed down to a crawl. The road was clogged with carriages and coaches and people on horseback, and more people walked on the uneven ground to either side of the road. The walkers were most often entire families, some with more than a few children.

"I think I'm beginning to understand why we started out so early," Jovvi commented as she looked out her window. "We're still moving, but only barely."

"The evil of the testing authority and government obviously knows no bounds," I commented back. "Imagine, being so heartless and cruel as to get us caught in a traffic jam. When I was young, my parents accepted an invitation from a business associate on a festival day. We'd always celebrated at home before, so we had no idea how bogged down it was possible to get. And we couldn't even turn around and go home. We were stuck for hours, and at the end of it we were limp rags."

"I seriously doubt if they'll let us be stuck for that long," Jovvi said with a chuckle for my comment and story. "The show can't start without us, after all, and if we show up exhausted we can always refuse to participate. But come to think of it, they don't yet know we can refuse. Ah, well, at least we have water, tea, and sandwiches to keep us fortified."

"Which we won't even sniff at until Lorand tells us it's safe," I reminded her. "If necessary, we can link up and ask him to do it."

"Yes, the distance between us and the men is no problem," Jovvi agreed. "We've Blended this far away from each other before, after learning that the formation was just a beginner's aid. The arrangement is needed inside our heads, not with our bodies. I wonder how many of the nobles running this thing understand that."

"Probably very few," I said after glancing at her. "What I'd like to know is how many of their Blendings have learned it."

She couldn't help but agree with that, and then we settled back into silence again. But the silence was only between ourselves, as the noise outside the coach had risen to a relatively high level. People were happy and excited, and some were even singing.

We inched our way forward for another few minutes, and then a different noise began to intrude. It resolved itself into the shouting of men, and shortly thereafter we began to move faster again. When we saw members of the guard chasing walkers away from the very edge of the road and hurrying vehicles along with impatient gestures, we understood what was happening. Any vehicle too slow to keep to a good pace—like the rickety, slanted old wagon filled with women and children being pulled by a single, tired, old horse—was being gotten out of the way onto the side of the road, letting the rest of us continue on.

After that there were no further delays, and when other coaches and carriages and riders were directed toward one of the outlying areas where vehicles and mounts were to be left, we were waved on. The amphitheater loomed large in the near distance, and people were streaming toward it on foot from many different directions. They all pointed excitedly toward our coaches, and some even began to run in an effort to keep up with us.

When we finally came to a stop near one of the private entrances leading to the interior of the amphitheater, there were actually crowds with guardsmen holding them back. One of the guardsmen helped Jovvi and me from the coach while our men got out on their own, and as soon as the crowd saw us they began to cheer. I noticed that none of them actually tried to get too close, but they did cheer with abandon.

The men waited until we'd reached them, and then we all began to walk toward the entrance. Lorand and Vallant grinned and waved to the cheering crowd, which helped to increase the noise. Rion simply put himself behind Jovvi and me, a rear guard we wouldn't have needed even without the guardsmen being present. But it was a sweet thing to do, and almost distracted me from what we were so casually walking into. . . .

Lord Idian saw Delin Moord and his group arrive, so he left the crowd around Adriari's group and hurried over to the new arrivals. Everyone was trying to curry favor with the soon-to-be new Seated Five, of course, and Idian would have been foolish not to do the same. But he had a chore to attend to, after which he'd be able to return to what he'd been doing.

"Good morning, Lord Idian," Kambil Arstin said with his usual politeness when he reached them. "It's a lovely morning, isn't it?"

"Yes, quite lovely," Idian said impatiently, wishing that whole thing were already over with. "An apartment has been prepared for the five of you, where you may rest and change your clothing before the competitions begin. I've assigned one of my assistants to show you the way, and also to fetch anything you might want or need. But before you go, there's one change in plans you have to be made aware of."

"And what change is that?" Delin Moord asked, his smile just as charming as ever. "Nothing that will really inconvenience us, I hope?"

"Quite the contrary," Idian told him, also adding a warm smile. "The Advisors met and discussed the matter, and have now told us that they wish to show their sympathy with and gratitude toward Lord Homin. The poor man has lost a stepmother and an uncle in a very short period of time, and yet has manfully carried on with his duty toward the empire. For that reason it's been arranged that your first opponents will be different from the group you expected to meet."

"That's their idea of a favor?" Homin Weil asked with a snort, actually looking annoyed. "Weren't they told that we've already researched the original group, and there's scarcely time to do the same with the new one?"

"That's the beauty of the favor, Lord Homin," Idian replied, putting a bit more snap into his voice to keep the boy in line. "There's no need to do research of any sort with this group, as they took their ten gold dins each and immediately began to spend them on one long good time. This morning they're barely recovered, I'm told, and may even find it impossible to Blend. The change all but guarantees your victory in the first competitions, which will affect your prestige and standing in a very positive way."

"That's really quite generous of the Advisors," Kambil Arstin said with his own smile while the others exchanged surprised glances. "Please give them our thanks when you can, and also our assurance that we'll do all in our power not to disappoint them. Now . . . you said there's an apartment assigned to us?"

"Yes, and my assistant will show you where it is," Idian said, turning to gesture to the boy who had been assigned to assist him. "His name is Glindil, and you need only follow him."

The five people nodded and went off after the boy, and rather than returning immediately to what he'd been doing, Idian stood staring pensively after the group. His chore was now done and he was, for the most part, out of it, but he couldn't help thinking about what would come afterward. Everything he'd said about the group's new opponents was absolutely true, but the same couldn't quite be said for the reason behind the change. . . .

It had been Lord Anglard Nobin, the Advisory representative, who had given Idian his instructions, and the man had been as coldly distant and unpleasant as ever.

"Why are we doing this?" Lord Anglard had said in answer to Idian's question. "The reason is perfectly obvious, once you understand that we've managed to eliminate all suspects in the murders but one. That one is Delin Moord, and the Advisors want very badly to make an example of the man. The first day of the competitions often leaves dead bodies on the ground, I'm told, and the Advisors don't want Moord dead so easily. His group can be defeated by one of *our* Blendings on the second or third day without taking casualties, and then Moord will find himself just where the Advisors want him."

Idian thought about that particular position for a moment, then turned back to Adriari's group before a shudder took him over. No matter how difficult the competitions turned out to be, they would be a pleasant delight compared to what the Advisors meant to come up with. One could almost feel sorry for Moord . . . if the man weren't so objectionable. . . .

FORTY-THREE

Lorand looked around at the interior of the amphitheater, trying not to gawk like a hayseed. The area they stood in was immense, much larger than the outside of the structure led one to expect. The inner tiers of seats must be suspended over a hollow, despite their having been carved out of stone.

"This place is a madhouse," Rion said, his near shout reaching only the five of them. "And it looks like we're the last to arrive."

"They're leadin' two of the groups toward that door," Vallant pointed out, indicating the area to their left. "The rest are bein' herded to the right, and herded seems to be a particularly good word."

"There's Twimmal, standing next to Lady Eltrina," Jovvi put in, also pointing. "Neither one of them seems particularly happy, and I wonder why."

"Maybe we'll find out," Tamrissa observed. "Twimmal has just seen us, and he's hurrying over."

The fat little noble was *trying* to hurry over, Lorand noted, but his gait wasn't nearly fast enough to be considered a true hurry. He waddled, actually, but did eventually reach them.

"It's certainly about time that you got here," he began without preamble, the petulance in his tone clear despite all the noise. "You were specifically instructed to arrive early, and—"

"Stop right there," Lorand interrupted coldly, in no

321

mood for taking nonsense from a fool. "If you wanted us here earlier you should have sent the coaches earlier, or possibly done something about the crowds we were caught in. If you people aren't up to getting this thing done right, you can't excuse your incompetence by blaming *us*."

"How dare you speak to me like that?" Twimmal asked in his high, squeaky voice, obviously deeply shocked. "You people are nothing, and I am—"

"A lot less than nothin', or you wouldn't have been tapped as an official flunky," Vallant finished for him, just as coldly as Lorand had spoken. "That means we're still better than you, so start flunkyin' and tell us what's goin' on."

"I don't know how I'm expected to bear this," Twimmal whined, still upset and apparently talking to himself. "First that nasty person is placed above Lady Eltrina, and now the peasants feel free to give backtalk. I shall resign my place at once, that's what I'll do."

"Isn't it time you woke up to the real world?" Tamrissa put in, the hard edge in her tone only just noticeable. "At this point no one will be allowed to resign, least of all you. Or haven't you realized yet that you know too much for your own good? Having knowledge of how a Blending is formed is usually punishable by death, and you're the only one among them who knows. If you don't make an effort to share your knowledge, you probably won't live long enough to see the end of the competitions."

Twimmal had turned absolutely white, and the fact that he hadn't fainted was due only to Lorand's efforts—efforts made only because Lorand finally understood what Tamrissa was up to. She'd had a good idea, and there was no sense in letting Twimmal ruin it by passing out. The fat little man wavered a bit, and then he staggered away without another word.

"That was evil, and I loved it," Jovvi said to Tamrissa with a chuckle when Twimmal was out of hearing range. "Once he snaps out of the shock he'll start to tell everyone the way to form a Blending, and that should cause a riot among the nobles. While they're busy trying to silence him and find out everyone he spoke to, they'll have less time to plot against us. And wasn't that interesting about Eltrina? No wonder she's so bent out of shape."

"It's typical of the breed," Rion put in, nothing of sympathy in his tone. "They let her do all the work, and now, at the last moment, they put in one of their own to take all the credit. Since she must have schemed a long time to get herself into the proper position, she's probably livid. But even I was told how these things work, so I'm surprised she didn't expect it."

"One of her schemes probably didn't work right," Vallant put in with distaste. "She strikes me as the sort who's too busy lookin' over the men around her to pay attention to every detail. Now she can look at the one they made her boss."

"I hadn't realized you'd noticed her attraction to you, Vallant," Jovvi remarked with faint amusement. "I couldn't miss it myself, but I decided against mentioning it. I could also tell how put off you were by her."

"Too bad she didn't notice the same," Vallant remarked dryly. "But now that we've sent Twimmal flutterin' away, we're stuck with just standin' here. Maybe we ought to remind them about our presence."

"They know we're here, and they're sending someone over to see to us," Jovvi disagreed, only glancing in the direction of the people she spoke about. "They're vastly annoyed with Twimmal for wandering off before his job was done, and I think he was supposed to bring someone over to us, but forgot. The man really is an incompetent, emptyheaded fool. . . . Ah, the someone is on his way."

Lorand glanced around casually and spotted a young man strolling in their direction. His attitude screamed to the world that he was a noble, and one who considered himself really important, at that. Just what they needed in that madhouse, someone else to rub badly against their nervousness. . . .

"Well, it seems that you people were abandoned," the young man said lightly when he reached them. "I'm Lord Ophin Ruhl, and I've been asked to direct you to the place where you'll wait for things to begin. By the bye, do you happen to know where Lord Twimmal has gone? He surprised us by disappearing like that."

"He didn't say where he was going," Tamrissa responded with complete honesty, then put her head to one side while showing a childlike expression of innocence.

"Twimmal can't possibly be considered anyone's lord, but you still use the title for him. Haven't you people learned yet how silly you all look, calling ones like him the same thing you call yourselves? Or can't you tell what a deficient Twimmal is?"

"It's—ah—something I believe they're looking into," Ophin responded with a great deal of discomfort. "Please follow me in this direction."

He indicated the way to the right before immediately moving off, and Lorand exchanged bland glances with the others before joining them in following. Tamrissa's wide-eyed, empty-minded questions had left Ophin with very little to say—even if the man had wanted to defend his position. Arguing with someone who's already shown herself willing to say anything but isn't terribly bright can be very frustrating, not to mention embarrassing. Ophin had taken the easy way out, leaving Tamrissa with her point clearly made—and the young lord already rattled.

They were led across the wide floor and through the crowds to the door in the right-hand wall, and once they passed through it the noise level dropped abruptly. They'd entered a lamplit corridor of some sort, and Lord Ophin walked almost to the end of it before throwing open a door.

"This is the apartment where you'll wait to be called," he said, gesturing them in past him. "Your robes will be brought to you in just a few moments, and you're to get into them as quickly as possible. Oh, yes, and ladies, no petticoats, please. You'll all be furnished with undergarments and sandals as well, and they're the only things to be worn with the robes. Tea and snack cakes have been provided, and if you require anything else, speak to the person who brings your robes. Good luck, and I'll certainly see you later."

And with that he strode away, obviously intent on putting enough distance between them that Tamrissa would find it impossible to ask any more questions. Lorand discovered that he wasn't the only one chuckling as he walked into the room to look around. Vallant had entered first, and now he returned to close the door behind all of them.

"I hope no one minds my hurryin' inside here," Vallant said then. "That big outer room had too many people, and the corridor was windowless and too narrow. This place at least has windows, even if they *are* too high up to be reached easily. I know I can reach them if I have to, so I can stand bein' in here.''

"If it becomes necessary, Rion and I will help you," Lorand told him simply. He'd tried to imagine what Vallant usually went through in small, enclosed places, and hadn't been able to do it. His favorite place as a boy had been small and close and almost airless. Picturing that safe and cozy place as a trap to be escaped from was completely beyond Lorand.

"At least this room is big, and there's another one just like it through this door," Tamrissa reported from the left, where she peered through the door she'd mentioned. "It has a narrow, lumpy-looking couch instead of those chairs, but it's just as big. And there's a far door that probably leads to privacy facilities."

"All the comforts of home," Jovvi remarked dryly, stopping in front of the large tea service. "Lorand, can you tell if they've done anything to the snack cakes and tea? I'll be happier if we can save our own supplies for later."

"They seem to be against taking any chances at all," Lorand replied after a brief moment of examining the cakes. "There's something mixed in with the other ingredients that looks an awful lot like headache powder. You know, the kind that relaxes you enough to relieve your headache? It's not enough to really incapacitate any of us, but it's still there."

"And it's probably there to distract us," Jovvi said with a nod. "If we're smart enough to check, we find that the cakes have been tampered with. That should convince us that they don't intend to try anything else, so we'll be off our guard. What about the tea?"

"The tea itself looks all right, but I can't tell about the water," Lorand said, already having checked. "Can you see anything, Vallant?"

"Yes, and I'm recommendin' that we don't touch it," Vallant responded, staring at the service. "Tea water is usually almost . . . empty, so to speak, except for the tea. This water's got somethin' in it that makes it crowded, and I don't like the looks of it. It reminds me of the drinkin' water in a port I once visited very briefly. Most of the townsfolk were sick to their stomachs, not plague-sick but bad-food–sick. Our cargo was already paid for, so we off-loaded it quick and got out of there—and got fresh supplies at the next port.''

"So that settles that," Tamrissa said, having finished her exploring and rejoined them. "We eat or drink only what we brought with us, and even then not until Lorand and Vallant look it over. How much time do we have left to wait?"

"Just under two hours," Jovvi told her after consulting a small pocket watch. "We ought to be able to survive that length of time without food or drink, so our supplies will be conserved anyway. I wonder how long it will be before they bring those robes. Changing our clothes will fill some of the time."

"And the special visitor we can expect will fill even more of it," Rion reminded them. "We haven't been given our instructions yet, and then they'll have to position us all before it turns noon. With that in mind, we probably have less than an hour to actually spend waiting."

Those points were too obvious for anyone to disagree, so they all chose chairs and sat. Lorand found himself more comfortable than he'd expected to be, but the presence of the headache powder in the cakes should have warned him. The powder and the chairs were supposed to combine to make them sleepy, ruining the sharp edge brought about by nervousness. The nobles seemed to be covering every possible contingency, in spite of the fact that they shouldn't need anything but the drug the group had already been given. Curious. . . .

By the time a knock at the door brought two servants into the room, Lorand had thought of a possible reason for the over-thoroughness of the nobles' preparations. The drug they'd been given could well be a last resort, to be used only if everything else failed. But that would hardly do for the group meant to face their chosen Blending. The nobles would want to be very sure of *their* opponents, so a visit from someone with orders ought to confirm the group's guess that they were indeed the ones. . . .

Except for size, the white robes and accompanying white

sandals were absolutely identical. The undergarments were slightly smaller robes made of silk, and felt cool and wonderful against the skin. Lorand had expected that Tamrissa at least would go into the other room to change, but all sense of embarrassment seemed to have left the girl. She changed with as little fuss as everyone else, and when they were through they examined each other.

"Now we really look like full participants," Jovvi said, the first one to comment. "And I'm surprised that these things are so comfortable. I expected them to fit badly, which would have been another distraction."

"The cakes and tea could have been put in here for any group they happened to assign to the apartment," Lorand said, deciding to share his guesswork. "The robes, though, were clearly made for no one but us. If they're this comfortable, we probably will get that visitor Rion mentioned."

He explained his thinking in more detail then, and everyone nodded their understanding.

"That means if we do get a visitor, we have to be sure to link up," Rion said then. "If the drug still held us we'd respond at precisely the same time; linking will let us do that without draining us."

Again everyone agreed, and, as it turned out, just in time. Another knock came at the door, and when Lorand went to open it he found the man who had been standing next to Eltrina Razas, waiting patiently.

"I'm Lord Simin Dolf," the man said smoothly with a smile. "I may be new to the ranks of those who have worked with you, but I'd still like to extend my good wishes. May I come in?"

Lorand felt tempted to answer, "No," and then close the door in the man's face, but that was just a fleeting whim. It would do no good at all to put off what the nobles intended to make unavoidable, so Lorand shrugged and then stepped back to allow Lord Simin entrance.

"Looking at all of you, I believe I'm beginning to feel truly excited," the noble said as he advanced into the room. "I hadn't expected to be so deeply involved in this twenty-fifth year, and now that I am, I'm as delighted as a child. I believe I'll sit here for a moment, so that I'm able to look at each of you well enough to remember details. This will be a tale to tell for the rest of my life.''

Lorand reclaimed his own chair as the noble took one to the left, which gave the man the overall view he'd mentioned. The rest of the group had been seated when Simin entered, and Lorand wondered if the noble felt insulted over the fact that no one rose respectfully. If so, Simin hid the emotion well.

"This is marvelous," he continued to burble, still looking from one to the other of them. "I can't tell you how much this means to me, as now is the time for all commoners to come to the aid of the empire."

Lorand froze where he sat as the Blending link instantly flared into being, Jovvi initiating the state with all the speed of her considerable talent. The very great temptation was there to Blend all the way to melding, but Lorand held it off just as he felt the others doing.

"Now that's a good deal better," Lord Simin said without the burbling, suddenly looking like an entirely different man. "You filthy little nothings imagined that you were getting away with not giving me the respect you owe to all your betters, but you were mistaken. Right now I have orders for you, and after you carry them out we'll see to your punishment for insolence. If you're still alive, that is."

Nice of him to tell us that our opponents will be out for blood, their Jovvi part sent while Simin chuckled nastily. *Let's see what else he lets slip.*

"The most important command that I have for you is that you're to understand you're no match for the noble group you'll be facing," Simin continued. "You will keep up the pretense of being ready to contend with everything you have, but on the inside each of you will know and believe that defeat is all there is in store for you. In point of fact you will assist in your own defeat, but not in any obvious way. The victory of your opponents is to appear as nothing but superior ability. Is all that clear?"

"At your command, my lord," Lorand said with the rest of the link, almost contributing to a chant. Simin's expression lightened, and he laughed with clear enjoyment.

"That is exactly what you useless peasants are, at the command of every one of your superiors," he said. "During the competition you will attack and defend with only enough ability to make your opponents look good, and then you will lose. If they decide to spare your lives, once you return to the gathering area you will report to me for your punishment. If they don't decide to spare you, well, then I suppose you'll get away with having been insolent. I now give you no choice but to obey."

"At your command, my lord," the chorus chimed out again, causing Simin to chuckle again. But if the noble had been able to feel what Lorand did from the group, chuckling would have been the last thing Simin would have wanted to do.

"That's my good little peasants," Simin drawled. "You'll obey me now, and later—if there *is* a later for you—you will obey me once more without question and without needing to be keyed again. And now you have my permission to return to the way you were . . . and so I'd like to thank you for giving me this opportunity. Now I'll wish you good luck in your attempt, and leave you alone to rest and relax."

By then the noble was back to burbling as he rose to his feet, and Lorand rose as well to follow him to the door. Jovvi had released the link when Simin believed he was releasing them, and apparently the ruse worked perfectly. Simin left still burbling, and once Lorand closed the door he turned toward the others.

"The fool isn't even standing outside the door to hear whatever we might decide to talk about," he reported. "His trace and life signs are strolling away back toward that open area, and in another moment or two he should be completely gone. . . . There. He just went through the door."

"I'd say that that answers our question about which of our groups will be facing their darlings," Jovvi said with a shake of her head. "If they were going to do the same to every group, he would never have come directly here and then left in the same way. Tomorrow will probably be another story, but today the privilege is ours alone."

"I suggest we pretend that he never visited us," Tamrissa said, her extreme annoyance still clear in Lorand's memory of the link. "The pretense will keep them guessing about what went wrong, and may even serve to get that useless garbage exactly what he deserves. If they think their plans are in ruins because of *him*, they may actually end him before they find out any better.''

"I'd enjoy seein' that," Vallant commented, his light eyes looking very cold to Lorand. "There are men who are my superior in any number of ways, but none of them simply because he *said* so. We've got to do somethin' about gettin' rid of those parasites."

"We'll have time to worry about it if and when we win the competitions," Jovvi told them all as Lorand joined Rion in growling agreement. "Right now we need to *relax*, so let's sit down and do it the way I taught you. We'll all be forcing ourselves to relax, but we'll gather ten times the strength we use to accomplish it. With me, now. One, two, three. . . ."

Lorand pushed aside thoughts of getting even and made himself join the effort to relax, but only because it was necessary. Once they won—and they *would* win—they'd go back to the topic of getting rid of parasites, and then they'd find the best way to accomplish it. That was something to really look forward to, almost as much as actually winning. . . .

FORTY-FOUR

When Jovvi felt the last of the others finally slide into the calm lack of thought of relaxed meditation, she dropped her defenses with a sigh of relief. Between everyone's nervousness—including her own—and the anger generated by that vicious pig of a noble, Jovvi had almost felt as though she were already under attack. If she intended to uphold her corner of the Blending, she needed the strength generated by relaxation even more than her groupmates. She forced herself to slide into it after them, and—

And the knock on the door roused them all. It seemed as though only a minute or two had passed, but Jovvi's watch told her it had been a little more than an hour. She felt marvelous and well rested, and the thoughts of the others showed they felt the same way. Simin had done them a favor by coming around so soon after the robes had been delivered.

"All right, people, it's time to go out there," the young lord Ophin Ruhl announced when Lorand opened the door. "Follow me, please, and be certain you don't dawdle. Tradition insists that the competitions begin precisely at noon."

There was still almost half an hour until that time, but Jovvi couldn't imagine dawdling even with twice the time left. She exchanged glances with the others as they all followed the idiot noble, relieved that no one seemed prepared to make an issue of it. Especially Tamma, who had pushed things a bit too hard for Jovvi's complete peace of mind. . . .

But leaving the apartment and reentering the very large gathering area erased all thoughts of other things. Two other groups in white were entering from the opposite side, and with the two already there and waiting they totaled the necessary five. It was actually getting ready to begin, and Jovvi knew that if she'd had to perform on her own, she never would have been able to do it. Her balance was tipping wildly between excitement and apprehension, and only the comforting presence of the others kept her from doing something ridiculous, like screaming at the top of her lungs.

"All right, people, I'm now supposed to tell you how you'll be arranged," Ophin said when they reached him where he'd stopped. Others like him, all wearing white scarves as armbands, were speaking to the other groups as well. "It's been decided by the coin toss that your groups will be positioned out there first, and then your opponents will be placed opposite you. Please remember to keep your hoods on at all times, as the sun at this time of day can be extremely draining. Now we can get into line."

Jovvi saw now that the others had been lined up in

groups, no two particularly close to one another. As she raised her hood in accordance with instructions, she also noticed that it was impossible to tell where Pagin Holter and his group were without using her talent. Only size differentiated one participant from any other, and there were several people the proper size. The others were very likely women, but even that was difficult to tell by sight alone because of the loose, shapeless robes.

"I feel odd walking around without petticoats," Tamma murmured as they took their places at the end of the line. "I feel as if I'm in a wrap and on my way to the bath house."

"We're probably heading for hot water at that," Jovvi murmured back, watching the first group being led out the wide doors which had been opened on the arena side. "If there's a delay in bringing out our opponents, guess who will be stuck out there in the sun."

"If there's a delay of more than ten minutes, we'll just have to lead everyone back in here where it's cool," Tamma replied with a small shrug. "Letting them get away with something like that after everything else would be stupid, so we just won't do it. You know, I'm glad we decided to bring two flasks each. They balance each other nicely where they're hung under my robes."

Jovvi nodded with a sigh, feeling the same not only about the flasks. Tamma was right about not letting the nobility get away with any more nonsense, but the entire situation touched Jovvi badly. There were pitfalls all around them, and if they happened to stumble into the wrong one. . . .

The line moved fairly rapidly, and from the very first it was possible to hear the cheering and shouting of the people in the tiers. The noise they made was more than deafening; it was possible to feel their vocal excitement vibrating in your bones, and Jovvi knew she wasn't the only one experiencing that. Everyone seemed to be rubbing their ears or shaking their heads sharply, not to mention rubbing their arms.

But the closer they got to the open doors, the easier it became to stand the noise. That might have been because they were moving out of line with the worst of the area's echoes, but whatever the reason it came as a great relief.

Then it was their turn to step outside, and the ocean of noise struck like waves during a terrible storm. There were thousands of people in the tiers, and their combined voice was very much like a descending curtain of stone.

Jovvi and the others—and their escorting noble—plodded heavily across the scattering of gray sand, but every step they took proved easier than the one before. Getting farther out into the open was helping, but then Jovvi noticed that the sand was getting deeper. Not too deep to keep them from walking across it easily, but deep enough to cover the ground thoroughly. They were led to a place at least thirty feet away from the next nearest group, Ophin wished them good luck, and then they were left on their own.

"I hadn't realized how huge this place is," Lorand said as he surreptitiously looked around. "No wonder we can barely hear ourselves thinking. There must be ten thousand people out there."

"I'd estimate more than that," Rion said, looking about in the same way. "And I would also guess that more than five pairs of Blendings are meant to compete here, but they've spread us out to disguise that fact. It's likely that the number of contenders now depends upon how many Blendings my former peers are able to muster."

"I'll take a big chance by goin' along with that theory," Vallant agreed dryly. "Do you remember what Lorand said some time back, about the nobles limitin' themselves by not insistin' that their offspring compete fairly? Well, it's occurred to me that they may have had no choice. If they didn't have a good stock of strength to begin with, all the careful breedin' in the world couldn't give it to them."

"So that's the *reason* they do all these things, not an excuse for it," Tamma said impatiently. "If you can't do the job you're supposed to get out of the way of someone else who can, but these . . . these . . . bloodsuckers refuse to let go. They intend to hang on just as long as they possibly can, and if they aren't stopped now they just might accomplish their aim forever—or until there are none of them left."

"I'm more worried about there being none of *us* left," Jovvi put in, having no intentions of calming Tamma. They would need her anger badly in just a few short minutes. . . .

"And speak of the aspect, here comes the first of our opponents. Now it looks as though they had our side come out first because of the noise. Why subject their people to all that cheering and yelling, when sending them out second spares them?"

What Jovvi had said wasn't meant as sarcasm, only as an easily observable fact. At the appearance of the first noble Blending, the crowd noise quieted as if by magic. A few voices here and there shouted and yelled as though in an effort to sustain the cheering, but the effort failed. Those commoners in the audience had no interest in showing support for members of the privileged class, and the nobles' own supporters were undoubtedly much too good to make a spectacle of themselves.

Jovvi joined everyone else in watching the opposing groups take their places, a good thirty feet away from the first arrivals. That still left a lot of unused room in the amphitheater arena, but some of it was used at least for a short time. A small group came out to stand in the very center of the area, one of the men stepping out to stand in front of the others.

"In a few short moments it will be precisely noon," the white-haired but robust-looking man said, and Jovvi had the impression that everyone in the amphitheater was able to hear him as clearly as she did. "When that moment arrives, the giant torches on two sides of this arena will be ignited at the same time. That will be the signal to begin, and we wish all our brave competitors the best of luck."

He turned and rejoined his party then, and they all exited to the sound of polite applause. There was also a growing murmur of excitement, despite the fact that most people seemed to have no idea about who had spoken. Jovvi didn't know either, but Rion's surprise took her attention.

"Rion, do you know who that was?" she asked. "He seemed to be a noble, but there was something . . . different about him."

"Something very different," Rion agreed, nodding his hooded head slowly. "That was Advisor Zolind Maylock, the most powerful of all the Advisors. He's such an important and influential a man, that almost no one beyond his own circle of associates and acquaintances knows him.

Mother pointed him out to me once, but when she tried to speak to him he snubbed her. To this day she probably hasn't forgiven him for that.''

"Well, at least she and I agree on that one point," Jovvi said, watching Advisor Zolind disappear under the tiers on the opposite side of the amphitheater. "I've never believed in forgiving a snub either, but that isn't very important right now. Those torches ought to be set off any moment, so we'd better prepare ourselves.''

Everyone heard and understood the suggestion, which was something they'd discussed the day before. From what everyone had said about Blending, the nobles apparently believed that the initial formation was necessary every time if a Blending was to take place. From what Jovvi and the others had learned during practice, that wasn't even close to the truth. But if that was what the nobility believed, it would be foolish to disillusion them.

So they all took their proper formation positions, Jovvi noticing in passing that the closest commoner groups were doing the same. There couldn't be more than a minute left before full noon, and that made Jovvi uneasy. The nobles thirty feet away were already in their formation, and their unmoving postures were disturbing. If they were already Blended and poised to attack the instant the torches were lit. . . .

Thinking about it any longer would have been idiotic, therefore Jovvi immediately initiated the connection with the others. They responded even more quickly than usual, and this time there was no reason to hold back from a complete merging. Jovvi went from one-of-five to a single entity so quickly that she would have blinked if she'd still been in her body.

But the entity had no body, nothing more than the five forms of flesh left behind when it emerged. It gloried in being whole and free again, felt delighted that it would no longer be held back—and then two things happened at once. The first was a double burst of flame shooting up from two places at the top of the amphitheater, and the second was an immediate attack by the entity formed of the beings thirty feet away.

The entity wasn't in the least surprised at being attacked

without warning, and because of that its reactions weren't delayed in any way. It immediately defended itself from the ravening flames billowing toward it, flames which were backed by a strength that seemed somewhat reserved. The enemy appeared to be cautious even in attack, a theory noted in passing.

But observation and theorizing also did nothing to keep the entity from responding. The part of itself that was ever on guard had thrown up a shield against the flames, and now thirsted to attack in turn. Attack was also the entity's desire, of course, but curiosity held it back. This direct enemy had been presented as the best of all the enemy entities, and the entity wished to know exactly *how* it was best.

For that reason it reached toward the enemy with all of its abilities. It snatched away air and deluged with water, then removed the water and sent sand-filled air. The enemy responded to each of the moves, but so slowly and awkwardly that it might as well not have bothered. It was then that the entity realized the truth: the enemy wasn't being cautious, it merely had very little strength to use. It also seemed less than adequately Blended, another flaw it had no hope of overcoming.

Those were the answers, then. The enemy couldn't possibly be the best in any group, therefore those who believed the lie were sadly misguided and mistaken. It was now necessary to correct the error in apprehension, and in a way that would leave no doubt of the truth.

So the entity reached out with the most spectacularly deadly of all its abilities. Yellow-orange flames flared into being all around the enemy, which was still in the midst of being distracted by the previous testing probes. The white coverings of its fleshly forms burst into flame first, distracting the enemy even further. The enemy entity should have responded in some way, made some effort at defense, but instead it disappeared, leaving nothing but the individuals who had birthed it.

And those individuals were completely incapable of defending themselves against the attack. Water magic attempted to douse the flames, but was halted by the entity's superior strength. Air magic also made a feeble attempt, as did Earth magic and Fire magic, but the screaming and fear flowing from their individual forms hampered their efforts even more. Even together they'd been no match for the entity; as individuals, their frantic efforts reached a peak and then ceased altogether. The forms had fallen to the sand, and now lay smoldering and smoking.

The entity watched dispassionately as its enemy became no more, and a trace of disgusted annoyance fleeted through it. Those inadequate forms should never have been set against it, not when it was so much stronger and more able. They had been sacrificed for no purpose, soiling the entity by turning it into an executioner. The sense of dishonor and anger was intense. . . .

And then it was Jovvi again, feeling the same anger their Blended selves had felt. Those nobles had been pitiful, and they'd died for nothing—except, obviously, to ease the fear of their superiors. Why choose a Blending that can *do* something, when you can slip one in that will never be a danger to *you*. . . .

"Look," Tamma said quietly, surprise rippling her own anger. "I'd say we aren't the only ones who were set against inadequate opponents."

Jovvi turned her head to see what Tamma meant, and it all became immediately clear. The confrontation itself couldn't have lasted more than a minute or two, not for them and not for the others. Of the five contending sets of Blendings, four of the five noble groups were at the very least down, most of them apparently dead.

Four common Blendings stood victorious in the first round, and the audience in the tiers began to scream and applaud like mad people. . . .

FORTY-FIVE

"... total disaster!" Delin heard as he and the others were escorted back into the vast gathering area beneath the tiers. "Don't you realize that the next Seated Blending is dead? Find out how this happened! Find that fool Twimmal, who seems to have disappeared! I want the ones responsible dragged in front of me in chains!"

The man ranting and raving was High Lord Embisson Ruhl, and Delin was fascinated to see that he was nearly foaming at the mouth. He screamed at the people around him, of course, most of whom were pale and unsteady. As was to be expected. . . .

"Finding out the identity of those responsible is secondary right now," another, calmer voice intervened, the voice of Advisor Zolind Maylock. "Our first concern is deciding what to do about this fiasco, what we're willing to do and what we *can* do. One point I'm able to speak for my associates on is that we will *not* tolerate having commoners on the Fivefold Throne."

"Then your only other option is to back *our* group," Kambil put in with light friendliness, drawing everyone's immediate attention. "We do happen to be the only noble Blending remaining, but as long as we survive, all is far from lost."

"That remains to be seen," Advisor Zolind countered, his voice quiet and showing nothing of emotion. "But since we discuss the matter, I'd be interested to know *how* you managed to survive when the others didn't."

"Possibly it was because our opponents were so poor," Kambil replied with a shrug of innocence that made Delin want to laugh. "They were barely able to Blend, and we had the distinct impression that they hadn't practiced much, if at all. Their strength was certainly adequate, but they had no idea what to do with it."

"Whereas you knew exactly what to do with yours," Zolind responded flatly, the expression in his eyes one of extreme unhappiness. "I now recall that your opponents were changed at the last moment, as a . . . favor to one of your number. We seem to have done you a larger favor than was intended, which means you may be correct about the options at my disposal. In any event our general plan has to be changed now, and it must be done quickly. If we try to delay tomorrow's competitions, that rabble out there will tear the city apart."

"My Lord Embisson!" a different voice came, and Delin looked around to see Lord Simin Dolf hurrying over—with an escort. From the pallor on Dolf's face, it was clear that he'd never have come *without* the escort.

"My Lord Embisson, I have no idea what's going on!" Dolf babbled as he reached his furious superior, his hands shaking visibly. "I did as I was instructed to do, and then I retired to see to . . . some private matters. The next thing I knew I was being accosted by these . . . these . . . glorified guardsmen, and dragged to this side of the amphitheater. I don't know why, but . . . where are the rest of our Blendings?"

"They're dead or dying, you incredible fool!" Lord Embisson snarled, glaring at his victim. "If you *had* done as you were instructed to, that would not be the case. And the chosen Blending would certainly not also be dead! I should have known better than to believe you'd gotten your womanizing under control! Your brother was obviously willing to swear to anything, and I—"

"No, my lord, please, that isn't so!" Dolf interrupted with bottomless desperation, now actually wringing his hands. "I keyed the peasants personally, not just the ones who would be facing the chosen Blending, but also a second group decided on at random! They all responded properly, so I *know* it worked! If something happened after that, it can't possibly be considered my fault!"

"I see," Lord Embisson replied with a nod, his voice now low and deadly. "We're to take your word for the fact that you keyed the peasants and they responded properly, and so we're to look elsewhere for the one who is responsible for this disaster. Well, *Lord Simin*, you wanted this position so badly that you had your brother pull strings and reclaim favors, so now you have it—along with the responsibility for its failure. Take this man away, and make sure that I never lay eyes on him again."

Dolf screamed as the members of Lord Embisson's private guard dragged him off, the sound echoing eerily through the heavy silence in the vast area. Lord Embisson had handed down his judgment, and *no one* would ever see Simin Dolf again. Delin exchanged a glance with Kambil, both of them knowing they had to talk privately. The peasants facing Adriari's group had obviously found a way to make use of the keying phrase Delin had sent them, but had they actually been so stupid as to share the information with their fellow peasants . . . ?

"All right," Advisor Zolind said when Dolf had been dragged away, once again capturing everyone's immediate attention. "I've come to a decision but I warn you that it's tentative, and it will remain so until I'm much more firmly convinced about this course of action. Your group and mine will have to have a long, serious talk this afternoon, but for the moment I'm prepared to make an offer."

If Kambil had made any sort of flippant reply to that, Delin would certainly have killed him on the spot. Delin's stomach was in so many knots that it was a miracle he could stand, and apparently the difficulty was shared, to some extent at least, by Kambil. The Spirit magic user retained his life by remaining silent, as did the others in the group, and Zolind nodded grudging approval.

"At least you're wise enough to listen rather than talk," the old man said. "That's an encouraging sign, and will also be discussed between us later. For now, I tell you without guile that my support must be earned. You will be required to compete tomorrow as well as the following day, and not simply compete but triumph. Should you join your peers in death, my support will do you no good whatsoever."

"The point can't be argued," Kambil responded with a

faint smile, "and your offer is fair. All things of value must be paid for, most often with something other than gold. Our group is prepared to make that payment, and we will be honored to join you for a discussion later today."

"A good beginning," Zolind allowed, his expression unchanging. "Have them take you back to your residence, and we'll meet later when I'm able to get away."

Delin joined everyone else in bowing before they withdrew from Zolind's presence, but the knots of his insides had changed in nature to smoldering nodes of fury. The miserable old man acted as though he were doing them a favor, when the obvious truth was that he had no choice but to back them. The way the peasants had swept the field had come as a great surprise to Delin and his group, but it had also been a delightful surprise. They were now the only nobly born contestants left, with no one of their own class to oppose them. . . .

Which meant that victory was all but in their grasp. Delin began to whistle softly, a rollicking battle tune from many years earlier. The song celebrated complete success, and that made it completely fitting. Nothing but lumpish peasants stood between them and the Fivefold Throne, and soon the peasants would be gone.

Then . . . *then!* . . . their dreams would finally become a reality. . . .

Zolind Maylock watched the five people walk away, for once finding it necessary to fight in order to keep his face expressionless. The only reason he'd been able to control himself at all was because it was the Arstin boy he'd spoken to. If he'd had to say even a single word to Moord. . . .

"Sir, do you really intend to support them?" Embisson Ruhl asked quietly, a tightness to his voice. As a High Lord, Ruhl was close to a number of Zolind's fellow Advisors and tended to behave accordingly. Zolind, however, regarded the man differently, and felt it was time to show the fact.

"You dare to question one of my decisions?" he asked just as softly, turning to stare at Ruhl. "Just who do you imagine you are?"

"Sir, I wasn't questioning your decision," Ruhl made

haste to answer, wilting under Zolind's stare as so many had before him. "I'm simply asking for enlightenment, as I'm aware of what close friends you were with Ollon Capmar. It was my understanding that you came here today primarily to get a good look at his murderer."

"And what a lucky thing that decision was," Zolind muttered, turning again to send his hatred after Delin Moord. "If I weren't here, you'd probably have ordered our last Blending executed for daring to survive their peers. I hate what I'm going to have to do, but at the moment there's simply no other choice. I intend to do a good deal of deep thinking, and while I'm engaged with that, there's something *you* must do."

"Anything, sir, anything at all!" Ruhl exclaimed without hesitation, understanding the matter of responsibility without being told. Dolf was in the process of paying for that fiasco with his life, but ultimate responsibility for the matter rested with Ruhl. Zolind felt tempted to mete out to Ruhl the same fate Ruhl had meted out to Dolf, but at the moment the man was needed.

"I have a conviction about this whole thing that as yet has no basis in detailed fact," Zolind said slowly. "In some way I've become certain that those people are the ones responsible for causing our near utter defeat today, and I'm ordering you to find the means of proving it. You have no more than a matter of days, as I'll want the answer before those five are Seated on the Fivefold Throne—if they survive to be Seated."

"If the proof is anywhere in the world, I'll find it," Ruhl said as though taking a blood oath. "And once I do, what will become of those five? If they've won the competitions in the meanwhile. . . ."

"If they've won the competitions but I have proof of their duplicity, my course of action will be effortless and satisfying," Zolind replied with a faint smile. "I'll simply disqualify them by having them executed, and announce that the retiring Five will remain on the Throne until next year, when the competitions will be held again. But in order to do that I need proof, so begin your investigations this instant."

"Yes, sir, this instant," Ruhl acknowledged, then the

man hurried off to do whatever it was that he'd decided on. He'd probably realized that his life depended on finding what Zolind wanted, but that incentive might not be enough if the man was an incompetent. Others would be sent out to search, others like Anglard Nobin, who never cared about who he caught, just so long as that person was guilty.

And, of course, Zolind hadn't mentioned the best option he had about what to do with an unwanted winning Blending. Those robes all the contestants wore . . . no one was really able to see faces under the hoods, so it wasn't possible for the rabble to tell one group of five people from another. Their last remaining Blending would do its best to win for them, and then, when they did, they would be replaced by five other people, ones who could be trusted to do as they were told. And ones who weren't terribly strong, or practiced as a Blending. Those with strength too often reached the point of deciding to use it, usually against those who knew the proper way of running an empire, as they did not. . . .

The five people comprising the last Blending had disappeared from sight, but Zolind continued to stare after them. Ollon Capmar had been more than simply Zolind's good friend, and Zolind refused to rest until his murderer had paid for what he'd done. Which would hopefully be soon now, but not soon enough to suit *him*. . . .

FORTY-SIX

If Vallant thought it had been a madhouse before in the gathering area, now it was complete chaos as well as insanity. People danced around screaming out their laughter, and were still being drowned out by the sounds from the crowd outside. It wasn't possible to hear even shouted conversation, at least until the outer doors were closed. Then it became clear that the servants and various observers weren't the only ones touched by jubilation.

"Man, we done it!" Holter suddenly came close to shout as he danced. "We done it, an' it's you we got to thank for makin' it happen! On'y one a them noble groups left, an' four a us! This time one a us'll do it, damned if we don't!"

Vallant felt like laughing at the sight of Holter dancing in his robe, but that wasn't something you did to a friend. Besides, he was feeling too good himself to want to put *anyone* down, even if the large gathering area was beginning to seem smaller and smaller. He was *not* going to let his problem control him, not after they'd been so successful.

"Well, here comes Eltrina Razas," Jovvi said, taking Vallant's attention as well as that of everyone else in their group. "She's wavering between a feeling of success and a feeling of failure, finding it hard to decide which to go with. I wonder why that is."

"Maybe her happy feelings are based on the fact that her new superior seems to have disappeared," Tamrissa commented. "I looked for him when we first came back in, wanting to see his expression when we didn't immediately report for that 'punishment,' but I couldn't locate him."

"That's because he isn't anywhere within my range," Jovvi said, obviously searching with more than just eyes. "His absence doesn't look good for his future health, and for the sake of our own we'd better remember that he never came to speak to us. If they even bother to ask."

The last of Jovvi's words were little more than a murmur, as Eltrina Razas had finally reached them. The woman looked more than a little harried, but apparently wasn't so distracted that she failed to give Vallant the sort of appraising look she usually did. Vallant hated that look, even though it had helped to make him understand why most women hated the same sort of thing from a man. The appraisal made him feel like less than a human being, more like a possession with no say over who did the possessing. . . .

"Has any of you seen Lord Simin?" Eltrina said at once, cutting short her usual inspection time. "He was here just a little while ago, and now I can't find him."

"Who's Lord Simin?" Tamrissa asked blandly, giving Eltrina a different sort of inspection. "Someone else who's come to congratulate us on our victory?"

"No, of course not!" Eltrina snapped, then belatedly got the message. "I'm the one authorized to give you all the congratulations you deserve, and I certainly do. Lord Simin is my . . . superior, and he was supposed to have introduced himself to you."

"The only one of your sort that we met was named Ophin," Tamrissa replied with a shrug, looking around to the rest of the group for confirmation. "He showed us to our apartment here, and then he disappeared until it was time for us to go out. What's so important about this other man you're looking for? Has he stood you up or done something equally as vile?"

"No, and it's not really all that important," Eltrina returned tightly, fury in her eyes over Tamrissa's use of the phrase "your sort." The suggestion was very strong that Eltrina's "sort" was totally useless and completely unimportant, and the woman clearly resented the implication.

"It's just that Lord Simin was supposed to tell those of you who won your encounters that you'll be housed here, in the amphitheater, tonight," Eltrina continued. "It's an honor reserved only for those who earn it, so—"

"We're not interested in being honored like that," Jovvi interrupted before Eltrina might take their agreement as understood. "We'll be returning to our residence tonight, where we can relax and celebrate properly."

"Out of the question!" Eltrina snapped, back to her original, touchy self. "You'll do as you're told, or you'll certainly come to regret your disobedience!"

"We're not slaves who belong to you, lady," Lorand said in a growl from where he stood behind Jovvi. "We're free human beings who have emerged victorious from the first round of these competitions, and we'll damned well be treated like it! Moderate your tone when you speak to us, or I'll do it for you."

"And I'll take a great deal of pleasure in giving him

assistance he has no need for whatsoever,'' Rion added as
Eltrina gasped out her insult. ''You and your friends are
fools to believe that nothing has changed, but you always
have been fools. Be wise for once, and bow to the inevitable.''

''We'll just see how inevitable your insolence is,'' Eltrina snarled as she tossed her head. ''I'll get the rest of
those fools sorted out, and then I'll be back with guardsmen
to see to *you*. If I were you, I'd spend my time until then
practicing my begging and pleading.''

And with that she marched away, her nose in the air and
her back very straight. Vallant joined the others in watching
her go, and then he shook his head.

''She really is a fool,'' he observed, stating the obvious.
''How did she miss seein' what we did durin' the competition?''

''I got the impression that she was busy making herself
indispensable to her new superior,'' Jovvi responded very
dryly. ''The time didn't take long, but neither did the competition. Let's follow along and see how she does with
'those other fools.' ''

Everyone considered that an excellent suggestion, so
they drifted after Eltrina. The woman had gotten the attention of a good number of robed figures, and now stood in
the midst of them.

''You're all to be sincerely congratulated,'' she said with
a smile that looked painful as she glanced around at her
audience. ''Now you're to be honored for your efforts, and
will therefore be shown to apartments here in the amphitheater for the night. There's a giant celebration planned,
at which you'll all be guests of honor—''

''I don't think so,'' a male voice called out while everyone else began to mutter. ''The only ones among us who
took your suggestion about celebrating the last time are no
longer living, which means the rest of us will be smart to
ignore it again. We'll just go back to where we belong for
the night, and you and your friends can celebrate without
us.''

''You can't refuse!'' Eltrina screeched as various forms
of agreement came from the others standing around her.
''It's already planned, and it's part of the tradition—!''

"Traditions come and go," another voice, this time female, called out. "We'd rather not do the same without a struggle, so we'll be going back to our residence also. If you and your people don't like it, you can have your last remaining noble Blending face itself tomorrow. Or isn't that allowed under the rules?"

Eltrina's face had reddened in a blotchy way, and she didn't respond immediately. One member of one of the other Blendings had discovered that no group could win the competitions by default, and had passed on the information to everyone else. If their four groups refused to step out tomorrow, the current members of the government would immediately be out of jobs, and their replacements would be responsible for straightening out whatever the trouble was before the competitions continued.

"I'll—have to let you all know if returning to your residences is permitted," Eltrina said at last, hatred and loathing in her voice. "You'll all just have to wait here until I can reach—"

"Aren't you able to understand simple speech?" Rion called out, extreme satisfaction in his tone. "We aren't asking anyone's permission, we're telling you how we want it. Right now we're going to change back into our ordinary clothing, and then we'll be leaving. If you have anything else to say to us, send a messenger with a note."

Supporting laughter came from all sides as everyone began to turn away. Vallant's last view of Eltrina was her frantic screeching in an effort to force everyone to obey her, something she still seemed incapable of understanding that she wasn't about to get. Then he was too far away to see or hear her any longer, a condition he intended to make permanent as soon as possible.

"The poor woman is apparently beside herself," Jovvi murmured as they walked toward the rooms where they'd left their clothing. "She was delighted that she seemed to be back in charge, but now that things have gone wrong again she has no one else to pass the blame to. Her people really do want us handily close tonight, and I'd rather not speculate about why. I'm just relieved that the others supported us."

"They knew they had no choice," Vallant told her, passing on what Holter had said. "It's perfectly clear that they'd want us handy only for a single reason: to make sure we don't win again. If we're goin' to lose, we all want it to be out there in the middle of tryin' to win. Gettin' it in the back from people we aren't supposed to be facin' isn't the same."

"But going back to our residence won't guarantee our safety," Tamrissa reminded them. "It only requires our enemy to come a longer distance to reach us, so we'll have to stay alert. We can take turns standing guard, or at least most of us can. My own perceptions of body heat won't work at too great a distance, so all *I* can do is watch everyone else be useful."

"Stop that," Vallant told her softly, drawing her close by an arm about her shoulders. "The way I remember it, the only reason our Blendin' entity—and our bodies—survived that competition was because *you* protected us from that first unannounced attack. You, all by yourself, callin' on no one's strength and ability but your own. That's earned you the right to rest tonight, but I still have a question. Did that protectin' harm you in any way at all?"

"It's odd that you should ask," Tamrissa replied with an expression of disturbance as she deliberately leaned into his embrace. "That Blending wasn't very strong at all, but their attack was a great deal stronger than anything sent at me during the testing. I—shouldn't have been able to hold it off alone, but I had very little trouble doing it. Is it possible that being almost constantly in full touch with the power has somehow made me stronger?"

"I hope it's so, but none of us really knows," Jovvi said as Vallant—and everyone else—groped for an answer. "We simply don't know enough about how our abilities work, and there's no one we can consult with about it. For now all we can do is move ahead, and hope there aren't any pitfalls in our path that we just aren't seeing."

"There are enough pitfalls that we *can* see," Tamrissa agreed with a sigh. "I really do have to stop borrowing trouble, not to mention asking questions that have no answers. I think I'll take a bath instead, as soon as we get home, that is. Anyone interested in joining me?"

Vallant chuckled along with everyone else as Tamrissa

looked at everyone but him. He liked it when she teased him, but somehow he sensed that her worry hadn't disappeared entirely. Well, he didn't blame her. His hadn't disappeared, either. . . .

"That stupid old man!" Delin raged as soon as they were back in their residence. "Telling *us* what we must and mustn't do to earn his support! Possibly he was too wrapped up in a senile snooze to notice, but we're his only hope. Without us he'll have a group of peasants to deal with, and he almost acted as though he would prefer that! And I'm the leader of this group! How dare he open negotiations with anyone else?"

"He doesn't know that you're our leader, Delin," Kambil replied reasonably, easing Delin's anger a trifle. "I'm sure if he did he would have spoken to you, but it's still a bit soon to tell him such things. He has no real need to know it yet and it's safer for you this way, but if it makes you feel better we can always tell him this afternoon. . . ."

"No," Delin decided reluctantly when Kambil's voice trailed off in a half question. "No, it's definitely a better idea to wait. He'll know soon enough, and I want to see his expression when he finds out. *After* we're Seated, of course."

"I don't understand why he's being so hard-line about this," Bron said from where he stood, pouring himself a cup of tea. The man was completely overlooking Delin's statement about being their leader, making no effort to challenge it. Delin had no idea why that was, but he was too relieved to question the gift. An argument with Bron was the last thing he needed right now.

"I mean, why is he insisting that we have to earn his support?" Bron asked. "It isn't as if he has anyone else to support, so why is he forcing us to compete every day? If he loses us, he'll be left with nothing."

"I think I understand the plan he has in mind," Kambil said, relaxing in the chair he'd dropped into. "We're the last noble Blending left, so we have a certain measure of survivor-sympathy working for us with the commoners. If we compete tomorrow and the next day and win, much of that sympathy will turn to active support. We'll have come from behind to become full contenders for the Throne, and that Zolind Maylock will be able to work with.''

''When you say 'work with,' do you mean manipulate on our behalf?'' Homin asked, waiting behind Bron at the tea service. ''If so, I hope he decides to work with us. We had no trouble at all with our opponents of today, but I think tomorrow will be a different story.''

''For that we have those fool peasants to thank,'' Delin grumbled, having taken a stronger drink than tea to a chair of his own. ''How could they have told all the others about the drug and the keying phrase? And don't say there's no evidence that they told *all* the others. Dolf chose a second group at random, and to believe that that second group just happened to be the only ones the peasants told would be asinine stupidity.''

''It so happens I agree with you about who the commoners told,'' Kambil said, again soothing Delin's annoyance. ''The only thing I can think of is that the commoners realized the truth of the old saying about there being safety in numbers. If they'd been the ones to survive alone against four noble Blendings, their position would have been quite impossible. This way they have a good deal of company—''

''And it's *our* position that's impossible,'' Delin interrupted, his temper flaring again. ''We expected to meet those particular peasants in the final confrontation, and now there's only one chance in three that it will be them. If it's a different group and they happen to be stronger than us, we could end up losing after all.''

''That's why we have to make sure that it isn't a different group,'' Kambil returned, still sounding calm and assured. ''It's the one point we'll have to insist on when Advisor Zolind Maylock comes to speak with us later this afternoon. Arranging it should be no trouble at all for him, and all we have to say is that we researched that group along with our original one. Pointing out that they have the most weak spots of all the commoners will be nothing but the truth, so hopefully the Advisor won't become suspicious.''

''And if he does become difficult, we'll simply have to offer to give up our place,'' Selendi said so calmly that Delin was startled. ''We'll be risking our lives out there, and if he refuses to give us that one bit of help, he can go out and face those peasants himself. It won't matter to *us* if we die at the hands of the peasants or are executed by our own people. Dead is dead no matter how it happens.''

"That's a very good point," Kambil agreed, smiling at her where she stood beside Homin. ''It sounds like something Delin would want us to keep in mind, but there's another point to go with it. The Advisor is extremely upset, and it won't take much to make him turn his back on us and look for another solution to his problem. For that reason he'll have to be handled very carefully, so I think Delin should do it.''

"No," Delin said at once, then forced a smile when the others all looked at him. "What I mean to say is, a good leader knows his limitations. If the Advisor is in that delicate a frame of mind, the one to deal with him should be someone able to reach his reactions. That means you, Kambil, so I'm giving the assignment to you to take care of.''

"All right, Delin, if that's the way you want it," Kambil agreed with a shrug and a sigh. "I happen to think that you would do just as good a job, but since you want me to see to it, I'll be glad to.''

Delin smiled and nodded, then took another swallow of the whisky he'd poured. His insides still twitched at the thought of his saying something wrong to Maylock, and thereby ruining their chance of success forever. He'd be much happier having Kambil do it, but the man had better not make any mistakes. If he did. . . .

Delin finished the last of his drink in one swallow, then got up to get another. He wasn't used to drinking this much, but today was a day to celebrate. He'd drink his drinks now, sit quietly while the Advisor was here, and then probably go to bed. But he still didn't much care for Kambil, so he'd have to see to the man as soon as they won. Happily, he was all prepared to do exactly what was necessary. . . .

FORTY-SEVEN

"At least there won't be any more of those messengers," I said morosely as I toyed with what was left of my breakfast. "I can't tell you how tired I am of hearing that our names weren't 'picked by lot to compete today.' Since it's the last day, we *have* to compete."

"I've decided I don't trust the 'luck' that left us for last," Jovvi said, sounding no better than I had. "Those people are up to something, and have been for the last two days at least."

"What they're definitely up to is eliminating our friends," Lorand put in, sounding no happier. "The last two groups may still be alive, but Warla said they were badly hurt when they were carried off the sand. We shouldn't have let them keep us from attending the competitions as spectators."

"How were we supposed to argue with that particular rule?" Vallant asked impatiently. "It's perfectly true that a Blendin' not competin' is a Blendin' free to interfere in what's happenin'. We would have screamed if a noble group was around to attend as spectators, so how could we complain about their not lettin' *us* attend?"

"We could hardly point out that our words are better than theirs, but it might have been amusing to try," Rion put in, but still sounding as far from amused as the rest of us. "What takes my attention the most is Warla's report that the competitions we missed took longer than the ones on the first day. After our first experience we felt completely undrained, but today won't be the same.''

"And our opponents will have been getting used to that in real life, while all we've been doing is practicing," Jovvi said in agreement. "We're doing considerably better than we did that first night, but I can't help thinking that we're still far from being really . . . practiced and experienced."

"But you aren't really, you know," Naran put in, her voice filled with its usual warmth and support. "You're all doing wonderfully well, and I happen to know that you'll win. Those people you'll be facing simply won't be able to match you."

"It's nice that *one* of us has a positive outlook," Lorand said with a smile the rest of us couldn't help echoing. Naran had turned out to be a really nice person, and Rion couldn't possibly have found anyone who fit into our group better. It didn't even bother her that she couldn't Blend with us, which wouldn't have been true of most other people.

"Well, I happen to like bein' positive, so I'm goin' to believe Naran," Vallant announced to us as he looked around. "Here's to victory, and all it will mean to us."

He raised his teacup in the proposed toast, and after only a second of hesitation the rest of us did the same. It was nice that Jovvi had made it possible for Naran, our resident ghost, to join us on a regular basis, as her raised cup made the wish unanimous. We all drank to it then, and the silliness even made *me* feel better.

"The coaches will be here for us soon, love," Rion told Naran after the toast was done. "I wish it were possible for you to go with us, but even disguising you as a maid could be dangerous. I'll be happier knowing that you're here and safe, and no matter what happens I'll be back with you before you know it."

"Yes, love, I know you will be," Naran answered as they held hands for a final time, her face showing warmth and love and absolute belief. "Don't let thoughts of me distract you, because soon we'll be together for the rest of our lives."

"That's the sweetest promise ever made me, and I mean to hold you to it," Rion responded with a smile. "Give me a final kiss, please, and then wait for my return upstairs."

"With pleasure," she said with a laugh, and after the

kiss she left without hesitation. We'd made it a practice not to have Naran walking around the house when we weren't there, as the commands Jovvi had given the servants not to see her might not have held if she weren't hidden in a crowd, so to speak.

"Getting there and then coming home again will probably take longer than the competition itself," I commented after making myself finish what had actually been a rather light breakfast. "It would be nice if someone thought of a faster, more comfortable way to travel."

"You might as well wish for wings or a personal cloud," Lorand replied, obviously amused. "What better way to travel can there possibly be?"

None of us could think of an answer to that, and as if the entire topic created a magic of its own, a servant appeared to tell us that our coaches had arrived. We glanced at each other but didn't hesitate, and a few short moments later we were on our way.

The trip didn't take quite as long as it had that first day, but only because the guardsmen along the way seemed to have gotten practice in keeping the traffic moving. The crowds themselves seemed even thicker, and the closer we came to the amphitheater the more campsites there were. Not everyone was able to afford the stay in an inn or hostel even if there'd been enough room to accommodate them all, but everyone apparently wanted to see the last of the competitions.

Jovvi and I didn't speak much during the trip, and I suspected that the men were just as silent. Even touching the power hadn't done much in the way of settling my nerves, and I would have enjoyed screaming out loud and breaking things just to relieve the tension. Actually, what I most wanted to do was burn things, but that had to be saved for the competition.

When we reached the amphitheater we were escorted inside again, this time through triple or more the number of people. Their cheering and words of support would have meant more if we weren't their last hope of taking the Throne away from the nobles, but it still felt good to have them there. Once we passed through the door into that very large gathering area, the only one there for us was our former guide, the young lord Ophin Ruhl.

"Welcome, people, welcome to the final day of the competitions," he said expansively when we stopped near him. "Today will see the choosing of our next Seated Blending, so let's get you to your apartment where you'll be able to rest for a short while."

"Where's Lady Eltrina?" Jovvi asked as we followed along behind the man. "I don't see her anywhere, and I was certain she would enjoy showing up to tell us that we were going to lose."

"Lady Eltrina is back in her husband's household where she belongs," Ophin replied in a very bland way. "An investigation of her efforts was conducted, and it was learned that much of what was supposed to be *her* responsibility had actually been delegated to others. That produced rather . . . unpleasant results, so Lady Eltrina no longer has her former position."

"All our groups refusin' to stay here must have been the final nail in her coffin," Vallant commented with barely hidden satisfaction. "What a shame that it had to happen to such a lovely person."

I felt the urge to cough rather loudly, and a glance around showed that the others felt the same. But we all managed to control ourselves, at least until we reached our assigned apartment. Once Ophin was gone with the door closed behind him we were able to laugh, but that didn't last long.

"What's this?" Lorand said, looking down at the table he'd stopped near. "Five envelopes, one addressed to each of us. Do they contain the sincere good wishes of the government, I wonder?"

"What else could they be?" Jovvi asked with a wry smile. "Have you checked them for anything that could harm us if we touch it? I don't really know what that could be, but I seem to be *made* of suspicion today."

"As far as I can tell, there's nothing on or in any of them but paper and ink," Lorand reported after a moment. "I checked each one individually, and they're all the same. That has to mean the trap, if there is one, lies in what each of them says."

"So maybe we ought not to open them," Jovvi suggested, looking from one to the other of us. "I can stand not knowing what mine says, and the rest of you can probably do the same.''

"There's only one trouble with that," I found myself being forced to say. "We have no way of knowing that these were left by an enemy. If they were left by a friend instead. . . ."

"You're thinking about that Lord Carmad," Jovvi said with a slow nod that suggested the same thing had occurred to her. "He never did come back, and he doesn't seem to have visited any of the other groups. I'd ask how he could have managed to leave letters for us *here*, but that's like asking how he found out the proper way to start a Blending."

"So what do we do?" Vallant asked, looking down at the envelopes as though they were living beings. "If we leave them untouched, we could be leavin' valuable hints and help behind. If we open them, we could be helpin' our opponents instead of ourselves."

"There's only one possible solution," Rion said, stirring where he stood. "We don't *all* have to open them, only one of us does. That should minimize any possible harm, and as the idea was mine, I claim the privilege of being that one. With the rest of you there to sustain me, I should come to little harm in any event."

The rest of us exchanged glances over that, but it wasn't possible to argue with the idea. It gave us the only practical solution, and Rion knew it. He therefore reached for the envelope with his name on it, opened it and removed the sheet of paper, then began to read. There seemed to be quite a lot of writing, but after a moment or two he closed his eyes and let the sheet fall to the floor.

"These letters are definitely not from a friend," he said in a dead, toneless voice. "And I was quite mistaken about their ability to do harm."

He put his hand over his eyes with that, seeing nothing of the way Jovvi bent to retrieve the letter. Vallant, Lorand, and I were in the midst of trying to comfort Rion when Jovvi made a sound of deep scorn.

"Those people would be pathetic if they weren't so disgusting," she said with anger in her voice. "Can you imagine—this was left here to tell Rion why his mother raised him in such isolation and turned him into a pet. It seems that Rion isn't fully human, because his father was a commoner who worked for his mother as a gardener. She took the 'peasant' into her bed and enjoyed him, and as soon as she had what she wanted from him—a child she could control all alone—she sent him away. Everyone of any importance knows all this, and they're so upset by such a disgusting act that they can't under any circumstances consider Rion one of them. His mother knew he would never be considered acceptable, but that just made things better for her own plans.''

"And that's *bothering* you?" I said to Rion once Jovvi had finished speaking. "I find that really hard to believe since that's the best news you could have gotten."

"I don't think I'd care to hear what you would consider the worst news, dear lady," Rion replied tonelessly without opening his eyes. "Considering that horror the best news means I could never withstand the worst."

"Rion, please stop emoting and start thinking," I said with all the exasperation I felt. "How many times have all of us—including you—pointed to something to show what miserable excuses for human beings those nobles are? Almost everything they do proves it, and I was beginning to feel sorry for you for having the same blood. But now we know you don't have the same blood, you have your father's blood, and that's why you're as wonderful—and *capable*!—as you are. Would you really rather be completely one of *them*?"

"That seems to be the major point," he said, disturbance in the eyes he'd now opened. "Rather than being one thing for certain, I'm now neither fish nor fowl. And it's all well and good to say I have my father's blood—whoever he might be—but I still have my mother's as well."

"So what?" Lorand asked, sounding honestly puzzled. "There's no difference between the person you are now and the person you were five minutes ago, except that you now know something new. I can't see how that's supposed to change you. You became one of us because of what's inside you, not because of who your parents are."

"I happen to love my parents," Vallant put in, "but I'm not an extension of them, I'm an individual. Knowin' who *we* basically were is one of the things my folks helped my brothers and me to learn about ourselves, includin' the fact that we didn't have to do and like what they did and liked. And they accepted us as we were without tryin' to change what couldn't be changed, just the way those of us here accepted *you*."

"And if nothing else, you no longer have to consider yourself an outsider among us," Jovvi said, delight now filling her voice. "Your father's sacrifice—that of not even knowing he had a son—can be considered full payment for full membership on your behalf. It's the least he'd want you to have, and he'd be very proud of you."

"Do you really think so?" Rion asked, and for the first time in a long while he looked like the innocent he'd started out as. "Mother always said my father had been killed in a tragic accident, and she always found it impossible to discuss any of the details without breaking down with grief. Now. . . . Do you think I might actually get to meet him one day?"

"Why not?" Lorand countered with a grin of relief that must have been just like my own. "Anything's possible, and there's a definite benefit in meeting a parent for the first time when you're already grown. If you don't happen to like him or her, you can simply shrug and walk away. Small children don't have that option."

I had to add my own copper's worth of agreement with that idea, and the discussion became one of the sort we usually had, rather than a case of most of us trying to convince one. It was marvelous to see Rion pulling out of the pit our enemies had dug for him, and the rest of us made sure to stay away from the other envelopes. As Jovvi had said, we could stand not knowing what they were there to tell us.

After a few minutes, Rion retrieved the letter he'd dropped and Jovvi had tossed to the floor again, and he refolded it neatly and replaced it in the envelope. Then he returned the envelope to where it had been, and the rest of us began to chuckle. There was no reason to let the nobles know that one-fifth of their plan had almost worked, and every reason to keep it from them.

We sat around talking for a short while after that, until two servants came to deliver our robes and sandals. The servants were enthusiastic but cautious as they wished us good luck in whispers but with big grins. Jovvi had already told us that we weren't being eavesdropped on, but we didn't mention that to the servants. They were happier to think they were getting away with something, and I couldn't blame them for that.

We had just enough time to change our clothing before Ophin came to call us, and I felt drawn absolutely tight. I couldn't wait for everything to begin so that it would be on its way to being over, but Ophin hesitated before leading the way back out into the corridor.

"You—ah—don't seem to have read the notes which were left for you," he observed much too casually. "I understand that they're from some rather important people, so you might want to glance at them before you go. We can spare the moment or two it will take."

"Why rush through reading them now, when we can read them slowly and carefully later?" Jovvi asked with a pleasant smile, the five of us having already walked to the door. "We're much more interested now in being out on the sand, so we'd appreciate your leading the way."

Ophin hesitated a very long moment before realizing that he had no choice but to let the matter lie, and when he finally gave in to the inevitable he wasn't a happy man. His movements were brusque and furious as he led us toward the gathering area, but none of us paid him any attention. We were all of us ready, and if we didn't win this final competition, it would certainly not be our fault.

FORTY-EIGHT

Delin stood with his groupmates, glancing around casually, but on the inside he was drawn so tight that he feared something might snap. The past two days had been incredibly nervewracking, causing him to come as close as he had to losing everything. The peasants his Blending had faced had proven much stronger than they had any right to be, and he and the others had nearly lost to them. Somehow they'd just managed to pull out their victories, but hadn't even been able to destroy their opponents. The Advisory representative assigned to them had been pleased about that, but Delin wasn't able to muster the same pleasure. . . .

Now they stood by the as-yet-unopened doors to the arena floor, waiting for the last group of peasants to join them. The Advisory man had insisted that they come to the peasants' side rather than having the peasants come to them, and there had been no arguing with him. It was all part of Advisor Zolind's plan, they'd been told, which meant the orders weren't to be argued with. Delin felt the urge to do more than argue, considering who these last peasants were. But at least they'd been subjected to the disabling bits of information and half threats Delin had himself intended to use. . . .

Thought of that brought a faint smile to Delin as he considered how his idea had been improved upon. Zolind's people had worked swiftly to learn everything there was to know about the peasants, and the resulting letters had been most interesting. That useless fool Mardimil had been told how common he really was, the Earth magic user had been told that the friend he'd come to Gan Garee with was dead, Fire magic had been told that she would be returned to her father's authority and possession, Spirit magic had been told that the woman sent to the deep mines because of *her* was slowly dying, and Water magic had been told that his family would be ruined because of him.

Not quite the way Delin would have handled it, but certainly effective nonetheless. The lowborn fools would be fortunate if they even managed to Blend, not to speak of doing anything effective. They would—

"I've just been given less than happy news," Kambil murmured after he turned away from a runner who had drawn him aside. "The commoners are on their way over here, making slow going of it because of everyone who wants to wish them luck. Ophin was therefore able to send word ahead that they haven't read the letters. The envelopes were all lying untouched just where they'd been left."

"How could they have done that?" Selendi asked with a frown as Delin's mind clanged with shock. "Don't they have anything of natural human curiosity?"

"They're obviously more suspicious than curious," Homin said with a shake of his head. "I, personally, wouldn't have touched something like that, which was why I disliked that method of passing on the information. A pity Zolind dismissed my opinion out of hand."

"Well, done is done," Bron said with a sigh. "They haven't read the letters, so we can't expect them to be badly out of balance. We'll simply have to win over them without that."

"How can all of you take this so calmly?" Delin demanded in a hiss, then let his voice turn into a growl. "It's all Zolind's fault for insisting on doing things *his* way, so I say let Zolind go out there and face them! I, for one, have no intention of being defeated by lowborn garbage!"

"If we don't compete, Zolind will take great pleasure in having us executed," Kambil said calmly and gently. "He'll find some way to keep the commoners from being Seated, but we won't be around to find out what he does. Is that what you want?"

"No, of course not," Delin was forced to say, a great coldness spreading inside him. "I want us to accomplish our dream, but how are we supposed to do that now?"

"We'll do it in the way we were meant to, by facing them and bringing them to defeat," Kambil said, briefly putting a hand to Delin's shoulder. "Since that's our only option, it's the one we'll take. Are you with us?"

Delin could do nothing other than nod, although he would have most preferred to scream out what fools they all were. They refused to see that they were about to lose everything, refused to try to find a way out of that mess. . . .

A stir in the crowds heralded the arrival of the peasants who, just like their betters, already wore their robe hoods up. It was difficult to pick out individuals like that, with faces shrouded in shadow. Delin had thought he might rattle Mardimil at least by *speaking* what the man hadn't read, but he couldn't pick out the fool from the other two men. Not to mention that the two groups were being kept separated from one another. . . .

And then the outer doors were being slid open, letting in the bright sunlight and the muted roar of the crowd—less muted once they noticed the doors being opened. It was nearly time when they would find out who their next Seated Blending would be, and their level of excitement was so high that Delin could feel it in the air like something tangible. But most of that excitement was on behalf of the peasants he and the others would face. If Zolind had really expected the masses to become more and more fond of Delin's group as the days and competitions went by, that was another part of the fool's plan which hadn't worked.

Delin joined the others in following their official guide out onto the sands, but he felt as though he were moving through a dream. The waves of screaming delight and applause washed over him, threatening to knock him down, making him believe that all the encouragement and support were for him. Sand began to enter his sandals the way it usually did, but this time he ignored it. All those people were waiting for *him* to fulfill their dreams, and he couldn't bring himself to disappoint them.

The guide took them to the designated place in the sand and then left them, just as the other group was left thirty feet away. The sun beat down on them mercilessly, hating the fact that they were all protected by white robes and hoods. The others of his group moved into position in front of him, preserving the myth that it wasn't possible to Blend otherwise. What the fools around them didn't know couldn't be used against *them*. . . .

And then the giant torches set on two sides of the amphitheater burst into flame, and Delin was swept up and devoured by the entity the five of them Blended into. His last thought was what a relief it was to be devoured so, and then the entity looked about itself. Just as it had expected, another entity waited to challenge it the way the previous ones had.

But this latest enemy made no effort to rush to the attack, so the entity did it for its opponent. Fire flamed out as sand was hurled with strength and water was added as air was taken away—but somehow none of that worked. Everywhere the entity thrust was a shield-barrier, invisible and intangible, but still incredibly there. This had never happened before, not in any of the three battles which the entity had fought.

And then a counterattack came, one which was so strong that the entity was nearly overwhelmed completely. Only by the expenditure of total effort was the entity able to defend itself, and even so, some of the fleshly forms of its components staggered. The truth was clear and as unavoidable as the attack: the enemy was far stronger than the entity, and the next attack would finish the matter.

Despair wasn't something the entity was truly able to feel, but echoes of the emotion came from one part of it. Defeat was merely something to be accepted if it came— but then the entity's attention was taken by an oddity. Without the entity making an effort of any sort, the enemy entity suddenly disappeared as its five separate components collapsed to the sand. And the components lay there unmoving . . . how odd, how very odd. . . .

And then it was Delin back again, aware of his individuality and completely stunned. Their opponents were down, apparently unconscious. . . . How could that possibly have happened?

"I'm delighted to say that the major plan worked just fine," Kambil told them all with a laugh. "Those letters were left in their apartment as a distraction, giving them something to think about even if they weren't read. The thing we wanted them to miss was the fact that their undergarments were impregnated with hilsom powder. At the first sign that we weren't able to defeat them, Zolind had the High Earth magic talents he sent here simply *shake* the undergarments. Their entity was so engrossed with ours that it never noticed, but it certainly noticed when they all breathed in the powder. They were immediately cut off from their individual abilities, and then the High talents were able to put them to sleep. They intended to use more than one High in order to reach the Earth magic member, I was told, and apparently whatever number they used was the right one.''

''Why weren't the rest of us told about that?'' Delin demanded as the others chuckled their appreciation. ''I was nearly beside myself, and might even have refused to compete!''

''There was no real danger of that, and we had to make our act look good,'' Kambil said soothingly despite the insanity now being produced by the crowds. ''If we'd all strutted out here without a care in the world, the commoner officials would have known that something . . . extralegal was planned. But this isn't the place to discuss it. Let's accept everyone's congratulations, and then go home.''

Delin's anger wasn't interested in waiting, but when the others threw their hoods off and headed back toward the gathering area, he had no choice but to do the same. That certainly wasn't the place for discussions, but once they reached some quiet spot. . . .

The promised discussion didn't take place for hours. First they had to accept the congratulations of every human being they passed, and then they were put in individual carriages and paraded up the roads and through the streets. Not many people shouted and waved in the peasant areas, but once they reached the more important neighborhoods things definitely changed. People of position applauded politely as their carriages passed, and servants shouted words of delight and support. To a certain extent it was truly gratifying, but Delin was still too angry to really appreciate it. And that was another unanswered question: why were they being returned to their residence rather than taken to the palace?

When they finally did reach the residence, Delin had long since decided how it would be best to handle things. For that reason he made sure to stroll into the sitting room first while the others stood in the front hall sharing the excitement and delight they hadn't been able to show earlier. While they made fools of themselves he took out the vial he'd hidden behind the cushions of a couch, poured himself a cup of tea from the service, then emptied the vial into the rest of the tea.

He had taken a chair and was sipping from his cup when the others stormed in, all of them acting like small children after successfully completing a prank. Delin added his own smile as he watched them all take tea, and when the last of them turned away from the service, he raised his cup high.

"To the newest Blending of the empire, long may we reign!" he toasted, and the others added, "Here, here!" before joining him in drinking—just as he'd known they would. He then waited until they'd all taken seats, after which he looked directly at Kambil.

"For your information, you've all just swallowed a good dose of Puredan," he announced amiably. "If the thought disturbs you, it shouldn't. The leader of a group is entitled to know everything, and if he can't get his answers one way, he has to get them another."

"What answers are you after, Delin?" Kambil asked without the least sign of agitation. "I'll be glad to tell you anything I can."

"Of course you're glad," Delin countered, letting some of his fury show through. "You have no choice but to be glad. Now we can start with why I wasn't told about what Zolind actually planned to do. He may not know I'm leader here, but you certainly do."

"You weren't told because you simply can't be trusted, Delin," Kambil replied pleasantly with a continuing lack of hesitation. "Even if you managed not to brag to someone, your arrogance would have been so thick that you would have given the game away. The commoners' observers were watching us very closely, so we couldn't afford that."

"Are you insane?" Delin demanded in complete outrage. "I don't brag about the things I do, and I've learned to be humble when humility is called for. You're just making excuses, so I'll give you a different question. Why are we here instead of at the palace? There are certain plans I mean to move ahead on at once, even before we're Seated."

"You're talking about arranging to have your father and mother killed," Kambil said with a nod, shocking Delin. "Yes, I know all about it, which is one of the reasons I agreed to Zolind's demand that we come back here rather than go to the palace as we're supposed to. Once we get there we'll be expected to separate, and I needed to finish up with you before that's done. We have much more important things to worry about than your vengeance against your parents."

"But what—what are you talking about?" Delin stuttered, suddenly noticing the way the others were calmly staring at him. "You can't know—you can't speak to me like—what's going on here? You're supposed to be drugged . . . !"

"Not many people can be drugged with plain water," Kambil commented with a smile after taking another sip of his tea. "And that's all you added to the service, plain water. The Puredan you paid quite a lot of gold for was never really Puredan, I made sure of that. Letting you have it would have been like putting a weapon into the hands of a small child."

"A completely insane small child," Bron added without inflection, still studying Delin. "I missed seeing it at first, of course, but it wasn't hard to make up for that blindness later. Insane doesn't necessarily also mean stupid, but you seem to be the exception to that rule."

"Which at least afforded us some amusement," Homin said, the faint smile he wore causing Delin to feel chilled. "In the beginning you thought you were controlling Bron by calling him our leader, and never once stopped to wonder why the rest of us saw through the farce, but he didn't. You simply grew tired of the pretense and made it clear that *you* were leader, and again never wondered why no one argued."

"It was because we were all humoring you," Selendi

told him, the gentleness of her tone like a slap in the face. "It was amusing to a certain extent, but when we saw how easily you might ruin everything, it stopped being funny. We told Kambil we thought he should control you completely, but he said it wasn't possible yet."

"Which, unfortunately, it wasn't," Kambil said, taking up the narrative again. "There's a definite . . . extra something . . . which comes from Earth magic in a Blending, but it doesn't appear if the Earth magic user is being controlled. You might even call it a hidden reserve of emergency strength, but whatever it is it definitely wasn't there when I took full control of you. I had to leave you mostly uncontrolled, then, but we did without the extra anyway. Your terror was so thick that it affected the Blending entity, so you almost caused us to lose all by yourself."

"I did no such thing!" Delin snarled, humiliation flushing his skin to the point of pain. "I don't get terrified and I certainly don't lose, but you people do make me sick! It isn't me he's controlling but the rest of *you*! I know you can't see yourselves from the outside, but you're not the same people you were!"

"And you're only just noticing that," Bron commented while Homin and Selendi showed those faint and horrible smiles again. "We remember exactly what we were like, but Kambil's been working with us practically from the day we were first put into this group."

"He just didn't let us show these much more efficient selves until there was no one around to notice and wonder," Selendi went on. "We love being efficient and capable, untouched by all those emotions which used to choke us and trip us. We're the same as we used to be—except for the petty problems we were hampered by."

"But I do actually regret something, even if the regret is faint," Homin said, taking his turn again. "It would have been marvelous to be able to show the new me to that offensive Elfini, but your sickness made that impossible, Delin. If not for you, she wouldn't have had to die."

"You know I killed her?" Delin demanded, his voice much higher and more shrill than he'd wanted it to be. "But no one was supposed to—I mean, you're completely mistaken. I did no such thing, so you'd better not say it again or I'll—"

"Tell your father?" Kambil suggested with sickening amusement. "Or possibly kill us as well? Save yourself the effort of planning our deaths, Delin. You're marvelous at making those sorts of plans, but you simply haven't got what it takes to carry them out. You're a bungler, and you've never killed anyone in your entire life."

"That's not true," Delin choked out, his head whirling so wildly that his vision had started to blur. And he'd dropped his cup of tea. . . . "I've killed more than once, Elfini and Ollon Capmar, and those sluts at the pleasure parlors. . . ."

"You did nothing at the pleasure parlors but faint," Kambil's voice came through the ringing in Delin's ears. "After the first time, you mumbled something before you came out of it about how happy you were to have killed the girl. The manager of the establishment took that as his cue about how to behave, and therefore told you that he'd discreetly gotten rid of the body. Your tip to him was so generous that he shared the information about your preferences with the managers of the other parlors you patronized, and thereafter he shared their own tips as well. They lied to you, you fool, and simply kept the 'dead' girls out of your way for a while. You never really noticed their faces, so there were some you 'killed' two or three times."

"No," Delin moaned, fists to his temples in an effort to stop the throbbing pain in his head. "I did kill them, I did! Them and Elfini and Ollon Capmar! You're lying, you're—"

"What I am is sick and tired of cleaning up after your messes," Kambil said from somewhere, unbelievably sounding annoyed. "I didn't trust you any farther than Selendi could throw you, so I followed you when you so generously agreed to help Homin. You were actually fool enough to go in and abuse that woman, after which you fainted as usual. If I hadn't been there, she would have summoned the guard and had you locked up and the key thrown away."

"She certainly would have," Homin agreed soberly. "She lived for power, so she never would have dropped the charges. You would have stayed under arrest, and we would have been given a Low or Middle talent in Earth magic to round out our Blending.''

"So I had to make her forget about what had happened,'' Kambil continued. "You were dreaming happy dreams as usual, but she was straining to recover what I'd forced her to forget. I could tell she'd recover the memories unless I stayed there and kept a constant eye on her, and that was completely impractical. So I gave you something else to dream about, and went back that night and killed her myself. Just in time, I might add, as she was close to remembering what had happened. That was the real reason she beat Homin's father so badly. The incident was beginning to come back, but she still felt confused about the identity of her attacker. Confused enough to think it might have been the man under her whip.''

"But I was there,'' Delin whispered, still writhing in pain in the chair. "I remember every bit of it. . . .''

"Every bit but the killing part,'' Kambil said with a sound of scorn. "I couldn't get your mind to accept that part of it, because it was reality rather than fantasy. You've never been able to handle that sort of reality, not after what your father did to you—and made you do. You did clean things up nicely, though, after I told you what had to be done. And while you thought it was your own idea. . . .''

"But you couldn't let well-enough alone,'' Bron said, sounding like a disapproving adult speaking to a child. "Your hatred of Rigos was so intense that you had to keep punishing him for being a better man than you despite his lack of talent. Kambil was busy working with us and the servants at the time, and we all thought you were safely off with one of your bored older women. They pass you from one to the other as a group joke, and all the time you believed it was your charm that got you into their beds.''

"Bron woke me when you were late getting back, so we went out searching for you,'' Kambil said. "It took a short while to pick up your mental trail, so by the time we caught up with you you'd just finished telling Ollon Capmar that you'd killed his sister. The man's obsession was much too strong for me to work through, so he had to die as well. This time I was able to give you the entire scene, because

I disguised it as daydreaming. I had you do everything necessary in the way of removing our traces and then kept you from going back into the room, but it was all wasted effort.''

"Because we didn't know that Rigos had killed himself," Homin said, his tone just like Bron's. "That ruined everything, of course, because instead of dropping the investigation with the death of the strongest suspect, they realized that Rigos was innocent after all. So they dug and questioned and checked and crosschecked, and now they know exactly who the real murderer is."

"You," Kambil supplied cheerfully while Delin fought to keep his head from breaking open. "Zolind told me so when he and I spoke privately, only he doesn't remember that he told me so. He also doesn't remember admitting that it would be impolitic on his part to let us lose in front of everyone, but he'll never allow us to be Seated, not as long as he lives. That's why our first concern has to be doing something about the condition."

"His continuing to live, Kambil means," Selendi said with a chuckle. "In point of fact we've decided not to let any of the Advisors live, and you'll do your part to help us end them. We won't need that something extra to accomplish their ends, so from now on you'll be under complete control. You'll even be under control when we destroy the present Blending. We've already checked, and their strongest member is no stronger than a good Middle."

"But first we wanted you to know how much trouble you've caused us," Kambil said, for the first time with vindictive satisfaction in his voice. "Your insanity runs much too deep for me to be able to do anything about it, even with Grammi's help. Oh, that's right, you don't know that my grandmother has been helping me. She loves me even more than I love her, and she'd never let anything terrible happen to me. The fact that she's also a High in Spirit magic has all but doubled my effectiveness."

"Which he needed when he had you under partial control," Homin said negligently. "We *had* to give the commoners the keying phrase to release them from the control of others, but you almost refused to send it. Kambil did some very thorough research when he was supposed to be napping all those times, and he discovered that our peers in the other Blendings were all incompetent fools. They were also not nearly as strong as we are, so if the commoners were freed they would eliminate our peers *for* us— leaving us as the only ones the Advisors could support in order to save everyone's face. Kambil also found out that that one Blending would not hesitate to pass on what they learned, so they had to be the ones to be given the information—which you regretted sending even while you were doing it. You just have no imagination or the courage to take a chance, Delin.''

"And now that we've had the pleasure of telling you the truth, you'll be put under Kambil's complete control,'' Bron said with the same smile that Homin and Selendi showed. ''You'll no longer have to be coddled, and you'll do exactly as you're told. You certainly won't like it, but you also won't be able to do anything about it. Goodbye, Delin.''

Delin had been trying to scream, but nothing in the way of sound came out. The ice of terror had formed all through him, and then it froze him solid—

FORTY-NINE

Lorand awoke—to a certain extent. His head ached in a way that he'd never felt before, the pain so intense that he wished he were unconscious again. And there was nothing he could do to stop the pain. Even if he'd been able to work around it—and the blurriness covering his mind—he couldn't seem to figure out where the power was. . . .

''Look, he's tryin' t' wake up!'' someone said, sounding alarmed. ''He ain't 'sposta try t' wake up!''

"So what if he does?" another voice countered, male like the first voice. "They got him so doped up that he won't even know what day it is. When you feed him later, you'll probably have to keep shaking him to remind him what he's about. But you better not let him start wasting away, or they'll skin you alive."

"Why?" the first voice demanded, a heavy whine to it. "I heared he's prob'ly all kindsa damaged like, 'cause a th' way he got yanked outta that Blendin'. Gettin' yanked out's 'sposta damage 'em real bad, so why'd they still want 'im? An' if he ain't damaged, how'm I 'sposta handle a High?"

"Why do you insist on worrying about things that are none of your business?" the second voice asked, sounding angrily impatient. "Even if he's left with no more than Middle talent, they'll still want to find that out for themselves. They'll be able to use him even like that, but if his talent level remains intact, he'll be much more valuable. They'll dose him with Puredan to make him docile, and then they'll use him until they burn him out. You, personally, have nothing to fear, because they'll transport him to where the army is before they let him come back to himself. Are you satisfied now?"

"Yeah, yeah, sure," the first voice muttered, and then there was silence again. But it wasn't silent inside Lorand's head, where fear joined the unending pain. He had no idea what the men were talking about, and couldn't even remember what had happened to him. He lay on something hard in a place with a terrible stench, but he didn't know where the place was. He was supposed to have been doing something, but he couldn't remember what that something was.

All he knew was that someone was going to try to burn out his mind.

A long moan escaped Lorand's lips as he tried to free himself from whatever held him down, but it suddenly came to him that he wasn't chained or even tied. Something insubstantial held him in its grip, but its lack of substance did nothing to limit it. It held him tightly, like the arms of a very strong woman. . . .

A woman. Hadn't there been a woman in his life somewhere? The memory of her hid just out of reach, teasing him with hints and suggestions. Had she been like that, a woman who teased? He'd always wanted to meet a woman who would tease him lovingly and gently. . . .

Gently. That word didn't fit anywhere in his world. He'd tried gently to open his eyes, but they'd refused to work. He'd wanted his head to pound more gently, but he couldn't make it happen. Nothing was working right. . . .

Working . . . was he working? Had he had an accident? Someone really should have come by to tell him what was going on, it would only have been common decency. Now. . . .

Now he wished he knew where he was . . . and what had happened . . . and who was he, anyway . . . ?

Jovvi felt as though she floated in a heavy sea, she herself heavier than usual. Everything around and about her was heavy, even the air almost too thick to breathe. It was a strain to draw that air into her lungs, and struggling to do it made her head hurt more. But it also seemed to thin the sea a bit, enough so that she could just touch the outer world. . . .

"Well, well, aren't you the adventurous one," a male voice murmured very near to her, and then a hand smoothed her hair. "You're actually trying to wake up, even though it isn't time for you to do that. First we'll find a place to make you nice and comfortable, then we'll wait for the first transport group that's formed, and then you'll take a nice long trip. You'll like that, won't you?"

Jovvi could almost understand the words being spoken to her, but trying harder was out of the question. Even lying wherever she lay was almost too much of an effort, so anything beyond that . . . except for taking a deeper breath. . . .

"Now, now, just settle down," the voice said, again almost clearly enough to be understood. "I know you're probably disappointed, but the lord who is Seated High in your aspect decided that he doesn't want you after all. To look at you, one might easily consider him mad, but then one would have to pause in thought. If a man of his strength doesn't even care to dally with you for a short while, you must be dangerous indeed. I am a man possessed of sufficient courage for all things, yet my sense of discretion usually surpasses the other. They'll make good use of your talents—whatever they may now be—in the place where you're awaited, and I'll find a less adventurous—and adventuresome—woman to do my own dallying with. Rest now, for when you get where they mean to send you, there will be no rest short of death—or burnout, whichever comes first.''

Jovvi thought she heard the word "burnout," and agitation began to build inside her. That word . . . it meant something beyond the ordinary, beyond what most words mean. She had to . . . do something she hadn't gotten around to . . . had to remember something specific . . . find someone important. . . .

Opening her eyes proved to be impossible, as was any sort of movement. And that hand, smoothing her hair . . . it made her want to rest for a while, to sleep until the sea rolled out and she wasn't so heavy any longer. . . . Heavy . . . sleep. . . .

"Yes, my darling, that's right," Rion heard, a woman speaking softly and encouragingly. "Try to wake up just a bit, my darling, so that you'll understand what I have to say."

Rion fought to open his eyes, but at first his vision was too blurred to make anything out. Blinking helped to solve the problem to some extent, but it was still necessary to focus. He finally did so, using the face which swam before him as an anchor, and once success was his he immediately wished he'd failed.

"No, no, darling, don't frown so," Mother chided, just as she always used to do. "It will put lines into your face and make you look older, and then people will think *I'm* older. We certainly can't have that, now can we?"

Rion tried to speak, to tell her just exactly what she would and would not have, but his tongue refused to operate properly. And his head ached so abominably that he winced at the concept of trying to form words into a sentence.

"Of course we can't," she continued with a smile and a pat on his cheek, just as though he'd agreed with her.

"Now that you're back beside me again, we won't allow anything into our lives that isn't perfect. No, don't try to speak, you won't be able to do that for some time yet. I'm going to keep you drugged for a bit, you see, to make sure you aren't able to keep yourself from being permanently damaged."

Permanently damaged . . . the words chilled him, even though he had no idea what they meant. Nothing could have happened. . . . he didn't remember anything happening . . . but where had that headache come from . . . ?

"Don't you worry about that now, darling," Mother went on, chatting happily. "The physician tells me that you're probably permanently damaged anyway, but there's a chance the damage can be minimized if you're able to work against it. But we don't want it minimized, not when that might let you imagine you can escape me again. You can't, you know, because you're mine and always will be. But please don't think you'll be given an allowance again, I'd hate for you to be disappointed. From now on Mother will control everything, and you'll be her loving, devoted, talentless boy."

Rion fought against it, but the tears rolled down his face anyway. He couldn't even remember what had happened, but he still felt a vast sense of inconsolable loss. It wasn't even possible for him to move, and that seemed to please Mother enormously.

"That's right, my darling, you have a good cry," she said, the expression on her face making him ill. "Cry all you need to and then you'll sleep, and when you awake everything will be the way it was before. Except that I'll never again allow you to leave my side. But then—there won't be any reason for you to leave, will there, my darling?"

Rion let his eyes close again, which did nothing to stop his tears. It seemed as though the crying came from a very small boy inside him . . . while a grown man tried to rage and fight. But that grown man had no strength . . . and the mists of sleep were closing in again . . . and couldn't be avoided even though they would trap him forever. . . .

*   *   *

I think I became aware of my heart beating first, which struck me as being odd. A person is rarely aware of her own heartbeat, unless fright causes it to quicken or to nearly stop dead. My own heartbeat was more than ordinarily rapid, but I didn't know why. . . .

"I said, lovely child, can you hear me?" a man's voice came, the words answering my previous question. The thud of my heart grew even louder, as I recognized the voice. It belonged to a man whose name I didn't even know, but the vague, unformed memory of his intentions was very unsettling.

"Your muscles have tightened a bit, so I presume you can hear every word despite your lack of verbal response," the man went on. "That suits me well enough for the moment, as I shall speak and you need only listen. Later, of course, you'll also be expected to obey. If you fail to do so, you'll be made to produce a verbal response other than speaking."

He chuckled at that, a sound which made my blood run cold, but for no reason easily understood. Who was this man, and what did he want of me?

"To begin with, I should explain that the pain I'm told you probably feel is the result of your having been damaged," he said. "It's highly unlikely that you'll ever be what you once were, but please don't feel relief just yet. My interest in you remains as high as it was, for you're still perfectly able to serve my purpose."

What purpose? I wanted to say, but the lethargy all through me didn't allow it. I had no idea what he was talking about, but for some reason it still frightened me.

"Now, I mean to keep you quietly sedated for a time," he said, "but not for too long a time. I find I'm truly eager to begin with you, and as soon as the Puredan is brought to me I'll have you drink it. After that you'll no longer need to be sedated, and we'll be able to begin."

He chuckled again. "There's something rather amusing that you should hear. Your father and some crony of his attempted to claim you, actually challenging *my* right to possess you. I put them off until tomorrow, but only to give myself time to prepare something really special for them. It will be the highlight of my dinner party tomorrow night, and I mean to let *you* be present to watch. No, don't try to thank me, I've already decided on how I mean to be thanked.''

His chuckling really bothered me, especially since I could almost remember something about my father and some friend of his. That memory was just as disturbing, even without any details. I didn't want to hear about any of it, and the best way to escape was in sleep. I felt sleepy anyway . . . sleepy and frightened . . . sleepy and miserable . . . sleepy and very lonely. . . .

''. . . know what they could do to me for this?'' a thin and trembling male voice demanded. ''They could end my career, and then where would I be? Please ask for something else, my dear, I beg of you.''

''But there isn't anything else that I want,'' a female voice responded, one that Vallant seemed to recognize. ''You owe me more than one favor, love, and if you don't pay up I'll just have to collect in another way. Would you prefer it if I did that?''

''No!'' the male voice almost shrieked, and then it quieted again. ''No, I would not prefer that other way. You leave me no choice but to do exactly as you wish.''

''Stop making it sound like the end of the world,'' the woman chided with a laugh. ''No one will be doing anything with him until it's time to send him on his trip, so he might as well do his waiting here. I have this perfectly lovely little box prepared for him, made out of steel so that nothing will be able to harm him. When he learns to beg properly I'll let him out for a while, but I won't forget to put him back again. That should satisfy your feelings of anxiety, shouldn't it?''

''Perhaps,'' the male voice allowed grudgingly while Vallant's insides began to twist and burn. He couldn't quite remember why he felt like that, but it had something to do with part of what the woman had said. And his head hurt, for some reason he also couldn't remember. What was going on here—and where in the name of chaos was ''here''?

''Oh, he'll be fine,'' the woman said with more laughter. ''I'm just going to put him to work for a while, and then you can have him back. I'm sure he thought he'd seen the last of me, but a person's power isn't always linked only to her career position. When I decide I want something, I never rest until I get it.''

''Well, now you have *him*,'' the male voice said, still sounding extremely unhappy. ''Just be sure you don't lose or damage him, or we'll both regret it. If I'm blamed for anything, I'll make certain that you're right there beside me.''

''Worrier, worrier,'' the woman laughed, then went on to reassure the man again in different words. Vallant tried to listen, hoping to find out where he was and what was happening, but everything both inside him and out began to lurch. Not sick-making lurch but sleepy lurch . . . as though he were being rocked in the arms of someone who needed badly for him to be there . . . even though he couldn't be there . . . wherever there was . . . sleepy lurch, back and forth, back and forth . . . out but not in . . . please, please, never *in*. . . .